LISA HELEN GRAY
MADDOX

A NEXT GENERATION CARTER BROTHER NOVEL
BOOK FIVE

Copyright ©
Copyrights reserved
2020
Lisa Helen Gray
Edited by Stephanie Farrant at Farrant Editing
Cover Design by Cassy Roop at Pink Ink Designs
No part of this publication may be reproduced or transmitted in any form or by any means, electronic or mechanical, including photocopy, recording, or any information storage and retrieval system without the prior written consent from the publisher, except in the instance of quotes for reviews. No part of this book may be scanned, uploaded, or distributed via the Internet without the publisher's permission and is a violation of the international copyright law, which subjects the violator to severe fines and imprisonment.

This book is licensed for your enjoyment. E-book copies may not be resold or given away to other people. If you would like to share with a friend, please buy an extra copy. Thank you for respecting the author's work.

This is a work of fiction. Names, characters, places and events are all products of the author's imagination. Any resemblance to actual persons, living or dead, businesses or establishments is purely coincidental.

FAMILY TREE

(AGES ARE SUBJECTED TO CHANGE THROUGHOUT BOOKS)

Maverick & Teagan
- Faith engaged to Beau
- Lily
- Mark
- Aiden

Mason & Denny
- Hope
- Ciara
- Ashton

Malik & Harlow
- Maddison (Twin 1)
- Maddox (Twin 2)
- Trent

Max & Lake
- Landon (M) (Triplet 1)
- Hayden (F) (Triplet 2)
- Liam (M) (Triplet 3)

Myles & Kayla
- Charlotte
- Jacob

Evan (Denny's brother) & Kennedy
- Imogen
- Joshua

MADDOX

PROLOGUE

AMELIA

THE BALLS OF MY FEET throb as I make my way along the cracked path. It has been a long, tiring day, and although I'm exhausted, nerves rattle in my stomach, pulling me forward and towards home.

Two more streets and I'll be there.

I'll talk to Cameron, and he'll tell me everything is going to be okay. He has to. Because right now, I'm scared, unsure of what our future will hold.

At twenty-three, I have only just finished my internship and nursing degree. I had my final exams and last shift at work today. A shift that ended far too early because I collapsed whilst putting away stock. With all the long shifts, the extra schoolwork, and a five-year-old daughter, I've been exhausted. It was bound to happen.

All I want is a day with my daughter, to relax. Just one. The last two weeks have been hectic, and I've hardly spent any time with her. But with Cameron still out of work, we need the money, so I've taken on the extra shifts.

Cameron hasn't been taking the extra time at work well, and has gotten angrier as each week passes. He's getting sick of being the one to do the cleaning—like he does any—and is tired of watching over our daughter. She can be demanding, but only in a good way. She loves having all the attention and is so friendly and loving. It's all slowly tiring him out, but he can't blame it on the cleaning because whenever I get back, it's worse than when I left for the day.

When we moved out here, Mum and Dad followed months after so they could help out with Jasmine. At first, it was only ever meant to be temporary, but they stayed longer, finding a home that was closer, wanting to help me.

A few years ago, they moved back home, so I no longer had their help. It was hard without them, and that was when things really began to get worse with Cameron.

My best friend, Scarlett, helped out when she could, but I didn't like placing that responsibility on her. She was the only one, out of all my friends, who stuck around after I announced I was pregnant. I didn't want to push her away by forcing my family on her.

A bench near our housing estate comes into view, and I practically whimper. I take longer strides before dropping down on it and shoving my face into my hands.

"You're pregnant."

Those words are a haunted whisper. I can't be pregnant. Not again. But the results don't lie. I took four tests, and each one came back positive.

Pregnant.

I'm not sure how Cameron is going to react to the news. I'm worried this will be the thing to tip him over the edge. He's been hard to read lately, and his temper constantly gets the better of him. And it's me who he lashes out at. I fear Jasmine will be next, and there is no way I'm going to let him near her. He needs to get his head on straight and re-evaluate his life.

"Nothing good will come from being with him."

Mum's warning had felt like the beginning of a countdown, and with each passing minute, the noise of it ticking on gets louder and louder, like it knows something is about to happen. A part of me has always worried she was right. His family doesn't have the best track record around town, which Cameron inherited. He isn't like his family though.

When I met him, he was different—at first. I loved him—I have since I was fifteen years old—and there wasn't anything anyone could have said to change that, especially back then. Whilst everyone saw a bad boy, I saw a boy who was struggling to get by, who worked hard to look after his family when his mother couldn't.

When I got pregnant at seventeen, it shocked us all, but we made it work. Cameron could have run scared, but he stayed, assuring me we could do it. I still managed to do all the things I had planned to do when I left school, just minus a few friends.

Jasmine is my world, and I wouldn't change her for anything.

But another baby...

I'm scared. I've just finished my exams, and depending on my results, I should be looking for a full-time position. Now, I'm going to struggle. No one is going to hire a pregnant woman who will have to leave in eight to nine months, and my contract at the hospital ended tonight, so I don't have that to fall back on.

Standing up, I exhale, then push myself to finish the journey home. I normally drive to work, however, when I do shifts that finish at eight in the morning, I opt to catch the bus or grab a taxi. There's no way I could drive home after staying up all night to do a twelve-hour shift.

However, I left in a rush tonight because I didn't want to leave Jasmine when she was acting out of character. In my haste to get to work on time, I left my purse at home, but even if I didn't, I wouldn't have had the money to pay the fare to get home.

Cameron blew the last of our money on his new game for the Xbox, leaving us with nothing but pocket change.

When I get to the house, I'm surprised to see Scarlett's car parked on the street outside. She knew I would be at work tonight, so the only reason for her being here, that I can come up with, has my heart racing. I run up the path that leads to the stairs to our flat, needing to get to Jasmine. She had a slight temperature before I left for my shift, and if she had taken a turn for the worse, Cameron would have called Scarlett if he couldn't get hold of me.

It's two in the morning, and I can hear her cries as I race up the stairs, my bruised feet long forgotten.

I fumble with my keys, my hands shaking, before finally managing to slide the right one into the lock. When the door sticks in its frame, I shove my shoulder into it and force it open. I hate it here, but on a tight budget, it's all we can afford.

I grit my teeth at the smell of weed. Cameron promised me he wasn't smoking it. I've questioned him a few times now, and each time he's had an excuse. First, he blamed the smell on one of the neighbours for smoking a joint while he had the window open, and the other times he told me it was one of his mates who had one on the balcony. Intuition told me it was him, but I blocked it out, choosing to believe him again.

I take a step into the hallway but come to a heart-stopping pause when I hear a moan coming from our bedroom. My heart sinks at the unmistakeable sounds of people fucking. I can't think about that right now, not when my daughter needs me.

I rush down the hall and push her door open, finding Jasmine curled up on her bed, her cheeks bright red and sweat trickling down her face.

Oh my God!

She looks up when I rush to her side, her expression filling with relief when she sees it's me.

"Mummy!" she cries, clutching her stomach. "It hurts."

"What hurts, baby?" I ask, sitting on the pink blanket next to her. Placing my hand on her forehead, I feel her temperature, shocked to find she's burning up. Her sweet face scrunches up in pain as a whimper passes through her lips.

"My tummy."

I feel her rigid stomach and she cries out, pushing my hands away. My heart is racing, to the point I feel like it's going to burst. I can't fall apart, not now. Not when she needs me the most.

"Right, Mummy is just going to tell Daddy, and then we will take you to see the doctor. Okay?"

I need to get my handbag and car keys from my room, otherwise I would have whisked her out without him knowing.

I want to break things, to scream at him for leaving our daughter to suffer like this. Out of all the sinister things he's done over the past few years, this is the worst by far. He can lash out at me, blame me for his own failures, but he can't neglect his child. She should be his first thought, his first concern. And he can't even use the excuse that he didn't realise she was sick, because he knew before I left. He should have been checking in on her.

I shouldn't have left.

"Make me better?" she asks, her big doe eyes staring up at me.

I lean down, kissing her sweaty forehead. "Yes, baby. All better."

I pluck her dressing gown off the end of the bed and place it, along with her slippers, next to her. Then I grab my house keys off the floor.

I race from the room, my stomach knotting, and walk down the hall. Everything in me knows what I'm about to walk into. I guess the part of me I've kept locked away knew downstairs when I saw the car. But denial is a tricky thing, and I have been in denial for a long time, not letting myself question what was right in front of me.

I didn't want to believe it, and maybe if I hadn't been so weak, so foolish for thinking I was in love, I wouldn't be here right now.

We have been together since we were fifteen, and although eight years isn't much to some people, it is to me. We have been through a lot and fought against all odds.

I can barely swallow past the lump in my throat as I grip the door handle. I know what I'm going to be walking in on, however, that doesn't make it any easier.

The sound of Jasmine whimpering has me steeling myself against the onslaught of emotions as I push through the door. I only give them a brief glance, my eyes welling with tears as I see him balls deep in my best friend, her nails digging into his arse as she begs him for more.

I can't feel anything. I want to express my disgust, my anger, but neither are worth it. Not anymore. They are dead to me.

A part of me wonders if my lack of action has less to do with my concern for Jasmine and more because it has felt like we have been over for a while. As soon as that thought comes, I remember the exact day I began to fall out of love with him. He had raised his voice in anger and shoved me against the door, then punched a hole through the wood right next to my head. All because I told him I didn't want to keep coming home to a messy house.

Or maybe it was because the minute we decided to live in our own place, our relationship changed. *He* changed.

It could have been from a million moments.

They haven't even sensed or heard me come in as I walk over to the dressing table, knocking Scarlett's bag to the floor so I can get to my keys in the bowl.

Tears course down my cheeks because what hurts the most is that Scarlett did this. We have been friends longer than Cameron and I have known each other. She was my best friend, the person I confided in, who I trusted.

Yet she is there, with my boyfriend's cock inside her like it isn't the first time.

"Amelia…" Cameron panics, seeing me for the first time. He jumps off the bed to grab his boxers, his face flushed. "It's not what you think."

"Oh my God," Scarlett cries. "Amelia, I'm so sorry—"

I switch the music off and grab my bag off the chair. "Fuck you!" I bite out, keeping my voice low so I don't scare Jasmine.

Scarlett struggles to cover herself with the bedsheet, but I can't look at her a minute longer. Bile begins to rise in my throat.

"It's not what it looks like," Cameron rushes out, his red eyes boring into me.

He is definitely stoned.

"It just happened," Scarlett rushes out. "It didn't mean anything."

"I don't care," I snap, stopping at the door. "I'm taking Jasmine to the hospital. If you cared less about getting your dick wet, you'd know she isn't doing well and is in pain."

His face turns concrete. "I hurt you. I get it. But don't call me a bad dad."

"You're fucking another woman while she's in the other room. Did you even care what this would do to her if she had walked in to get you? She was calling out to you and you didn't even hear her. And don't get me started on the smell of alcohol and the stench of weed and smoke in here."

I storm down the hall, blocking the pain. I can be a single parent. Lots of mum's do it every day and I can do the same. I don't need a man to make us a family. I'm done trying to keep us together. He's had chance after chance, and he blew it.

"Amelia, wait," he yells, and I hear him pulling on clothes.

Walking into Jasmine's room, I wrap her dressing gown around her, pushing her Stitch slippers onto her feet. I lift her into my arms, cradling her as I run a soothing hand down her back.

"It's okay, baby."

"Why's Daddy mad again?" she asks, her voice trembling.

"We should talk about this," Cameron snaps, blocking the doorway when I turn to exit.

"Move!" I snap, cuddling Jasmine to my chest. Her little arms wrap around me, her face tucked into my neck.

"Mummy," she whimpers.

He slams his fist against the door, the veins in his neck bulging. "You aren't taking my daughter."

For the first time, I really look at him, seeing past the red in his eyes to his dilated pupils. He's on something. Something more than weed.

Jasmine grips me tighter. Normally when he gets like this, I put her in her room and turn the television on for her. We don't have time to placate him right now. We need to go, and he is in our way.

"Move!" I yell. "She needs to see a doctor."

"She's fine. She's just being a baby, like always," he snarls, and I clutch her tighter when she whimpers.

I fear this isn't the first time he has said something cruel about her to her face.

"Cameron, let them go," Scarlett says, dressed now. Her face is pale and apologetic but all I feel is disgust towards her.

"And I want you gone by the time I'm back," I warn him.

His gaze sharpens, something lethal, deadly, shining through the haze. "No. I'm fed up with you constantly telling me what to do. You aren't my boss."

"I'm not your mum either," I snap, trying to push past him, but he keeps blocking my path.

"You bitch," he roars, slapping me around the face.

I nearly drop Jasmine, and the only reason I don't is because of how tightly she is clinging to me.

"Cameron," I whisper, feeling blood trickle down my chin.

"Cameron," Scarlett gasps, stepping between us, but he pushes her away. Her head smacks against the doorframe and she collapses to the floor.

I step back, my heart racing for another reason. "Cameron, don't do this. Let us go."

His fists clench at his sides and he takes a step forward. "You aren't taking her from me."

"Baby, get down for me a minute," I whisper, my entire body shaking. She lets go and I quickly place her in her book corner behind me before stepping in front of him, blocking his view from her.

My fear for her health thrums through me, but fear of what Cameron is going to do is just as bad. It wouldn't be the first time he has hurt me, but it will be his last.

I can't do this again. I fought for so long for our family, to keep us together, but I can't do it anymore.

It's no longer about keeping our family together. I lied to myself in thinking I could. Each time I forgave his transgressions was me giving him more power. Power to hurt me, to hurt us.

Right now, it's about protecting my little girl. I should have left him sooner.

I hoped he would change. He hasn't. And now I'm taking a stand, something I should have done the first time he hit me.

"I'm asking you to move, Cameron. I need to take Jasmine to the hospital," I tell him, trying to keep my voice even, calm.

A scream bubbles from my throat as he reaches out for me. I try to jump out of his reach, but it's too late. He grabs me by my hair, and with a rage I didn't know existed inside of him, he attacks.

The next thing I remember, apart from the excruciating pain, are flashes of blue lights as my head rolls to the side. A man in a green paramedic uniform sits forward, gripping the bar of the bed I'm lying on.

Memories come flooding back, and I begin to struggle, needing to get to Jasmine.

"Amelia, you need to calm down. You've got extensive injuries," he orders gently, pressing down on my chest to get me to lie back down, which isn't hard as the pain is too much for me to bear.

My gaze darts around the ambulance before going back to him. "J-Jasmine," I croak out, my lips swollen and cracked. I try to say more, to tell him she's in danger, that she's not well, but I can't open my mouth.

"Jasmine is the little girl?" The small room blurs when I nod. "She's in the other ambulance. She's being taken care of."

Relief courses through me as I let the pain take over, falling into a deep slumber.

ONE

MADDOX

THERE IS NOTHING LIKE DOING a food shop when you're starving. The possibilities are endless. The only trouble is, I want everything for dinner tonight. I can't pick just one meal. I'm craving everything I lay eyes on.

There is always a midnight snack, I muse to myself.

And those chocolate bars will go down a treat once I've had dinner.

I grab the **BBQ** sauce off the shelf, grinning. This will go great with the potato wedges I picked up before.

The pickles are looking tasty too.

Decisions.

"This isn't fucking Tesco," Dad barks, slamming the cupboard door shut, nearly taking my nose off.

"Watch the face." I pout, stepping back. "Mum said I could come back any time."

"Not to steal my food, kid." Dad drops his work bag down by the backdoor before turning to lean against the counter. "Put it back."

"Maddox, baby, you're here," Mum gushes, leaning up to kiss my cheek.

"Mum," I whine. "Dad said I can't have this food. I'm starving and I've not had a chance to go shopping."

Mum glares at Dad. "Let him take some bits. I'll go to the shop tomorrow and grab us some things," she tells him, before turning to me. "I'll grab you some things too and will unpack them at yours tomorrow."

I grin, winking at Dad, who growls low under his breath. "You are the best, Mum."

"I know. Now, what has brought you here?"

"Our food," Dad growls, pulling a cup down from the cupboard and flicking the kettle on.

Trent, my younger brother, walks in, glaring. "Are you stealing my food again?" he snaps.

"*My* food," Dad grumbles.

"Can't your son just come by to say hi?" I tease before arching my eyebrow at Trent. "Still jealous she loves me more?"

"You wish," he mutters, grabbing a Snickers out of the bag of food I have near my feet.

"Hey, they're mine," I snap, snatching it out of his hand.

"Mum," he whines.

She rolls her eyes, opening another cupboard. Dad takes a step forward as if to stop her, but it's too late. She pulls down a Bueno and hands it to Trent.

Dad, seeing me eyeing the shelf I missed, glares at me. "Don't even think about it," he warns.

"Play nice," Mum scolds. "I'm just going to get the bedsheets out of the tumble dryer, but I'll be back. No fighting."

Once she leaves, Dad clips me around the head. "Next time I'll be coming to yours to steal your food."

Laughing, I push his hand away. "Like there's any food to steal."

Trent chuckles, jumping to sit on the side. "Dad, you won't have to do anything to get payback. Madison will."

Dad's glare doesn't waver. "Yeah, speaking of, Madison is pissed at you."

I glance through the window, over at next door. It used to be our grandparents' house, but now a few of the family stay there. Madison is one. I forgot about yesterday. Still…

"In my defence, she knows who I am. We're twins. And the chick was hot."

Trent snorts, rolling his eyes. "They're all hot to you."

"What can I say, women are beautiful," I tell him, reaching up for a Bueno, ignoring Dad's snarl.

"You owe her money."

"I'll give her the money back," I assure him.

Me, Madison, Hayden, Clayton, Lily, and Jaxon went out for a meal. Stupidly, in a drunken stupor, I offered to pay the tab. When the others left, leaving me and Madison, I went to break the seal. That's when I bumped into Sophie, or Chloe. *It had an 'E' in it, I'm sure.* "In my defence, I got distracted. She had a rocking body."

"When are you going to settle down? You're twenty-two years old now, Maddox. You've got a successful business whereas most guys your age are still figuring out what they want to do with their life."

I narrow my gaze dangerously. "Would you be having the same conversation with Madison?"

"No, because she's my daughter and she's the sensible one," he tells me straight.

"And the thought of a man touching her makes you want to commit murder," Trent adds, hitting the mark.

"All this 'cause I took your food?" I argue.

He rolls his eyes. "This is like talking to Max. I'm just saying. Maybe if you stop sleeping around, you'll find someone to cook and clean for you."

I muse over it for a minute. The thought holds merit but… "Dad, stop worrying about me. I have too much going on in my life to have a relationship."

"It's because he can't get one," Trent taunts, arching an eyebrow at me.

"I could totally fucking get one."

Dad grunts. "Women aren't chocolate bars you get to pick off a shelf. You have to work to get one and then keep them."

"Whatever," I grumble. I could totally keep a girlfriend. I just don't want one. I have a lot to give, and it's a waste to women all around the world to settle down now with just one. I still have years of being a bachelor left in me before I pick one who is worthy. Right now, I'm happy being the best part of a woman's night. I make their dreams come to life and their fantasies come true.

Who the fuck would give that up?

Trent, still sniggering, jumps off the side and looks at Dad. "Your life savings to be left to me when you die says he never settles down and dies of some sexually transmitted disease."

"Have you even had a sex education lesson yet?" I ask bitterly.

"Probably know more than you," he taunts.

"Like you know what to do with it," I reply, opening the fridge. I pull out the milk carton, unscrew the lid, and gulp down a quarter of the contents.

Dad, a cunning look in his eyes, gives Trent a smirk. "Nah, some girl will knock him on his arse, and she'll reject him. He'll regret ever being a player and will come crying to his mum for help."

"Like you were a saint," Mum tells him, stepping into the room. She gives him that 'I love you' smile as she cuddles up against him.

Frowning down at her, he gives her a kiss, making me groan. "None of them were you."

Sighing dreamily, she says, "No, they really weren't."

"I'm going out," Trent groans. "Jacob text me earlier."

"I need to go too," I hastily rush out, grabbing the bags off the floor before giving Mum a pointed look. "See you tomorrow."

"I won't forget."

"She will," Dad calls out, but I shut the door, blocking out Mum's reply.

Dad's words hang in the air. *Will someone knock me on my arse?* The pregnant chick from a few weeks ago comes to mind. As quick as the image comes, the quicker it leaves.

I am never settling down. I feel happy for those in my family who have, but that damn curse they've projected onto the Carter line isn't reaching me.

Dad said it started with him. Once he found Mum, the rest of them followed, finding the love of their lives.

It seems history is repeating itself, because until Faith found Beau, not one of us had a desire to settle down. Now, Lily is married, Faith is engaged, Aiden has a kid and a missus, Hayden is shacked up with her guy, and Landon is loved up.

Landon.

He is the one person in my family who I thought would never settle down again after his ex, Freya, died. Now he is with a Hayes, of all people. Though Paisley isn't so bad.

I shudder. Yeah, definitely not settling down. No one has ever grabbed my attention or interested me enough to even contemplate it.

If they couldn't garner that, then they weren't worth another fuck, let alone a relationship.

My truck bounces over the potholes on my road. I put the car back into second, slowing down until I pass them.

When I bought the house here, I had high hopes. It had been a quiet street, and at eighteen, I didn't know how to look beyond the silence of the morning. Even when I was doing the house up, it had been peaceful here. After growing up around such a large family, I needed that tranquillity.

It was all a lie.

Once the work had been done and I slept in my home for the first time, I hated every second of it. A new family had moved in next door and the music blared all through the night. And it has been like that for a few years now.

Instead of being able to sleep in after those long nights, I got woken up by dustbin men who thought people woke up at six every morning, or I had to get to work.

The first night it happened, I blew up. It was around five in the morning that time, and in anger, I cut their power off. I had a new business to run, jobs to start that I needed to make a good impression on, and I wanted to prove to my mum and dad I'd be okay. They were proud of me for taking on college early, working on the side for construction companies to learn the trade, and taking a night-time business course.

Now I dread coming back here each evening. And with Lily's place now out of bounds, I have nowhere to go for silence, somewhere to just sit back and relax.

Pulling onto my drive, I put my truck in park. I grab my phone and wallet out of the pocket in the dashboard before making my way out of the car.

Strolling around to the back, I check the new lock I installed, not wanting my personal work tools to be robbed again. It's locked.

Ready to grab the bags of food I robbed from Mum and Dad's, I'm stopped by a noise that comes from across the road. I look up to see the new tenant Uncle Maverick rents the house to.

She is stunning. Beautiful. And every time I get a glimpse of her, she is on her own; her rounded stomach a reminder of why I have to stay away.

It looks like she's moving in today, what with her car filled with more boxes. Her red polka dot dress blows around her knees as a light wind travels down the street. Her generous cleavage is out on show, probably giving every man she comes into contact with a hard on.

I can't look away.

She lifts a box out of the back of her car, wobbling back on her feet, which nearly causes the box to slip from her grip.

I'm going to regret this, but my mother didn't raise a fool.

I jog across the street, coming up behind her. "Let me take that," I offer.

She screams, dropping the box to the floor. The sound of ceramic smashing has me wincing.

"I'm sorry. I didn't mean to startle you," I rush out, bending at the knee to pick up the contents that have fallen out.

I look up when she doesn't speak. Her head is tilted down, her lips parted and her eyes unblinking as she stares me. Her pale complexion begins to pinken slightly, giving her cheeks a rosy colour.

The sun glows behind her, and when her body sways to the side, making the light reflect off her hair, something stirs inside of my chest.

"Mummy," is cried in excitement, and I fall back on my arse, staring at her stomach in horror.

It's not until the tiny pitter-patter of feet approach the side of the car that I exhale, getting up off the floor. I dust off my jeans, along with my dignity.

A little girl with black hair as glossy as her mum's bounces to a stop at her side. Snapping out of her daze, the woman runs her hand over the dark locks, a smile on her face.

Fuck, she is stunning.

It's a shame she's taken, because for her, I'd rethink my rule not to go after single parents. I could look past kids for that face and body.

When I first saw her, I never got a good look at her, but up close, she is even more beautiful. Her hazel eyes hold flecks of emerald green. It's hard to look away.

"What is it, baby?" she asks, her voice like velvet, sliding down my spine.

"My room is pink," the little girl gushes. She goes to say more but jerks when she finally spots me. She moves closer to her mum, wrapping her arms around her legs.

How I want those legs wrapped around me.

I swallow past the lump in my throat at the look she gives me and put on a brave face. I grin, winking at the little girl. "Hello."

"Who are you?" she asks bluntly, making me chuckle.

"I'm Maddox. I live across the street."

Her nose scrunches up as she eyes the house across the street that has music blaring. "You should turn your music down. It's not very good and it's really, really loud."

I chuckle; I can't help it. The kid is okay. "I don't live there but you are right. They should."

I turn to her mum, arching an eyebrow. She has yet to address me, and I don't like how much it's bugging me.

"That's good then. They were saying naughty stuff to my mummy."

That has me tensing. "Did they?"

She nods, but before she can speak, the woman composes herself, rushing forward with her hand reaching out to me. "I'm Amelia. And this is my daughter, Jasmine."

"It's nice to meet you, Amelia," I greet, letting her name roll off my tongue as I wrap my hand around hers.

When she tries to pull her hand away, I tighten my grip, not wanting to let go. Her gaze locks with mine, her tongue running along her bottom lip as something inside my chest tightens.

"Um, my hand," she tells me.

I clear my throat. "Uh, yeah, sorry."

She wipes sweat off her forehead, pulling her white cardigan around her as if it's a protective barrier.

"I'm sorry for screaming earlier. I didn't hear you approaching, and it startled me."

I give her a firm nod then glance at the car filled with boxes. "You really shouldn't be picking up heavy stuff."

Jasmine leans forward, her fingers curling in indication for me to bend down. "Grandpa said to wait until they were back to do it, but Mummy didn't listen."

"He did, did he?" I muse, straightening.

Amelia fiddles with the cuffs of her cardigan, looking anywhere but at me. "I'm just trying to get as much done as possible before the baby comes."

I don't look down at her stomach, but instead ask the question I'm dying to know. "Where is your boyfriend or husband?" I ask, even though I already clocked her bare ring finger.

"We shouldn't talk about him," Jasmine whimpers, curling into her mum's legs again.

I tense at how pale she gets, and although it's none of my business, I still look to Amelia for an answer.

"He, um…" She pauses, closing her eyes, but not before I see a flash of pain behind them. "It's just us."

Had he died? Is that why she is here moving heavy boxes by herself?

"Well, I'm free for the evening. I can help carry these into your home," I offer, not giving her an option. I can't let her carry them inside by herself.

"That's okay, I've got it," she tells me, reaching for the box.

I take it from her, hoping she gets my warning look. "I'll do it. It will save me from listening to my neighbours' obnoxious music."

Amelia giggles. "Still… we don't know you."

"You should let him. He can see my room," Jasmine orders. "He's my new best friend, Mummy."

I bristle but cover my reaction before she can see it. I shrug at her mum, grinning wide. "See, we're best friends now and friends help friends."

"Not mine," she mutters under her breath, grabbing a stack of pillows.

When she goes to walk off, I reach up and slam her boot closed. She gives me a questioning stare. "Never leave it unlocked. Some people have sticky fingers."

Her gaze goes across the road and she gives me a single nod, not saying anything more.

TWO

AMELIA

My fingers gently part the blinds to give me enough space to peek outside. Mum has popped to the shop, and I'm telling myself I'm watching out for her. Really, I'm watching Maddox clean his truck.

It's a Friday night. He should be out clubbing with his friends, not cleaning his truck. My tongue runs along my bottom lip as I watch suds of soap cover his naked and muscled chest. My fingers play with the necklace around my neck, my chest rising and falling at the sight of his muscles glistening. I'm riveted by the sight of him—have been since the first time I stopped by to see what decorating needed doing to the house. He was with another girl who looked a lot like him. At first, I was jealous, seeing the beautiful couple laughing and joking as they walked down the driveway. He was every girl's fantasy. It wasn't until I saw the familiarity in features that I realised she wasn't his girlfriend, and I found myself giving him a longer look. He was beautiful, strong features with a sharp jawline and exceedingly good looks.

This is the first time I'm seeing him without a shirt and I can't help but be captivated. It's the pregnancy hormones doing it to me because any other male repulses me. Even pregnant, guys flirt with me, and I recoil at their advances or touches.

But him...

He helped me with the boxes that day. He even came with us for the second load, and not once did I feel scared or repulsed by him. When I thought he wouldn't hurt me, I never second-guessed that feeling. He wasn't Cameron, which I found hard to categorise with other men I came into contact with.

So, what made Maddox different to all the other males?

After everything I went through with Cameron, I was sure something inside of me was broken.

Maddox awakened it that day, and I wanted him.

I wanted him so badly I couldn't find my voice.

"You know, it's a crime to spy on people," Dad quietly whispers in my ear, causing me to jump.

"I-I wasn't spying."

"You were spying," Jasmine confirms, her smile wide. I lean down, kissing the tip of her nose. She looks adorable with her missing tooth.

"I wasn't."

A car pulls to a stop outside, and before I can stop her, Jasmine runs out the door, screaming, "Grandma's back."

I race after her, warmth filling my chest when Mum grabs her around the waist, lifting her into the air. She looks over Mum's shoulder, waving frantically.

"Maddox! Maddox! Look!" she yells at the top of her lungs, and he stops at the side of his car whilst the girl I saw him with before gets up from the lawn chair. "Come meet my grandma and granddad."

"Jasmine," I lightly scold. I force out a laugh and call back to Maddox, "It's okay."

He says something to the girl standing next to the chair before he begins his stroll over here. She puts down her magazine, following him with a curious expression.

Oh God.

Having no other option, I head down the drive, stopping at the end to greet him.

"Hey."

He gives me a chin lift before his attention turns to my daughter, who leans forward to tap his glistening chest.

"This is the best grandma in the world. Grandma, this is Maddox. My best friend."

"Is he now?" Mum asks, indulging my daughter.

"I didn't have a choice," Maddox jokes, before giving me another look, his heated gaze running down my body.

Jasmine's bottom lip trembles. "You don't want to be my friend?"

"Maddox," the beautiful girl next to him hisses, whacking him in the stomach.

"I couldn't ask for a better friend," he rushes out, paling.

"I'm Madison, Maddox's twin sister. It's really nice to meet you," Madison greets, waving at my daughter.

"I'm Nita. This is my daughter, Amelia, and this is my husband, Gareth."

"It's nice to meet you," Madison replies.

I rub my stomach when the baby kicks out, wincing when a foot digs into my ribs.

"You okay?" Dad whispers.

I give him a nod, continuing to watch my daughter stare at the newcomer, open-mouthed.

"You're so beautiful," Jasmine whispers, gripping my mum's jacket.

Madison smiles wide. "And you look like Snow White."

I look at my daughter's raven black hair and milky-coloured skin, and smile. She really does look like a mini Snow White.

Jasmine doesn't seem to like the compliment though. Her nose scrunches up. "I like Elsa more."

Madison nods. "Girl power. She doesn't need a man to make her happy."

Jasmine grins, showing her missing tooth. "I'm going to get a prince when

I'm older, but I want to be strong like Elsa." She takes in a deep breath before leaning in, whispering, "And she has powers."

"Who's Elsa?" Maddox asks, his eyebrows pulling together.

Jasmine gasps, clapping her hands. "We can totally watch it together, best friend."

He gulps, looking at everyone, searching for someone to save him. Dad chuckles, stepping forward. "Maybe another time, sweet girl. We need to get that floorboard nailed down."

Mum slowly lowers Jasmine to the ground. "And I need to get dinner on."

My stomach grumbles, loud enough for everyone to hear, and my cheeks burn with embarrassment when they all look to me.

Maddox chuckles, shaking his head in amusement before a frown creases his forehead. "What floorboard?"

Dad growls low in his chest. "Bloody loose floorboard. Could have really hurt my granddaughter."

"What?" Maddox asks, looking between us with a slight panic in his eyes.

I nod. "It must have a nail in it or something that wasn't inserted right. It's pulled up the carpet."

"It did more than pull it up. Tore right through it. My granddaughter could have stepped on that board. We put her bed up yesterday. It was fine. But then as we started to organise her room, we piled boxes on her bed. The floorboard came right up."

Maddox's gaze hardens, and for the first time, a shiver of fear races down my spine. He looks livid. "Give me ten minutes and I'll fix it. I just need to fire someone first."

"Oh no," Madison mutters, watching her brother with a grimace.

"What?" I ask, feeling like I'm missing something.

"My uncle owns this home. My crew fixed this place up. There shouldn't have been anything wrong with the place. I'm really sorry. I'll fix it and replace the carpet. And double check everything."

"Was it Joey?" Madison asks.

"Yeah."

"You really don't need to do this," I tell him, kind of feeling bad for Joey.

His gaze meets mine and neither of us can look away. He steps forward, rubbing my arm just below my shoulder. Lust fills my lower abdomen, and my knees knock together. His pupils dilate slightly, and he removes his arm, breaking the spell.

"I'll fix it," he promises.

I give him a nod since it's hard to form words. I can still feel his touch on my arm, feel his gaze on my flesh.

"I'll be back," he tells us before leaving, his sister following. He has his phone out by the time I turn to my dad.

Eek.

"He doesn't seem happy," Mum comments, a small smile on her lips.

"He's going to fix my room," Jasmine whispers in wonder before racing off into the house, squealing with joy.

Dad is still staring in Maddox's direction. "He seems like a good fellow."

"He seems nice. He's the one Jasmine was telling you about."

"I'm glad he helped you," he tells me, before giving me a stern look. "Even after I said I'd do it when I was back."

My eyes water. "You guys have done so much for me. I needed to do this."

Mum takes my hand as Dad wraps his arm around my shoulders, kissing my head. "You're our daughter. We'd do anything for you."

"I let you down," I whisper, and look away, ashamed.

"You didn't let anyone down. You were in love. What he did…" Mum shakes her head, forcing the memories away. "It wasn't your fault."

"But you warned me," I argue.

And they did. They didn't like Cameron when I first introduced them to him back in high school, and they certainly didn't like him when he made us move to where his father lived a few hours away because his dad had gotten him a job.

Mum and Dad uprooted their home and moved close to help me when they could see juggling school and being a mum to a new-born was taking a toll on me. And they did this believing we wouldn't truly last.

I can't let that nightmare surface again. Not here. Not in my new home, in a place *he* hasn't tarnished. He can't touch me anymore, so he isn't worth thinking about.

"Let's go inside. Those neighbours are watching again."

My hair slides over my shoulder as I turn that way, watching as the mum greets her friends, who are holding beers as they walk up her path.

I inwardly groan. I'm not looking forward to another sleepless night listening to their blaring music. For an hour I stood by my front door, slippers on my feet, my coat on, ready to go over and ask them to turn it down. I couldn't do it though. They are loud, boisterous, and at times, fights break out.

There was no telling what they would do or how they would react, so I left it, opting for a sleepless night.

"Let's go see what madam is up to."

I walk ahead of them, holding my stomach when another sharp kick has me gasping.

"That's the fourth time you've stopped for air," Dad warns. "Are you sure you're okay?"

I smile, taking his offered arm. "Dad, I'm fine. The baby is just really active at the moment. I still have another three weeks left."

We step into the house, and I laugh at what I walk in to when I enter the living room. Jasmine's headfirst in a box, her legs dangling in the air. "Found it," she wheezes, kicking her feet.

I waddle over, helping her out. She holds up her Elsa doll, beaming. "He can meet Elsa now too."

There's a short tap on the door before Maddox and Madison come into view. "Hey, I hope it's okay that we just walked in."

"It's fine," I assure him.

"Look!" Jasmine demands, holding her doll up to him.

I watch with a sharp pain in my heart as he bends down to her level, nodding and listening intently to what she's telling him. Madison laughs, taking the doll from her hand, agreeing to play.

These strangers have shown so much kindness, but seeing Madison sitting on the floor, playing with my daughter, reminds me too much of the friend who betrayed us. Scarlett would sit for hours entertaining Jasmine. They would braid each other's hair and watch cartoons. She chose to sleep with Cameron knowing it would destroy our relationship, and that betrayal still burns inside of me.

Maddox gets up from the floor, walking over to us, his eyes never leaving mine. "Which room?"

My eyes go round, my cheeks heating as I sway in a daze. "Room?"

Mum beams as she takes my arm, pulling me towards Maddox. "Amelia will show you, won't you, honey?"

I inwardly groan when I nod. "Yes, follow me," I tell him, giving my mum a 'you are *so* dead' look. We reach the stairs, and the silence begins to make me uncomfortable. "So, it's your uncle who owns the home?"

"He does."

I turn my head at the sound of his deep voice, and I'm greeted with him staring at my arse, his lips tight.

I trip on the stairs in a rush to get from in front of him, and just after I hear a thud, he catches me, his hands warm on my hips. I hiss in a breath, closing my eyes as my arse presses into his chest. "Crap!"

"Are you okay?" he asks, concern in his tone.

Other than being humiliated again, yes. "Yeah. Sorry."

His hands don't move from my hips as I straighten, pulling my top back down over my bump. His touch burns, and I can't help but find pleasure in it. It feels good to be touched again. It's gentle, kind, and I relish in it.

"Are you sure?"

"Yes, why?"

He grins, his eyes sparkling. "Because you haven't moved."

I jerk, heat filling my cheeks, and quickly rush up the stairs, leaving him to pick up his tool bag. I take him to the first room on the right.

The bathroom is the next one over, and the baby's nursery and my bedroom are on the other side of the hall. I want to be close to the baby once they are in there and I don't want him or her waking up Jasmine. I don't like that she's at the other end of the hall and closest to the stairs, but her room would never fit my belongings inside. I would have kept looking but it was the nicest house we could find within my budget.

The council have a large waiting list to home people, and since I wasn't seen as a priority, I didn't even warrant getting a band to bid on anything. So, when Hayden said she knew someone who could rent me a house, I took her up on her offer. It was within my budget, which was a plus, but I have a sneaky suspicion Hayden was the reason for that.

When we walk into the bright pink room that has one wall wallpapered with a butterfly pattern, I take a look at the mess and feel shame.

The cream carpet is torn next to the bed and boxes now line the walls, some half emptied, some still closed.

"I'm sorry about the mess," I tell him, fidgeting with the sleeves of my top.

I wanted this to be the first room to be completed, but Dad swapped Jasmine's junior bed with a single and we had to wait for it to be delivered.

Jasmine has been sharing my room with me, which isn't in a much better state. When the bed came yesterday, we were excited to set it up. Then the drama with the carpet happened and we put it on hold again.

Dad isn't exactly handy when it comes to DIY. I've been worried he will make it worse, and then we'll be kicked out.

He was a lorry driver until a few years ago, when he retired due to his back. His gift now is gardening. He has a knack for it and now spends his time in his and Mum's garden, or comes to see his daughter and granddaughter.

I am their only daughter, the surprise of the family. Mum had me at forty-two, and my brother, who is thirty-four now, in her thirties. Stephan joined the Army at twenty-five and hasn't been back for three years now. I think it's why they spoil me rotten. They miss him terribly, and I guess I'm a way to compensate for that.

If he were here, he would be doing this for me right now. He'd fix it all. Including the list of things that need to be put together in the nursery and around the house.

I couldn't keep any of the furniture from my old life. The only things that came with me were my personal effects that had no tie to Cameron, and all of Jasmine's things. Everything else was left. Slowly, with each pay cheque, I have been buying something new for the home I had hoped we'd get, and for the baby. And thanks to my parents refusing to accept any money towards bills, I had managed to concentrate on that and paying off the bills Cameron built up—which I am still paying for.

"Are you sure you're okay?" Maddox asks, clicking his fingers in front of my face.

I give him an apologetic smile. "Sorry. I've got a lot on my mind. What did you ask?"

"I said I have some purple carpet that should fit this room. My cousin Aiden overordered when he did his daughter's room. I still have it. Or I can buy some of what's already here."

"Are you sure he won't need it?"

His eyes soften. "No. He doesn't."

"Then the purple is fine. It will go with the butterflies."

He grins and bends down to his tool bag, pulling out a drill, then screws down the problematic floorboard. "They must have forgotten to nail this back in. The electrical installation was outdated when my uncle bought it, so we had to rewire the entire house. I'm sorry this happened."

"It's okay," I assure him, since no damage was done.

"It's not. I informed Maverick about it, and he said he's giving you next month's rent free."

I suck in a breath. "No, that's not necessary."

"Trust me, it is. The junction boxes are under this board. If Jasmine had found them and started pulling, it could have ended badly."

His jaw clenches as he finishes with the last screw. My heart tightens at the thought of what could have happened. I hadn't even thought of that. The worst I imagined was a scraped knee or a bruised head if she tripped.

"Do you mind if I check out the other rooms while I'm here?" he asks, pulling me from my thoughts.

I really need to stop making a fool of myself. He's going to think I'm weird—if he doesn't already.

"No, no. Carry on."

He grabs his tool bag off the floor and carries it with him as he leaves the room, heading to the next one, which is the bathroom. I don't follow him in. It isn't a large space, and cramming myself into a small room with him… it would be torture. He smells heavenly.

He walks out, his gaze going to my stomach before quickly shifting elsewhere. He heads into the next room, the baby's room. The yellow and mint-green walls stand out like a summer's day, matching the white curtains decorated with yellow and mint green stars. I don't know the sex; the baby was positioned in a way that we didn't get to find out.

Tears gather in my eyes when I think of what Cameron nearly did that night. My hand automatically goes to my stomach, rubbing the large bump soothingly. He or she is thriving, and although their start in life hasn't been a good one, I'm going to make sure he or she is raised with love and adoration.

"You've not set up the cot?" Maddox asks, as he takes in the room. His fingers run over the mark Dad made when he was trying to put shelves up, and I giggle.

"My dad isn't exactly good when it comes to DIY. I'm going to do it tomorrow, after I've finished work. I just wanted to get Jasmine's room, the living room and kitchen done first."

"I'll do it tomorrow," he tells me, seemingly surprised at himself for offering.

"You're kind, but this really isn't necessary. You've already gone out of your way to help me. And I'm grateful."

He shrugs, picking up the instructions. "I have time on my hands in the evenings."

I take a step further into the room, watching his expression. He looks sad, like he's missing something or someone. There's a longing there and it hurts to witness.

"How come?"

He looks up, a smile erasing the turned down lips he had. "My best friend traded me for a husband. She's family, so I forgive her, but him… I don't. Can you believe he keeps me from going there?"

I'm completely lost and startled by the change in his tone. "Um, no?"

He nods like I've answered in a way he understands. "I know. I used to go round to play on my Xbox, but she gave it away to the kid who lives next to her. I replaced it, but then he gave that one away too because the kid broke the first one." He snorts, pulling the changing table box away from the wall to see the picture of it on the other side. "This will give me something to do. I mean, you can tell me to fuck off, but I'm telling you, you'll regret it. I am awesome at DIY. It's what I do—except for being sexy and handsome."

I laugh, rubbing a hand over my stomach when the baby pushes down again. "I don't think anyone could be as bad as my dad. I have to fill that hole up now."

He grins, his gaze going to mine. "I own a construction business. I'm good at what I do. And I don't mind helping. I've done this before."

"You have kids?" I ask. I'm surprised. I've not lived here long, but I would have thought I'd have seen him with one by now.

He pales, shaking his head. "God, no," he blurts out, and I flinch. He grimaces, letting out a groan. "Not that kids are bad. They just scare me."

"You seem good with Jasmine," I tell him softly, trying not to laugh at his expression.

He shrugs. "She's a good kid."

My smile spreads now. "She is."

At a loss for words, he takes another look around the room. "My offer is there. I'll get my dad to come and help me with the carpet tomorrow, so it's done as quickly as possible. I'll just throw this together then. My niece's room didn't take us long. *Once I got there*," he adds, smirking.

I tuck a strand of hair behind my ear, giving him a nod. "If you're sure, then I'd appreciate it. But let me give you something for helping."

His eyes darken as his gaze runs over my body, causing me to shiver. His posture changes to show more swagger and confidence, as he opens his mouth then closes it, shaking his head as if to dismiss his thoughts. "Do you bake?"

Um, okay. That was random, but I answer anyway. "I do. Do you like cakes?"

He licks his lips. "Who doesn't."

Giggling, I'm surprised at how easy it is to be around this stranger. "Then I'll have a cake baked for you and your dad."

He frowns. "Not my dad. He has diabetes. He can't have sugar."

"I'm sorry," I tell him, feeling guilty. "What can I make for him?"

"Nothing," he rushes out. "He'll just appreciate being out of the house. He doesn't get out much."

"Wait," I tell him, turning before I can exit the room. "Your father isn't the crazy guy who turned up at the office where I met with your uncle, is he? He started yelling at Hayden when she met me there. She took his muffins again or something."

"No," he tells me, his lips twisted in disgust. "I'm too good-looking to be his kid."

My shoulders sag and I reach out, squeezing his arm. "Phew! He was kind of scary."

"You have no idea," he whispers, before following me out of the room.

THREE

AMELIA

I waddle my way out of Mr Archie's room and rest against the wall, taking deep breaths. He is one of our best residents, but he is also one of the most demanding.

"We'll play chess next," he calls through the door.

An unbearable pain shoots up my back, taking the wind right out of me. Sweat runs down my spine, and I clutch my stomach, feeling it tighten.

Fuck, this hurts.

This morning, the midwife said the baby was head down, ready, and that everything was looking fine. When I asked about the pain in my back, she explained that they were Braxton hicks, which are common in this stage of the pregnancy. There was no evidence I was in labour, and the pains weren't regular. In fact, they've been hardly here or there, which is why I haven't been overly concerned. However, when one does come, it's agony, much like it was during my labour with Jasmine—if not worse.

Hope, one of my favourite colleagues, steps out of the room a few doors down from me. Her uniform hugs her slim figure, making me a little envious. She's gorgeous, and right now, her expression is pulled tight.

Heading my way, she asks, "Are you okay?"

I straighten from the wall, the pain now gone and forgotten. "Yes. I'm fine. The little one just knows how to give a good kick."

"Are you sure? You looked a little in pain when I walked out."

I smile, rubbing a hand over my stomach. "I'm sure."

"I heard your aunt tell you to take maternity leave. You should really take her up on it. You're due soon, right?"

I nod. "I am, but I need to work all the hours I can. Soon, I won't be able to."

"But you get maternity leave, right?"

Flustered at her question, I duck my head. I can't tell her my ex left me with debt. The catalogues and loans are all in my name, and I'm still paying them off.

When Cameron did work, he would lie to me about how much he got paid. Whenever he brought new purchases home—video games, trainers, and so much more—he would say he bought them with the extra money he made. Back then, I didn't know any different, not until the debt collectors' letters began to arrive. He kept all the other letters from me.

I was dumb and stupid not to question him, especially when those things miraculously turned up even after he lost his job. I'd get angry at him for spending money we didn't have, and he always made sure I paid for it. I lost a part of myself every time he hurt me.

I was blind to a lot of things when it came to him, and I hid so much from people, which I feel stupid about now. I lied to my parents whenever they asked me if I was okay, or if I needed anything. I lied to myself when I said he hadn't done anything wrong. I lied to my daughter when I said he was sorry.

But I've learned from my mistakes. My eyes are wide open, and I'll never let anyone treat me like that again.

"Sorry, I'm being nosey," Hope rushes out, tucking a loose strand of blonde hair behind her ear.

"No, you aren't. I, um—I'm paying a few things off, and with the baby on the way, I want to be prepared."

"If you ever need anything, call me. In fact, the next time we have a day off together, we should go and grab lunch or something."

Her hopeful expression tears me up inside. I desperately want to be friends with her. When I started working here, she was the first person to be nice to me; who didn't talk behind my back or try to sabotage my job.

I just don't know if I can put my trust in another person, one I know I could become great friends with. Scarlett was my friend for a long time. I trusted her with everything, even my daughter, and she destroyed that friendship for a guy, who, in the end, hurt her too.

Why the hell not. I have nothing left to lose.

I have gotten over a lot of stuff since that dreadful night; it's now time to start trusting people again. I have no friends here, and I'd be lying to myself if I didn't admit I miss having someone to talk to.

I've gotten to know Hope a lot over the months I have worked here, and not once have I compared her to Scarlett. She's too nice. She doesn't bitch, even though some of our co-workers deserve it, and she always makes sure everyone is taken care of.

Taking a leap of faith, I give her a smile. "I'd love that."

My aunt steps around the corner with my mum and Jasmine in tow. Jasmine, who is clutching her Elsa doll, has her head down, dragging her feet instead of bouncing up the corridor to greet me.

I force a smile at my mum, who turns her gaze back down to my quiet daughter.

I bend down, letting my knees fall to the carpet as I take her in. "Baby, did you have a good time at the childminder's?" I ask, keeping my voice gentle.

"No." She pouts, her lip trembling and eyes watering when they meet mine. "That mean boy tripped me over again."

"Did you tell Mel?" I ask, checking her over for injuries. The graze on her knee has been cleaned, but still, she has been hurt again.

I pull her to me, giving her a kiss on the cheek, breathing in the scent of her apple shampoo.

This isn't the first time she's been hurt or bullied there. Mel is good with the kids, but she looks after a few that have no manners and are rough with the little ones. She promised me another incident like this wouldn't happen again. I'll need to have another word with her about it.

"I'm okay, Mummy. I was brave."

I run my gaze over her lovingly, threading my fingers through her tangled mass of black locks. "I bet you were. You're the bravest girl I know."

I take Mum's hand when she reaches down to help me up. I giggle, giving her a hug in greeting. "Thank you for picking her up, Mum. I know you had plans today."

"I'll always have time for my girls. I've got to rush off, but I'll be around again later to help sort your room out."

"Thank you." I give her another kiss before looking down at Jasmine, my stomach rumbling with hunger. "Would you like a McDonald's for dinner?"

She squeals, clapping her hands. "Yes, yes, yes!"

My aunt laughs, along with Hope. "I guess that means she'd love to."

"I'll see you Monday," I remind her, before grabbing Jasmine's lunch bag. "Let's go, baby."

I LAUGH AT the sight of my daughter's face covered in tomato sauce. She couldn't wait until we got home to eat, so I opened her Happy Meal and let her eat it in her car seat.

Jasmine holds up the toy that came with her Happy Meal, laughing at whatever is in the tiny ball.

"What did you get, baby?"

"It's a light-up ball. But it won't work," she explains.

I give her another quick glance in my rear-view mirror. "I'll have a look at it when we get home."

"After you eat your food," she tells me in her bossy voice.

"Yes, missy," I tell her, rolling my eyes.

As we pull into our street, the first thing to catch my attention and make me groan are the cars outside the house across the road. It seems that for people who don't work, they can afford to party day and night, and if alcohol wasn't expensive enough, they always seem to have fags in their mouths.

Too busy planning on my quick escape from the car to the house before they can cat-call or yell crude things across the road, I miss the car parked next to my drive.

Something inside of me nearly keeps going, but I don't want to give anyone else the power of knowing I'm scared ever again.

"Baby, I'm going to take you inside the house and then I need you to stay in the front room until I'm back. Okay?"

Not missing a beat, she looks out the window, her eyes widening when she sees who is waiting. Her bottom lip trembles as she meets my gaze in the mirror. "That's Grandma Hudson."

"It is."

"Will she hurt you again?"

I close my eyes briefly as I put my car into park. I hate that she witnessed the altercation between me and Cameron's mum. She hasn't cared or bothered about him his entire life. The only time she remembered she even had a son was when she needed him to get a fix for her or to look after her kids. She never congratulated him on our pregnancy, or when he passed his GCSE's.

She was in his life, but she wasn't. Until the day he was charged. Since then, she has been a thorn in my side. The first time, which was the time Jasmine witnessed her slap me, was when I had been released from the hospital and we went back to our flat. While Mum and Dad were helping me pack, there was a knock on the door. It was Carol, and before I could utter a word, her hand was across my face. I already had bruises from her son, so the slap hurt more than it should have.

Her weathered face pops in front of the passenger side window, her lips twisted in a snarl as she taps her knuckles across the glass.

Her yell has me grimacing. "Bitch, I want to speak to you."

"Remember what I said?" I warn Jasmine, turning a little in my seat.

"We go inside," she tells me, her voice shaking.

I quickly exit the car, leaving my food and bag on the passenger side floor. I move as fast as my large stomach will let me after grabbing the house keys.

"I want a word with you," Carol snarls, as I get out of the car.

"Let me get Jasmine inside," I tell her, giving her a pointed look to keep it down. She doesn't. And neither does her sister, who comes storming up behind the car.

"Don't you dare take that child away from her again."

I ignore them and quickly unbuckle Jasmine from her car seat, pressing a kiss to her forehead. "It's going to be okay, baby."

She nods but doesn't speak. We head around the car, intending to make it to the house, when I'm blocked by the sisters.

Carol looks to have aged ten years, but that's to be expected, what with the amount of alcohol, drugs and cigarettes she consumes. Her dark roots are stark against her bleach blonde hair that looks more orange than blonde. Her twin sister is no exception.

"Oi, I said I wanted a word with you," Carol barks.

Trying to keep my tremors at bay and hold my cool at the same time, I force a smile. "And I said, give me a minute to get Jasmine inside."

Her sister, Karen, snorts. "Look at you, thinking you can keep her grandbaby away from her."

"You want to see your grandma, don't you?" Carol asks Jasmine, who tucks herself behind my leg, her tiny body shaking. When Carol meets my gaze, she's livid. "You turning her against me? Like you turned her against her daddy?"

"Carol, I'm going to ask you again: please let me past so I can get Jasmine inside. She doesn't need to witness this."

"No," she snaps. "I want some time with my grandbaby. Cameron wants to see her too. He's allowed visitation. You can't keep her from us."

My blood runs cold at the news because it will be the last day on earth before I let him near her again. She knows that. The courts know that. And Cameron knows that. He nearly killed our daughter that night. By keeping me from taking her to get medical care, she nearly died. Her appendix had ruptured as she got to the hospital. If the neighbours hadn't called the police when they did, we would have both died that night. He was a danger to us both.

"You've wasted your time in coming here because he isn't allowed visitation with her. You know that. The courts denied him any access. I have full parental control."

"Because you lied," she spits out.

Seeing they aren't going to let me pass, I bend down a little to Jasmine. "Why don't you go play over there with your ball while I speak to Carol and Karen."

She nods, rushing over to the small patch of grass. I straighten, turning to the two sisters. "I don't care why you're here, but I want you to go. You know what happened with Cameron, and you're deluding yourself if you say otherwise. I'm tired of doing this with you. Let me raise my daughter in peace. She's seen and been through enough."

"You're denying her a family," Carol argues.

"She has a family," I shoot back. "You've seen her, what, three times now? You're just angry because Cameron can no longer give you my money. He can no longer get drugs cheaper for you."

I hadn't known what Cameron did behind my back. The drugs, the dealing, it was something he swore he wouldn't touch. And then he did, saying he needed the weed to help him sleep. When he promised me he wouldn't do it again, I believed him.

When I finally got all the bills, I saw the destruction of what Cameron had done to my finances. Growing up, I know his mother relied on him. He had brothers and sisters he helped raise because his mum couldn't or wouldn't. He did everything he could once he turned eighteen to make sure they had everything they needed. His mum had maxed out his credit and got him blacklisted, so I knew when we got our first store card, it would have to be in my name.

"Because you never let me around."

"No, not when you were intoxicated or high, which happened to be all the time. But you also never made the effort to come."

Her lips twist into a cruel smirk as she eyes my stomach. She turns to her sister, arching her eyebrow. "I wonder if the courts knew she cheated on him and got pregnant. I mean, that would be reason enough as to why he got uncharacteristically angry and hurt her." She turns to me, flashing her yellow teeth smudged with red lipstick. "That's why he was angry, right? I bet the courts will bail him out beforehand."

My stomach tightens in knots. Although sentenced, Cameron still got a light one. Four years. Four years for the damage he had done to not only me, but Jasmine and Scarlett. He got off lightly and they knew it.

"You know that isn't true. I found out I was pregnant the night he got arrested. He didn't find out until much later—when it came up in a police interview. I'm done explaining to you what happened that night. It wasn't the first time he hurt me," I tell her, hearing a car pull in across the road. I don't look to see who it is, already aware of prying eyes.

"Well, I'm not done with you," she snaps, shoving her hand on her hip. "My boy is in prison and you're here, living it up. You always did think you were above my boy." She looks up at the house, her lip curling. "I didn't want to believe it when Karen said she saw you shopping around here. She followed you home, said you lived in a big fancy house."

That explains how she knew where I lived. We called the police so many times when they kept coming to my parents' house. It was another reason I knew I had to leave there. It was unfair they had to deal with them.

"I don't care what you think, Carol," I tell her, stepping back when she comes forward. "I want you both to leave, and the next time you come, I'll be phoning the police."

"I say we take the child now. She's not fit enough to look after her," Karen orders, crossing her arms over her chest.

The blood drains from my face. "I don't think so. If any of you even think—"

"Mummy, look, it lights up," Jasmine yells, bouncing the ball again. It bounces away, and before I can open my mouth to yell at her to stop, she's rushing after it.

"Jasmine," I scream, my stomach cramping as the squealing of tyres sounds from the road.

In horror, I watch as the silver vehicle that is normally parked across the road, speeds up the street, heading right for my daughter.

My screams are lost over the pounding bass music coming from the car.

"No, stop!" I scream, freezing in fear as the car nears. I try to move, try to scream louder, but there is nothing but paralyzing fear.

My body jerks forward when, suddenly, she's swept up in a pair of arms. Water gushes from between my legs as relief consumes me. A sob breaks out as I reach for my daughter, keeping my eyes on Maddox for a moment.

"I don't know where you came from, but thank you. Thank you so much."

Jasmine cries into my shoulder and I lower us to the floor, clutching her to my chest. *She's okay. She's okay.* I press my hand over her chest, feeling her heart beating. "You're okay. You're okay."

"See, this is why we should have her," Carol snaps, stepping closer. "Give us the girl."

"Who the fuck are you?" Maddox growls, just before he was about to turn and leave.

"I'm her grandma, and she's keeping her from me."

"From where I stood, it looked like you were keeping her from her daughter. Now, I suggest you leave before I make you leave."

"We don't have an issue with you," Karen begins, but Maddox steps forward, clenching his jaw.

"Lady, it would seem you have more issues than the local paper. I don't give a shit about those either, so do one and leave Amelia alone."

Carol, not happy with being told what to do, goes to say something, but Karen pulls her back, stopping her. "Let's go."

"I'll be back," Carol warns, her intent clear. "You won't get away with what you've done."

She wants to make my life hell.

I'm about to thank Maddox once again, but his back is to me and he's in the road, pulling the lad out of the car.

A cry escapes me, and my grip tightens around Jasmine as pain shoots through my abdomen.

FOUR

MADDOX

Dad finishes typing away on his phone before giving me his attention. "I've called in reinforcements."

"Dad, it's a few jobs. I don't need that much help," I tell him, rolling my eyes. "Once you've helped with the carpet, you can head home. I'll do the rest."

"I want to meet this woman Madison told us all about."

I snort, my attention going to the two middle-aged women on Amelia's drive, both looking like they stepped out of an episode of *Shameless*, with their roots on show, their knock-off trainers, cheap gold jewellery, and torn jeans. And not in the fashionable sense. It looks like they're blocking her path.

Absently, I reply to Dad's comment. "Madison thinks she knows everything."

"Madison said you couldn't stop staring at this mystery woman."

Putting the truck into park, I turn to Dad. "Dad, don't make this out to be something it isn't. She's pregnant and has a little girl called Jasmine. You know my rules."

His eyes harden a little. "Nothing wrong with being with a woman who already has kids."

I shudder, although there is no mistaking I don't see Amelia the way I have other single mums. The scream that shakes the car has my stomach turning. I take a minute to look at Dad before racing out of the car.

I know that sound.

It's the sound of fear. The same fear I hear whenever Lily has one of her nightmares or episodes.

Fuck!

I hear the car first. Kayne, one of the older kids who lives next door, has his music blaring as he races down the street. I watch as he leans down to grab something, and when he comes up with a can of Carling, taking a swig, fear runs up my spine.

"No, stop!" Amelia screams.

My feet are moving before it even registers. Dad tries to wave down Kayne, but it's no use. Just inches away from hitting the little girl, I manage to swoop her up in my arms, getting her out of harm's way.

Tweedledee and Tweedledum step back when I rush Jasmine to Amelia. I avoid looking down at her wet scrubs and keep my gaze on her face.

I think I'd piss myself too if my kid had nearly been roadkill. I'm not going to judge.

There is a certain warmth that expands inside my chest when her gaze meets mine, boring into me. "I don't know where you came from, but thank you. Thank you so much." Her voice cracks at the end as she cuddles into her daughter.

There's nothing I can say in this moment. I feel like I'm invading on a moment between mother and daughter as Jasmine cries into Amelia's chest.

Anger runs through my veins when I think of what could have happened had I not been here. I turn to leave, to go to my dad, who is being blocked from one of the guys next door. His nostrils flare, and he looks moments away from exploding. The guy doesn't know who he's messing with.

I'm not shocked to find the mum still sat in her green plastic chair, laughing uproariously as her son struggles to open his car door.

About to show them how pissed I can get, I take a step towards them, but hearing, "See, this is why we should have her," come from one of the women behind me, has me pausing mid-step.

"Give us the girl," she orders, like she has every right to.

I growl low in my throat, and take a step towards them. I stand in front of Amelia and Jasmine, blocking them from view. "Who the fuck are you?"

Shocked that I spoke, the woman scans me over, curling her lip. "I'm her grandma, and she's keeping her from me."

Yeah, that bullshit isn't going to fly with me. "From where I stood, it looked like you were keeping her from her daughter. Now, I suggest you leave before I make you leave."

If these two hadn't been pulling Amelia's attention away from Jasmine, then she would never have run into the road. I've only met them a few times, but I can say with one-hundred percent certainty that Amelia is a good mum.

"We don't have an issue with you," the bigger of the two snaps, looking like she wants to take a swipe at me. Seeing pain etched on Amelia's face, I take another step forward, gritting my teeth.

"Lady, it would seem you have more issues than the local paper. I don't give a shit about those either, so do one and leave Amelia alone."

I arch my eyebrow, daring the peroxide grandma to say something. She opens her mouth, but wisely, the mess beside her pulls her back, leaning in to say, "Let's go."

"I'll be back," she warns, her intent clear. "You won't get away with what you've done."

Hearing a commotion behind me, I quickly rush to my dad when I see a guy with a badly drawn dragon tattooed on his neck and chest come at him. Dad pushes him with such force it knocks the guy on his arse.

Knowing Dad has it handled, I head straight to the car. I grab one of the lads by the back of his jacket and shove him to the side, out of my way.

The door makes an awful groaning sound when I pry it open. Kayne stares up at me, his eyes not really focused. He looks high, his eyelids narrowed into slits.

"You could have fucking killed a kid," I growl, gripping his jacket and pulling him out of the car. Darkness courses through me when I smell lager on his breath. "You've been drinking."

Blinking up at me, the situation seems to dawn on him, and his eyes begin to widen. "Only a bit, man. I didn't see her. She came out of nowhere."

I couldn't hold back my reaction even if I wanted to as I take a swing at him. My knuckles crack open when they hit his lip piercing, knocking him back against the car. "I fucking saw her, and I wasn't driving, arsehole."

"Hey, get off my son," his mum yells, getting her lazy arse out of the chair.

"Back off," Max, my uncle, booms, swinging a baseball bat over his shoulder, looking like he's on the set of a street gang movie.

I groan. This situation went from bad to seriously bad on an epic scale. I give my dad a side look, and he shrugs, his expression blank. Thankfully, my uncle Myles is here too, along with Maverick and Mason. If anyone can control Max, it's them.

Kind of.

When I glance at Dad, silently asking him why they're all here, he shrugs. "They wanted to meet her too."

Wankers.

"Look, Granddad, get out of our face and out of our business," the tattoo guy yells, throwing a drink all over my dad.

Dad, calm as always, glances down at his shirt, his jaw clenched. When he looks up, his pupils are darker, deadlier, and I wince when he leans his head back, before bringing it forward, slamming it into the guy's forehead, knocking him clean out on the floor.

Max jumps, swinging his fist in the air. "And that is why you don't fuck with a Carter."

When they go to go after my dad, the others step beside him. Maverick shakes his head, his lip curling. "Unless you want to be picking up your pride and licking your dignity off the ground, I suggest you all fuck off and go back inside."

A scream vibrates through the air, and I swivel around to the sound, finding Jasmine hovering over her mum, who is curled onto her side, clutching her stomach.

I quickly turn to Kayne. "I'm not done with you."

His eyes widen, and he shakily lets go of my elbows, nodding. I run over to Amelia, kneeling on the ground next to her.

"Did those bit—" I force a smile to Jasmine before clearing my throat. "Did they hurt you?"

"Have you pissed yourself?" Max asks, glancing over my shoulder. When I go to push him back, he lets me, paling. "Oh my God, please tell me you've pissed yourself."

"Seriously? Accidents happen," I snap.

"M-my w-waters have broken," she wheezes, sweat pouring down her face. Her expression tightens as she screams out.

I lean in, whispering, "Is that code for you've pissed yourself? Because I meant what I said: accidents happen. I've not pissed myself before, but I've woken up after a night out and found I've pissed—"

"I'm in labour," she screams, her beautiful face scrunched up in agony.

"Mummy," Jasmine whispers, rubbing a hand over her mum's head.

Panting, Amelia forces a smile and manages to run a hand over her daughter's head. "It's okay, baby. We talked about this, remember? It means your baby brother or sister is coming."

"But you didn't say it would hurt you," she whines, bending down to the large stomach. "Stop hurting our mummy."

Realisation hits me, and I glance up at my dad, in a panic. "Do something!"

He grunts. "What do you want me to do? Give birth for her?"

"Oh God," she groans, rolling onto her back. "I really need to push."

"Don't push," Max screams, pulling at the ends of his hair.

"Let's get her inside," Maverick orders, and I nod, pushing one arm under her knees and the other around her back. She screams when I lift her into my arms.

Jasmine slaps my leg. "Don't hurt her."

Myles kneels next to her. "Do you know who we can call?"

I ignore her reply, holding the woman in my arms tighter, feeling her pain like it's my own. I can feel her entire body tightening with every scream she releases.

Dad, grabbing the keys off the ground, heads up the path, before opening the front door for us.

"What do I do?" I ask, standing in the middle of her living room. Apart from the television set and the sofa, everything else is still in boxes.

"Lay her down on the floor," Maverick orders. "I'll go get some towels."

"Oh God, I need to push," she strains out, the veins in her head popping out.

Christ, that can't be natural.

"The paramedics are on their way," Mason reveals, looking at me with a pale face. "He asked how many centimetres dilated is she?"

"Dilated?" I ask, swaying slightly.

"Yes, dilated," Amelia screams, taking me aback.

"No need to shout at me," I yell, gripping my hair.

She begins sliding her scrubs down her legs, and frantically, I crawl back, staring at her in horror. "This can't be happening right now," she groans, before a noise, so loud and so feral, escapes up her throat.

Jesus. This is something out of an exorcist's movie.

"Put them back on," I cry out, but she kicks them off, going for her boxer shorts next. "God, no."

"Close your fucking legs," Max snaps, covering his face up.

"Will you get out," she screams. "I don't need this right now."

"*You* don't need this," he screams, thumping his chest. "*I* don't need this. I came to see who my nephew had the hots for, who my niece said was different from the others. I didn't come for this. I've been through this before. I still have nightmares."

I glare at my uncle. "For the last time, I do not have the hots for her." Taking a calming breath, I then ask, "Isn't birth meant to be beautiful?"

He points at Amelia, narrowing his eyes. "Does that look beautiful to you? *Does it?* Because I'm telling you now, my boy, they fucking lie."

"Why don't we go and find some toys," Myles orders gently, steering Jasmine out of the room before glancing over his shoulder. "Her mum is on the way."

Face covered in sweat, her cheeks and neck bright red, Amelia glares at me, panting heavily. "I'm giving birth, and whether I like it or not, I've got you. Now I need you to look and tell me what you see."

She sounds so rational, so at ease, like she's asking me to look in the fridge. I'm far from rational right now. In fact, I feel like I'm slowly losing grip on reality.

She is giving birth.

To a baby.

And for some reason, I'm the one situated between her legs, ready to catch the fucker.

My pulse races as Maverick comes back in with a pile of crème towels, placing one over her lap.

"I can already tell you what I'll see. A vagina." I try to find an excuse to get out of this but there are none. "Isn't birth meant to take hours?"

"Please," she begs, pushing at her boxer shorts.

Fuck!

Max steps forward, slicing his hand across his neck. "Don't do it."

I had pictured this moment in a completely different setting and scenario. I never imagined the time I got her naked would be because I was waiting on the tiny human to exit her vagina.

Manning up, I grip her boxers, sliding them down her thighs whilst keeping my gaze averted from that area.

Her warm hands grip my wrists when I get past her knees, and I panic, thinking I misheard her, until she screams in my face, straining below.

"I never wanted to go through this again," Max whispers shakily, as I quickly place the boxers beside us.

"You aren't going to be there for Hayden?" Maverick asks.

Why are they all acting like this is normal? Can they not see what is happening right in front of them?

"Do you want to go grab a beer while you chat?" I grit out.

"Sounds like a good idea," Max murmurs, heading towards the kitchen. Calling back, he yells, "And Hayden loves me. She understands the pain I went through when she was brought into this world."

"He's deluded when it comes to his kids," Maverick mutters to Mason.

"Are you okay?" I ask softly, helping her lie back down on the pillows someone placed behind her back.

"Do I look okay?" she barks, before grimacing. "Sorry."

"If there is any time to forget pleasantries, this would be it."

She begins to cry, her fingers sinking into the carpet. "It wasn't meant to be like this. None of it."

Maverick taps Mason on the shoulder. "Why don't we step out?"

I go to leave, but she pulls me back down, grunting. "Don't you dare leave me."

"I won't, I swear it," I promise, but there might be a chance I pass out before it's over.

Max walks in, swaying in the doorway. My gaze goes to the cake and fork in his hand. "Um, she doesn't have any beer, so I'm, um, going for some air."

"Put that cake fucking back," I snap.

He growls, clutching the plate to his chest. "I eat my feelings when I'm anxious. Fuck off."

I glance over at Dad, who begins to sneak out behind him. "Don't you dare leave me alone in here."

He arches his eyebrow at me. "I'm just going to see if the ambulance is here."

That lying bastard.

"Dad! Dad!" I yell, but he's gone, leaving me alone with her.

"Can you see anything?" she asks, straining as her body tightens. She seems to be weakening, but I'm grateful she's no longer screaming. Slowly, with each one, she was breaking me.

As soon as the ambulance comes, I can leave.

"Why don't we wait for the paramedics?"

She moos. Actually moos. Or what sounds like a moo. Straining so forcefully, I have to lean over to wipe the sweat away before it runs into her eyes.

Face red and bathed in sweat, she scowls. "Fucking look, Maddox, now."

Snapping to attention, I can't help but look down, and what I see has bile rising in my throat. "Oh fuck."

"What?" she asks, straining once again.

I squeak when something bulges from out of her vagina before popping back in. *Are all vaginas this big?*

"Oh my God," I squeal.

"What is it?" she screams, before concentrating on pushing.

Now that I'm looking, I can't look away. "I think I see the head. I hope it's the head. It could be anything. I mean, there's a lot going on down there right now."

She tries to laugh but it comes out gurgled. "Does everything look okay?"

My breath hitches a little. "*Compared to what?*"

She pants out, "Just tell me what you see."

I look again, only seeing specks of blood, clear fluid and a lot of angry skin. "Do you really want to know?"

"Oh God," she cries out, pushing so hard I'm surprised she doesn't burst a blood vessel. When she does it again seconds later, the head slides further out.

"Come on, it's nearly here," I encourage her, gripping her knees.

Blowing out a breath, she then draws in another, before pushing with so much force the sound that crawls up her throat startles me, but not as much as the head that pushes through, ripping the skin around her vagina.

"Dad!" I roar, not knowing what to do as my hands hover over the wrinkled bundle.

He races through the door as the body slides out. I might not know what to do, but my body does. I reach for the towel, wrapping the tiny boy in the soft cotton.

"Oh fuck!" Max groans, before his eyes roll to the back of his head and he collapses to the floor, the empty plate now beside him.

"It's a boy," I whisper, staring down at the miracle in my hands. He is so tiny, so precious, and I can't help but marvel at the fact she has just given him life.

"A boy?" she whispers, tears streaming down her face now.

"He has something sticking out of his stomach that's, um, still up your, um—"

"Paramedics are here," Dad reveals.

My shoulders drop, and I look up to a worn-out Amelia, beaming at her. "You did it. You really did."

She reaches out to take her boy. Her fingers touch the material of the towel, just as a sharp intake of breath escapes her and she collapses back, passed out.

FIVE

MADDOX

I'M STILL HOLDING THE BABY, rocking him gently in my arms, while the paramedics finish sorting Amelia out.

Once she woke up, I handed her the baby, but it wasn't even a minute before the paramedics were passing him back to me. I guess I looked like the most trustworthy one in here.

It feels bizarre holding him in my arms. I can't explain it. I came here to do some work and instead, I delivered a baby. *A baby.*

"Sir, we're ready to leave. Would you like to come with mum and your son?"

I open my mouth, yet no words come out. I clear my throat, answering, "He's not my son. I'm not the father," I explain. "I live across the street."

"Jasmine," Amelia panics. "My mum isn't here."

I stand, careful with the life in my hands, meeting Myles when he takes a step forward to answer Amelia. "Your mum got stuck in traffic. She's closer to the hospital so I told her to meet you there."

"But Jasmine," Amelia replies, her gaze darting from my uncle to me, panicked.

"I can watch her, if you like. I'm a social worker. She'll be safe with me," Myles offers with an assuring smile.

She still looks hesitant, biting her bottom lip as her gaze darts back to me again. "I—I don't know."

"I'll watch her," I offer. I shrug at everyone's surprised faces. I can tell what they are thinking: that I can't look after a loaf of bread, let alone a kid. But how hard can it be? Aiden does it every day and he couldn't keep a goldfish alive when he was younger.

"I mean, I can watch her while I wait for your mum to come back from visiting with you. They said you need to stay in for observation, so you won't be coming back tonight, and your mum can't stay after visiting hours. I can wait here until then."

Her doubtful expression has me smiling. "You would do that?"

I smirk. "I just delivered a baby. Babysitting will be a piece of cake. Plus, you still need me to put the cot up, otherwise this little guy won't have anywhere to sleep."

"Now I'll need a new carpet in here," she murmurs, a little smile reaching her lips. "Can I have my baby back now?"

Jasmine giggles down by my leg. "He's going to keep him."

I quickly hand the baby over to Amelia, giving her an impish smile when she giggles. "I'm not."

She coos down at the bundle now dressed and wrapped up warm. I pause to watch her, seeing the same look Aiden gets when he looks at Sunday. It's more than love. I've seen love in the way my parents look at each other, but the way Amelia is looking at her son… it's as if she's holding the universe in the palm of her hands.

"Are you ready to go?" the paramedic asks, strapping her to the gurney.

I can understand her reluctance to leave her daughter in the care of five strangers. She doesn't know us. But I do, and I'd never let anything happen to her.

"I'll make sure she's safe. I swear it."

Hope taps her knuckles onto the door, letting us know she's here. "Hey, Dad called… Oh my God, Amelia," Hope gushes, when she sees her on the gurney. *They know each other?* "I didn't know this was your house. I thought you rented the one closer to the care home."

Amelia's lips part. "Hope?"

"My dad called me to say I might be needed, but I didn't know it was you. I got stuck in traffic," she rushes to explain, before leaning over and running her finger along the boy's head. "He's absolutely beautiful. Congratulations."

"Thank you."

"What did you call him?"

"I'm not sure yet," she whispers, her gaze briefly darting to me.

"We need to go," the paramedic announces again.

Hope steps back to give them room.

"Jasmine will be safe here with me," I promise her as they begin to push her out.

Hope narrows her gaze on me before looking down at Amelia. "I'll be here too."

Nodding her head, relief written all over her expression, she relaxes against the pillow. "Thank you. I'll get Mum back here as soon as possible."

"Just concentrate on you and the little one," Hope orders.

The paramedics wheel her out and Dad walks over to me, his expression blank. "You need to watch out for those neighbours. They're eyeing the house like a prize possession."

"They're lucky Amelia went into labour before we could call the police. He needs a kickin'."

"Yes, because Max could give a good explanation to the police as to why he had a bat in his hand," he replies.

Jasmine pulls on my hoody, and when I look down, she presses her hands together in prayer. "Can we watch a movie please?"

"Yeah, sounds good." I grin, slapping my dad on the back. "My dad here is going to set up your room for you while we watch it."

"Am I now?"

"Yes, and be a darlin' and grab the other roll of carpet from my garage. It was meant to be for my spare room, but you may as well use it for in here." I flop back on the sofa, dodging the blood stains on the floor, and pat the seat next to me. "How do you feel about action movies?"

"She can't watch—"

I stop Hope with a look. "Why don't you go help sort the baby clothes out or even help with Jaz's room."

Jasmine giggles. "My name's Jasmine, silly."

I grin down at her, before tapping my finger against her nose. "Now it's Princess Jaz."

She cuddles up to me on the sofa, and I stiffen, grimacing down at her. *What is she doing?* Hope laughs at my expression before leaving me on the sofa.

"Can we watch Frozen?"

Blanching, I shake my head. "How about a football game? I'm dying to watch tonight's game, and you, my friend, can be my new footy companion. I've been needing a new one for a while now. You'll be perfect."

She pumps her fists into the air. "Yes! I like football."

I grin at the kid. I wonder if Sunday will be this cool when she's older. Right now, all she does is steal your food and slobber all over you.

I THINK I BROKE the child. Manchester United just scored, and after two hours of watching the other games, she's really into it. Which is why I put the football highlights on.

Now, she's running around the living room, her jacket over her head, screaming, "Goal!"

Mum, who came after Hope called the family tree to come and help, rubs a hand over my shoulder, laughing at Jasmine. "I remember when you and Madison used to run around like this."

"Maddy liked football?" I ask, teasingly.

We get on better than most siblings, and I think that's because we are twins. However, it doesn't mean we don't argue back and forth. One thing we argue over is having the footy on the television. She hates it, always wanting to watch one of her rom-coms.

"She's a good kid."

I watch as Jasmine jumps on the sofa, shaking her behind in the air. I chuckle. "They nearly finished up there?"

"Why? Are you going to go up and start telling them they aren't doing it good enough again?"

"Mum, he was tiny," I argue. "He could get hurt easily if they don't set it up right."

Smiling, she replies. "I can't believe you delivered a baby."

I puff out my chest. "Mum, the rest of them were crying and cringing the whole time. What could I do but help her?"

"That wasn't what happened at all," Max argues, walking in and dropping himself next to me on the sofa. He swings Jasmine up before dropping her on his lap, tickling her.

"Stop!" she squeals, laughing uproariously.

He grins, letting her go. "Your son was crying for his daddy the entire time."

Growling low in my throat, I send him a lethal glare. "And what were you doing?"

A light pink tinge lights up his cheeks. "I was monitoring this one."

Jasmine pouts. "No, you weren't. The other you was reading me a story, and when we came down, you were sleeping on the floor."

Laughing, I high five Jasmine. "You tell him."

"Oh, Max," Mum giggles.

Max shrugs, not caring. "It's a medical issue, you know. I get PTSD. Thank God no one in our family is pregnant right now. I might have a heart attack."

"Mum, watch Jasmine for a second while I go see if the room is okay?"

She gives me a nod, ignoring Max's snort. "Go on. The girls have nearly finished putting away all her things in the kitchen."

The place looks more like a home and a lot less like one of Jaxon's storage units. I did good, and Amelia will be proud.

Heading upstairs, I hear my dad, Mason and uncle Maverick arguing in Jasmine's room. I peek around the door, my eyebrows bunching together as I see them holding parts of a toy.

"Did you break that?" I ask, eyes wide.

Dad drops the toy to the floor, groaning before taking a look around the room. "He bloody left."

What the fuck?

"Um, someone want to fill me in on what's going on?"

Maverick, shoving a toy behind his back, grimaces. "Your uncle kind of roped—or should I say—goaded us, into having a race with these wind-up toys. Your dad kind of lost it when Max's toy knocked his over. Now we can't put it back together."

I arch an eyebrow at Dad. "Really, Dad?"

Lips set in a straight line, he narrows his gaze on me. "I can't help it. He pushes the right buttons. I swear, I'll go out and buy her some new toys."

"Can I leave you alone for a few moments to go check on the nursery or should I get Mum up here to supervise?"

He grunts. "I'm not Max. Plus, we're done up here."

I look at the new carpet, and the set up. It looks good, although, if it were my kid, I'd have a swing in here, near the window, coming down from the ceiling beams. And there's a lot of pink, but I guess everyone has their faults.

"I'll be down in a minute," I tell them, going to leave.

Maverick's voice stops me. "Tell Lily I'll take her home in a minute."

"I thought she was sick?"

Was it wise for her to be touching stuff? I mean, the baby could get sick if she spreads germs on his stuff.

"She said she's feeling better."

"She's been sick for a bit now," I remind him, biting my lip. I hope she's okay. I hate seeing her sick. "I'll see you downstairs."

I exit the room, making my way down the short hallway to the baby's room. Lily is standing over the cot, her fingers running along the light green blanket someone has folded at the end.

Her expression makes me pause. She looks deep in thought, and I wonder if she's picturing herself as a mother. She doesn't confide in many people, but she does me, and I know one of her fears is becoming a mum and not being the best parent, like her first mum. Lily was adopted by Maverick—who is biologically her brother—at four. The woman who raised her for those few years of her life was abusive and as cruel as they come. Because of that, Lily suffered with panic attacks. No amount of therapists or love from all of us could make it go away completely. As painful as it is to admit, Jaxon, her husband, healed her in a way we couldn't.

"You're thinking awfully hard over there," I call out lightly, causing her to jump.

She places a palm over her stomach, her lips downcast. "Sorry, I was just admiring the room. They did really good."

They did. The white furniture looks good against the yellow and mint walls.

"What's on your mind?"

When she looks at me, I can see the hesitancy, and I'm not going to lie and say it doesn't hurt, because it does. She used to tell me everything, but I hurt her when I beat the crap out of her husband. I was a dick, but I was just looking out for her. She was too kind, and others tried to take advantage of that. None of us wanted her to experience any more pain or heartbreak.

"I was just wondering if I'd be a good mum."

I wrap my arm around her shoulder, pulling her against me. "You'll be the best, Lily. Never doubt that."

"Jaxon says that too, but I don't know. I still have panic attacks and black out sometimes from them. What if I do that when I have a baby to look after?"

I can understand her fears, but they're pointless. She's never really understood her worth. "Lily, I truly believe that when the time comes, your mind will somehow reset. These fears you have... they'll be gone and be replaced with new ones you'll have for your child. Never be scared of being a mum, Lily. You're going to be the best."

Her smile doesn't quite reach her eyes. "I don't want to let Jaxon down."

A growl threatens to surface but I tamper it down, knowing she'll only dislike me for it. "Jaxon loves you. Never worry about that." I give her a minute to absorb my words before asking, "Lily, is that all that's bothering you? It seemed like there was something else on your mind."

She fiddles with the hem of her blouse, unable to look at me. "I'm not sure. Once I know, I'll tell you."

"That wasn't cryptic at all."

With a giggle, she leans into me. "Sorry."

I kiss the top of her head, enjoying having this time with her without Jaxon there glaring because she likes to cook for me. "I'm always here if you need to talk. You know that."

"This room is really beautiful," she comments, changing the subject. "I still can't believe you delivered a baby."

"Neither can I," I murmur, wondering how mum and son are doing.

She tilts her head up. "Is she nice?"

"I don't really know her. From what I've learnt, yes. She seems to have some problems though. Two women came around earlier, causing shit for her."

Her lips part. "No wonder she went into labour."

I let out a dry chuckle. "I think that had to do with Jasmine nearly getting run over."

She gasps, reaching for my hand. "Oh God, what happened? Was she hurt? She didn't look hurt."

"Hey," I rush out, rubbing her arm. "She's fine. I got to her in time, but it could have ended badly."

"She must be worried then—not being with her daughter."

I hadn't thought of that. "Maybe."

"Hey, Madz, Nita, the grandma, is here," Maddy announces.

"Come on," I gently order, letting Lily go out first. She takes one last look at the room, a wistful sigh escaping her.

Maverick is waiting by the front door when we reach the bottom of the stairs. "Lily, you ready to go?"

"Yes," she answers, striding towards him. She backpedals at the last second, turning to me. "Thank you for talking to me."

Something is bothering her, but until she's ready, I know she won't talk. "Any time."

Maddy arches her eyebrow. "What was that about?"

"I'm not sure. She never said."

She sighs, her shoulders dropping. "Like you'd tell me, anyway."

I grin, lightly punching her shoulder. "Aww, don't worry, I tell you all my secrets."

She pouts. "No, you don't, but then, I don't care. I don't tell you mine either."

"What secrets do you have?" I ask, my voice high-pitched. I clear my throat, lowering my voice. "You're bluffing."

She shrugs, a wide grin on her face. "Wouldn't you like to know."

Yeah, I really would.

"Maddox, thank you so much," Nita gushes, tears running down her face. I get a second's warning before she's enveloping me in a tight hug. "You saved my granddaughter, delivered my grandson, and you've unpacked and organised her entire house."

"I'm a giving man," I tease, slightly uncomfortable with the praise.

"He had help," Max yells, lying over the sofa.

Nita pulls back, and cups my cheek. "I don't care. My daughter…" She shakes her head, wiping away her tears. "She's been through so much. She's a survivor. You doing this for her, it makes me happy. It will restore the faith she lost after what her ex-boyfriend did to her. I don't know how I can ever repay you."

What her ex-boyfriend did to her? So he isn't dead?

I can see the others are dying to ask too, but remarkably, they keep quiet.

"Do you bake?" I ask, not wanting to know about Amelia's previous life. I can't get too involved. She isn't for me. And she has kids.

Smiling, she pats my cheek then takes a step back. "I do, but my cooking is better. Amelia's the baker."

I lick my lips, my stomach grumbling. "Well, next time you're here, bring me over a plate."

She rushes at me again, squeezing me into a tight hug. "You're a good man."

I glance up with her still in my arms. Max is laughing uproariously on the sofa, Dad is giving me a knowing smirk, and Mum, for some reason, has tears in her eyes.

"I really didn't do much."

"That's not what my daughter told me. She said you were a hero for saving her daughter, for getting rid of the witches, and for delivering her son."

Stepping back, I rub at the back of my neck. "Well, um, you're welcome?"

"You've probably all had a long day but please, pop by again. Amelia would love to thank you for the work you've done."

"It's our pleasure," Mum answers her, grabbing her bag from the floor. "Jasmine has fallen asleep on the floor. She, um, she got overexcited about football and tired herself out."

Nita's nose scrunches up. "Did she have a screaming fit to get it turned off? My Gareth puts in on and she screams down the house until you turn it off."

Everyone, including me, is stunned. I give her an impish smile. "Um, not quite. She kind of got into it. At one point, she was running around the living room with her jacket covering her face, screaming 'goal'."

Nita opens her mouth, closes it, then opens it again before shaking her head. "Well, that's never happened before."

"We'll let you get her to bed," Mum tells her on a chuckle.

"You raised a good boy," she tells my mum, causing her to beam.

"I did," she agrees.

"It was touch and go," Dad jokes, causing Max to laugh harder.

"Dad!"

"You're his dad?" Nita asks, surprised. "I thought the man on the sofa was."

I groan, covering my face. Any hope that Max didn't hear goes out the window when he jumps up from the sofa, laughing his head off. "Nope. I'm too good looking to be this one's dad. Although, he does get all his best personality traits from me."

"I'm sorry. When Amelia asked last night if I had any recipes for cakes that were safe for people with diabetes, she also mentioned your dad didn't get out much either. When that woman was yelling at him for eating the muffins, I assumed it was because of his diabetes."

"What cake?" Dad asks, giving me a side glance.

Fuck!

"She offered to make one to say thank you but then Maddox said you had diabetes," Nita helpfully explains.

"Did he now?" Dad mutters, glaring at me. "My son is mistaken."

"Let's go," I demand, quickly turning to Nita. "Congratulations on becoming a grandma again."

I push Max out the door, ignoring his bickering as my dad apologises for our abrupt departure.

We hit the end of the path and come to a stop. I growl at the blaring music coming from my neighbours, and the sound of loud voices echoing through the open windows and doors.

I turn as a hand slaps down hard on my shoulder. Dad grins. "Son, you're fucked."

"What?"

He's not going to mention the cake?

"She's going to make you love her until it hurts, and I'm going to enjoy every single minute of you falling for her."

"Shut the fuck up."

He walks off with Mum, his hand going to her arse, making me gag. "Call it payback for trying to keep the cake to yourself," he calls out in twisted humour.

Arsehole.

He's wrong. There is nothing between us. We're practically strangers. My thoughts feel sour, and instead of waiting to say goodbye to everyone, I storm across the road, not stopping when they teasingly call my name.

"Fuck all of you," I yell, giving them my middle finger.

I'm not going to fall for her.
No way.

SIX

MADDOX

Pulling up outside Lily's, I put the truck into park. I scrub my face with both hands, the events of yesterday still going through my head.

Someone out to get the Hayes' business had the property they were working on, set on fire. Lily was in that house, and they were trapped. Knowing I could have lost her... I shake my head, not wanting to think about it. It's still going unanswered as to why she was there in the first place.

When I tried speaking to her the other day, a few days after the day I delivered Amelia's baby, she couldn't speak. She was too busy being sick. And from what was said yesterday, she wasn't all that well then either.

So why was she there? She should have been at home resting.

Jaxon has a lot to answer for. If he doesn't sort this Andrew Black business out, and soon, we will do it for him. If it wasn't for the fact that we respect the need to deal with shit ourselves, we would have already stepped in.

When Lily called, telling me to come over this morning, I dropped work, leaving Todd—my site manager—in charge. We normally have Sunday's off, but with our schedule for the next few months, we want to get on top of everything.

Sliding out, I slam the car door shut, staring up at the house. Maverick's car is parked behind Lily's, and unease pricks at my skin. I'm not the only one she called, so it must be bad.

Slowly, I make my way up to her door, before gripping the handle and pushing it open. I paste on a fake smile. "Honey, I'm home."

Maverick steps out of the living room, closing the door behind him. "Upset her, and I'll break your legs."

"Well, good morning to you too, cherry."

"This is no time to play games," he warns me.

I give him a closer look, seeing his eyes are glassy from tears. I swallow past the lump in my throat. "Is she okay? She said the doctors were happy and she was fine."

"She's…" He stops, exhaling. "Just go listen to what she has to say."

Striding past him, I push the door open, stepping into the front room. One glance at Teagan and my gut clenches. She's crying, but she's also smiling.

Lily, who also has tears in her eyes, looks up at me, quickly getting up and out of Jaxon's arms. "You made it."

"I told you I'd be here," I remind her. "What is it you want to discuss?"

She reaches out for Jaxon and he takes her hand, getting up to stand next to her. "We were going to wait, but after last night and the close call, we thought it would be wise if our parents knew. It was hard for me to keep Mum and Dad out of the room last night."

I'm completely lost.

I scan her body, seeing no visible signs of injury. She's pale, though, and her hands are shaking. *Is she sick?*

"I'm lost," I tell her truthfully.

Taking a deep breath, she straightens her shirt. "First, we need you to promise that what we tell you doesn't leave this room. I wanted Mum and Dad to know, and we are going to tell Jaxon's mum and Faith next, but I wanted you to know before the others." Her eyebrows pull together. "Except Wyatt and Reid, but that was an accident. We didn't tell them; they overheard. But no one other than you guys can know. Not yet. We want to wait."

Laughing at her nervousness, I joke, "If you're going to tell me you and Jaxon are getting married, you're too late. I was there, remember?"

She giggles, sagging against Jaxon. "No silly. I'm pregnant."

I stagger backwards into the chair, my arse hitting the soft cushion. "What? How? When? Holy fuck!" I glance up at her in horror. Flashes of pain, and the sounds Amelia made during birth run through my mind. "Lily, I don't think you know what you're getting into."

"Maddox!" Teagan snaps.

Seeing Lily's bottom lip tremble and Jaxon take a step forward, his expression livid, I hold up my hands. "No, no. I'm happy for you. Seriously. I meant what I said the other day, Lily. You're going to be a fantastic mum, but—"

"What do you mean, but?" Maverick snaps. "I thought we were over this crap?"

I hold up my hands, feeling my cheeks heat. "A lot happens down there," I yell, pointing to her crotch, then shoving my hand down at my side. "It's not going to be pretty when you give birth. Don't listen to anyone who tells you otherwise. It looks painful too. *Really* painful. To the point I think I'd rather have bamboo sticks shoved under my nails."

Teagan, shoulders dropping, lets out a giggle. "Maddox, birth may be painful, but the minute you hold your baby, it's forgotten. It's one of the best moments of your life."

I doubt that.

A thought occurs to me; Amelia didn't hold her baby right away. Was she still remembering the pain?

"Maddox, women have been doing this for years," Lily tells me, pulling away from Jaxon to stand in front of me.

I reach for her hands. "Lil, you're too small and delicate." I pause, something Mum once said coming to mind. "If they give you another option to give birth, go for it."

"So, you aren't mad? You aren't going to…"

Her gaze goes to Jaxon as she bites her bottom lip, and realisation dawns on me. She thought I'd kick off and beat the shit out of him again. As tempting as that is, I can't deny how happy she is with him. I learned my lesson the first time. Not having her in my life… it killed me.

I reach for her, gently pulling her into my arms and kissing the top of her head. "Will you still be my best friend?"

Her eyebrows pull together. "Of course."

"Will you still cook for me when dick face isn't here?"

Smiling, she rolls her eyes. "Yes."

"Will you still let me come over, even though the kid will love me more than they love Jaxon?"

Laughing, she wipes away her tears. "Yes."

Jaxon grunts but I ignore him, my smile spreading. "Then I'm overjoyed for you. Worried? Yes. But I'm happy for you. You'll be the perfect mum. I've seen you with Sunday. I've seen you with the brats next door. No one is as loving as you, except for me."

She slaps my arm gently. "You don't even pick up Sunday unless she's freshly washed and changed."

I snort, waving her remark off. "I have good clothes. She has a thing for wiping slobber and snot all over them. I'm still her favourite uncle." I exhale, continuing to answer her previous concern. "But that just proves what a good mum you'll be. You don't care when Sunday slaps one on your lips, even though she's covered in shit and snot."

Giggling, Lily takes a step back. "Thank you. It means a lot that you're okay with this."

"Not that you had a say anyway," Jaxon adds, his expression hard.

As much as his comment pisses me off, he's also right. "We've only ever wanted what's best for you. For you to be happy. There's no denying you're happy."

"Thank you," she breathes out, her glassy eyes sparkling with tears. "We aren't ready to tell the rest of the family yet. We want to wait until I'm further along."

"I won't say anything, I promise."

Teagan begins to blubber into her tissue. She looks up, tears streaming down her face. "My baby girl is having a baby."

"Mum," Lily giggles, stepping into her arms. "Faith could be next too. They might be able to grow up together like we all did."

Maverick falls against the doorframe. When he sees us all staring, he slowly straightens, looking pale. "Let's not jinx anything. Our family is already large enough."

My phone rings from my pocket, pulling me away from the conversation. I pull it out, seeing Madison's name flashing on the screen. "Hello?"

"Um, Madz, you might want to go home."

Hearing the apprehension in her voice has me tensing. "Why? What's going on?"

"I went to yours to see if you were doing okay. I know you said you were fine after the fire, but I'm your twin; I'm allowed to care," she rambles.

I cut her off before she can continue. "It's four stiches, Maddy. I'll live. Just tell me what's going on." A kid blindsided me when I ran around the corner to help out the others. Apparently, they were there to smoke them out of the house and then beat them to a pulp. We were lucky we turned up when we did because Reid had been stabbed. Well, it was more like a scratch, but he was being a baby about it.

"Well, next door egged your house. I didn't stop because of, you know, what happened the last time."

I release a string of curses and all eyes come to me. I force a smile, turning my back to them. "It's because I turned their electric off again last night."

"I thought you said that wasn't working?"

"It's not, but at least Amelia didn't have to listen to it her first night home."

"Aww, you really care about her."

"No, I fucking don't," I rush out, feeling my face heat. "Why you all keep going on about it is baffling me. I don't even know her."

"You delivered her baby."

"And? The guy at McDonalds delivers me food but that doesn't mean he's in love with me."

"I'm just saying. She's different. You were different when you were around her. You didn't even give her one of your sleazy chat-up lines."

"That's because if you hadn't noticed, she was pregnant and has a kid."

Laughing, she says, "She isn't anymore, and you're practically BFF's with Jasmine."

I smile thinking about our game night, but then frown, not wanting to go there. "I'll be home soon. I'll figure something else out to get them out of that house, even if I have to knock the entire thing down."

"I get it. I'll drop it for now. But don't push her away before you even give it a chance," she tells me, and I groan.

Anyone would think I'd known this chick years. I haven't. I don't even know what her last name is, if she's a good cook, if she likes footy, what she tastes like.

"Is that all?"

"No. I also called to tell you I spoke to a friend in the shop today. He said if you want a quicker way to get them evicted, have a petition signed from all the neighbours."

I muse over it, wondering if I have the time to do it. I do. A smirk pulls at the corner of my lips. "I may even be able to get them to sign it."

She laughs. "Definitely. I need to go, but I'll pop round in the week."

I growl when she ends the call without a goodbye, then turn to the room. Maverick and Teagan are smirking, Lily looks worried, and Jaxon seems bored. "What?"

"Is that about Amelia?"

"If you must know, it was about my neighbours. Maddy caught them egging my house."

"She didn't try to stop them, did she?" Maverick asks, taking a step closer.

"No," I sigh out. "She learnt her lesson the last time, when she got stuck trying to climb from my window to theirs."

"I could have sworn you mentioned Amelia," Teagan muses, her lips twitching.

"The lady who gave birth?" Lily asks, her eyes sparking.

"I'm going," I yell, moving towards the door. "Congratulations on the pregnancy. I'll be by tomorrow for lunch."

"Bye," she yells back.

I DIDN'T WANT to give them the pleasure of seeing me seething over the state of my windows and doors, which is why I didn't go straight home after Lily gave me the news. However, I made the wrong decision, because now they're all out the front, and I can't hide my rage over the mess they have made. Not only is there egg all over the front door, but the partial glass in my door is cracked.

I walk around to the side of the house, grateful my jet wash is still connected to the outdoor tap. I drag it around the front before spraying the windows and door. It washes away most of the mess, but not all of it.

"Ew, can you smell egg, guys?" Kayne asks, loud enough for the other neighbours to hear. He pretends to gag, causing his friends snicker.

I feign a pitying stare his way, meeting his gaze. "I had a friend once with the same issue. Toothpaste and a shower worked like a charm in the end."

His expression grows turbulent. "Are you saying I smell of fucking egg?"

I hold my hands up. "Hey, you don't need to be ashamed. We all have issues. Yours just stinks."

"You fucking prick," he roars, jumping off his front doorstep.

I don't move. Instead, I cross my arms over my chest, tucking my hands under my armpits. "Do you really want me to embarrass you with all your friends watching?"

He pauses just shy of the property line, where the fence once was before he knocked it down. "I'll kick your arse."

I laugh, throwing my head back. "Kid, come at me, I dare you. I'll even let you have the first shot. After your friends watch me beat the living crap out of you, they'll leave, too ashamed to be near you. Maybe then I won't have to listen to your fucking music all night, so do it. C'mon."

Shakily, he takes a step back, trying to straighten his spine and be tough. "Nah, you 'ent worth it."

Grinning, I lean forward. "That's what I thought."

"Next time, I'll fuck you up," he tells me, and it's my turn to step back.

"Dude, even if I was into guys, you wouldn't be my type," I call back, loud enough for his mates to hear me.

"What the fuck you on about?" he yells, paling. "You're a sick fuck."

"So the ladies tell me," I taunt, leaving him to stew as I put the jet wash away in my garage.

When I reach the drive again, the car across the street pulls my attention away from the bickering going on beside me.

Amelia helps Jasmine out of the car before going to the other side. A part of me wants to go inside and ignore the fact that I've seen her, but my body makes the decision for me, and in seconds, I'm striding across the road.

Jasmine sees me first. "Maddox! Maddox! Come meet my baby brother."

I smile at the little girl, catching her in my arms and swinging her up. "Hey Jaz."

She giggles at her nickname. "Princess Jaz."

"Princess Jaz," I confirm, grinning. Her mum, who has frozen near the car door, turns red. "Hey, how are you doing?"

"She has a sore lady bum," Jasmine whispers, causing Amelia to turn redder.

I grimace, only imagining what it must feel like down there. "I bet."

"I've been meaning to come over—"

Wailing from inside the car stops Amelia from whatever she was about to say. She gives me a small smile before opening the car door, cooing gently at the baby. I step forward, trying to look in without intentionally meaning to.

When she steps backwards, I take one back, getting out of the way. When I see her knuckles turning white around the handle of the car seat, I step forward, reaching for the handle.

"I'll help you inside."

She pauses for a moment, but then nods, letting go. "Thank you. I wasn't sure how to get the shopping out as I didn't want to leave him in the car after…" Her gaze goes across the road, and I know what she's thinking. I don't blame her. I informed Beau of what the kid did, and he's told me to report him next time.

"You can stay for dinner," Jasmine announces, taking my free hand.

My stomach grumbles in response, and Amelia laughs as she slams her boot closed. "I do owe you a thank you."

"You don't, but I never turn down food." I grin, but it drops when a thought occurs to me. "You can cook, right?"

I've learnt my lesson: don't believe something tastes good just because it looks good. Charlotte taught me that the first time she cooked for me. The other times I fell for her food doesn't count.

And if Amelia's a good cook, maybe we could become good friends. Since I never see Lily now, I have time to spare and no one to feed me.

"I can," she reveals. "And I do owe you a thank you. I put you in an awkward position. What you did for me, for us, I'm grateful." She pauses, stopping to give me her full attention. "I still can't believe you managed to unpack and arrange everything how I would have it. You even sorted his room out for me. Thank you doesn't seem enough for what you have done."

When he begins to stir again, I bring the car seat up higher so we're nearly eye level. His tiny face is scrunched up, his bottom lip trembling. He has his mum's eyes, yet somehow, darker.

"Be good for your mum," I tell him, taken aback when he suddenly stops, his lips puckering as he sucks on nothing. I glance up at Amelia, answering her. "Don't mention it."

Heat creeps up my neck when I think of what I saw that day. No guy should ever witness that.

From the stories I heard from my relatives, they had all been by their other half's side when they were in labour. But then, my family are nuts, so no wonder they volunteered to witness that torture.

No wonder they say, once you have kids, your sex life is ruined. I've not been able to fuck anyone since. Tammy, the chick I fuck on a regular basis, was ready to go the other night. I had my trousers down to my ankles, condom rolled on, but the minute she spread her legs, all I could picture was Amelia giving birth. I had to make up an excuse that I had to feed the cat. It didn't matter that she knew I don't have a pet. I had to get out of there.

She pushes the door open, letting Jasmine run ahead of her. I follow her into the kitchen, watching as she places the bags down on the counter.

"Mummy, I'm hungry," Jasmine whines, as I hear the television start up.

When the baby starts to cry again, Amelia sags a little against the counter, looking utterly worn out.

"Do you want me to help with anything?" I ask before I can stop myself. There's just something about seeing her look so tired, so rushed, that has me wanting to help.

"You've done too much already, and I'm still unsure why," she announces as she bends down, giving me a line of sight down her top when she unbuckles the baby. Her tits look bigger than I remember, and they were generous before. I inwardly groan and force myself not to react when she straightens with him in her arms. I place the car seat down on the floor and step back to watch as she gently rocks him until he settles.

"Mummy," Jasmine cries. "I'm hungry."

I chuckle, moving further into the kitchen. "What does she have for dinner? I'll put it on."

She arches an eyebrow. "You can cook?"

Sheepishly, I give her a one arm shrug. "Not really but it's always edible."

There's laughter in her eyes when she glances at me. "Here. Hold Asher."

I go to refuse but the baby is in my arms before a breath escapes through my lips. "W-what? Why don't I cook?"

He's as light as I remember and fits perfectly as his head rests into the crook of my arm, his body the size of my forearm.

"He's so tiny," I murmur.

"He's lost a little weight."

My head shoots up at that. "Is he okay?"

Smiling as she turns the oven on, she nods. "It's normal."

I nod, relaxing slightly. His eyes sparkle up at me, and he's now blowing raspberries. I smile, rocking him gently. Then what she says penetrates. "Asher?"

I like it. It's a manly, strong name; not some name that will guarantee he spends his school years getting bullied.

"Yes," she replies quietly.

"And he has your name," Jasmine announces, walking into the room. She jumps up onto the stool, reaching for a strawberry out of the bowl.

"What?"

Amelia reddens. "My grandfather's name was Asher. It meant a lot to my dad that I gave him that name. And you delivered him," she explains, shrugging. "When he asks who he's named after, I'll get to tell him about his grandfather, and about the guy who delivered him and did something so huge for me and his sister. This house would never have been ready for his arrival if it weren't for you and your family. I'm not even sure who I should be thanking or how I can ever repay you all."

A lump forms in my throat as I stare down at the bundle in my arms. "Asher Maddox," I whisper before looking at his mum. "You don't have to thank anyone. They wanted to help. Although, I will warn you, my mum is wanting to meet you."

She smiles, staring longingly at me, and I can't look away. What she's done means a lot. The intensity isn't lost on either of us.

Her gaze, soft and relaxed, goes from me to Asher, and a flash of sadness resides there. "I'd love to meet your mum."

"So, are we eating?" Jasmine asks, breaking the tension, and I chuckle, walking over to ruffle her hair.

"Yes. I'm starving."

Amelia snorts. "Then I guess I should get cooking."

SEVEN

AMELIA

I can't believe he's here. Embarrassment floods my cheeks whenever I catch him looking at me. I just keep picturing the horrified expression he had when he looked between my legs. A part of me is just amused, but the other, the part that is extremely attracted to him, is mortified. Out of all the people I could have gone into labour in front of, it had to be the hot neighbour.

I still don't understand my attraction to him. How can I be attracted to someone after all I have been through? But the evidence is there, seeping between my legs, and I get butterflies in my stomach whenever I catch a glimpse of him. How can a stranger—a beautiful stranger—become someone I am so drawn to?

He is charming, and he is funny, but I had someone before with those qualities. I know how someone can hide their true colours.

And yet, even as those thoughts run through my head, I know deep in my soul that he's different. He isn't hiding who he is—even though he is a little nuts.

Mum has been on at me to date for months. She said even if I don't want a relationship, I have to try to get out there, to socialise. I'm terrified of being with another man, but yet, I can't deny there is something inside of me that needs to prove I can move on—even if it's only a dinner date.

I don't want to live my life scared, petrified I'll never feel sexy again, that I'll never feel intimacy or love. But mostly, I'm scared Cameron not only damaged me physically, but mentally, and I'll forever let my past rule my future. I don't want that for myself, and I don't want it for my kids.

Right now, I'm glad I don't have to think about any of it. I have a new home, and two beautiful children to concentrate on.

It still doesn't stop me from being attracted to Maddox, however hard I've tried not to be. And what makes him more appealing is everything he did for me that day, rearranging my home and unpacking. It's the way he held my son and the way he looked at me like I handed him the world when I told him Asher's full name. To me, giving Asher his name wasn't enough appreciation or recognition, and I wish I could do more.

Setting the plates down on the table, I take a deep breath. "Dinner's ready!" I call out.

A smile spreads across my face as Jasmine's feet stomp towards me. She skids to a stop at the table, smiling wide. "Cottage pie." She pumps her fists in the air. "Yes!"

"That smells amazing," Maddox praises, walking in. He stops at a chair, his pupils dilating somewhat at the food set in the middle.

"Are you okay?" I ask, a little concerned.

He licks his lips and reluctantly looks away. "Sorry, it's been a long time since I've had a home-cooked meal."

Instantly, I feel bad. Since we got back from the hospital, I've been meaning to go over and invite him over for dinner. I don't have much to give, but cooking I can do. It was the fear of him thinking I might be coming onto him that stopped me from heading over there to invite him. I heard him tell his uncle he didn't find me attractive. It was humiliating. I don't think I could handle another rejection, even if it was a misleading one.

"If I'm not working, you're more than welcome to come for dinner."

He grins, taking a seat. "Thanks. I will." He piles a large portion on his plate before frowning. "Is Asher okay on his own?"

Smiling at his concern, I nod. "He is. I'll hear him if he—" Asher picks that moment to start crying. I wait for a minute, hoping he'll go back to sleep. When he doesn't, Maddox goes to get up, but I stop him, waving him off. "I'll go feed him. I thought he'd go back to sleep. I won't be long."

His brows pull together. "Feed him here."

I pause before leaving, wondering if he's serious. Not everyone is comfortable with women breastfeeding. "Are you sure you're okay with that?"

He's seen everything else, so seeing a part of my breast will be nothing in comparison.

He grins. "We're eating, it's only fair that he eats too. My cousin tried to wait until Sunday was fed before he ate, but he learnt early on that if he did, the food would be ruined."

My shoulders sag with relief. I wasn't looking forward to eating heated up cottage pie. "I'll go get him. Be back."

I make a beeline for the living room, where Asher is wailing from his Moses basket. A smile pulls at my lips when I see him kicking his arms and legs out. His dark hair is fluffy, sticking up at the top. I cradle him in my arms, and he calms somewhat, his mouth searching for milk. I chuckle at his determination as I head back into the kitchen.

Our dining table is only a small one, since the space in here isn't that big, but it's perfect for me and Jasmine and one or two guests if we have any.

I take a look at Maddox and ask him one last time. "Are you sure you don't mind me feeding him?"

He lifts his fork, waving it before diving back into his food. "This is so good," he mumbles, taking more from the main dish.

Pulling the strap of my top down, I unclip my bra, freeing my breast. I wince at the discomfort when he latches on, going to town like he wasn't fed only a few hours ago.

Maddox begins to choke on his food, his eyes bulging out when he looks up from his plate. "W-what!"

I knew he'd be funny about it.

"Is there something wrong with my breast?" I ask, keeping my tone light.

He chokes again, and he slams his fist over his chest as he reaches for his glass of water. He clears his throat, straightening in his seat. "No, you, um, you've got great—" He stops, glancing at Jasmine. When he realises he's holding his hands up to his chest like he was cupping a pair of boobs, he slaps his hands down on the table. "Sorry."

"I can go upstairs," I murmur, going to stand.

He waves his hand, gesturing for me to sit down. "I didn't think you'd, um, you know, get them out. I thought you would have a bottle."

It's amusing how he keeps trying to avoid looking but is failing. It isn't like he can see much. Asher has my entire nipple in his mouth.

"You've gone a little red," I admit, reaching for my fork.

"I just didn't expect it. Then again, Aiden is male, so we never ran into this issue. Sorry if I'm being awkward."

"You're staring," I point out, my lips twitching.

He groans. "Sorry. He's just really going at it. It's hard to look away."

I chuckle, shifting Asher in my arms so I can dig into my food. "I got it a lot with Jasmine too. I'll pump once I have the equipment and bottles."

"You don't have them?" he asks, surprised.

"Not yet. I—" I take in a breath, unable to look at him. "With the move and stuff, I need to wait."

When I glance back up, he doesn't say anything, just stares at me in an unnerving way. I begin to fidget, not liking that it feels like he's reading into me. I couldn't bear it if he asked me about money or if I was struggling. Because the truth is, moving wasn't really the best choice for me to make right now. Mum and Dad offered for me to stay there, but I needed my independence back. I needed to set up a home for me and the kids.

Sometime during my relationship, I lost of a piece of myself. It started as a tear inside of me, but then after the attack, I was left with a gaping wound.

After I was released from the hospital, I was not only recovering from the injuries he inflicted, but from the emotional abuse I endured over the years. It wasn't until I met with other women in my group sessions, who had been through the same, that the signs were pointed out to me. I felt ridiculous for not seeing them beforehand.

Mum and Dad were my safety net. I relied on them to make me feel something other than a failure. They picked me up when I was down, raised my daughter whilst I was recovering, and was doing what any good parent would do: being there for their child.

But I couldn't let it go on anymore. They had already sacrificed so much for me, and I couldn't let that happen anymore. I needed to prove to myself I could do this.

Instead of asking what I assumed he would, he asks, "Where did you live before?"

"With Grandma," Jasmine says, piling more food onto Maddox's plate. "You need to eat more. Granddad said it helps you grow."

He grins and my stomach flips. "Good looking out, kid."

"You're welcome," she sing-songs, before going back to her own plate.

"We lived with my mum and dad before. With Asher due, I knew it was time to find somewhere."

He nods. "I understand that. I have a large family. First chance I got, I moved out and got my own place. But I was kind of lucky. Our nan left us money, and my mum was left money as a teenager from her parents. She put it into an ICER account for us, and she gave it to us when we turned eighteen under the condition we used it wisely."

"So, you bought a house?"

"Yeah, and started a business. Sometimes I miss my mum's cooking though." He pushes his empty plate away from him, sitting back. "Where did you live before your parents, or is this your first home?"

Jasmine leans into him, and I can see it on her face that she's going to say something, but Asher chomps down on my nipple before I can stop her, causing me to wince.

"We got hurt really badly at the old house and couldn't go back," Jasmine whispers.

Seeing her empty plate, I unlatch Asher and cover my breast whilst I wind him. "Jasmine, baby, why don't you go wash your hands and then put on a movie."

She bites her bottom lip, looking from me to Maddox. "I'm sorry, Mummy."

"Hey, you have nothing to be sorry for," I assure her. "Once I have Asher down, I'll bring you some pudding, okay?"

She's hesitant at first but then nods. "Okay, Mummy."

Once she's left, I can't avoid Maddox's stare any longer. "What?"

He opens his mouth but then shakes his head. "It's none of my business."

He wants to ask, and I don't blame him. He's only got an inkling of the story and it must be bugging him. "Just ask."

"It's none of my business. I'm not going to ask."

"But you want to?" I guess.

He shrugs. "I do. Your mum said something the night you gave birth, so I can only guess what you've been through."

I force out a laugh. "And you'd probably still be wrong," I tell him before I jokingly say, "Maybe if we were best friends, I'd tell you."

A grin teases his lips. "Amelia, Amelia, Amelia. I'll be the best friend you've ever had."

At a loss for words, I'm grateful when Asher lets up wind, causing Maddox to chuckle. "I'll go wash up while you finish feeding him."

"No, I can do that."

"Hey, if we're going to become best friends, I need to do my part. You cooked, I'll clean," he orders, grabbing the plates off the table.

"Maddox—"

He gives me a stern look, stopping me from saying any more. "Please don't make me go home. They're playing club music and I can't take it anymore."

Laughing lightly, I say, "You mean they aren't playing the classics?"

He groans. "Oh God, no. Although, nothing is worse than their karaoke nights. They've ruined some of my favourite tunes."

I can agree there. "When that kid dressed up in that red tracksuit and sang Eminem?"

Maddox groans as he flips on the hot tap. "I've not been able to listen to Eminem since. I cut the power to their house that night."

I gasp, turning to face him. "Oh my God. Was it you who did it the night I came back from the hospital?"

He chuckles, rinsing a plate off. "Yeah. I've been trying to get them out for a few years now."

"Have you been to the council?"

"Every week," he admits.

I grimace. "I'm sorry. The noise is bad over here so I can't imagine what it's like living right next to them."

"Hopefully, they'll be evicted soon. I'm more determined now that I can't crash at my cousin's."

"Is this your best friend too?" I ask, my lips twitching when I remember his ramblings about her.

He presses his hands against the edge of the sink, his muscles bulging. "Yeah. But I get it. Kind of."

"And your cousins with Hope and Hayden?"

"I am. Don't hold it against me."

I chuckle, unlatching Asher from my breast to wind him again. "You have a big family then. I can remember Hope telling me about some of you, and Hayden is always talking about your family getaways."

"We do. And we're all close," he tells me. "You'll love my mum though. She's awesome."

"I like that," I tell him. "I'm close to my parents. For me, they were the best people to be around growing up. I'd get picked on because I liked doing family stuff with them."

"Do you have any siblings?" he asks, drying his hands on a towel.

I look down at my son wistfully. Stephan hasn't had a chance to Facetime with us yet, so all he's had is a picture. I really want him to meet Asher. "I have a brother, Stephan. He's in the Army, so I don't get to see him much. He's a lot older than me too."

"You miss him?" he guesses.

"I do."

Jasmine comes running into the room, holding her game. It's a Frozen edition of Pop-up Pirate, and she loves it.

"Maddox! Maddox! Come play with me."

He turns to me, silently asking if it's okay. I shrug. "Go ahead, if you like. I need to get this one up to bed, but you can play if you want."

He beams, turning to Jasmine. "Get ready to have your arse whooped. I'm a pro at this game."

"Nuh, uh. I'm the best at it. Mummy tells me all the time."

"She is good," I warn him, standing from my chair.

"We'll see," he murmurs, following her into the living room.

I follow behind, leaving them on the floor, and carry on upstairs, heading for my room. Asher has another Moses basket inside. Until he's sleeping better through the night, I'm keeping him in here. I want him close to me.

I wind up his projector mobile after placing him down in his coat. He'll wake up again soon, and I'll change and bath him.

His lips pucker, causing me to smile. "Night, baby boy," I whisper, pulling his blanket up to his waist.

I turn on the monitor before heading downstairs. When I enter the living room, both Maddox and Jasmine are laying on their stomachs, the pop-up toy in the middle of them.

"You're staring," Jasmine whispers, not taking her eyes off the device.

I have a million things to do, but I can't help but sit down to watch them.

"Scared?" Maddox taunts.

"Nuh, uh," Jasmine mutters, before slowly sliding out a crystal stick. She lets out a breath when Olaf doesn't pop out.

Maddox rubs his hands together, eyeing the barrel in concentration.

"Scared?" Jasmine taunts back, giggling when Maddox frowns at her, sticking his tongue out.

"Kid, I've got this. Watch the professional."

"Famous last words," she sings as he reaches for a crystal.

I laugh when Olaf pops off the top and onto the carpet. Jasmine squeals, rolling onto her back to kick her feet and hands up in the air. "Yes!"

Maddox is frozen, staring at the game. "No. No. No. Let's do this again. I let you win."

She rolls back onto her stomach, shaking her head. "Of course you did."

"Put it back together. It's on," he tells her, narrowing his gaze.

I laugh, sitting back to watch them. Seeing Jasmine laughing and giggling has warmth spreading through me. For the first time since her father left, she looks truly happy. She doesn't have the same hesitancy she normally has when being loud and playful. She hasn't stopped to look at the door, wondering if her dad is going to walk in and tell her to be quiet. She is finally free to be a child.

And I have to wonder, who is Maddox Carter and where did he come from?

EIGHT

MADDOX

Slipping my boots off inside the door, I shake the rain from my hair. Ella, Paisley's cook for the bed and breakfast, beams when she spots me walking in.

"Have you come for your lunch?"

Winking, I give her a firm nod. "You know it. What did you cook for us today, gorgeous?"

Ella is an easy going, gifted cook in her fifties. Her food is phenomenal.

Since the work is still ongoing for the new addition to Paisley's establishment, she has given Ella longer hours, so me and the boys have food at lunch.

I reckon it has more to do with Landon hating that Paisley was cooking for us, and personally, I don't care. I get fed, and that's the main issue. Most jobs we work at we have to go out in search of lunch.

"Beef stew today, Maddox. Perfect for the weather."

It is. A storm is brewing, and it won't be long until the rain pours. It will be welcome, since it has been muggy all day.

Mark trails in behind me, slipping off his own muddy boots. I reach for a bread roll as he leans in, kissing Ella's cheek. "Smells good, Ella."

She swats his arm. "Away with you, boy. Go sit in the dining room. I'll bring the pot out in a minute."

"You want a hand?" we both ask.

She arches an eyebrow, giving us both that unnerving stare. "No. Because it will be gone before you sit down."

I grin, and around a mouthful of bread, I mutter, "You still love us."

"Go," she orders.

Taking that as our cue, we exit the kitchen and head into the dining room, where a few of the others are already seated.

Paisley has closed the doors to the area, giving us privacy, away from her guests.

"So, what happened to you last night?" Mark asks as we join Landon and Paisley at their table.

My eyebrows pull together. "Nothing happened to me last night."

Landon grunts but doesn't say anything. Mark, however, doesn't have the same hesitancy. "Then why did you bail on drinks at The Ginn Inn?"

Really? That's what this is about?

"Bro, I know we're family, but it doesn't give you a right to know my every move. I get it, you can't survive without me to liven up the party, but you'll have to live with it."

"You're a dick. You know that, right?"

I grin. "Yep."

"You aren't going to tell us where you've been then?" Landon asks, groaning when Ella brings in the slow cooker filled with beef stew.

"Food," I rumble, flying out of my chair.

"Don't break anything," Paisley yells as Landon bumps me out of the way. "Wanker!"

"Prick," he snaps, elbowing me when I reach for a bowl first.

I fill my bowl up until it's filled to the brim, then look around for the bread. Ella notices, and smiles. "I'll bring it over."

Bending down, I kiss her cheek. "You're the best."

I give Landon a smug smirk before making my way back to our table. The others follow, taking their seats.

"I don't get it. You're always the one who is first at the pub."

I bailed once. *Once.* "I had a better offer." I spoon more of the beef out of the bowl, savouring the taste that explodes on my tongue.

"A better offer?" Mark asks, his spoon paused halfway to his mouth. "Like what?"

For fuck's sake. They aren't going to drop it. "I had a roast dinner cooked for me. It was the full works."

Landon nods like he understands. "I'd skip the pub for that too. God, I've not had a roast in—"

"Since Sunday, Landon," Paisley reminds him, rolling her eyes.

I chuckle under my breath. "Wait, who cooked you a roast? Because it wasn't my mum or any of the aunts. I'd have known."

I snort. "Of course you would."

"I would. I'm their favourite."

I arch an eyebrow at him. "Does that help you sleep at night?"

He snatches a roll off the plate Ella places in the centre of the table, growling low in his throat. "Why so evasive?"

"Why such a dick?" I mutter, grinning around a mouthful of bread.

Landon grunts, sitting back in his chair so he can give me that unnerving stare of his. "You were with a girl."

"Was it Amelia? Charlotte said you've been spending a lot of time there," Paisley comments.

It was. And I have been. She's pretty cool. And so is Jasmine and Asher. Plus, the kid has my name; he has a right to know where he got his kickass name from.

"It is," Mark states, grinning.

I shrug. "Yeah, and? She's cool. And she can cook."

Mark frowns, straightening in his seat. "Wait, doesn't she have kids?"

My lips twist. "Yes, so?"

I want to punch his smug grin off his face. "Didn't you have a rule for not fucking single mums?"

I throw the spoon at him before picking up a clean one. "I'm not fucking her. We're just friends."

Landon grunts. "Yeah, right."

"It's true. Look, I'll be honest, it's hard for her to keep her eyes off me, but we have a mutual agreement. She feeds me, and I let her ogle my sexy as fuck body."

"I'm sure she's over the moon," Paisley utters dryly.

I nod, finishing the last of the stew. "Said it's the best thing to ever have happened to her."

The door to the dining room slides open and Louisa, Paisley's receptionist, pokes her head through the gap. "Paisley, you need to get out here. Cluck has damaged one of the guest's cars and it won't start. Something has come loose. Now he's chasing Rex around the car park, scaring some of the kids."

"Fuck!" Landon growls. "I'm going to kill that damn bird and give it to Ella to cook."

"Landon," Paisley exhales, her eyes bugging out. She turns to Louisa, forcing a smile. "Tell them to come in and grab something to eat. I'll call my brother to come and take a look at the car."

Once Paisley and Landon leave the room, Mark and I share a look before nearly tipping our chairs over to get a second bowl. There is no way her guests are eating my lunch.

A group of people are walking in when we retake our seats. The kids go off into the corner where Paisley has set up a little play area whilst the adults walk to the food bar, eating all my food.

"So, what's so special about this Amelia chick?" Mark asks as he dips his bread into the stew.

"Does there need to be anything special about her?"

"Yes. Like I said, you don't do single mums."

"I'm not fucking her," I snap, a little more heatedly than I meant to, causing him to grin.

"But you want to."

"Can't a guy just be friends with a girl without all this crap?"

"You, friends with a female?" He chuckles, shaking his head. "Nah."

"Are you forgetting my best friend is a female?"

"She's also your cousin," he reminds me, shrugging.

"You lot need to get your own lives and stay out of mine."

"Whatever," he mutters, typing away on his phone. I leave him to it, my gaze wandering over to where the kids are playing. There is a little girl the same age as Jasmine playing in the small play area. A little boy with bright red hair storms over, snatching the plastic pan the little girl was clutching out of her hand. Her bottom lip trembles for a few seconds before she begins to wail, the noise echoing over the sound of my men chattering.

If that had been Jasmine, I would have told her to snatch it back and smack the kid over the head with it. I guess parents don't condone that shit or something.

Kids scared me before. Sunday was okay, but she was also family. However, Jasmine isn't, and I like the kid. She's cool. I'm still not sure if I want kids in the future, but then I'm still really young. The only commitment I ever make is to food.

"Can I join you?"

I snap back to the present at the sound of the seductive voice purring close by. I glance away from the screaming child to turn to the owner of the voice. A gorgeous brunette with high cheeks bones, rounded chin, and a face caked with makeup, doesn't wait for a reply as she sets her bowl on the table, taking a seat between Mark and I.

"Hey," Mark greets, and I turn my gaze back to the children, watching as the little boy pushes the girl to the floor. He has to be about eight or nine, way older than her, the little fucker.

Where the fuck are her parents?

A little boy even smaller than the girl begins to scream at the boy, stepping in front of her like a little hero. He lifts his hand, catapulting a chocolate bar towards the bully. It hits him dead between the eyes. I chuckle under my breath, silently cheering him on.

"Leave my sister alone, you big meany," he cries out.

"God, if I knew screaming kids would be allowed in here, I would have gotten a room somewhere else."

My attention snaps her way, a low growl rumbling up my throat. "They're kids."

Her lips twist in disgust. Clearly, she's not clicking on to my annoyance. "The owner should think twice about letting them in," she tells us with a chuckle before looking up at me with a flirtatious smile. She licks her bottom lip, lowering her lashes. "I'm Alice, by the way. You could make my stay better by coming to my room with me. Maybe you could help me drown out that God awful sound."

My gaze hits Mark with an 'are you hearing this' look, before turning back to her. "No thanks."

"What do you mean 'no thanks'?" Alice asks, her tone sharper.

Mark chuckles. "Maybe you should go."

Her eyes bulge out when my gaze goes back to the kids fighting. "Oh my God, they aren't *yours*, are they?"

My lips press together. "No, and even if they were, I'd still let them do what the fuck they wanted."

She forces a laugh, waving me off. "But you've got to agree the owner shouldn't let them in. It should be a place to relax."

"Um," Mark grumbles when I stare down at the woman, my eyes narrowed.

She keeps on, not feeling the tension in the room. "And she needs to get a better cook. Jesus. This is vile."

"Get out!" I grit out.

She drops her spoon into her bowl, turning to face me. "What?"

"I said, get out. You can bitch about the noise, you can even bitch about how this place is run, but don't, and I mean *don't*, bitch about Ella. She feeds me."

"Ella?" she asks, slowly scanning the room when she notices the chatter has stopped.

"Yes, Ella. There is not one thing fucking wrong with her cooking."

"I brought muffins," Charlotte sings, stepping into the room. She spots me and Mark and heads over to us, dropping the large box down on the table. All the others groan, most of the men scattering out of the room. "There's some new cupcakes in here too."

She opens the first box, and I know from experience not to be deceived by the smell or decoration.

"They look amazing," Alice gushes, still here.

Charlotte tucks her hair behind her ear, bouncing on her feet. "Help yourself. I have loads more in the car."

"Yeah, you should have one," I tell the girl, before turning back to Charlotte. "Are you okay?"

"Yeah, why?"

"Because you only cook this much when you have something on your mind."

She loses her smile, scanning the room. "It's nothing."

"Charl—"

Alice suddenly pushes away from the table, spitting muffin all over the table before getting up. "What the fuck is in that?" she screams.

Charlotte's bottom lip trembles. "Were they too sugary?"

"It has a tub of salt in it," Alice screams, her face reddening.

"I guess you should go wash your mouth out," I murmur waspily.

She pushes her bag over her shoulder. "Where is the manager?"

Paisley steps through, cuddling the bird to her chest. "Can I help you?"

Alice squeaks, stepping back. "You bring flea-ridden pets in here?"

Charlotte bites her lip as Rex runs up to her, rubbing his snout up her leg. "Rex doesn't have fleas. He's well taken care of."

"I wasn't speaking to you," Alice spits out. "And I was on about the duck."

"Cluck is harmless," Charlotte assures her.

"Why are you still talking?" Alice snaps, curling her lip at Charlotte.

Paisley's face tightens. "I'll not have you speaking to my guests in that manner."

"I'm your guest. But not anymore. This place is a joke."

"Then go," Paisley retorts. "No one is stopping you."

Gasping, Alice grits her teeth. "I'll be leaving a bad review."

Paisley shrugs. "I'm sure you will."

After watching her storm out, Paisley then turns to us, narrowing her gaze. "What did you do?"

Mark huffs. "Nothing. She was just one of those whiney bitches."

I notice Charlotte pale when she hears 'whiney bitches'. "Charlotte? You okay?"

She steps away from the table, unable to meet my gaze. "Yeah. I need to go. I forgot to feed Katnip."

Before we can stop her, she's gone, brushing past Landon on her way out. "Charlotte?" he calls out. "Wait, I'm done." Turning back to us, he gives us a questioning look.

"She's been acting weird a lot lately."

He rubs the back of his neck. "Shit! I need to spend some time with her."

"I'm telling you, it's that new bloke she's got," Mark puts in.

"We've not met him," Paisley admits.

Even though his attention is still on the door where Charlotte left, Landon says, "Because she knows I'll wring his fucking neck."

For some reason, Amelia comes to mind, followed by the cryptic words from her mum and Jasmine. I'm not stupid. Her ex did something to her. Her mum practically said as much. But her mum also doesn't seem like the type of person who would sit back and let her child get abused.

But Amelia... Amelia is the type of person who would do anything for those she loved, even keep secrets.

Charlotte is a romantic with a huge heart. If some guy was playing her, she might not even know it until it was too late. And she would do everything to keep someone she loved. Hell, she kept her cat even though it tries to kill her every night.

"You don't think he's hurting her, do you?"

Landon slams his fist down on the table. "I would know. She would tell me."

I grimace. I don't want to make him feel like shit—he looks like crap already—so I keep my mouth shut.

Mark, however, doesn't care. "No offence, but you've been kinda busy lately. I hate to say it, but *would* you know?"

I cough into my hand, shifting my gaze away from Landon. "Never start a sentence with 'no offence'. Ever."

"Fuck off," he mutters.

"No, I'd know. She's just adjusting. She isn't used to change. She likes things how they are. You know Charlotte."

"We do, which is why I know something is going on with her. But then again, I pay attention."

His lips twist as he snarls at me. "Like you paid attention to Lily? Oh no, wait. She had a relationship behind your back."

I throw a breadstick at him, growling. "Stop bringing up the past, Landon. It's not me you're pissed at, it's yourself."

"No, it's definitely you."

I grin, flashing my teeth. "No one can be pissed at me. I'm the fucking bomb, baby."

With an aggravated sigh, he turns to Paisley, looking torn. She smiles, squeezing the duck closer to her chest. "Go. I'll get someone out to look over the car."

He nods, bending down to kiss her cheek. "I won't be long."

Paisley leaves with the duck, Rex following behind obediently, like he knows he's going to get a treat.

"Wait a goddamn minute," I snap, crossing my arms over my chest. "She might be your boss in your personal time," I comment, to which he just snorts, "but today, I'm your boss, and I need you on the rendering."

"Get Spencer on it," he retorts. "You knew I was going to be doing less shifts since I bought into the gym."

He leaves without another word, and my attention is brought back to the kids screaming again. This time, the chubby kid is trying to rip a toy gun out of the little lad's hand, the one who stuck up for his sister earlier. He's holding his own, refusing to be intimidated by the kid twice his size and probably three times his age.

I lean into Mark, still watching the kids, as I pull out a twenty. "Twenty the little kid wins."

Mark chuckles, slapping a twenty over mine. "Nah, the ginger is being a little dick and doesn't look like he plays fair. I reckon he'll win."

"Game on," I tell him, sitting back and watching it play out.

When the parents come to pull the little guy off the ginger kid, I turn to Mark in triumph, holding my hand out for the money.

NINE

AMELIA

My feet are dragging along the pavement. Asher isn't settling, and normally, a walk or a drive will get him off to sleep. Since going for a drive was out of the question because I'm beyond exhausted, I decided to walk up and down the street.

It's keeping Jasmine occupied too, as she rides her scooter next to me. I'm not sure if I can make another trip up and down the street, but Asher won't settle, and every time I stop, it makes him worse. He isn't hungry, and he isn't wet. He's tired.

And it's because of the music playing all night across the road. I can't keep doing it. I've reached a point where I'm contemplating looking for another place. I haven't been this exhausted since I started my temp work at the hospital and began doing late shifts. And the music will start again soon, since it's getting on. I've noticed they sleep until five-six each evening, then party like the world is going to end tomorrow for the rest of the night.

It needs to stop.

As soon as I have the energy, I'm going to look online to see who I need to speak to about the noise. The police certainly aren't doing anything.

We're nearing our house when I spot Jasmine getting too close to the curb again. "Jasmine, baby, move away from the road."

"Yes, Mummy," she calls back.

"Please, Asher, go to sleep for Mummy," I plead, tucking his blanket back in. He keeps kicking it off, and it's a little chilly.

"Oh no," Jasmine whispers, coming to a stop beside me.

Lifting my head, I spot the woman who lives across the way, storming across the road. I inwardly groan.

I don't have the time or energy for this.

"Shut that fucking brat up," she snarls, coming to a stop in front of the pushchair.

"Excuse me?" I'm worried I heard her wrong, but if the twisting of her lips is anything to go by, I'm not hearing things.

"You heard me," she yells, as Asher's wailing gets louder.

I rock the pushchair back and forth. "I did. And I'm sorry if it's bothering you, but your loud music kept me up all night."

She snorts, getting a fag out of a packet before lighting it up. "Are you trying to blame me for this?" I open my mouth to reply, when she blows smoke my way. I move Asher out of the way, trying to grip on to my last bit of patience. "Because my kids slept through music just fine."

"Can you step back if you're going to continue to smoke in front of a new born?"

She begins to laugh, stunning me. I don't see what's funny here. "Look at you, thinking you're all prim and proper. My kids weren't hurt by any smoke either."

Her kid is also an alcoholic, probably a druggie, and doesn't know how to tie his shoelaces. But she's right; it probably doesn't have anything to do with inhaling smoke.

"Maybe if you kept the noise down, he wouldn't be so unsettled during the day," I argue, praying she keeps it down tonight. I'm not sure how much more I can take.

"Now, listen here, you little—"

"What's going on here?" Maddox asks, and the sight of him has me sagging against the pushchair.

Although he's made me nervous by always showing up, his attendance right now is welcome. In fact, he has a habit of turning up whenever I need another adult to make me feel human again. Being a single mum is hard, and keeping your identity when you're responsible for two living souls is harder. It's nice to have someone to remind me.

"This has nothing to do with you, pretty boy."

He stares at her unnervingly, before, as quick as lightning, he snatches the fag out of her mouth and chucks it to the ground, stomping on it. "Don't smoke around the kids."

"Hey! That was my last one," she snaps.

"Then go get another," he growls, gesturing for her to leave.

She looks from him to me, her face tightening. "Shut that fucking baby up during the day."

"Leave," he rumbles, a lethal air about him.

When she stomps back across the road, I watch as his entire personality changes. His shoulders relax, his facial features soften, and he grins. "Miss me?"

"Loads," Jasmine squeals.

He frowns into the pram, and like he has every right, he unstraps Asher and picks him up. I go to take him, but I'm stunned by the silence. After listening to his wailing for so long, the silence is deafening. Asher cuddles into Maddox, suckling.

"How did you do that?" I breathe out.

He winks. "Magic."

I don't even care. I'm just happy Asher is finally calm. And it's as if his silence gives my body permission to finally relax. A yawn escapes me, and I try to fight back the exhaustion.

"Are you coming to watch a movie?" Jasmine asks.

He has been coming over a lot lately, and although it isn't a bother, I have to wonder why. He must have better things to do than sit with two kids and a single mum.

But he's there. Always inviting himself and asking personal questions. I'd ask them back to get to know him a little more, but he never gives me a chance. He just volunteers the information without being asked, revealing his life story.

It's unnerving at times.

I'm intrigued by him. The stories he's told me about his siblings and family… they're crazy. However, he tells them with love and affection. He really cares for them all.

"You bet'cha," he answers, before turning to me, watching me closely. "I'll order pizza to give your mum a break from cooking."

"Good. Because your cooking isn't very nice," Jasmine admits in a sweet voice.

He mocks outrage. "I thought you loved my toast?"

I chuckle at her expression. We bumped into him one morning and he had half a piece of toast in his gob and another four slices in his hand. He gave Jasmine one like a granddad would give their grandchild a pack of sweets, before patting her on the head and telling her to have a good day. It was pretty funny. And sweet.

"It was kind of burnt," she whispers, scraping the toe of her foot along the pavement.

"Lies," he cries out, before turning to me, his face turning serious. "Just don't tell me you have pineapple on pizza because I'm not sure we can be friends if you do."

I shiver. "God no!"

His shoulders drop dramatically. "Thank God, because I'm starving."

With a blink, I realise what's just happened. "Um, don't you have other things to do?"

His eyebrows pull together. "No."

I'm learning he doesn't do subtlety, so I decide to be straight. "You keep coming around and you hardly know us."

"Of course I do. You're Amelia Taylor, and you have two kids. You're a good cook, it's still debatable about your music choice, and you work in a care home. You aren't a B.I.T.C.H., and you can cook."

My lips twitch. "You said 'cook' twice."

He shrugs. "It was worth mentioning twice."

"I just don't get it. I really don't. Do you push your presence on everyone you meet?"

His lips twist and his eyebrows pull together. "I don't push my presence on anyone. They love me being around."

I roll my eyes. "You know what I mean."

He exhales heavily, rocking Asher side to side. "Can I be honest?"

"Why, have you been lying this entire time?" I ask, ignoring the rapid beat of my heart.

"Ha, ha," he mumbles. "I need a friend."

"And you don't have any?" I ask, arching an eyebrow. I thought for sure someone like him would have plenty of friends.

He snorts at my reply. "Of course I do. I'm an amazing friend to have, but I need a *best friend*."

"A best friend?" I repeat, at a loss.

He nods. "Yes."

"And what does that have to do with me?"

He looks at me like I should already know. "Because you are that new BFF."

"Me?"

"Are you always this difficult?" he asks, watching me curiously.

I wipe the tiredness out of my eyes. "So, you come around a lot because you want to be best friends with someone you hardly know, who has two kids that take up all of her time?"

"We've already covered this," he groans, exasperated. "Jasmine doesn't have an issue being my best friend."

"She's six," I argue.

"He's the best, Mummy," Jasmine helpfully adds.

Maddox grins, winking down at her before addressing me. "Plus, I've learnt you can be best friends with someone and not really know them at all."

He has that right. I thought I knew Scarlett until I found her fucking Cameron. "I guess."

"It's true. Look at Lily. I thought I knew her. I thought what we had was tight as fuck. I *thought* I knew who she was. Now, I've not got a clue. She's dating the enemy, a guy who doesn't let me stay over in *my* bedroom at hers, or lets her feed me. Who does that?"

I let out a chuckle at the redness rising up his neck. "Alright, deal. It's not like I couldn't use a friend."

He wraps an arm around my shoulders. "I'll be the bestest friend you ever had."

And that's what I'm afraid of.

He's hot. True. But there's something about his personality and charm that draws me to him.

The one thing I can't do is begin to have a crush on him. I'm not even sure I have the head space for that.

"Can we have pizza, Mummy?" Jasmine pleads.

I roll my eyes. "Yes. I need to feed Asher too."

Maddox suddenly perks up, and his smirk is devilish. "Let's hurry up then."

Jasmine rides up the path, and once I know she won't hear, I lean in closer and say, "I hate to break it to you, but my mum bought me a shawl."

"What's that?" he asks, as a frown creases between his eyes.

"It's to cover up the baby while they feed."

He hums under his breath, not looking too happy. "Let's order pizza."

I chuckle, clicking the breaks on the pushchair so I can open the door. Jasmine dumps her scooter by the door before running inside. "Can we watch Moana?"

"Go ahead, sweetie," I tell her, letting Maddox go first before bringing the pushchair in after him.

"Go sit down. You look dead on your feet," he tells me, handing over Asher. "I'll order pizza."

I nod before grabbing his wrist, stopping him. "Thank you for intervening outside, by the way. That woman scares me."

"I think she scares everyone," he admits. "One way or another, I'll get them evicted. I'm starting a petition tomorrow. My cousin is going to print out the forms."

"Really?" I ask with a little too much enthusiasm.

He chuckles. "Really."

"Let me go up and change Asher, then I'll be back down to feed him. Help yourself to a drink."

"Do you still have my beer from the other night?" he asks.

I chuckle, remembering him turning up the other night with four cans and a puppy dog expression. "It's in the fridge."

He nods, leaving to head straight for the kitchen. I hear Jasmine tell him about Moana and how cool Maui is, and I chuckle to myself.

Smiling, I head up the stairs, pushing through the exhaustion so I can at least get Asher fed in case I pass out.

I JOLT AWAKE to the sounds of singing. In my fog, it takes me a minute to realise I fell asleep during Asher's feed.

I pat my chest, realising everything is back in place and Asher is no longer there. Sitting up, eyes wide, I glance to the floor, where Maddox is sitting. He has Asher laying on a blanket between his legs.

"And when you get a chick to—"

"Um, what happened?" I ask, although I already know the answer.

Maddox jumps, turning to me. "Hey, you're awake."

"Um… I was breastfeeding Asher."

"Three hours ago," he reveals, picking Asher up. "I think his nappy may need doing again. Jasmine and I tried. Well, I did. But I dunno; it didn't look right. Mum said it was piss easy, but she wasn't here—"

I hold my hand up, rubbing my eye with the palm of other. "Maddox, I was breastfeeding Asher. I was—"

Realisation dawns and he rubs the back of his neck. "Oh, that."

"Yes, that," I tell him, feeling a little vulnerable.

"Don't worry, I didn't see anything. He was making wheezing noises and I kind of panicked. Then you wouldn't wake up and I... I lifted him off and kept the blanket thingy over you."

"My top is up," I remind him. He must have touched me.

He grins. "I'm a skilled guy, but I have to admit, I didn't think I'd pull off putting clothes on a chick."

"Maddox," I groan.

He holds his hands up. "Jasmine helped me."

I look around the room, my mind still foggy. "Where is Jasmine?"

"Asleep in bed."

"Oh God, I'd better go check on her and get her changed," I announce, getting up.

"Stop," he orders gently. "I got her some clothes out because she said she wasn't allowed to touch the drawers."

I nod. "They aren't screwed into the wall yet. I don't want them tipping over on her."

His eyes widen a tad. "Jesus. I didn't even think of that." He pauses for a moment before continuing. "I grabbed what I could and left the rest to her."

I sag back against the sofa, feeling utterly devastated. "I'm so sorry. I can't believe I fell asleep. Then you fed and looked after them, and I'm being a bitch."

"You aren't. In fact, you took it better than I thought you would. When I realised I had to get Asher off you, I kind of had a meltdown."

"A meltdown?"

He grins sheepishly. "Yeah. I didn't want to invade your personal space. You wouldn't wake up, and Jasmine wouldn't get Asher, so we kind of had a whispered argument on who should do it, and then, if you can believe it, she threw the adult card at me."

"The adult card?" I ask, my lips twitching.

He blows out a breath. "Yeah. And she drives a hard bargain."

"Oh dear," I murmur, more relaxed now.

"You're telling me. She took twenty quid off me just to lift your top back up after I grabbed Asher. Poor guy's mouth was stuck in an 'O' shape."

Laughter spills out of me. "I'm sorry for falling asleep."

"It's okay. There's a first time for everything," he teases, winking.

"Are you okay to watch Asher a little while longer while I run up and check on Jasmine?"

"Go on. We're cool." He turns to Asher, grinning. "We were just talking about how to get a chick into bed."

I shake my head, getting up from the sofa. "Stop corrupting him."

I head out of the room, and as I reach the stairs, I quickly straighten my top, chuckling to myself when I see my bra isn't clipped back on.

Stepping into Jasmine's room, a smile slips free at the sight of her. She's lying half under her blanket, half out, her hair a tangled mess, and drool is dripping down her chin. She snores lightly, and as I bend down to pull the covers over her, I notice she has on mismatched pyjamas, and they're inside out.

Happy she's safe and sound, and now tucked in properly, I reach down by her bed to flick her night light on before turning the main lamp off.

Since I'm up here, I rush into my room, grabbing a jumper out of my wardrobe before heading into Asher's room for some clean pyjamas.

Back downstairs, Maddox is still there, his eyes on the television. "You're pretty hooked onto Enchanted."

He ducks his head, chuckling. "I had to watch it twice," he admits.

I chuckle as I take a seat on the floor, gently reaching for Asher. He coos in excitement, kicking his little feet around. I drag his changing box close and pull out a fresh nappy, wipes and a nappy bag.

Just as I unpop the first button, Maddox places his hand around mine. When I look up, he's pale. "There's something I need to tell you, and you can't get mad."

My heart stops, and I feel the blood drain from my face. "What?"

"When I was changing him, he, um… he had something on his stomach. Jasmine said it was meant to be there."

"Maddox," I call, my lips twitching.

"But, um, when I was pulling his vest back down, it kind of, um…" He runs his hand through his hair, ignoring me.

I raise my voice a little more, trying to get his attention. "Maddox."

He throws his hands up in the air. "It fell off! Okay! I know. You're gonna hate me. But I swear, he didn't cry."

"Maddox!"

"I'm not even sure what it's—"

"Maddox," I call out, forcing myself not to laugh. "Stop. It's fine."

He shakes his head. "I was gonna tell you when you woke up, but then you mentioned your tits and—"

"Stop," I tell him, laughter spilling free. "It was going to come off any day now."

"What?" he asks, falling back against the sofa.

"It's his umbilical cord. I'm surprised it didn't come off sooner."

"So, I didn't do anything wrong?"

"No," I tell him, keeping my voice soft. He looks genuinely worried.

He leans over Asher, letting him grip his finger. "Hear that, little man, it's all good."

I quickly get him changed, laughing when I see the mess of the nappy. Moments later, I lift him against my chest. "He's not even winging for food."

"He had me to occupy him," Maddox explains, grinning. Suddenly, his grin slips, and he begins to frown. "I'll order you some food."

"You didn't eat?" I ask. "What about Jasmine?"

"Um, yeah, we did, but we ate it all."

I wave him off. "There's no point in ordering just for me."

He shrugs. "I'm kind of hungry myself."

My eyes widen. "You sure?"

"Yeah. Maybe we can put something else on the tele though."

"Deal," I tell him, smiling.

"I'll have to buy an Xbox to leave here," he mumbles, heading over to his phone to order.

I just shake my head, still not knowing what to make of him. I guess in time, I will.

TEN

AMELIA

It's three in the morning and Asher is awake, wailing, and showing no signs of stopping.

And again, it isn't because he's hungry—he's not long been fed. It isn't because he's wet either. It's because he has gone past tired and is irritable. The music blaring from across the road is shaking the walls, so we aren't getting a moment's peace.

I'm seconds away from having a breakdown. I'm desperate for sleep, more than my little man at this point.

Keeping Asher resting over my shoulder, I peek through the blinds, gritting my teeth when a guy jumps off the hood of his car and onto the ground, singing 'Eye of the Tiger'. He isn't only keeping us awake, but he's killing one of my favourite songs.

A group of girls, who must be around eighteen-nineteen, are dancing in the weeds. One is standing on a chair, holding up a bottle of Lambrini.

Classy.

When they begin cheering for the mum to down a can, I step away from the window. I've seen enough, and I'm at my wits end now. The police aren't doing anything about it. They just arrive, issue a warning before waiting for them to go inside, then leave. As soon as it's clear, the music is back on and they are at it again. I think it's gotten to the point where people have stopped calling.

Tonight, it's a zoo over there. They are always loud, but the amount of people there has doubled the noise. I'm so sleep deprived, I'm willing to sell my soul to the devil to get them to turn the music off.

"Come on, Asher, go to sleep for Mummy," I plead gently, feeling the back of my throat tighten.

I'm shattered. My eyes sting from the lack of sleep. I'm barely functioning. I'm almost regretting not taking my mum up on her offer to stay and help out. The only reason I said no is because it would have been pointless. The noise wasn't going away, and the only reason Asher wasn't sleeping was because of it. And I refuse to change our sleep routine for him. Plus, I still have Jasmine to watch over in the day.

A sniffle escapes me, and my nose begins to burn. I'm meant to start back up at work in a few weeks, and if this keeps on, I won't be able to. And if I don't go back to work, the debts won't get paid. I'll have to move back into my parents', and I'll be back at square one.

I can't let that happen.

Tears slip free as I gently bounce Asher in my arms. Each time the bass drops, he screams louder.

A frustrated growl escapes me. I badly want to go over there, but there is no way I'm leaving Jasmine unattended, not even for a second.

Tomorrow, all bets are off. I'm banging on that damn door and demanding they turn their music off at night.

A light tapping sounds from the front door, and I startle, a small yelp escaping me. Shaking, I take a step away from the door, clutching Asher in my arms.

"Shh, baby. It's okay," I soothe, kissing his head.

There's another tap at the door, just as my phone vibrates with a message. I pick up my phone from the coffee table, seeing a message from Maddox.

Maddox: Open the door.

My shoulders sag, and I step over to the door and unlock it. I pull it open, seeing him in tracksuit bottoms and a grey T-shirt. His eyes have dark circles underneath and his jaw has a shadow of growth.

"Maddox," I call out, surprised.

"I can't do it," he grumbles, pushing his way inside and locking the door behind him.

"Um…"

"I've tried. I've tried everything. I'm going to go around with those damn forms tomorrow and I'm going to get them out of that house," he growls, gently taking Asher from my arms. "Shush, little man. I got you."

He immediately settles, and I stand in the doorway, frozen, as Maddox makes himself at home, kicking his feet up on the sofa.

A sob breaks free and I crumple against the doorframe. He looks up, his eyes widening. "I swear, if I could get them out now, I would. Please don't cry. You're making me anxious."

"How do you do it?"

"Be so calm and rational? It's a gift. One I got from my father."

I shake my head as I wipe my nose unattractively with my sleeve. "No. How did you get him to settle? I've been trying all night."

He glances down at Asher, who is sound asleep, and falls back against the sofa, getting more comfortable. "Now the kid is talking my language."

"Maddox, what are you doing here?" Not that I'm complaining. Asher is finally asleep. But it's the middle of the night and we aren't there in our friendship. Or clearly, I'm not. Maddox doesn't seem to have the same qualms.

Maddox opens one eye, looking at me. "What's it look like I'm doing?"

"Um, going to sleep on my sofa?"

He gives me a curt nod, closing both eyes. "The music is quieter over here."

Quieter? The sound is vibrating all over my walls. I'm glad Jasmine's room is at the back of the house. It isn't so bad there. It also helps that she sleeps like the dead.

"*You're* sleeping *here?*"

"Shush," he grumbles. "Tired."

"But this is my home." I step closer when his lips part, a light snore escaping him. "Maddox? Maddox?" When I get nothing, I groan, running my fingers through my hair.

This can't be happening.

I've never met anyone who didn't understand boundaries before. He doesn't do it to be a bully or use it as power; he just does it to achieve what he wants. He fits himself into places without invitation, without design or tact. It's kind of admirable.

Kind of.

Resigned to the fact I'm going to have someone I barely know sleeping on my couch, I take a step forward, my hands going around Asher. I barely lift him when he starts wailing again.

Maddox presses him closer to his chest. "Shush, little man, it's sleep time."

And as if he understood the command, Asher's eyes close, and he falls back to sleep.

I run my fingers through my hair, my eyes drooping as I watch them both sleep like there isn't music blaring.

Can I leave him here? Can I leave Asher in his arms?

A yawn escapes me, and feeling my body weaken, I know I can. I really can. I have been trying for hours to get him to sleep, to stop his crying, to no avail. It's been breaking my heart.

Knowing what I should do, I drag my body up the stairs, quickly checking in on Jasmine before heading into my room, grabbing my blanket, throw blanket, and a pillow.

When I'm back in the living room, I place the blanket on the floor near the sofa. Maddox has a firm grip on Asher, but I'm not taking any chances.

Pulling the other throw off the back of the sofa, I place it over them both, smiling when Maddox lets out a contented sigh.

He's a gorgeous man, but sleeping, he is simply beautiful. His features are relaxed, and yet the lines tell a story, one of a man who has lived laughing. I straighten away from the man who has wormed his way into our lives, and walk over to the light switch, turning it off. The room is lit by the warm glow from the lamp in the corner, and with that, I head over to the chair, curling up into a ball with my pillow and throw blanket.

Asher will be up again soon, and I need to get as much sleep as I can.

As much as the music grates on me, I let the bass pull me into sleep, tuning out the sounds of them laughing and singing. I'm too tired to even care at this point.

"Psst," I hear, and groggily, I rub sleep from my eyes before blinking them open, finding Maddox kneeling in front of me, holding Asher like he's Simba from the Lion King. "Your son is hungry and it's kind of awkward that he keeps going for my nipple."

What?

What is Maddox doing here?

"Am I dreaming?"

He grins, flashing his pearly whites. "Why? Do you normally dream of me?"

I groan, sliding up into a sitting position and stretching the kink out of my back.

In a daze, I take Asher from him, coming fully awake. "What time is it?"

"It's seven in the morning."

It doesn't feel like I've been asleep an hour. And yet... wait, what? "No, it can't be?"

"It is," he announces.

"No. Oh my God, I'm going to be late," I rush out.

"Late?"

I quickly stand with Asher in my arms, heading over to the changing box. I grab everything he needs before lifting my head, yelling, "Jasmine, it's time to get up."

"Um—"

"Did he not wake once?" I ask, spinning around to face Maddox.

He takes a step back, holding his hands up. "Was he meant to?"

I nod. "He's been feeding every few hours. But then, he's not really slept during the night since the night after we got back. The music has kept him up."

"No, I woke up to him sucking on my chest," he explains, rubbing the back of his neck. The move causes his T-shirt to rise, showcasing his muscled abs. I lick my lips, seeing a fine trail of hair leading down to his groin. He clicks his fingers in front of my face. "Aren't you going to be late?"

"Shit!" I yell, racing upstairs without another word. I quickly make it into Asher's room, working on getting him changed before heading into Jasmine's room. "Jasmine, wake up, baby. You need to have breakfast before school."

"No," she moans, hiding her head under the pillow.

I roll my eyes, stepping further into the room, and walk over to her bed. I pull her blanket away from her, dropping it on the end of her bed. "Now, missy."

She rolls out of bed, her hair a static mess all over the place, and drags her body out of the room. I follow, keeping an eye on her as she dazedly walks into the living room. I chuckle when she knocks her shoulder into the doorframe. She grunts, walking around the room before heading straight for the kitchen.

I'm shocked to find Maddox still here, leaning against the kitchen counter with a cup of coffee in his hand.

A thud has me looking away and over to the table, where Jasmine has rested her forehead against the wood.

"What are you still doing here?" I whisper, wondering how I'm going to explain it to Jasmine. She won't understand, and I know she likes Maddox, but after everything her father put us through, I'm not sure if she would want him around like this.

He gives me a 'duh' look, holding his mug up. "Coffee. I've got a long morning ahead of me."

"What time do you start work?" I ask, forgetting my earlier dilemma for a moment.

"Now, but I'm taking the day off to get something done about that family," he growls, taking a large swig of his coffee. "I think he needs feeding."

I glance down at Asher, who is fussing in my arms, then back at Maddox and Jasmine. "Go, before she wakes up."

"She's not awake?" he asks, his eyes wide.

"She's not a morning person. It takes breakfast and the drive to school to get her to wake up, otherwise she's a zombie."

He chuckles. "She's dribbling all over the table."

When Asher begins to cry, I lift him higher in my arms. "Maddox, you need to go before she wakes up."

"Why?"

"Why?" I repeat. I thought that would be obvious.

"Yeah, why? She likes me," he tells me. "Yo, Jaz, you like me, don't you?"

My eyes widen, and I stare at my daughter in horror, scared she's going to be upset. She surprises me by jolting from the table, nearly falling from the chair. "Maddox?"

He grins, walking over to take a seat next to her, ruffling her hair. "Kid, you look like a puffed-up house cat."

I take a seat on the other side of her, pulling my dressing gown apart and unclipping my bra. Asher immediately latches on, and I grimace from the discomfort.

"How do you get a break?" Maddox suddenly blurts out.

"What do you mean?" I ask, my heart racing for some unknown reason. Is he going to ask me out?

"Well, you're the only one who can feed the little guy. What are you going to do if you want to go out for a meal with friends, go back to work? Does he go with you?"

I duck my head, gazing down at Asher. "No. I'm hoping to have the pump by then so I can do bottles. That way others can feed him too."

"You've not got one?"

He asked me this before. "Not yet."

"Maddox," Jasmine breathes. "Did you come to see me?"

He grins, leaning down so they're eye level. "I did, but you were snoring like a gorilla."

She giggles. "I was not."

"Were too."

"What would you like for breakfast?" I ask, already resigned to the fact we're going to be late. It's a thirty-minute drive to her school. By the time I get her fed, washed and dressed, then get everything together for Asher, we're going to be at least forty minutes late.

"Cereal, please," she murmurs.

"I wouldn't mind some scrambled eggs and toast."

"Yummy," Jasmine breathes. "Can we, Mummy?"

"Baby, we're running late."

"I'll drop her off, under the condition you make me breakfast," Maddox offers.

My lips part, close, then part again. "No, it's fine. I'll call the school and explain we're running late."

He waves me off. "No need. Feed Asher, get madam ready, and I'll drop her off. Then you can do what you gotta do."

"I—"

Jasmine pouts up at me, fluttering her lashes. "Please, Mummy; can he?"

I go to decline, but something in her expression stops me, and I turn to Maddox. "Are you sure?"

He nods. "Yeah. I can go grab those forms from my cousin on the way back. There's something else I need to do after too."

I turn to Jasmine. "Go up and get washed and dressed. You can brush your teeth after breakfast."

"Then Maddox can take me to school?" she asks excitedly.

I grin. "Yes."

She closes her hand into a fist, holding it out to Maddox. He chuckles, fist bumping her. "I'll quickly run back and get changed."

Jasmine pauses half off the chair, turning to Maddox, her excitement gone. "But you'll be back?"

He frowns, nodding. "Of course."

"You'll definitely come back and take me to school?" she pushes further.

Recognition flashes across his expression, and he bends down, knocking her chin with his knuckles. "One thing you should know about me, kid; I don't break promises. I promise I'll be back, and I promise it will be the best school run you've ever been on. We can listen to really loud music."

"Can I bring my CD?" Jasmine asks, her excitement back.

He winks. "Of course."

She races out of the room to get ready, and I turn to Maddox. "Thank you. You keep helping at every turn."

"I'm getting fed in return, and she's a cool kid to hang out with, so it's a win-win for me." He eyes me up and down, causing my cheeks to heat and my stomach to flutter. "Her mum isn't so bad either."

I ignore his comment, not knowing what to make of it. "Still, thank you."

He takes a swig of his coffee. "Hey, after I'm finished doing what I've got to do, do you want to help me get these forms filled in?"

I shrug. I have nothing but cleaning to do. "I don't mind. I'll do anything to not have to listen to *that* for another night."

"The guy I spoke to after my sister mentioned the petition said it should work. It's not like they don't have complaints against them already. I also gave them a list of housing they could go in, where they wouldn't have neighbours to disturb."

"Then I'm in," I agree, giddy at the thought of a peaceful night.

And maybe spending time with Maddox.

ELEVEN

MADDOX

"Strap in, kid," I order gently, lifting her easily. She drops her bag down on the floor, jumping into her car seat.

"Be a good girl," Amelia orders, standing close to my truck. Asher is in her arms, making gurgling noises.

I walk over to him after putting Jasmine's seat belt on her, and let him grab my finger. I chuckle. "Be good for your mum, little man."

"Are you sure you're okay taking her?" Amelia asks, biting her bottom lip.

"Sure. I need to go out anyway."

She arches her eyebrow. "So you said."

I grin. "Scared you'll miss me?"

"Come on, we're going to be late," Jasmine calls from the truck.

I wave. "We'll get there."

"Without speeding," Amelia emphasizes.

"Always safe," I tell her.

She nods once, lifting Asher higher in her arms. She's still in her pyjamas and is waiting for us to leave before she goes to get ready. "If she, um… if she tries to talk you into dancing with her, say no if you're driving."

I give her a sharp nod. "No dancing and driving." I groan once I realise what I just said. "Not words I thought would be in my vocabulary."

She chuckles, waving me off as I jump into the truck. "Have a good day."

"Bye," Jasmine yells as I get into the truck, starting it. "Sheesh, talk about not letting go."

Laughter spills out of my mouth. "She's going to miss you."

"Yeah, but I'm a big girl now."

"Right, so what are we listening to?" I ask, knowing she brought her own CD. Luckily, my truck has a disc player.

She pulls it out of her bag, then pops out the disc and slides it into the player. When classical-like music begins to play, I turn to her in horror.

"You're going to love this."

Something tells me it needs to be a desired taste.

I pull onto the next street, wondering what I should say or do. "So, um, school. Do you like it?"

"It's okay. I miss my old friends."

"Old friends?"

"We had to move when me and Mummy got out of the hospital."

"When you were born?" I ask, taking my eyes off the road briefly.

Her voice is shaky when she replies. "When Daddy hurt her," she reveals, blowing me off guard. All of a sudden, she smiles wide. "You can learn the dance we're doing for our school play."

I force a grin, my mind still on her words. My assumptions were right about the dad. "Not while I'm driving."

Her head tilts to the side, her lips in a pout. "Mummy says that all the time too. It must be an old person thing."

She begins to wiggle in her seat while I stew over her earlier words. I grit my teeth. I don't know why it's affecting me so much that he hurt her. But it is. She's a good person. And seriously fucking hot. He was a fool to treat her like shit.

Men like that baffle and sicken me.

I'm not sure how long I listen to her sing or have to stop her from nearly pushing herself out of her seat from dancing, but as the next song comes on, I swear a tear leaks from my eye. It's more Disney. These aren't cool songs. And I'm pretty sure this one is about letting it go, or letting one go...

"You said we could have this loud," Jasmine mutters for the tenth time.

People are staring already as we pull into the area her school is located. "Um, what about a bit of Tupac or Eminem?"

She folds her arms over her chest. "Nope. My music first."

I grin at her spunk. "Alright, kid, turn it up. Let's give them nosey fuc—fudgers something to stare at."

She claps her hands, singing so loud I'm afraid she's pierced my ear drums. I don't care. She's more fun than some of my mates. "You're going to love the next one."

"It's not another one about water is it?" I ask, my lips turning down.

She giggles. "No, it's the best one, apart from this one," she explains, giving me nothing.

When the song ends and another begins, a grin spreads across my face. "I love this song."

"I told you!" she screeches.

Hakuna Matata starts playing through the speakers, and as soon as the words begin, I'm belting out the lyrics alongside her.

We pull up outside the school, just as the song comes to an end. Onlookers openly stare, but I don't care. When I turn to Jasmine, she's grinning from ear to ear, bouncing in her car seat.

I turn the music down, looking over at the school. "Do I have to do anything?"

She unclips her belt before grabbing her bag off the floor, swinging it over her shoulder. "No. I've got it. The teacher is right there."

The woman she's pointing at looks around twelve. "*That's* your teacher?"

Giggling, she nods. "Yes. She works with our other teacher. She's so cool."

I eye the girl in question, my lips twisting. "I dunno. She doesn't seem mature enough to look after you."

She tries to push open the door, and I chuckle when it doesn't budge. I shut the car off before sliding out and running around the front. When I open her door, she exhales. "Phew, that door was heavy."

I wink. "A princess should always wait for her door to be opened."

I help her out of the truck and place her safely on her feet. She pats my stomach. "Thanks for the lift to school," she tells me, tucking a piece of hair behind her ear. "Next time, I might let you play your music."

I ruffle her hair, chuckling. "Go have a good day, kid."

She scrunches her eyes and nose up. "It's Princess Jasmine to you."

I created a monster.

"Princess Jasmine," I repeat, bowing a little.

I watch her run through the gates and up to the incompetent teenager. I keep my gaze on them until she begins to lead a row of kids into the school. Once she's inside, I start to relax.

When I head around to the driver's side, a woman greets me, holding her hand out. "I'm Natasha, Lucas' mum. He's in Jasmine's class. I haven't seen Jasmine with her father before. I assumed Amelia was a single mum."

She say's 'single' like it's a bad taste in her mouth. I don't like her tone or the way she practically made out being a single mum is a bad thing.

I snort in the woman's face, rolling my eyes. I don't even give her a reply as I get back into the truck. She says something as I shut the door, but I tune her out, blasting Jasmine's Disney CD.

I have one more thing to do before I can head home to get those forms sorted. And I need my mum's help.

WHEN MUM WALKS up to me with Dad at her side, I inwardly groan. "Do you not have a job?" I ask him, arching my eyebrow. He'll tell the others. He's worse at gossiping than the mum's sometimes.

Dad grins. "It's my day off, and I wanted to know what was so important that you needed your mum to take time away to come and meet you outside Mother's World.

I glance at Mum, who has the audacity to look away. "Really?"

"He's your dad. Whatever is so important, you can say in front of him."

I throw my hands up. "He wants payback for the food I took a few days ago."

She chews on her lip before glancing at Dad. "Don't embarrass him."

He sighs, rolling his eyes. "Why are we here?"

I give him a glance. "I didn't invite you. I invited Mum."

"Maddox," Mum warns.

I exhale. "There's something Amelia needs, and I'm not sure what to get."

Mum's eyebrows pull together. "What do you mean?"

"She's mentioned it before, but I've got a feeling she can't afford to splurge on one."

"It must be tough for a single mum," Mum agrees.

I shake my head. "It's more than that. I don't know how I know, but I do. Will you help me?"

Her expression softens, and she smiles. "What is it you think she needs?"

I relax, but then feel my cheeks heat. "Well, I'm not sure what it's called, but it's something to help others feed Asher. She, um, she breastfeeds."

Realisation dawns on her expression. "Ah, she needs a breast pump."

Dad groans. "I wish I stayed at home."

"Can you come in and help me? Do they come in sizes? I mean, she'll need bottles too, right?"

Mum chuckles, slapping Dad on his shoulder when he groans again. "Let's go inside. I'll show you what you need to get her," she starts, but then pauses at the entrance, a grin lighting up her face. "Oh, we can buy him some baby clothes and maybe some little toys."

"Mum," I begin, but she waves me off.

"No, we can—"

"Harlow," Dad warns.

She huffs. "Let me buy *some* stuff. It will give us an excuse to go over and meet her. Maybe she'll even let us babysit sometime," she rambles, walking into the store. "Teagan never shares babysitting Sunday, and is always telling us about the stuff she's buying her."

"Mum," I whine, yet smile.

She spins around. "She does. She got her this cute outfit the other day."

"Alright, but if it makes Amelia uncomfortable, you have to take it back," I warn, giving her a firm expression.

She exhales before relenting. "All right."

When she grabs a shopping trolley, I can't help but chuckle under my breath.

"Do you know if she has the correct nursing bras?" Mum suddenly asks.

I rub the back of my head. "What are they?"

"It's to make it easier to feed the baby when you're on the go. It pulls—"

"Down," I finish, feeling my cheeks heat when my dad begins to bore his stare into me. "Yeah. She has one. I don't know how many though."

"We can pick some up just to be sure," she tells me as she leads us down an aisle.

When she comes to stand in front of a section of different devices, I begin to wonder if I made the right choice in doing this. Each box has a picture of a mum breastfeeding, and one even has a device attached to the nipple.

"That can't be right," I murmur, pointing to the box. It looks painful, but the woman is smiling.

"That's a breast pump. That's what we need," Mum explains.

I suck in a breath. "So, she literally gets milked like a cow?"

A woman scanning over the products next to us, clucks her tongue, giving me a dirty look. "Sorry. He has no filter," Mum apologises. "We're looking for a pump for his friend."

The woman smiles, her expression softening. "It's fine. If you are looking for the best one, I'd go with that set there," she declares, pointing at a large box on the top shelf. "It's a little pricey but it's more comfortable on the nipples."

Now this woman knows what she's talking about. "And it won't hurt her?"

She shakes her head, her lips tugging into a smile. "No."

"And the bottles included—are they safe for the baby?"

"Yes."

Mum steps up, rubbing my arm. "It looks just like a nipple."

It looks nothing like a nipple to me. "Yeah, I'm not going to comment."

"Bloody hell," Dad groans.

"Thank you for your help," I tell the woman, giving her a wink.

"You're welcome," the lady replies, but then stops before moving away. "Word of advice: don't call mothers breastfeeding 'cows'."

I give her a sharp nod, turning back to Mum. "What else will she need? I don't want to give her that and it turns out she can't use it because she doesn't have enough."

Mum rolls her eyes. "Grab the box. I'll grab extra stuff that is included in the box, so she has enough. And grab some different flow teats."

"Different flow—what?" I ask, my eyebrows pulling together.

"Yeah, you had fast flow because you were a greedy little fucker. Madison, on the other hand, was happy to take her time," Dad explains.

I puff out my chest. "I was a growing boy."

Dad grunts. "You were greedy."

"No, he just loved being cuddled to his mother's chest."

"Yeah, I didn't need to hear that," I tell her, grabbing the box down. I don't care that it costs nearly two-hundred quid. She needs it.

"Are you sure she'll be okay with you buying her this? You've not known her long," Dad warns.

I give him a dirty look. "Of course she will be fine with it. She likes me. We're friends."

He snorts. "You've not known her long."

"I've known her long enough."

"As kind as I think this is, and I'm not talking you out of it, but I think your dad's right. What's going on with you?"

"What do you mean? Can't someone buy a friend something they need?"

She nods. "Of course. But you don't do this with anyone else."

"I did it with Lily."

Realisation dawns on her face. "You do know she's still your friend. She just has other priorities now."

"I know that," I tell her, a little too harshly.

Dad slaps his hand down on my shoulder. "I think what she's trying to say is you don't have to buy someone things to be friends."

"I've got loads of friends."

"So, Amelia is different?" Mum concludes.

I shrug. "Yeah. No. Yeah." I run a hand through my hair. "Can we not talk about this? We are just friends."

"If you say so," Dad mutters.

"I say," I bark.

"Then let's spoil your friend and her kids," Mum states.

"Mum," I warn, but it's too late. She's throwing things into the trolley left, right and centre.

TWELVE

AMELIA

Maddox text me to let me know he got Jasmine off to school okay, but I haven't heard from him since. He said he was coming back over so I could help with the petition, but as I sneak glances through the blinds, I wonder if he's had second thoughts.

He's been pacing at the back of his truck for what must have been fifteen minutes now. Each time he talks himself into whatever it is worrying him, he'll step away from the boot.

Moving away from the window, I leave him to it and place Asher down in his bouncer, strapping him in.

My phone ringing distracts me from Maddox, and I walk over, answering my mum's call.

"Hey, Mum."

"Hey, sweetie," she greets. "How are you?"

"A little tired," I admit.

"Asher still didn't sleep last night?" she asks, sounding a little concerned.

"Um, not at first," I tell her, my voice sounding almost robotic.

"Amelia Taylor, what aren't you telling me? You didn't listen to your father about the whiskey, did you?"

I force out a laugh. "No, I didn't. Maddox, my neighbour—he came over."

"What?" she screeches.

"It's not what you think. It was the early hours of this morning. Across the road were blaring their music. I think he came over to crash, but then he saw Asher crying, took him from me, and within minutes, they were both asleep on the sofa."

"Amelia," she warns softly.

"We're just friends. I don't ask him to come over, and he doesn't ask permission."

She chuckles. "I do like him."

"We're just friends," I warn. "He even took Jasmine to school today because we slept in."

"Maybe you should give him a chance. He's a nice bloke, has values, is family orientated, and isn't bad on the eyes at all."

He's gorgeous and she knows it.

"He doesn't like me like that."

"I'm sure that's not true. He'd be lucky to have you."

I let out a sigh. I know she just wants me to be happy, but… "Even if he does like me, I just had a baby. I'm not ready for any kind of relationship."

"Let me set you up on a few dates."

"No, Mum." There's a light knock on the door, and I interrupt her before she can speak. "Someone is at the door. I've got to go."

"Think about it," she yells.

"Bye, Mum."

"Bye, darlin'."

I shake my head, wondering when she will stop worrying about my dating life. She wants me to be happy, I get it, but I think she's more afraid that I've let Cameron put me off relationships for life.

But if that was the case, I wouldn't have let Maddox into my life; someone who is intimidating, strong, powerful. And I wouldn't be attracted to him.

Pulling open the door, my lips part at the sight in front of me. Loaded with bags on each arm and carrying two large boxes, Maddox forces a smile. "I got you some things."

"W-what?"

"Can I come in? I'm strong but these are heavy."

On shaky legs, I push away from the door, opening it wider to let him through. He walks straight into the living room, giving a quick 'hello' to Asher before stepping into the kitchen.

"What is all this?" I ask, even though I can already see what he has.

It's a breast pump kit with a steriliser and even a bottle warmer. What is in the bags is a mystery, but I can only guess it's more baby stuff.

He drops the last bag to the table, stepping back. "I got you a breast pump," he declares.

"That is more than a breast pump," I murmur.

"Did I get the wrong one?" he asks, swallowing hard.

I glance up at him, struggling to find the right words without sounding rude or ungrateful. "Maddox, this was generous of you, but I can't accept all of this."

"Why?" he asks, his brows pulling together.

"Because I didn't pay for them," I tell him. "And you shouldn't have got them. I know we're friends now but this is too much."

"Don't worry. I didn't get it all," he tells me, grinning now. "My mum and dad bought some too."

"What?" I ask, my lips parting.

He nods, rummaging through one of the larger bags. "Yeah. Mum helped me pick this stuff out. I chose this though," he reveals, holding out the most adorable outfit ever.

Grey bottom dungarees with a white shirt. There's even a matching little cap.

"Maddox," I whisper, choked up by his kindness and generosity.

"And this one," he continues, pulling out another outfit. This one has 'mama's boy' written on the T-shirt, and dark grey bottoms. The woolly hat is gorgeous. "It says, 'mama's boy'. Can you believe they don't do a T-shirt that says, 'my mum's best friend is awesome'?"

I stop him from getting anything else out, my heart racing. "Stop."

His brows pull together. "Did I get the wrong sizes?"

"Why are you doing this? You come over all the time for dinner. You got my son to sleep last night, and let's not forget you stayed over. You took my daughter to school this morning and now you're buying all this," I tell him, gesturing to all the bags. "Stuff I would never have been able to afford and will never be able to pay you back for. You aren't their dad."

When his expression drops, I feel like shit. "I, um—"

I pinch the bridge of my nose. "I'm sorry. That came out wrong."

"I thought we were friends," he murmurs. "Friends do this kind of thing."

"We are. We are," I rush out to assure him. "But this… it's a lot. We haven't known each other long. I don't expect you to do all of this."

"I wanted to," he states. "If you don't want to be mates, say so now. I'll fix it."

I chuckle at his blunt honesty. I've never met anyone so determined before. "I'm not good at this friend thing. I had one before who did all these things. She took Jasmine to school sometimes, bought her toys and played games with her."

"Yeah, but I bet she didn't rock a school run like I did, or give her burnt toast in the morning, or get her into football," he states.

I chuckle. I can't help it. He is so damn adorable. "No, she didn't. She was fucking my ex for years behind my back."

He waves at me dismissively. "Well, you won't have to worry about me doing that, will you."

"No, I won't," I whisper, amazed at how indifferent he can be. He is truly a breath of fresh air. He doesn't judge. He doesn't pity me. Half the time I worry he doesn't hold any logic or sense.

"And good riddance, if you ask me," he tells me, rummaging through another bag. "You shouldn't have bitches around Jaz."

I giggle, stepping closer. "But, Maddox, it still doesn't make this okay. It's not your responsibility."

He turns to me, his bottom lip trembling. When his eyes begin to water, I start to think I've truly upset him. "I knew you wouldn't like them."

"I do. I do," I assure him. "I just know how much these things cost."

"But I spent so much money, and I don't have the receipts. Please, let me do this."

When his chin begins to wobble, my shoulders sag. "Alright."

He grins, his facial features straightening. "Good, because you are going to love what I got Jasmine."

My eyes narrow into slits, and I have this overwhelming sense I've just been tricked. I feel cheated. "You played me."

He winks, pulling out a remote-control sledge with 'Frozen' written on the box. "I always get what I want. I got two so we can race."

"You mean you wanted to play?" I muse.

He shrugs, not caring. "Yeah."

"Thank you. For all of it. I don't know how I'm going to repay you."

"Just keep feeding me," he declares seriously.

"Maddox," I warn, because there is no way I'm letting him buy me all of this. I'm not sure how I'm going to afford to pay him back, but I'll do it.

He leans against the kitchen chair, his easy-going expression gone. "I don't want anything in return. I didn't do it for that. I don't do anything I don't want to. I'm not sure what happened to make you refuse help when it's given to you, but I'll fix that in time."

I throw my hands up in the air. "Because everything comes at a price. Everything. I don't have it in me to be played with, Maddox. I just don't. You keep giving and giving, and as normal as this is to you, it's new to me. You have to admit, it's strange you're doing this for a person you haven't known long. I mean, the longest interaction we've had was you screaming at my vagina."

"There was a lot going on," he yells, but there is no heat to his tone; it was more in embarrassment.

Laughing, I grip the chair to stand upright. "You are such a complicated man, Maddox Carter."

He shrugs. "It runs in the family. Which reminds me," he starts, grimacing. "My mum has invited you three to dinner tonight. She really wants to meet you."

How can I say no? These people have done so much for me, and I haven't gotten the chance to thank them.

And I know I'll be safe with him, no matter what.

"Okay," I agree.

"Do you want to check the pump out?" he asks, his gaze going to my chest.

I slap his shoulder, chuckling. "I'll look later."

"Good, because I was hoping you'd help me get these signed," he declares, pulling out a clipboard with forms on.

I ROCK ASHER in his pushchair with one hand, my attention on Maddox banging the hell out of his neighbour's door.

He bet me the last slice of chocolate truffle cake that he could get the mum to sign the form. I didn't think they would answer the door. But he isn't giving up.

The mum, who I heard someone call Cassie, opens her door. Her hair is frizzy and sticking up all over the place, and her makeup is smudged down her face.

"What the fuck do you want?" she snaps.

"I was wondering if you could sign this petition. It's to give everyone a say on what they do on the street."

"No," she barks, going to slam the door.

Maddox sticks his foot in the doorway, blocking her from shutting it. "Please. Whatever street gets the most signatures wins ten grand."

She pulls open the door, her eyes widening. "Ten grand?"

Maddox nods. "Yeah. Per person," he lies.

He holds out the pen and she takes it, signing her name and putting in her details. "Now fuck off." When she spots me at the end of the pavement, her lip curls. "And make sure that brat stays quiet."

She slams the door, and Maddox grits his teeth as he walks back to me. "Bitch."

I laugh, glancing down at the paper. "I can't believe she actually signed it."

He grins, winking down at me. "Told you I could get her to," he gloats, before looking at the house in thought. "Wait here. I have something I need to do."

I nod, watching him run to his truck. He grabs something out of it before he lets himself into his house. Moments later, *Let It Go* is blasting through the windows, and I chuckle.

It's Jasmine's CD.

When he rushes back out, grinning, I can't help but shake my head. "You're so bad."

"It's on repeat too," he states, rubbing his hands. "Let's go."

I laugh at his pun as we move down to the next house, and this time, we go to the door together. Just as the old man opens the door, next door's window opens and the kid, Kayne, shoves his head out. "Shut that fucking up," he roars.

Maddox and I share a look before bursting into laughter.

The guy, who must be in his eighties, chuckles with us. "My great-granddaughters love that movie."

"My daughter too," I admit.

"The song gets annoying after a bit though," he states.

It really does.

Maddox chuckles. "Which is why I have it on repeat and at top volume."

"I'm glad I have hearing aids, son. I've heard the commotion when I've gotten up during the night to get a drink. I'm glad I have a choice to take them out and not have to listen to that awful racket," he tells us.

I pout in envy. "I wish I could do that."

He chuckles at my expression. "I bet," he says, before turning to Maddox. "What can I do for you today?"

"I've started a petition to get them evicted. I know you've had trouble before, so I can understand if you don't want to—"

He snatches the pen from Maddox. "Happy to."

Maddox grins. "If the music from mine becomes a bother, just let me know and I'll turn it off. I'll be at the house across the road."

"Will do," he answers, before something occurs to him. "You should do the street at the back of us. I know the bloke whose garden meets the back of theirs, and he's had enough of the parties too."

"They can hear it from there?" I ask, open-mouthed.

He nods. "Terrible. No respect these days. It was a nice quiet street before they moved in."

"Well, you take care," Maddox pipes in.

"You too, boy."

I wave goodbye before pushing Asher down the path. Maddox turns to me at the end, tapping the tip of the pen against his chin. "I think we should walk the other street first. You up for it?"

"I am. He's not due for a feed for another hour."

"Good. Hopefully we can get everyone to sign. I might have to catch some people tomorrow evening after they've finished work though."

"You'll do it," I tell him.

"There's something I want to ask you, but I'm not sure if it's appropriate."

His comment takes me off guard. "You? Appropriate?" I tease, but then my smile falls when I see he's serious. "What did you want to ask?"

"Jasmine, on the way to school… She said something, and I guess I'm a nosey fucker because I want to know if it's true."

I jerk a little, wondering what she said to him. With my mouth now dry, I force myself to reply. "What do you mean?"

"She said her dad hurt you. That you were both in hospital," he states, and I look away, gritting my teeth. I didn't want anyone to know. "It's okay. You don't have to tell me anything. I just want to know if everything is okay."

I exhale, and nod my head. "It's something I don't like talking about," I whisper.

"But you're both safe, right?"

His kindness has my heart melting. "Yeah," I whisper.

"You okay?"

"Remember when I told you my friend was sleeping with my ex?"

His expression tightens. "I do."

"I walked in on them. That was the night he put me in hospital. Jasmine nearly died; her appendix ruptured," I explain.

It was rare Jasmine talked about it, but there were times when little things slipped out, things I didn't know she remembered or saw. I know there will be another time she'll say something, so it's best to get it out in the open.

"Fuck, I'm so sorry."

I shrug. "I don't like talking about it. My relationship wasn't the best, and I hate being reminded of what a failure I was."

"That's not true."

I force out a laugh. "You don't know anything about it."

He grabs the pushchair, pulling it to a stop. "But I've seen you with Jasmine. You're a good mum. What he did is on him, not you. I hope he got what he fucking deserved."

I snort. "He got off lightly. His prison sentence wasn't nearly long enough."

"And those women who came to the house the day you went into labour?"

"His mum and aunt. They haven't bothered with him his entire life, but they love causing drama."

"I'm sorry."

"You have nothing to be sorry for."

"I do. I shouldn't have brought it up."

"It's fine," I assure him.

He gives me a sharp nod before saying, "If you ever need to talk, I'm here."

I smirk. "Because it's what friends do?"

He bumps his shoulder against mine. "Yeah. And I'm the bestest friend you'll ever have."

I smile to myself. He doesn't know how true that statement is. I cherished my friendship with Scarlett. Trusted and shared my secrets with her. But with Maddox, it's different. He seems like the sort of person who would keep your secrets even if revealing one would save his life. Scarlett, I knew, had always been the kind of person to put herself first. And I didn't begrudge her for it. It was just who she was. I just hadn't imagined I'd be the person she ended up betraying.

I'm not sure if I'm ready to bare my secrets with another person like I did her. I trust Maddox as much as I can.

But to trust him completely… I'm not sure if I could be vulnerable like that ever again.

I guess time will tell.

Just as we reach the end of the street, a loud scream echoes from down the road.

"Turn that fucking off!"

Maddox and I share a look before bursting into laughter.

Yeah, time will really tell.

THIRTEEN

AMELIA

Maddox drums his fingers over the steering wheel of my car, bobbing his head to Jasmine's Disney CD.

"You do know I can drive," I tell him, although I already said this to him when he snatched the keys off me.

"I like driving," he replies. "And I wouldn't have fitted everyone in my truck."

I tap my foot on the floor of the car, glancing out of the window. We have been driving for ten minutes, and he said it only took ten-to-fifteen minutes to get to his parents' house. We're close.

I smooth the palm of my hands over my thighs. It wasn't until ten minutes before leaving that it occurred to me that I didn't know why his parents wanted to meet me. *Do they think we're together? Did he tell them we're a thing?*

I want to ask but I don't know how. My anxiety is going through the roof. I deal with strangers every day at work. This won't be any different. And yet,

I'm nervous about meeting them. And then it hits me. I want to make a good impression.

I just don't know why. It's bizarre, since we're only friends.

"Why are you nervous?" Maddox asks, turning the music down.

I grin at the sound of Jasmine's groan. "I'm not."

"You are," he states, not taking his eyes off the road.

I link my fingers together, placing them in my lap. I have to pull on my big girl knickers and just come out and ask.

Shifting in my seat, I face him a little. "They don't think we're an item, do they?"

My shoulders hunch when he begins to laugh. "They wish. Don't take it personally though. They've been trying to get me to settle down for years."

"You don't want to?" I blurt out.

He gives me a quick glance, shrugging his shoulders. "Not really. I like my life how it is. I'll never have time for a girlfriend anyway."

I twist my lips together. "You don't have a problem seeing us," I point out.

He grins. "Yeah, but you aren't my girlfriend. You're my friend." *Ouch.* "And you're fun to be around. You don't boss me around. You try to, but it doesn't work."

I shake my head at his logic. "You don't listen, that's why."

"Are we having a domestic?" he asks, his lips twitching as he pulls into the next street.

"No, because you'd have to be my boyfriend for that, and that would *never* happen," I declare, hoping he doesn't hear the bitterness in my voice.

I'm not even sure why I'm so hurt that he laughed. But I am. At least I know he's around for friendship and nothing more. Because honestly… as attracted as I am to him, I don't think I'm ready for another relationship. Of any kind.

I just wish he would stop doing all of the things a boyfriend—or at least someone interested—would do. It's making my crush on him even worse.

Damn, he's frustrating.

"Why? I'd make a good boyfriend," he cries in outrage.

I chuckle under my breath as I lean over and pat his arm. "Sure. If you say so."

"What is *that* supposed to mean?"

I shrug, glancing out the window as he slows down, finding a spot to park. "You're more friend material than boyfriend. I dunno."

He puts the car into park, turning to me sharply. "I'd make a brilliant boyfriend."

"You are a bit silly," Jasmine puts in. "Maybe you like boys."

"Jasmine," I call out, failing at hiding my amusement.

He turns round in his seat, his eyes wide. "I am not into boys, and even if I was, they'd love me too."

Jasmine unclips her belt and leans forward, patting his forehead. "It's okay. Maybe when you're a bit older. My mummy is always telling me to wait to find a boyfriend until I'm older too."

He sucks in a breath as he turns to me. "I would so make a good boyfriend to a woman *or* a guy."

I push open my door, my nerves now eased. "Maybe you're just doomed to only be friends with the opposite sex. I mean, it will be lonely not having someone to share everything with, who will cook for you, who you'll go to bed with each night." I lean in, whispering, "And sleeping with a different chick each week will just get predictable and boring."

"It is not once a week," he hisses, getting out of the car.

I watch him over the car as he gets Jasmine out. I pull open the back door, grabbing Asher, who is strapped into his car seat.

"Where do your parents live?" I ask as he takes the car seat off me.

He jerks his chin to the house we're standing in front of, and he groans. "I apologise in advance."

"What do you mean?" I ask, rushing to take Jasmine's hand.

"It's not just my parents who are there. It seems they have visitors."

Jasmine pulls on the sleeve of his jacket. "Do they have children?"

"My uncle Max isn't here, but you liked him, right?" he asks.

"Yeah, he was okay. He isn't as funny as you."

Maddox chuckles. "Please tell him that the next time you see him."

She gives a quick nod. Maddox reaches up to knock on the door, but it's pulled open by a beautiful brunette with hair to her shoulders and soft, flawless skin.

Her smile is blinding as she greets us, Malik—Maddox's dad—stepping up behind her. "You came. It is so good to meet you. I'm Harlow. This is my husband, Malik."

I give her a small wave. "Hey, I'm—"

"Mum, I'd make a good boyfriend, right?"

His dad chuckles, shaking his head. "Why not let everyone get inside before you start?"

His mum rolls her eyes, opening the door. "Come on in."

"Thank you for inviting us," I tell her as we walk through, stepping left into the living area. My shoulders sag when I see Hope sitting down on the sofa. "Hey."

"It's so good to see you. When Harlow told my mum you were friends with Maddox, I had to come and see for myself. I thought that when he delivered Asher, it was a coincidence."

"We're—" I stop mid-sentence, interrupted by Maddox once again.

"Mum, I would, wouldn't I? Tell her."

I snort. "Just drop it already."

"Drop what?" Madison asks, before beaming at Jasmine. "Hey, princess."

"Maddy," Jasmine squeals, letting go of my hand to run over to her. "Can you plait my hair again?"

Madison pulls out a pack of Frozen bobbles from her pocket, grinning. "Of course. I got these just for you."

Clapping her hands, Jasmine jumps up and down.

"Why don't you come and say hello to everyone else?" I tell her, arching an eyebrow.

Jasmine's nose scrunches up. "But I already met them, silly."

She has me there.

Harlow comes to a stop beside me. "It's fine. Would you like a drink?"

"I'm good for the moment, thank you."

"Does no one care that she thinks I'm not boyfriend material?" Maddox cries out, pointing a finger at me.

"He likes boys," Jasmine whispers, making me chuckle.

His dad claps Maddox on the shoulder. "Bite you in the arse."

Maddox's eyes narrow into slits. "This isn't that. I'm not in a relationship. But I could be if I wanted to."

"Of course you could," Madison replies sarcastically.

"This is abuse," he argues.

"Take a seat," Harlow gestures, and I take a seat next to Hope.

"Sorry," I tell Hope, facing her. "To answer your question, I didn't get a choice. He was like a cat. He kept coming back."

Maddox snorts, taking a seat in the armchair and picking Asher up out of his car seat. "She wanted me to."

"He's beautiful," Harlow murmurs, holding her hands out to hold him. When Maddox ignores her, she arches her eyebrow at him. "Let me hold him."

He shakes his head. "Let him get used to the room first. He might cry."

I nod in agreement. "He probably will. I think he's attached to Maddox."

His mum eyes him disbelievingly, and he puffs out his chest. "Try."

He hands her Asher, and within seconds of being held, Asher begins to wail. Harlow's eyes widen, and she turns to Malik in shock. "Maybe it's because you were the first one to hold him."

He shrugs, taking him back. "He just likes me. Give him a while and he'll be okay."

When his mum gives me a questioning look, I shrug. "I don't have the answers either."

I hear a door being opened somewhere at the back of the house, right before a gorgeous man, who looks similar to Malik, and a blonde bombshell walk through from the dining room.

"Hey," the woman greets.

Hope points to the new couple. "That's my dad, Mason, and my mum, Denny. They live in the house down the garden."

My eyes widen. "Down the garden?"

She nods. "Before it got strict with restrictions, they managed to get planning permission to build a house there. They had the land to do it. The gardens are huge."

"Impressive."

Harlow begins to make introductions, and just as she's finished, there's another knock on the door. It's Denny who replies. "That is probably Kayla and Charlotte. The guys went out to a hockey match, so I told them to come over."

Seconds later, Malik walks through, and two stunning women with bright red hair step through the doorway behind him. One is an older woman, but the other seems to be my age or younger. She's gorgeous.

"That's our cousin, Charlotte, and her mum, Kayla."

I can't look away. It isn't because she's beautiful either. It's something else. Something I can't quite put my finger on.

She's nervous, which seems weird since she's amongst family. And not only that, but she looks tired and filled with sadness.

"Charlotte, you should come meet Asher Maddox Taylor," Maddox announces.

She jerks at the sound of his voice, and I stiffen. I know that reaction all too well. When I turn to see his reaction, his jaw is tight, and he doesn't look happy. I catch him share a look with his sister before forcing a smile. They noticed it too it seems and aren't happy.

"He's beautiful," she murmurs, her voice a melody.

"I gave birth to him," Maddox boasts.

Her lips twist as she stares at him. "Maddox, you didn't give birth to him. That's impossible."

His eyebrows bunch together. "I meant delivered him. Same thing."

"It's really not," she answers, smiling when Asher begins to coo up at her. "Hey, little guy."

"I think he likes you," Maddox declares, handing him over to her. She gently pulls him into her arms, and the second she smiles, I'm blown away. Her entire body smiles with her.

Turning away from them, I glance to Harlow. "Thank you for everything you did the night I gave birth. All of you. I wasn't sure I was ever going to get unpacked. What you've done means everything to me."

Harlow's expression relaxes and a warm smile reaches her lips. "You're most welcome."

I clear my throat, nervous about bringing this up in front of everyone. "And thank you so much for your gifts today. They are extremely appreciated."

She steps closer, squeezing my shoulder. "Again, you're welcome. We've been dying to meet you and the kids for a while, but Maddox said you were busy."

"Busy?" I ask, and when my attention goes to Maddox, he begins to whistle, glancing around the room. "Maddox?"

"You were my friend first," he argues, throwing his hands up.

I chuckle, shaking my head at him. Only he would monopolize someone's time in a juvenile way.

Jasmine leans forward on Madison's lap. "You were my friend first."

He winks. "Always."

"How long have you known each other?" Harlow asks.

"Not long."

"Mum," he warns, "we are just friends."

She throws her hands up. "You can't blame me for wanting my son to settle down with a nice girl."

"You've got another son. Pimp him off," he orders.

His brother, Trent, coughs into his hand. "Scaredy cat."

"I'm not scared," he yells, slapping his hands down on the arms of the chair.

His dad grunts at him before giving me a look. "I can see why you don't want him."

"We aren't... We haven't..."

"I don't blame you. He's hard work," he tells me again, his expression serious.

"I am not," Maddox snaps.

Dinner has been amazing. Harlow cooked homemade pizza's, garlic bread, and wedges that had a spicy taste to them. I couldn't eat another bite if tried. And I had tried. She had made enough to feed an army.

Nearly everyone stayed seated at the table, but Malik and Mason went to watch a game of football downstairs, taking an eager Jasmine with them. Trent went to his room.

I wince when Asher sucks a little too hard. My nipples are cracked, sore, and are hyper-sensitive right now. He isn't going easy at all.

"You work with Hope, right?" Charlotte asks, reaching for her water.

"I do. My aunt co-owns the home, but I only recently started there," I explain.

"You didn't bake any cakes today, Charlotte?" Harlow asks, and Kayla gives a small, subtle shake of her head, like she shouldn't bring it up.

She wrings her fingers together. "Not today."

"Are you still with Scott?" Maddox asks.

She smiles. "Yes. But he's busy a lot with work."

"What does he do?" Hope asks.

Charlotte shrugs, her brows pulling together. "I'm not sure."

"You didn't ask?" Kayla asks, concern written over her face.

Charlotte beams. "It's fine. We're still getting to know one another."

"Shouldn't you have known this before?" Maddox questions.

I watch as her bottom lip trembles, and she pushes away from the table, getting up. "Maybe he doesn't want me either," she snaps.

From everyone's expressions, I'd guess this was new for her. Each of them look shocked by her outburst.

Kayla stands, reaching for her daughter. "Charlotte."

"It's fine. I need to go," she whispers. "I want to check on Kat-nip."

Kayla follows after her, and I startle when I hear a door slam in the distance. Madison grits her teeth, staring at her brother. "Please tell me you've found out who this guy is."

"No. But she's changed since they got together."

"I don't think it's that," Harlow announces, giving them a pointed look.

"Please, she jumps at her own shadow, cries a lot, and didn't bake anything to bring to a meal. Something, I may add, we've been trying to get her not to do for years," Maddox argues.

Harlow reaches for the plates still on the table, and gets up. "You know she's a kind soul. She feels everything. Her empathy to others is what makes her who she is. But right now, it's messed her up. You know how much she has wanted to get married, to have a family."

Madison's lips twist. "You think she's settling?"

Harlow shrugs. "I don't know. She's losing everyone around her to their other half. Out of everyone, she has craved what they have the most. She has wanted to be a mum, a wife, and has made that known for as long as I can remember."

"I don't think losing Landon has helped much," Hope agrees.

I keep my lips shut. I don't want to tell them my suspicions. There were no marks I could see that would indicate she is being hurt, but she most definitely is, either physically or mentally. I could see it in her eyes. Although she remained silent through dinner, it was a deafening silence. She was hurting. And yes, that could be because she was feeling left behind and was with a new guy who didn't bring her up to speed with everyone else's love life.

Trent steps through the door, takes one look at me feeding Asher, and freaks out. "Fuck!" he cries out, spinning around. He goes to escape, but smacks his head against the doorframe before falling back on his arse.

My shoulders shake as I watch him slowly crawl out of the room. "Sorry."

Maddox guffaws, slapping his thigh. "I guess that answers if he's seen a pair of tits before."

"Maddox," Harlow retorts, her lips twitching.

I lift the blanket that has slipped down, fighting hard not to laugh. "It's a shock to most people. They see a mum breastfeeding and immediately look away. Or stare, if they're anything like Maddox."

He holds his hands up. "He was going to town on them. It was hard not to."

Hope giggles. "Did you go bright red?"

He grins, shaking his head. "Not my first pair of tits."

"He was awkward," I tell them, giving him a gloating smile.

Malik walks in holding Jasmine by her ankles. "I think she needs a break from football," he explains, then grimaces when he turns to me. "She may have picked up a swear word and then yelled it at the television."

"Jasmine," I call out, astonished.

Her face is bright red when he straightens her, dropping her to her feet. She folds her arms over her chest, her face scrunched up tight. "The guy *was* an arse. That was a foul."

Malik chuckles, stepping away. "She's all yours."

I slowly turn to Maddox. "What have you taught my daughter?"

He rubs the back of his neck. "She's a quick learner."

"Jasmine, sit down in that chair. When you are ready to apologise for using foul language, you can go watch television in the living room."

She huffs out a breath as she takes a seat in the chair. "I'm not saying sorry. Our team are losing."

"Jaz, girls don't swear," Maddox tells her. "You should listen to your mum."

Still sulking, she glares up at me through her lashes. "Sorry, Mummy. I won't say arse again."

Maddox struggles to hide his chuckle, and I jab him with my elbow. "Go sit in the living room."

She gets up but pauses when the front door flies open. Harlow pushes away from the sink, turning towards the door.

Max, the guy who scared me the first time I met him at Maverick Carter's office, comes storming into the dining room. He gapes at the room, his lips parted. "Oh, I see how it is."

"Max," Harlow groans.

He waves her off. "You know I like my pizza. Did you invite me? No. But you let Mason come."

"How did you even know?" she asks.

He holds his phone up. "Mason Instagrammed me a picture of the food to rub it in."

She rolls her eyes as she dries her hands on the dish towel. "And how did you get in?"

He sniffs, looking away. "I lived here once. I still have a key. I wanted to catch you in the act."

When he takes a seat, diving into the leftovers still on the table, I gape. He lived here?

"Over twenty years ago, Max. How do you still have a key?"

He talks through a mouthful of food. "I have keys to everyone's house."

Jasmine steps over to Max, pulling on his T-shirt. "Will you let me watch football?"

"No," I rush out.

"Nah, the game was crap. They lost."

"What?" she screeches. "You spoilt the whole game."

"Calm down," he tells her, grinning. "I can do one better, kid. We can go outside and kick a ball around."

Jasmine jumps up and down. "Yay."

Maddox turns to me, grimacing. "I did tell you they were a little crazy."

He really did. But it's the good kind. The best. It feels great to be a part of something again, to be me and not just a mum.

Maybe my mum was right. Maybe putting myself out there will be good for me. For the first time in a long time, I feel like me again.

FOURTEEN

MADDOX

"**A**RE YOU NOT GOING TO CHEER the fuck up?" Mark asks, glancing over the rim of his glass of beer.

I rest my ankle over my knee, sitting back in the chair. "I am fucking cheery. I just don't get why I couldn't go," I argue.

"Dude, really?" Liam calls out, chuckling.

I slam my hand down on the table, rattling the beers. "Fuck off. And so what if I was dusty from work."

I'm more than dusty, but that isn't the point. I feel neglected, pushed out, and these arseholes are making fun of me for it. But to tell me I couldn't even step through the doorway was a joke. She used my work attire as an excuse to not let me in, and the fact she had people over. Like I was an embarrassment or something.

"It's called girls night for a reason," Mark states. "You've been glancing at your phone every two minutes since we arrived. Get over it already."

Because she kicked me out. When I saw all the cars out front, I went straight over instead of showering before like I normally do. I do it every day when I finish work because she likes to cook me dinner.

But *no*.

Tonight, it's no men allowed. I argued about Asher being there, but apparently, he's exempt because he's a baby.

Whatever.

I'm fucking exhausted, and all I want to do is sleep. I haven't slept much for nearly a week now, and it's catching up with me.

"I'm not the only one on their phone," I point out, flicking my gaze over to Aiden.

He looks up, frowning. "Are you in the doghouse? Do you have a kid? No. So shut the fuck up."

"What did you do now?" Mark asks his brother, his lips twitching.

He sighs, leaning back against the chair. "I ate the cookies she was making for the day care Sunday goes to. They're doing this bake sale thing to raise money," he mumbles. "In my defence, she knew who I was before I moved in. She shouldn't have left them on the side."

I chuckle under my breath. "Pussy whipped."

He glares over at me. "Say's the guy who's whipped by a girl he isn't even fucking."

"I am not whipped," I snap.

Mark and Liam begin to chuckle. "You both are," Mark states.

"I am fucking not. She's a mate. That's all."

"Who you want to be more," Liam argues.

My lips twist into a snarl. "No actually. I don't. Why can't a man or a woman just be friends?"

Mark holds his hand up, stopping me. "We aren't saying they can't. But, bro, you are fucking gone when it comes to this chick. I can't wait to meet her."

"You aren't," I bite out. "She won't like you."

"Everyone likes me," he declares, smirking.

I roll my eyes. "Not everyone."

"And let's not forget, we haven't seen you take a chick home since you met her," Liam points out.

I haven't. But it has nothing to do with Amelia. I just haven't had the time. "I'm too tired. With the neighbours partying like the world is ending tomorrow each night, I'm exhausted. Our workload has gotten heavier, and I'm trying to keep up. Plus, I'm having to get Asher to sleep each night before I go home to sleep—or lay awake plotting next door's demise."

I don't have to, but I know he likes to say goodnight before I leave.

Aiden chuckles. "I nearly believed you for a second there, but then you mentioned Asher and ruined it."

I shrug. "He loves me."

"Just admit you have a thing for his mum," Mark orders, dodging my punch when I go for him.

I groan. "You guys are fuckers. This is why I don't come out anymore. You're boring."

"Would you have had more fun watching a movie with Amelia and the others?"

Honestly, yes, I would have. She's probably bored shitless without me there to keep her entertained. And what will she do if Asher wakes up needing a feed, and they're in the middle of the movie? I won't be there to feed him.

I should have fought harder to stay, but my sister is scary when she gets angry. They all are.

"Fuck off," I mutter, answering his question after a moment's hesitation.

He laughs, throwing his head back. "I thought you would never settle down."

"We aren't together," I bite out, wondering how many more times I'll have to tell them this until they believe it.

Liam arches an eyebrow. "I hate to tell you this, bro, but you are. You just aren't getting the benefits of being with someone."

I reach for my phone, finally seeing a reply from her.

Amelia: You do realise women have been multitasking for years now. I am capable of feeding a baby and watching a movie.

Grunting at her message, I begin to reply.

Maddox: I thought we were friends? Are you not bored without me?

"See, whipped," Mark announces, chuckling.

"Fuck off," I mutter, glancing down at her reply.

Amelia: No. Actually, I'm having a really good time. Are you not having a good time with your cousins?

Maddox: No. Because I'm hungry and Jim won't let us bring in our own food anymore. Say's it's bad for business.

Amelia: Will it make you feel better if I save you some food?

I snort. That's never going to happen with my family there. Not one of them know what leftovers are.

Maddox: Are there any leftovers now?

Amelia: Um...

Maddox: Exactly.

Amelia: I think Madison is still hungry. I'll order extra and save some for you.

Maddox: Don't do me any favours.

Amelia: Are you really that upset about this?

Maddox: You were my friend first.

Amelia: So, you don't want food?

Maddox: I didn't say that. Stop twisting my words.

Amelia: LOL! See you later.

Maddox: Maybe.

When she doesn't reply, I shove the phone in my jacket. When I look up, all three are staring at me.

"What?" When they all burst out laughing, I grit my teeth, downing the rest of my pint before getting up. "I'm getting a fucking drink."

"I'll have another," Mark announces, holding up his half empty glass.

I ignore him, walking up to the bar and standing next to two chicks who are sitting there. I hold my glass up to Jim and he nods, grabbing a fresh glass from under the bar.

"I can't believe he would do this to me," the girl sniffles next to me. "I thought we were forever."

Her friend reaches forward, rubbing her arm. "He's a loser. You don't need him in your life."

"I know. But how am I supposed to move on?" she whispers.

I grab my wallet, handing Jim a tenner, when I feel eyes boring into me. The girl with red-rimmed eyes scans me up and down. "Hey, handsome."

My eyebrows pull together. She was just crying over her boyfriend. "Hey," I greet back.

"What are you up to tonight?" she purrs.

I give her a side glance, and at a quick note, she is someone I would have normally taken home. Or, well, her home. Boyfriend or no boyfriend issue.

However, I'm never in the mood for anything if I'm hungry. And right now, I'm fucking starving.

"Just enjoying a pint, then heading home to put the boy to bed."

"The boy?"

"Asher," I explain, placing my pint back on the bar. I pull my phone out and go to the pictures, bringing up one of Asher that I took the other night. He's smiling. Amelia said it was wind, but personally, I think she's just jealous it was me he smiled at first.

"Oh my God, he's so cute."

"He is, isn't he."

"I'm sorry for coming onto you. I didn't know you were married."

I draw back. "I'm not."

"Oh, *with* someone then."

"I'm not."

She shares a look with her friend. "Sorry, I assumed because of the baby—"

I shrug. "No biggie. Enjoy your night," I tell them, grabbing my pint.

Liam gapes openly as I make my way back to our table. "Are you kidding me?"

"What? I pay you enough to buy your own drinks."

"You just turned down a hot chick," Mark states, shaking his head.

I glance back towards the bar, forcing a smile when I see them still watching me. "And?"

"You never turn down a chick."

I roll my eyes at Mark. "Yeah, I do, plenty of times."

Liam chuckles. "Yeah, okay."

I sigh. "This is shit. Can't we do something?"

"You want to crash the movie night, don't you?"

I pout. "I do."

"Let's go then."

I grin, downing most of my pint before dropping it down on the table. It's the best thing he's said all night, and I'm not waiting around for the other two to decline.

"Fuck!" Liam breathes out, sitting forward in his seat.

I glance between the two headrests, mirroring his reaction. "Fuck!"

Mark quickly puts the car into park, and we all race out to chaos. "Who invited Hayden?"

"My fucking toe is bigger than your dick," Hayden screams, being held back by Hope and Madison.

One of Kayne's mates grabs his junk. "Want to see?"

Liam grabs his sister around the waist when she goes for him. "Someone pass me a magnifying glass," she screams.

"What did you say, you little sket," says a girl with hair dyed different colours, the top a really dark brown.

Hayden pulls the sleeves of her top up. "Don't think I won't take you out either, fried eggs."

"Fried eggs?" I ask.

"Her tits," Madison answers for me.

I chuckle under my breath. In all honesty, what did they expect? The girl has no meat on her at all. She's all bone.

"Are you fucking high?" the girl asks, scrunching her nose up before turning to her mates. "Can you believe this ugly bitch?"

"Me, ugly?" Hayden snaps. "Voldemort wants his nose back, you little bitch."

"What the fuck is going on?" I ask, stepping up beside a pale Amelia.

She shakily lifts her head, her mouth opening and closing. "It happened so quick."

"What did?" I ask, glancing towards my sister for answers this time.

"Hayden was getting pissed. You know what she's like. She went over to ask them to turn the music down, and that girl," she explains, pointing to a woman slowly being helped off the floor, "started mouthing off. Hayden laid her out and it went from bad to worse."

"There isn't any music playing," I point out.

Hope grimaces. "Hayden tore it from the plug socket when the woman—Cassie, I think they called her—started yelling abuse at Amelia."

My entire body tenses. "What?"

She nods as I pull Amelia into my arms. "She was accusing her of starting a petition. Apparently, they were told someone was starting one and she thinks it was Amelia."

Blood rushes to my ears, and I step away from Amelia. "I don't fucking think so."

"Don't," Amelia panics. "It will just make it worse."

"Leaving it will make it worse. They'll fuck with you, and I'm not having that."

"Maddox," she whispers.

I give my sister a pointed look before crossing the road to Cassie's. Her son stands from his chair, narrowing his gaze on me. "Get your fucking family off our property."

"No," I tell him. "Get your mum out here."

"Your family started this."

I step forward, grinding my teeth so hard they ache. "Get your fucking mother."

"What do you want?" Cassie snarls, stepping outside a moment later.

"None of you touch Amelia. None of you. One thing happens to her, her kids, house, or car, and I will personally make your life a living hell."

"She's trying to get us kicked fucking out," she snaps.

I cross my arms over my chest, leaning in a little. "No. *I am*. And half this goddamn neighbourhood is too. We're sick of the music, sick of the noise from you lot practising for X-Factor. We're sick of the shit."

She narrows her gaze on me. "I have kids. Where will we live?"

"Hopefully in the middle of fucking nowhere so you don't disturb the peace," I snap. "And your kids are old enough to look after themselves."

"I have young teenagers," she barks.

I glance around, searching for them. I know she has a lot of kids, but I haven't seen any of them other than Kayne. "And you live like this?"

"Are you saying I'm a bad mum?" she screams, storming down the steps. I don't budge, but luckily, her son intervenes, pushing her back. "Mum."

"I ain't scared of them," she yells.

I feel my family step up behind me. "It's done. You play that music tonight and I'm done being nice. I didn't want to give a bad impression on my other neighbours, and honestly, until now I've not cared to overstep, but all bets are off."

"You threatening us?" Kayne asks, his nostrils flaring. When I catch his gaze going to the bat lying against the wall of the house, I narrow my gaze on him.

"I wouldn't even think it," I warn him.

"Yeah, he's got a mean left hook," Liam calls out.

"Let me fucking at 'em," Hayden screams.

"You want to play your music? Carry on. But expect repercussions."

"We 'ent scared of you," Cassie yells. "My son and his mates will have you."

I wave over my shoulder as I head across the road, the others following me. She doesn't scare me. None of them do. The only reason I haven't acted until now is because they weren't important to me. Annoying? Yes. But other than that, they weren't worth it.

Now, all bets are off.

FIFTEEN

MADDOX

Amelia is clutching the baby monitor to her chest as I stomp over to them. She looks a little shell-shocked, her gaze darting around as if she's trying to absorb everything that just happened. I feel bad, but she's taking it better than I expected. I would have thought she would freak out over the violence, but apart from looking a little stunned, she seems to be taking it in her stride.

Still, she shouldn't have witnessed that at all, and they shouldn't have been giving her grief over the petition, especially since it was posted anonymously.

I clench my fists. "Are you okay?" I ask, my eyes crinkling into slits.

She nods mutely, and it's Madison who speaks up. "You need to do something about them."

I jerk my head into a nod. "I will."

"Fucking scrubber," Hayden spits out. A car pulls up, and when she turns, her lips tighten, and she groans. "Who called Clay?"

Charlotte raises her hand. "I thought he could come and stop you from being arrested."

She forces her expression to stay neutral. "I didn't do anything wrong."

"You knocked the woman out. You said you weren't going to get into trouble again."

"You were humming *Eye of the Tiger*. You know that's my fighting song," Hayden argues.

Charlotte throws her hands up. "It's a habit now when you go off on one."

"But did you really have to call Clayton?"

Her bottom lip trembles. "I didn't want you to get arrested."

"Thank you, Charlotte."

Charlotte visibly relaxes. "You're welcome." She takes in a breath before facing Amelia. "Thank you for the invite. I'm going to head home, but I hope we get to do it again some time."

Amelia nods. "Of course."

Hayden steps forward. "I'm getting a lift with Charlotte, but hopefully I'll see you again soon."

"Any time," Amelia answers.

They pass Clayton as they leave. "What did you do?" Clayton asks.

Hayden stomps her foot, crossing her arms over her chest. "Why do you assume it was me?"

He arches an eyebrow, his lips twitching. "Hayden."

She rolls her eyes, snorting. "Whatever. They deserved it."

"I bet."

She takes his hand, turning to the rest of us. "Catch you guys later," she tells us before her gaze meets mine. "You need to talk to my dad."

I groan because she's right. If anyone can get rid of the family, it's him. "I'll talk to my dad first."

She nods and leaves, Clayton close behind her. When it's just us, I stand next to Amelia, pointing to Mark. "These are my cousins, Liam, Mark and Aiden."

She waves, smiling. "Hey. I've heard a lot about you."

"Because he doesn't shut up, right?" Mark states.

She chuckles, shaking her head. "He does love the sound of his own voice."

"Dude," Aiden calls out, chuckling. "She has you there."

"Fuck off," I bite out.

When Asher's cry comes through the baby monitor, Amelia holds it up, grimacing. "I'd best go. It was nice meeting you all."

"I'll come and grab my bag in a sec," Hope announces, smiling as Amelia leaves.

As soon as she's through the door, she glares at me, poking me in the shoulder. "If you hurt her, I will cut your dick off."

The guys wince, stepping away from her. I hold my hands up, stepping back. "What are you talking about?"

"She doesn't deserve to be played."

"What are you on about?" I ask, utterly at a loss.

"I know you've been spending a lot of time here, and you were messaging her tonight."

"And?"

She sighs, throwing her hands up. "It's clear you like her. How could you not. She's amazing. But she doesn't deserve to be hurt, and I sense she's been through enough."

"Hope—"

"No, Maddox. The longest relationship you've had was with that footlong hot dog."

I grin, licking my lips. "That was a good hot dog. It couldn't be rushed."

She points at me sharply, groaning. "That right there. She doesn't need this. I love you, but you can be a bit self-centred."

"I take offence to that," I tell her, arching my eyebrow. "And as much as I appreciate you looking out for her, I swear to you, nothing is going on between us. We are friends. And as her friend, I only have her best interests at heart."

She rolls her eyes. "You'd better, because your neighbours will be the least of your worries."

She heads up to the house, and I slowly turn to the guys, my eyes widening. "Is it me or are they getting meaner?"

Liam nods. "Hayden threatened to poison my food the other day, all because I took the last piece of bacon."

Mark grunts. "I accidently spilt a beer over Ciara's white coat the other week when she was visiting Faith and Lily. I thought she was going to stab me right there."

Aiden makes a noise at the back of his throat. "Faith set her dog on me. Chased me down the street."

"Why?"

"Because I ordered food while I was at hers because Bailey doesn't want me eating so much crap. I was starving and rushed to the kitchen to dig in."

I smirk. "You told the delivery guy Beau was paying, didn't you?"

He chuckles. "Yeah. In my defence, I forgot my wallet. I had time to grab the rest of the bag before she set Roxie on me."

"I'm gonna go head in, but thanks for coming back with me," I tell them.

"Yeah, I'm hungry now that I've mentioned food," Aiden answers.

"Me too," Liam mutters.

Mark just shakes his head in amusement. "I'll take you to get something."

"Are you going to kiss me when you walk me to the door as well," Aiden asks, fluttering his lashes.

Mark snorts, rolling his eyes at his juvenile behaviour. "And it still shocks me that you take care of my niece."

"Whatever," Aiden mutters.

Mark turns to me. "Anyway, they're right. Something needs to be done about your neighbours. You've put up with them long enough."

"I know, and I'll sort it."

"Alright, well, we're here to help. I haven't gotten into a good scrap in ages," he tells me, rubbing his hands together.

I grin. "I'll keep that in mind."

"See you later."

I wave goodbye, waiting until they're in the car before heading up the path. The door is open a little when I reach it. I walk in, hearing Hope and Amelia chatting in the front room.

"Tracey said you're going back to work next week. I assumed you'd take the whole six months maternity."

"I wish," Amelia admits. "But I need to go back. My mum has said she'll look after Asher while I'm there and Jasmine has school. I'm going to take shorter shifts and less days, but I have to do something."

"You're going back to work?" I blurt out, stepping into the living room.

But she hasn't long had Asher. Aren't they meant to be resting, bonding, or some crap like that?

A faint blush rises in her cheeks. "I am. Next week."

"Isn't that too soon? You should be with Asher."

Her brows pull together. "Maddox, we're friends, but don't overstep the mark. If I could stay home with Asher, I would."

"Shit, I didn't mean it like that," I rush out. "Or to upset you."

Hope punches me in the arm, narrowing her gaze on me. "I'll speak to you soon," she tells Amelia, before giving me a warning look.

Amelia gives me her back, rocking Asher in her arms. I duck my head, feeling like shit.

Why did I open my mouth?

"Will you tell me why you're going back to work when you don't want to? I'm not judging," I assure her, leaning against the doorframe. "I'm just curious."

She turns, her eyes glassy. "Because I'm in a mountain of debt thanks to their father. Because I have two little people to provide for. It's not easy, Maddox. I'm not the priority here. They are. And if that means taking shifts so soon after giving birth, which means being away from my son and losing more sleep, so be it."

"Hey," I call out, taking a step into the room. "I didn't mean any offence to it."

She exhales, glancing away. "I know. I just don't like being judged."

I take another step into the room. "It's okay. You can judge me. I've been meaning to ask if my arse looks big in these jeans." I spin around, showing her my backside, and she chuckles before bursting out laughing. I pout, feigning hurt. "What about if I do this?"

I stick my arse out, giving it a little wiggle, and she laughs harder. "Please stop."

I straighten, smirking at her. "Too hot for you?"

"It's something," she murmurs, struggling to keep her face straight.

"I'm hurt."

"You look it," she retorts.

"Where's my food? I need to eat my feelings," I tell her, glancing around the room.

"It hasn't arrived yet," she explains, just as there's a knock on the door.

My nostrils flare as I inhale deeply, before groaning. "Indian."

Her eyes widen. "How could you possibly know that?"

I don't answer as I race to the door, pulling out my wallet. The guy startles with the force that I open it, taking a step back. "Soz, mate, you scared me there."

"How much?" I ask, snatching the food from his hand.

"It's fifteen—"

I shove a twenty at him. "Keep the change."

I kick the door shut with my foot, heading past Amelia and straight into the kitchen. "Maddox, seriously, did you not eat today?"

I pause with a takeout box in my hand, my eyebrows pulling together. "Of course, I did."

She grins as she pats Asher's back. "Are you sure?"

"I never go without food. I just haven't eaten in a few hours," I explain, bending down to grab a plate out of the cupboard.

"You would never know," she tells me in amusement.

I pile it all onto my plate, grabbing the papadums and naan bread before heading over to the table.

I finish chewing, when her stare begins to burn into me. "You didn't want any, did you?"

She takes a seat next to me, chuckling. "I'm okay."

I shrug. "How was your night, apart from the crap going on outside?"

"It was good. I knew Hayden was feisty and outspoken. I've heard her argue with the residents at the home. I've seen her sit with them for hours—even after her shift has ended—because she didn't want them to beat her at a staring competition. But I've never seen her like that before."

I chuckle. "You should see her when one of her brothers piss her off."

"It happened so quickly. I put the subtitles on first because I didn't want to wake the kids up by turning it up. Plus, we were laughing and joking around anyway. But then Hayden shot out the house like it was on fire and it just kicked off."

"What happened when she got out there?"

"This woman started mouthing back off at her. Hayden laid her out on the floor and then Cassie started coming at me. She heard why Hayden was there and then said I was the one who had dobbed her in."

I snort. "She dobbed herself in too."

She chuckles. "I don't even think she realises it yet." She pauses, blinking up at me through her lashes. "You have a really good family."

I pause midchew at the sorrow in her words. "So do you."

"I do. But you guys are more than family. You're best friends. There's a connection between you that's rare between other families."

I chuckle because we get this a lot. We're all tight because of the way we were raised. We've heard the stories about what our parents went through, whether it be from their mouths or from rumours on the streets. Our parents were honest in helping us understand. It hit each and every one of us, and we didn't take them—family—for granted. "I guess, but we have our bad days too. We still argue and sometimes fall out, although nothing major."

"You mentioned you fell out with Lily," she states.

I give her a quick nod. "We did."

"How come?"

I shrug, shovelling more food into my mouth. Once finished, I push the plate away. "It doesn't matter. She missed me in the end."

Her easy-going expression drops. "What? Tell me. You're always forcing me to answer crap I don't like talking about."

I wiggle my eyebrows. "I'm good at getting women to open up."

She snorts. "You pig."

I grin. "It doesn't matter."

"Tell me," she orders gently. "I'm always telling you about me."

I pick at the naan bread, contemplating just lying, but I would hate for her to lie to me. And it isn't anything really bad, just something I feel bad about. "I don't want you to hate me."

"What did you do?" she asks, her tone wary.

"I fucked up. I made a stupid decision, thinking I was protecting her, and it blew up in my face. She's hated me ever since."

"I'm sure that's not true."

I grunt. "Don't be so sure. She's the most forgiving person you could meet, but I know she can't forgive me, not fully."

"I can't help if I don't know what you've done," she tells me.

I groan, leaning back against the chair. "Her boy—husband… our relationship was tense. We fought all the time. We couldn't even be in the same room as each other without a fight breaking out. I hated him.

"For weeks, Lily was acting weird. She kept bolting her door, hiding away, and stopped messaging me back. And before, we spent most of our time together. When I found out they were together, I lost it. She had been through so much, still suffered from some of it, and I thought he had taken advantage of her."

"And he didn't," she surmises.

I shake my head. "He didn't. I beat the shit out of him, along with a few of my uncles, and she had to watch the entire thing. She wouldn't eat, sleep or speak to me for weeks. Her Christmas was ruined because of me. I never want to see that look on her face ever again."

"But you're okay now, right?"

I shrug. "I guess. We just aren't as close as we once were." I stand, pushing back from the chair. I take the plate over to the sink, swilling it off before putting it on the side. "I'd best go."

"Maddox," she whispers, following me.

I force a smile, stopping her. "It's fine. I'm just tired."

"Are you sure?"

"Yeah."

I let myself out, rushing down the path as I pull my phone out. I really had fucked up when it came to Lily. She's my best friend, family, and I hate the distance between us. She didn't deserve my reaction, any of ours, and I hadn't done much to make it up to her. Speaking to Amelia made me realise that.

"Hello," Lily greets.

"Hey, Lil. I was just calling to see how you were doing. How's the pregnancy?"

"I'm still being a little sick, but other than that, it's going fine. We have our dating scan next week, so I think we will tell everyone else then."

"That's good. They're going to be happy."

"You okay? You sound funny? You aren't drunk, are you? Because if you've fallen down a manhole again, I don't think I can come help this time. I could ask—"

I chuckle. "Lily, I'm not drunk. I just called to see how you were and to ask if you wanted to do something Sunday."

"Jaxon and I are taking the Merin kids ice skating. Can you remember the little girl, Alex, who I told you about?"

"Yeah."

"Her parents are meeting us there. She's doing really well."

"Okay, maybe another time," I tell her, leaning against my truck. It's like this all the time now. She's always too busy. And although I love seeing her blossom, I miss her.

"Are you sure you're okay?"

"Yeah, Lil. I'm always okay."

"Okay, I need to go. Jaxon just got back. But call me in the week. We can do something then."

"Yeah, maybe we—"

"Bye Maddox," Jaxon calls out before the line goes dead.

I run my fingers through my hair, gritting my teeth. I fucking hate him sometimes.

I glance back at Amelia's, letting out a breath. I want to go back over to talk to her. She fills in the days I'm alone. She's good at letting me forget for a moment. It isn't why I go there—I don't have that answer yet—but it's one of the reasons. Plus, I love being around her and the kids.

I push off from the car, letting myself inside. The house I once loved because of the tranquillity and freedom it gave me, just feels empty and cold now.

The novelty of moving out of my parents' and getting space from my large family has worn off. Hell, I think I kept my neighbours around because it gave me an excuse to stay over at Lily's and not be alone.

Now I'm not so sure what I want. And admitting to others I may have rushed into things is something my pride won't let me do.

SIXTEEN

AMELIA

The wind whistles outside the window and the rain smacks against the glass as I stand, tired, trying to get Asher to sleep. I can't even blame it on the neighbours tonight, since the weather is drowning out most of their music. It would have been heaven if it hadn't been for Asher wailing into the night. I can't get him to feed or settle.

Tears leak down my cheeks. I'm failing at being a mother. Cameron was right when he said I'd never be able to raise two kids on my own. I can't even get my son to stop crying. I will be starting work next week, and I'll get even less sleep than I do now. But if I don't go, I won't be able to pay the debt Cameron put me in. And if I pay them, I won't be able to afford rent. And if I can't afford rent, I'll lose the house. I could go back to Mum and Dad's, but what if Cameron's mum and dad call social services like they promised and they declare me unfit? Living with my parents because I'm unable to provide for them won't look good. I feel helpless and worthless.

I exhale, dropping down on the bed as a sob tears from my throat. "Please, Asher. Please sleep for Mummy."

My phone lights up and I glance over, sniffling. It's from Maddox. After earlier, I didn't think I'd hear from him again. He seemed really upset that I brought up his argument with Lily. He looked so sad, so vulnerable in that moment.

MADDOX: Open the door. I'm tired.

Lifting up from the bed, I head downstairs, not even replying. He knows I'm awake; he would have seen the lights on in my room.

Asher's wailing gets louder as I reach the bottom of the stairs. I pull open the door. Maddox takes one look at me and gently puts a hand to my stomach, pushing me further inside. He shakes the rain from his hair, shoving his coat off before draping it over the end of the banister.

"What's wrong?" he asks, taking Asher out of my hands.

When he begins to settle somewhat, only sniffling or winging here and there, I bend at the knees, sobs raking through my body.

"I'm failing. With Jasmine, I had all this help. I had my mum and dad. I kind of had her dad. But now… n-now I can't even feed him. He hates me. I hate me. I can't do this."

"Hey," he coos gently. "You can do this. He's only a few weeks old. They're meant to be up at all hours."

"You don't even have kids. What would you know?" I snap, wiping my nose on my dressing gown as I straighten. When he arches his eyebrow, my shoulders drop. "I'm sorry. I'm tired. I'll be fine tomorrow."

He stares at me intently for a few moments before clicking his tongue. "Up to bed."

"W-what?"

"Up," he orders, shifting Asher higher on his shoulder.

I puff out a breath, before turning and stomping upstairs. My stomach flutters when I realise he's following behind me.

When I reach my room, I turn to him. "What are you even doing here?"

He glances away from the window. "You can't hear anything," he murmurs.

"Only because it's raining," I mumble under my breath.

He jerks his head toward the bed. "Get in."

"I can't. Asher needs feeding but he's not latching on. And if you're staying again then I need to get you some blankets and pillows."

"Where are the bottles?"

I sniffle before wailing. "I was too tired to make them."

He grunts, walking over to gently shove me down on the bed. "Get in."

"I just said—"

"I know. You need to feed Asher, but you look dead on your feet. And although I've said this to plenty of women, I've never said it for this reason."

"What?" I ask, wiping under my eyes as he grabs my feet, swinging them up on the bed.

I watch as he walks around to the other side of the bed and lies down. "Get your tit out. He's relaxed now. Once he's finished, I'll wind him so you can sleep."

"I'm not doing that," I tell him, yawning.

And it isn't because I'd be lying here with my tit out in front of him. At this point, I couldn't give a shit if he saw me naked. He's practically seen everything anyway. And honestly, he's never given off a creepy vibe. He doesn't stare in the same way other men have.

My lips part when it hits me. I trust him. It's not bothering me or making me feel weirded out because I trust him.

He rolls his eyes. "You've fed around me plenty of times. I know what to do."

I nod, taking Asher from him and pulling my top back down. He begins to fuss, his mouth opening and closing around my nipple, but he doesn't suck.

"See," I point out.

My breath hitches when Maddox reaches out, stroking his finger over Asher's cheek. My lips part when Asher immediately latches on.

"I wonder why he does that?" he murmurs.

I don't care anymore. I'm just glad he's settled. I yawn, moving to get comfier. "I'm sorry for upsetting you earlier."

"You didn't," he replies quietly.

"I did. You don't have to try to make me feel better. If I knew it was a touchy subject, I would never have brought it up."

"It's not that," he explains, pausing for a moment. "It just made me realise I never tried to make it up to her. It might not be that Jaxon's the reason for our distance. It could be me. I haven't forgiven myself for hurting her and vice versa."

"She probably already knows you're sorry. I've only met her briefly, when she came to the home. She seemed kind and gentle. Someone like that doesn't hold grudges."

He grins, watching as I press down on my boob, guiding my nipple back into Asher's mouth. "Does it hurt?"

"Not really. It can be uncomfortable at times but that's it."

He moves away, letting Asher feed. "What's your brother like?"

"He's a good man. Funny. But he can be serious to the point he could make a gangster piss himself. I wish he'd stay home more. We miss him," I admit, lying down and turning on my side, keeping Asher glued to my chest. Maddox does the same, resting his hand under his cheek.

"How come you never ask for help?" he asks out of nowhere.

I'm taken aback by his question. "You mean with the kids?"

"With everything," he replies.

I shrug. "I guess it's a pride thing. When I found out I was pregnant, my parents weren't exactly ecstatic. They supported me and my decision, but they wanted me to finish school first. I wanted to prove to them I could do it all. But it's hard. They've offered to pay for the debt Cameron raked up, but I can't do it. He was *my* mistake. I need to be the one to fix it."

"I get that. I do. But it's the same with the kids. You said your mum will have Jasmine for you on the days you're at work, but what about anyone else?"

"I don't trust anyone else," I tell him, meeting his gaze dead on.

His pupils dilate. "You trust me."

"Yeah," I whisper.

He pulls his gaze away, clearing his throat. "If you need any help when you go back to work, let me know. If I'm free, I will. And I reckon Jasmine will get a kick out of our work site."

My eyes widen a tad because I can tell he's being serious. "Maybe don't take her to a place with heavy machinery."

He nods, smirking. "Probably safer for my men."

A yawn escapes me. "And what about Charlotte? Did you talk to her?"

"Not yet, and it's not because any of us don't want to."

"What's stopping you?" I ask, staring at him.

He exhales heavily, his brows pulling together. "Because we made a mistake when it came to Lily. Although none of us think we are wrong this time, we can't take that chance. We need to be dead sure."

"Have any of you tried talking to her since her outburst?"

"Her mum, Kayla, did. I'm not sure what was said, but her dad and uncles are getting antsy."

"And her cousins."

He grins. "And her cousins."

"You're very protective of each other," I comment, ducking my gaze. I envy that. My brother would do anything for me, but he would have to be here to do it. He loves his job, and I'm proud of him, but sometimes I wish he had been here to look out for me. Maybe I would have listened, maybe I wouldn't have. We will never know.

"Our family comes with drama. My dad and uncles had a shit childhood. It got better when they moved in with our great-granddad, but it was still tough on them. They've each fought battles and moved mountains for the women in their lives. Their loyalty and love was passed down to us, but then again, so was the chaos of finding their other half."

My lips twitch into a smile. I'm intrigued to find out what he means by chaos. "What do you mean, chaos?"

He rolls his eyes. "My dad said all of them were happy to be single until they met their other half. Dad met Mum first, and from there it was a domino effect. Mason and Aunt Denny got together next, then Myles and Aunt Kayla, then Evan and Aunt Kennedy, Max and Aunt Lake, and then Maverick with

Aunt Teagan. Now, Faith has Beau, Aiden has Bailey, Landon has Paisley, Lily has Jaxon, and Hayden has Clayton. It's only a matter of time before the next one happens, and it always ends up in disaster."

"Really?"

He nods. "Faith got robbed by an online dating guy while she was out to meet him. Then kept it from everyone. She ended up making a report to the police and that's when all that crap blew up.

"Aiden found out he had a daughter the day her mum gave birth and passed away. He then met Bailey, who had a hearing impairment and never left the house because she was bullied badly. That was kind of crazy.

"Landon was kind of a jerk at first to Paisley, without really wanting to be. She got pregnant, he got stabbed, she lost the baby, and then that ended up with him taking down the guys who attacked him as well as a criminal organization."

My eyes widen in shock. I thought he was going to say they broke up because something happened, then got back together, or that they had a partner before. Not this. Stabbed? I can't believe it.

"And Lily?"

"None of us knew about Lily and Jaxon until the end. We beat the shit out of him, she hated us all and herself for putting him in danger, and the rest is history. They got married on New Year, last minute, and have been blissfully happy ever since."

"And I guess Hayden's was about the corrupt cop? I remember reading about it in the paper."

He nods. "Kind of. Hayden's chaos is within herself, so it was always bound to be a difficult ride."

I chuckle, adjusting Asher on my breast. "She's not that bad."

He arches his eyebrow. "Tonight was nothing. Wait until someone steals her food."

"You steal her food, don't you?"

He nods, his chest puffing out. "I do," he admits, grinning impishly. "What about you? Will you tell me more about your ex?"

I frown, wondering if I can tell him more. He pulls Asher off me, and I lift up my top as he begins to burp him. I roll onto my back, letting out a sigh. "He wasn't popular, but he had a lot of friends, and then those who feared him. His family never had the best rep around town.

"I was just me. I was neither a nerd nor popular. I was in the middle. When he took notice, I felt special. He had a tough life at home with his mum. She was always drunk or off her face on drugs. He took cash-in-hand work just to feed her habit. He said it was worse at home when she didn't get them.

"He looked after his younger brother by three years and his sisters, making sure they were fed. I guess seeing the guy be responsible made me fall for him more. He didn't get into any of the stuff his mum did, or his mates. He stayed straight and worked on his grades, although there were times when he got into it with people.

"When I got pregnant, he changed. Not at first. It was slow. Then he made us move closer to his dad so he could work while I went to college, and it went to shit. He would get angry at the most ridiculous things. I let it happen," I tell him, ducking my head in shame as I roll back on my side.

He places Asher back down next to me, lifting him a little until he latches on. When I meet his gaze, there isn't pity or disappointment. It's something else. "No guy should ever hit a woman. Ever. You didn't let it happen; he did."

"I guess. After the last time, I knew neither of us would be safe. I'll never be able to forgive him."

He runs a finger down my cheek before snatching his hand back. He clears his throat. "I know this is probably something you don't want me bringing up, but, um, my mum… she's a councillor for women who have been through a traumatic experience."

My eyes widen. "I'm not talking to your mum about this."

He holds his hand up. "You don't have to if you don't want to. But she will listen if you want to talk about the stuff you've just skipped out on."

"It would be weird, what with her being your mum," I murmur.

Mum and Dad pleaded with me to talk to someone about Cameron. I held a lot of guilt inside, a lot of blame, and felt like a failure. But I couldn't do it. Admitting what I let him continue to do without telling anyone… I'm ashamed. My group sessions helped me in a different way. I got to see abuse through a different perspective. It gave me some sort of closure.

"My mum was attacked when she was in high school. He nearly raped her," he tells me, shocking me. "We were told when he was released from prison, and our parents wanted us to be careful."

"Oh my God."

"It was hard to hear. She was our mum. But he didn't just hurt her. There were other girls he had hurt badly, my aunt Kayla included."

"That's awful. I'm sorry."

"What I'm trying to say is, she knows about misplaced blame. She felt guilty for what happened to others. She also hated that my aunt Denny got kidnapped by his brother, so she wouldn't testify."

"Your family really have been through a lot."

He grins. "Yeah, but none of them fucking beat us. We're stronger together," he reveals, and I hear the pride in his voice.

"I'll think about it. Thank you for sharing that with me."

His gaze softens. "I hope it helps."

I yawn again, my eyelashes fluttering as I struggle to stay awake. "You should go," I whisper. "He's asleep."

"Your couch is bad for my back and I'm too tired to move."

"Maddox," I warn.

He closes his eyes, pulling Asher from my chest once more. "Let us sleep."

"You can't stay in bed with me."

"Why?" he asks, turning to look at me.

"B-because," I splutter. I don't have a good reason. He isn't touching me. Hell, he isn't even under the blanket. And this isn't romantic.

"Go to sleep. You need the beauty sleep."

My eyes close. "Arsehole."

His chuckle shakes the bed. "Night."

"Night, Maddox."

SEVENTEEN

MADDOX

I CRACK MY EYE OPEN, taking in my surroundings—or try to. Black, wild hair is blocking my view of anything. Gurgling and cooing comes from the left of me, and the realisation of why it feels like I'm burning up, hits me. On my chest, my hand cupping his bum, lies Asher, happily trying to lift his head up.

On the other side of me—in the middle of the bed—is Jasmine. From what I can see, her head is on my shoulder, and her legs are all over her mum.

As I take Amelia in, I chuckle to myself. Her hair is just as tangled as her daughter's. Her lips are parted, a light snore echoing into the morning.

"Hey, little man," I whisper, lifting him further up my chest. "You wanting a feed?"

He continues to babble, and I nod along as if I understand.

Then it hits me.

I bolt up, keeping Asher in my arms as I slide out of bed. I take in the bed, the two girls sleeping soundly, and panic hits me.

This is too much responsibility. It's too domestic. And that isn't me. The only time those words were used to describe me were when someone would say, 'He isn't domesticated.'

My chest rises and falls with each heavy breath as I slowly back out of the room.

What were you thinking?

She's going to get attached. She's going to fall in love with me, and then I'll lose the friend I desperately need. Or she needs.

It's going to be a disaster.

I breathe a sigh of relief when I escape the room, slowly shutting the door behind me. Maybe if I leave before they notice, I can say she dreamt me coming over and falling asleep in her bed.

Women dream about me all the time.

I slowly move from the door, when Asher begins to babble. I freeze, my eyes widening as I hold him out in my arms.

Fuck!

I just kind of kidnapped a kid.

I glance back at the door, struggling with what to do. It isn't like I can take him with me.

Can I?

I narrow my eyes down at him. "Way to go, kid." His arms start flapping around, the babbling getting louder. "Sheesh, you have a lot to say this morning."

A resigned sigh slips through my lips, and I reluctantly push the door back open. Amelia hasn't moved position, but Jasmine now has her feet in her mum's face and her head at the end of the bed.

I chuckle, stepping further into the room. Maybe I can let them sleep a little longer. It's Saturday, and neither has to be up yet. Plus, it isn't like Asher is screaming for food. He seems settled just being in my arms, like always.

It's just past eight, and already I feel like I've had the best sleep in the world. It's the longest I've slept in a long time. And strangely, the first time I've stayed the night with a girl who isn't family. Whenever I went back to a chick's house, I woke up a few hours later and left without a spoken word to the person whose bed I was leaving.

I guess I was exhausted because I can't remember stirring once last night.

Voices break through the silence, coming from somewhere outside. I head to the window, but before I can make it, loud, thundering banging on the door shakes the house.

Shit.

"Amelia," a woman screams.

Double shit.

My gaze shoots to Amelia, who begins to stir. I carry on to the window, peeking through the curtains to see the old bats from a few weeks ago.

The banging gets louder, and Amelia shoots up in bed, pushing her hair out of her face. "W-what? I'm coming."

"Shush," I hiss, keeping my voice low.

"Maddox? Am I dreaming again?"

I smirk, sitting on the edge of the bed. "You've dreamt of me before?"

Her eyes widen a tad before she masks it, snorting. "What is—"

When the banging continues, I grimace. "You don't want to get that," I warn.

"Is it the police?" she whispers. "About last night?"

"Shush, it's not time to wake up," Jasmine groans, and I chuckle as she immediately begins to snore again.

"No. Worse," I reply.

"The Army?"

"No," I answer, dryly.

"Is it the special police force?

I chuckle, shaking my head. "Where are you getting this?" I ask.

She drops her hand on the bedsheet pooled at her waist. "Who is it? Please tell me it's aliens."

"It's, um, the Sanderson sisters. And a clue: one of them isn't the hot blonde."

Her lips part. "What?"

"I want lots of eggs," Jasmine grumbles.

"What the hell do they want?" she asks, sliding out of bed. She grabs her dressing gown, sliding it on.

I shrug. "I'm good, but I'm not that good. Whatever it is, they aren't happy about it. Maybe you shouldn't open the door."

She sighs, sliding her feet into her Ugg slippers. "They won't leave until I answer anyway. If it gets out of hand, I'll call the police."

"Want me to answer it?" I ask, inwardly groaning as she stretches to put her hair up. Her top rises, showing the skin on her stomach.

"God, no. They'll have a hissy fit then try telling everyone you got me pregnant."

"What?" I hiss loudly, causing Asher to startle.

I follow her down the stairs. She pulls open the door, causing the trio to step back. "What do you want now?" she asks, then turns to the guy, her face paling somewhat. "What are you doing here, Devon?"

"See," the goofy-looking woman yells, pointing her finger towards me. "She's a slag. I told you she couldn't keep her legs closed."

"What are you on about, Carol?" Amelia asks, pinching the bridge of her nose. "It's too early for this."

"You know exactly what she's talking about, you little cunt," the sister with the darker roots snarls.

"We are having Cameron's case appealed," Carol reveals, stuffing her nose into the air. "He doesn't deserve to be in there and you know it. He's suffering while you fuck anything that looks at you."

"This isn't the best environment for a kid," Devon murmurs, grimacing. "She needs stability."

Amelia huffs out a breath. "Are you kidding me?"

"Amelia, they said—" Devon begins, but she holds up her hand.

"They told you a bunch of lies like they normally do, and yet you came anyway."

The woman with something green on her teeth steps forward, wagging her finger. "Now wait a goddamn minute. You are keeping her grandbabies away from her. You aren't fit to look after them. We should be their guardians."

Amelia's knuckles turn white as she grips the door, her body tensing. "This isn't about Cameron or the kids at all, is it?"

The mum tenses, her guilt-ridden face turning red. "T-this is," she stutters out.

The lad slowly turns towards her, his expression tightening. "What is she talking about?"

When she doesn't answer, Amelia does. "She wants the child benefit money, and most likely the income support she'll get since she doesn't work."

I watch the woman's reaction, and I shit you not, Amelia hit the nail on the head. You can see it on her face.

"Is that right, Mum?"

"Of course it's not," she snaps. "She's trying to change the subject because she knows what she's done is wrong." She bangs at her chest. "My boy. My precious boy is in prison because of her. Suffering. She deserves to pay. She hasn't even gone to see him."

"Because he nearly killed me," she screams, her eyes glassing over with tears. "And our daughter. I don't need this every time one of you feels like it."

"He did not hit you," Carol scoffs.

"Do they allow shower gel in prison?" I blurt out before Amelia can answer her.

"What has that got to do with anything?" she sneers, eyeing me up and down.

I feel violated and itch to take a shower.

I shrug. "Just wanted to point out he's safe if they do. He gets fed, doesn't need to pay bills, has a bed to sleep in, doesn't get arse raped because he has soap, and there aren't any women in there for him to beat on, so he won't get into any more trouble. Seems to me he's got it fucking easy, and you shouldn't be worried."

"Maddox," Amelia hisses, but I can see her struggling not to laugh.

My brows pull together. "What? I'm right. So, it's not about her son. In fact, she probably likes the drama."

"I know that, Maddox," she replies, rolling her eyes.

"Yeah, but does she know that?"

"I don't know," she retorts, throwing her hands up.

"Hello," Carol calls out.

I turn back to the Sanderson sisters. "Goodbye," I snap. "Don't come knocking this early in the morning again. No one does that. It's plain rude and insane. And leave Amelia alone from now on. She clearly has a good reason for not wanting you near her kids."

"I'm her grandmother," she snaps.

"You're a nuisance."

"Morning."

I groan at the sound of the voice. Amelia pales next to me, arching her eyebrow questioningly. I shrug. "I didn't know."

"Liam said Hayden got into it with some trollops," Max reveals, grinning. "Are these them?"

"Who are you?" Karen barks.

He rears back, his lips curling. "God, you remind me of the Sanderson sisters. And not the hot blonde."

Amelia turns to me, leaning in. "Are you sure he's not your dad?"

I suck in a breath. "Take that back," I hiss out, before turning to Max. "What are you doing here?"

He shoves his thumb over his shoulder, gesturing to the trio as he comes to stand inside the door. "What are they doing here? Don't they know it's rude to come to a house this early in the morning?"

"It really is," I tell him, nodding.

"I can see this isn't a good time," Devon announces, watching my uncle warily. "We just want to be a part of their lives."

"Devon, I appreciate that, but they don't know you. I haven't seen or spoken to you for nearly a year."

"I didn't think you'd want to see me after—"

"After lying about your brother?" Amelia questions, before lowering her voice. "You know I didn't lie."

"You did lie," Carol yells. "I always told him you were a snobby little bitch."

Devon closes his eyes, exhaling. "Mum, just go wait in the car."

She huffs out a breath after realising she isn't getting anywhere. He gives her a pointed look and she storms off, taking her sister with her.

Amelia holds her hand up before he can get a word out. "I'm done with them. Done with that part of my life. I closed that chapter the minute I opened my eyes in the ambulance. Each time they come round they make me feel worse about myself. I hate it. I want to forget everything that happened; not relive it."

"She has a point though, Amelia. You've got men here, one holding your baby. Bringing men into Jasmine's life is only going to confuse her when her dad gets out."

"He's not allowed to see her, Devon. The courts gave me rights. And right now, she's scared of him."

"Think of what this will do to her," he snarls, and I hand Asher to Max before coming to stand behind Amelia.

She points at his chest, her body vibrating with anger. "No. Nearly dying while her dad fucked her mum's best friend did something to her. Witnessing him beat the crap out of her mum and friend did something to her. Him yelling at her while I was at work, smacking her, and hitting me, did something to her. This isn't about him. It's about her and what she wants. What she needs. And right now, she doesn't need this. *I* don't need this."

"You're making a mistake. You aren't going to cope with two kids on your own," he tells her, and her body tenses.

"She isn't alone," I snap.

"And who are you? Someone who will be gone in a week, I guarantee it."

"He has more stamina," Max adds, before making baby noises at Asher.

Devon's face scrunches up in disgust. "You've changed," he points out, staring at Amelia.

"No. I haven't. I'm just not a pushover like I once was."

"I don't know what to do. Cameron isn't going to be happy once I tell him about this," he tells her, gesturing between Max and me.

"I don't care. It's not up to him. These guys have done more for me in the time I've known them than Cameron ever did."

"You know he was going to make it right once he was released."

"No, he was going to do what he always does. Say sorry, thinking it makes everything better. It means nothing. The only way that ended was because I ended it. I should have done it a lot sooner."

"You aren't thinking right," he starts.

"No, you aren't. You aren't even listening to her," I snap. "She's here telling you what your sick brother did to her, and you're placing the blame onto her. That's no different to what he did to her. We didn't even know some of what she just said, and yet to get her point across, she's blurted it out. That clearly means you don't listen."

"This has nothing to do with you," he growls.

"It has everything to do with me," I tell him, narrowing my gaze on him. "They're my friends. Now I suggest you leave before I set my uncle on you."

"I am not a goddamn dog," Max snaps.

I arch a brow at him. "There's cookies in the kitchen. Fetch."

He licks his lips, racing away to the kitchen.

"There are no cookies," Amelia whispers.

"He doesn't know that," I whisper back.

We both stare at Devon, who watches her like she's a foreign object. "I'll go, but you should know they weren't lying. He's doing good in there, and his lawyer said that will work in his favour."

Amelia begins to shake. "Good for him. But if he does get out, Devon, keep him away from me. From us. Because I will call the police."

He jerks his head before heading down the path. I turn Amelia and pull her into my arms. "You okay?"

She rests her forehead against my chest. "No. But I will be."

Footsteps pad along the landing upstairs. We turn, watching as Jasmine comes to a sudden stop. "Did we get the eggs?"

I chuckle as she sways at the top of the stairs, still half asleep with her hair a knotted mess.

Yeah, life with these guys will definitely be interesting.

EIGHTEEN

AMELIA

I slowly shut the door, resting my forehead against the cold wood as Devon's words penetrate. *Appeal.*

I know they're playing with my head, but those words, they're my worst nightmare. I've known from the day he was sentenced that he would eventually be released. My mindset then was to deal with it when it came. Right now, there is too much going on in my life to even think about it.

I never want to be near him again. Ever.

"Let's give your mum a moment," Maddox tells Jasmine softly.

"Has she been naughty? Is that why she has to face the door?"

Maddox chuckles, and I find myself smiling at her comment. "She's just waking up is all."

As their footsteps leave, my mind rushes through scenarios of what will happen if he *is* let out. Do I think he will come looking for me? Yes. Do I think he will make a scene? I'm not sure. He's normally all charm and kindness for the first couple of weeks of trying to make it up to me. But it's different this time. I'm not the same person I once was. He doesn't get to tell me what to do or make me feel like shit when I don't think the same way as he does.

We are also broken up, and it's permanent. There is nothing he could do to make me go back to him or make me forgive him for what he did. There's no fixing this—not that I'd ever want to. I'm free of him.

I'm stronger, even though at times I feel like breaking. Like now. Just the thought of seeing him again petrifies me. I want better for Jasmine, for Asher. I don't want their childhood filled with drama and abuse.

I give myself another minute to pull myself together before stepping away from the door. I need to be stronger for Jasmine, for myself. I have a life now; one he isn't a part of. I have friends who, although new, care for me like I care for them.

When I open my eyes and turn to face the living room, Maddox is standing in the doorway, watching me with an intense expression, like he's trying to read my thoughts. "Are you okay?"

I let out a dry chuckle, running a hand through my hair. "Honestly? I don't know. If this had been before I had Asher, I would probably have moved back in with my mum and dad to get away from it. But I'm done being scared. I shouldn't have to hide away anymore."

He looks up from his shoe, his face scrunched up in concern. "He nearly killed you both?"

"I told you some," I start, swallowing past the lump in my throat. I hate that he had to find out like that, or at all. "He had never hit me that bad before. It was mostly verbal abuse or a slap here and there. There were a few times it got bad, but that night changed everything for me. I could have lost both Asher and Jasmine."

"And he hurt Jasmine?"

My chest tightens when I think of that night in the hospital. It had been a few days after her operation, and social services had come in to talk to her. "I didn't know," I choke out, tears gathering in my eyes. "I hadn't known. Otherwise, I would have left long before I did."

He steps forward, pulling me into his arms. "I know you would have, Amelia. You don't need to explain yourself to me."

I cling to his shirt at the sides, breathing in his musky scent. "She told social services he yelled and smacked her a lot. She never told me a thing, and told them it was because he hurt me too. It's why he lost his parental rights. If he gets... if he's let out..."

His body tenses beneath me, and he pushes me back slightly, staring deeply into my eyes. "You don't have to worry about him. Ever."

I snort. "Yeah, I do. I have no idea what to expect. Before, it was different. We were together. Now we aren't, and I'm worried what he will do. He's used to getting his own way."

His brows pull together. "But you don't still love him, right?"

I push him away, glaring. "Of course I don't. I made a mistake staying with him for so long. I was stupid."

"I'm sorry. That was callous of me and it came out wrong."

"It's fine," I breathe out, running a hand over my face. "I'm tired of all of this. I just want to get on with my life, and I can't do that with them constantly knocking on my door. The only good thing to come out of it is that they aren't banging down my parents' door."

"You are getting on with your life. It's them who aren't. And nothing is stopping you from continuing to do it. Not all men are like him, Amelia. You'll have someone who loves you and your children, who will treat you like princesses. You were too good for someone like him, and he probably hated it. Hated that you were a better person. Now he's probably kicking himself for letting you and the kids go. You're gorgeous, and it's only a matter of time before someone snaps you up," he explains, sounding distracted towards the end.

My lips part at his words. *He thinks I'm gorgeous.*

A moment passes with us unable to look away. I shake my thoughts away, ignoring the pitter patter of my heart. "I know that. I do. It's just hard, especially when I have two children."

"And any fucker will be lucky to have them in their life too."

"Maybe Devon was right. I shouldn't have men coming and going from their lives. He was right about me not being able to raise them on my own. I'm struggling now," I point out.

"No, you aren't. You are doing everything possible to give them what they need. Don't sell yourself short."

I arch an eyebrow at him. "I can't even get my son to sleep. You do."

He grins, winking at me. "And I'm always at your service."

"I bet your future girlfriend will be happy with that."

He goes silent for a minute before shaking his head, focusing on me. "I told you; I don't do girlfriends."

Max comes storming around the corner, interrupting us. "There are no cookies anywhere. Even the kid said there weren't any."

"Max," Maddox groans, pinching the bridge of his nose.

"And where's the food?" he screeches, pointing back towards the kitchen. "I don't see anything. How do you survive?"

Maddox's lips twist. "You were eating breakfast snack bars when I left Jasmine with you."

"Where's the real food?" he snaps.

"I'm supposed to go shopping later, but I might have to take Jasmine out for breakfast first."

Asher starts winging in Max's arms, who's eyes widen suddenly at the sound. He takes slow, steady steps over to me, handing him over like he's handling a bomb. "I've already done the kid thing," he tells me before taking three quick steps back.

"I'll go tell Jasmine to get ready," Maddox announces.

"I'll feed this one," I tell him, heading into the front room with him. I cuddle Asher to my chest as I take a seat on the sofa.

Max looks up from his phone. "Everyone said to meet them at RJ's café."

"You messaged the others?" Maddox asks, stopping in the doorway to the kitchen.

Max nods. "We're going to brainstorm on how to get rid of your neighbours."

"I've done a petition."

Max waves him off. "Yeah, but they can contest that. We need to make them want to go, and I've got a few ideas."

Maddox sighs. "Okay, but no vermin or anything this time. Dad said you tried to get rid of your neighbour with mice, and it was you who ended up with the problem."

Max snorts. "Your dad is such a chatter box. And I got rid of the neighbours in the end."

"They moved to be closer to her mum because she was sick."

"Like I said, they left," he repeats, shaking his head at Maddox like he's the one who's lost it.

Maddox sighs. "Whatever."

WE PULL INTO the car park and I glance up at the dark grey sky, biting my bottom lip. I'm not sure if I packed the rain covers to Asher's pushchair, and it looks like the sky is going to open up soon.

Putting the car into park, I turn to glance back at Jasmine. "Wait until I've got Asher out first."

She gives me a nod, not looking up from her tablet that's playing Pepper Pig. I get out of the car, giving Max and Maddox a quick wave as they pull in behind us. Maddox still looks like he's in a sour mood from being made to ride with him. Apparently, Max had something important he needed to discuss. From the look on Maddox's face, it wasn't that important.

It's confirmed when he opens the door to the car, growling, "I am not helping you get payback on Dad for not inviting you to a dinner," he snaps.

"Your mum made pizza," Max growls, slamming his shut. "She always invited me before."

"Not my problem."

"You were never this grumpy before. Family life has done something to you."

Maddox stops, turning to glare at his uncle. "Max," he warns, the tone causing me to shiver.

"Whatever," Max sighs.

I open the boot and heave the pushchair out, dropping it to the ground. By the time I have it unfolded, Maddox is by my side. "Want me to get Asher?"

"Please," I wheeze out, flicking the last clip on.

I hear the car door open as I pull out the changing bag. "You getting out, Jaz?" Maddox calls through to her.

I sigh in relief when I see the rain cover. I reach for it before shoving it under the pram.

"I'm waiting for my door to be opened. I'm a princess, remember," she calls back.

"Jasmine," I groan. "Don't be a brat."

I take the car seat from Maddox, loving how his chuckle caresses my skin. I love hearing it.

"We can't keep the princess waiting," Max calls out, bowing dramatically outside her door. He pulls it open, and seconds later, she's taking his hand and jumping out of the car.

"Thank you, kind sir."

Max chuckles. "Always for the princess."

I finish attaching the car seat before glancing over at her, my brows pulling together. "What's made you all high and mighty, missy?"

She crosses her arms over her chest, pouting. "Maddox told me—"

"Well, that says it all," Max interrupts, swinging her up into arms and then over his back. "He says a lot of things."

"I'm sorry," Maddox murmurs once Max leaves. We follow behind, heading to the café where we're meeting the others. I have to admit, after the drama with Hayden and the neighbours, I'm a little intrigued as to what they are going to come up with to get rid of them. However, I'm petrified of meeting them all again. They are a crazy bunch.

"Amelia," Harlow calls out, rushing over to us as we reach the doors. Malik walks at a slower pace.

"Hey, Harlow. You doing okay?"

"I'm good. Where's Jasmine?" she asks, before bending over the pram, giving Asher a smooch on the cheek.

I look up, my gaze darting around in search of them. Maddox slaps his forehead, groaning as he points inside. Jasmine is now on Max's shoulders as they stand in front of a buffet table. Max is arguing with the guy on the other side, but I don't think it's in anger because Jasmine is doubled over, laughing.

"If he gets us kicked out again, I'm going to pretend I don't know him," Maddox warns. "I'm starving, so he better not ruin this."

"Me too," Malik growls.

"Surely they won't. He just looks like he wants food," I add, as Malik holds the door open.

Harlow places her hand over mine on the handle of the pushchair, grimacing slightly. "Just pretend you don't know him if he does get kicked out. And never try to resolve the issue."

"Um, okay."

We head inside and a change overcomes Maddox. He grins, placing his hand on my lower back. "There's someone I want you to meet."

When we head towards Lily, realisation hits me. A small smile pulls at my lips. We've already met, but I guess he's forgotten.

"Lily, this is Amelia. Max has her daughter, Jasmine, and this little guy is Asher Maddox. Amelia, this is Lily."

She gives me a small wave as she struggles not to laugh. "Hello, Amelia."

"Hi, Lily. It's nice to see you again."

"You too. This is my husband, Jaxon," she explains, wrapping her arm around his waist. The guy is gorgeous. Extremely gorgeous. And where she is light, he is dark, but somehow their pieces fit.

"It's nice to meet you," I tell him.

"You—"

Maddox makes a sound in the back of his throat as he takes my hand. "Lil, will you watch Asher so we can go grab some food?"

Her entire expression lights up with happiness. "Of course. Can I get him out?"

I can feel his warm, calloused hand over mine, so I'm too stunned to do anything but nod. He pulls me away, and as we get close to the counter, he leans down, whispering, "We aren't Team Jaxon, remember."

I step forward in the queue, leaning in closer as he lets go of my hand. "I thought you were making amends?"

He pouts, looking adorable as hell. "Do I haff'ta?"

I let out a chuckle, and glance up at him. "Yes."

"Just don't, I don't know, be happy to see him," he tells me, his brows scrunched together.

"Jealous?" I tease.

His eyes widen for a second before he shakes his head, grinning. "Have you met me? It's me people should be jealous of."

I roll my eyes. "Of course."

"Two large breakfasts please."

"I'm not going to eat—"

"But I will," he explains, tapping his card on the machine.

He grabs the two plates from the cashier and hands one to me. He lets me go in front of him, and the things I don't put onto my plate, he does, making sure I have an overflowing plate by the end of it.

When we head back to the table, I feel my cheeks heat. I don't want people to think this is the amount of food I eat. But as I take a seat next to Maddox, opposite Max and Jasmine, I realise my plate is small compared to the rest.

My eyes widen as I take in the heap on Jasmine's plate. She digs in, her eyes glazed over as she absorbs everything.

"Oh dear," I murmur, trying not to laugh.

Maddox chuckles, watching her like me. "She fits in perfectly."

She really does.

I glance down the table and notice Lily hold Asher close to her, her entire face lit up. I feel like I'm invading in on a personal moment when she tilts her head up, sharing a loving look with her husband. Her eyes glaze over with tears, and Jaxon smiles, leaning down to capture her lips in a kiss.

"Can you not do that in front of Asher?" Maddox calls out.

Lily jumps, letting out a giggle. "Sorry."

"As long as she doesn't get any ideas," Max grumbles, watching her with Asher.

Her cheeks redden, and across from her, Maverick, the guy I rent a house from, begins to choke on his food.

Max, none-the-wiser, glances at Maddox. "So, your neighbours. I've been thinking a lot about this—"

"You only got told about Hayden last night," Maddox retorts after swallowing down his food.

"I said I'm handling it," Malik calls out, glaring at Max. "Which is why I told you to leave it alone."

Maddox sits back, slamming his hands down on the table. "I can do it myself."

The dads give him a pitying look, but it's his father who speaks up. "No offence, but what you're doing isn't working."

"Which is why I should—" Max begins, but is cut off by Malik again.

"No. If you get involved, it will escalate. Let me sort it."

Max glances down at my daughter, letting out a huff. "They never listen."

She sighs, shaking her head as she leans back to pat her stomach. "Kids."

"What are you going to do, Dad?"

Malik shrugs. "What I always do. Sort the problem out."

Harlow leans forward, her eyes soft when they land on her son. "Let him sort it. You've gone on long enough listening to them."

"Okay," Maddox concedes. "Just don't do anything to my house."

"Is my name Max?" he retorts, earning a snort from Max.

"You wish, bro. You wish."

"This is going to end badly," Maddox whispers.

"It could be worse," I tell him, and he turns, giving me a doubtful look.

"How?"

I grin. "You could be living next door to them for years."

His expression tightens, and he turns to his dad. "Do whatever you have to."

"Me too?" Max asks, sitting up eagerly.

"No," everyone yells.

NINETEEN

MADDOX

THE TYRES GOING OVER THE GRAVEL clink against the car as I take the turn up to Paisley's bed and breakfast. I wince, hoping I haven't caused any damage to the paint work. I forgot I was driving Amelia's car and not my truck. Taking a quick glance in her direction, I'm glad to find she doesn't seem affected.

"Are you sure you aren't mad?" Jasmine asks for tenth time. In my rear-view mirror, I grin at Landon. He looks uncomfortable squeezed between the two car seats, his large shoulders scrunched forward to fit in.

Amelia turns around in her seat, wincing. "I'm sorry. He's just—"

Landon grunts. "I know, and it's fine," he tells her before turning to Jasmine. "No, kid. I'm good."

I smirk, turning my attention back to the road. When I realised it would be me dropping him off, I got a little payback for him turning up late and then taking the last of the bacon. I wanted seconds, but by the time I got up there, breakfast was coming to an end and you could only take what was left on the hot plates. That fucker pretty much stole the lot. Which is why he is now squeezed in the back, and not Amelia.

"But you look really mad. Is it because they broke your car?"

He grunts again, and I inwardly chuckle. "I'll fix it."

"It's bad luck you left your tools here," I mention as I put the car into park.

"I swear, Reid is going to get it when I see him. I know it was him. He might as well have recorded himself doing it and sent it me the video."

"What did he send you?" I ask.

As we were leaving RJ's, we heard a ruckus in the car park. We turned to find Landon kicking the wheel of his car. He couldn't get it started, and the tools he needed—which none of us had on us—were here in Paisley's storage room.

Max, his dad, offered to bring him, but if Reid was home, Max would intervene. It wouldn't have ended well. So we squeezed into Amelia's car and drove here. Before we left though, Landon got a message.

"An emoji of a blue car."

I turn in my seat, grinning. "Want help getting him back?"

Landon chuckles, shaking his head. "Nah. It will be fun to watch him sweat as he waits to see what I'll do."

"Call me if you change your mind," I tell him, before turning to Amelia. "Want to meet Paisley and take a look at the work I'm doing?"

"Sure," she murmurs, shrugging.

"I'll get the pram," I tell her.

"No need. I've got a baby carrier in the boot. There's no point dragging the pram out, and he's awake."

"Wow, look how beautiful that dog is," Jasmine murmurs, staring out the window.

"He's not beautiful. He's fierce," Landon comments, waiting impatiently for me to let him out.

"Beautiful," she whispers, earning a grunt from Landon.

I get out at the same time as Amelia. I open Jasmine's door, letting her jump out before going round to the boot, where Amelia is. She's struggling to strap something around her back. My brows pull together, wondering what she's trying to achieve.

"Here, let me," I offer, taking the clips. I hold the two in my hands, wondering where the hell they go, because the two I'm holding don't go together. There are four other clips too, but it's too complicated to figure out. I clear my throat. "Why don't you put it on me. At least then you'll know it's on properly."

She lets out a laugh. "All right."

In less than two minutes she has the thing strapped to my chest and Asher tucked in. I'm impressed. I chuckle as I tuck his ears back under his hat.

We head over to the bed and breakfast, just as the duck comes flying out of the entrance. Jasmine screams, followed by Amelia, both of them running behind me for cover.

"Get back here, Cluck," Paisley screams.

I squint, noticing the little shit has something in his mouth. "That bird is gonna be roasted," Landon growls.

"She has a duck?" Amelia asks, smoothing her hands down her coat.

"Kind of."

"Did she name it?"

"She's a nut," Landon answers her question.

"Is that a bra?" I ask, squinting to see what it is.

We watch as Paisley trips over a log trying to catch the damn bird. Jasmine giggles. "I want to play."

"She'll never learn," Landon sighs.

"Cluck!" Paisley screams, getting up off the floor. She wipes the dirt off her knees before turning to go back in. She comes to a sudden stop when she spots us, and I chuckle at the red blush rising over her cheeks. "You're back."

"Your damn brother broke my car."

She grits her teeth. "I'm gonna kill him."

"Can I pet your dog?" Jasmine asks sweetly.

Paisley's expression softens. "Of course you can."

Landon whistles through his teeth, and Rex comes barging over, coming to a stop by Landon's legs. "Sit."

Jasmine walks over, slowly reaching her hand out to stroke behind his ears. "He's so soft," she whispers. She giggles when he begins to lick her hand, then her face. "He's licking me!"

Amelia giggles as she watches. "He's gorgeous."

"He's fierce," Landon argues.

"Paisley, this is Amelia, her daughter Jasmine, and her little guy, Asher."

Paisley holds her hand up in a small wave. "It's nice to meet you."

"You too," Amelia replies. "Do you really have a duck?"

Paisley wipes her hands down her jeans. "Kind of. He wasn't always like this. I think being around my brothers and Landon's family has given him a complex. He likes to play pranks."

"Pranks?" Landon comments, arching an eyebrow at her.

She wraps her arm around his waist. "Pranks, Mister."

"What was in his mouth?" I ask.

She lets out a heavy sigh. "A guest's bra. I swear, at this rate, I'll either have guests coming to specifically see Cluck or I'll lose guests because of him."

"Why not get rid of it?" I ask.

Landon grunts. "Because he has a way of making everyone feel sorry for it when we try. Sometimes I want to drop him back on Charlotte's doorstep, but I'm worried it will end up dead then."

"Her cat attack her again?" I ask, nodding like I understand.

Landon lifts his chin. "And keeps escaping. He'll go out and taunt her. Once she reaches him, he'll rush off and hide again."

I chuckle, turning my attention to Paisley. "Do you mind if I show Amelia around? I want to show her the place and what we've been working on."

"Can I stay with Rex?" Jasmine pleads, glancing up at her mum.

"Sure," Paisley tells me, then gazes down at Jasmine. "Only if it's okay with your mum. Ella is making some cupcakes if you want to come and help us."

Seeing the conflict on Amelia's expression, I nudge her with my shoulder. "She'll be fine here. I swear it."

Amelia slowly nods. "No leaving Paisley," she warns.

"She'll be fine with me," Paisley assures her, reaching out to take Jasmine's hand.

"Cluck won't eat me, will he?" Jasmine asks.

Giggling, Paisley shakes her head. "No. He's a softy really. Just don't let him eat your cupcakes."

Jasmine straightens. "I won't. I swear."

"She just had a big breakfast," Amelia whispers, holding back laughter.

Rex barks, following behind them. Landon exhales, turning to me. "Thanks for the lift back."

"No problem," I reply. "Do you need help getting back to your car?"

"Nah. I'm going to steal Reid's car and leave it there after. Let him sort it out."

"Alright, I'll see you later then."

He gives us a chin lift before heading into the house. My eyes widen as I remember Paisley's words. "Don't go eating all those cupcakes, you fat bastard."

He turns, walking backwards, and a grin spreads across his face. "I had a small breakfast. They'll go down a treat."

"Prick," I grumble.

"So, what have you been working on because this looks finished," Amelia comments once he's inside.

I begin to walk, and she steps up beside me. "We're doing the new addition around the back. Before she opened, her vision was for a rustic farm feel. But she wants more, so we are doing a mini spa out the back. I think further down the line, once she has enough profit coming in, the plan is to build a function room to have parties and stuff."

"The place is beautiful. Is this her family's farm?"

I nod. "It is. It's a huge piece of land, and they all own parts of it. I know Jaxon is having his company relocated to a secure piece of land. He's having trouble with some guy wanting their company."

"Sounds interesting," she murmurs, taking in the new addition in front of us.

"I'll have to take you to Faith's one day too. Her place is across from the entrance of here."

"I'd love that," she tells me.

Mark strolls out, clipboard in hand. He looks up, hearing us approach, and grins. "Well, well, well. We didn't get to formally introduce each other the other day. I'm Mark. His cousin."

Amelia smiles, reaching out to take his outstretched hand. "I'm Amelia. It's nice to meet you."

"You too," he replies, before turning to me, his eyebrow arching at the sight of Asher. "I never thought I'd see you with a baby."

"I never thought you'd make it through college but here we are," I mutter dryly.

He laughs, blowing it off. "Whatever. I need to go. Ella is doing us an early lunch."

My stomach grumbles, and I turn back towards the house. "How is the work going?"

Mark shrugs. "It's going okay. I think the new kid is going to be a fast learner. He got the boards up and plastered the office area."

"Good to hear. After everything Joey did, we need someone like him," I tell him.

"Joey? The guy who did mine?" Amelia asks.

"Yeah, we had to fire him. It wasn't the first time he fucked up. He wasn't training either. He's been doing this for years and should know by now what to do."

"It's no loss. This new kid, Sam, is good."

"We're going to go in and take a look around. Everyone else inside the bed and breakfast?"

He nods. "Yeah. I'll catch you later."

I give him a nod before pushing through to the open reception area. Amelia takes slow, steady steps inside, walking around in a circle to get a look at the room. "I bet she can't wait to get all this done."

"She's excited. We've been so busy between other jobs we had to put the work on hold for a bit. She understood since we fitted her in at the last minute."

"What's going to be through there?" she asks, pointing to the left.

"That is going to be some green room. She saw it on a television programme. It will be filled with plants and recliners," I explain before moving on through the right door, down a short hallway, pointing to each room. "Down there will be the two massage rooms and where people can get facials. These rooms are going to be for mani's and pedi's. This, once the equipment comes, will be a changing room. The men's will be just down the hall." I lead her outside, through the archway we built in for shelter. This is the part I'm most proud of.

There are five handmade huts scattered in places on the grass in front of us, with a cracked, stone path leading up to each hut. The outside of each one has a seating area that has a smaller fence to give privacy. Inside the huts, the walls are bigger and have wooden stairs leading up to a hot tub.

Each hut is decorated with plant features or something that fits into the theme Paisley has been going for.

"This is amazing," Amelia rushes out, walking inside the first hut we come to. "What's going there?"

I glance to the wall she's gesturing to. "A place to put speakers. It's so guests can connect their phones to play music."

"You built all of these?"

I nod. "I did. All of the outside I designed myself, and took the plans to Paisley to confirm. Mark helped me put it together."

Her smile is warm when she turns to me. "You seem proud."

I shrug. "I like building things."

I follow her outside as she follows the path to the left, where a larger hut is built. This one has a small bar, and a seating area. "She's going to have a bar?"

"If she can get a liquor licence she will. If not, she's going to put a juice bar up."

She points to the longest wall in the bar. "I guess that is going to be for a tele."

I grin because she's not wrong. "It is. If all the females can get pampered inside, then the men can come out here to watch a game and have a drink."

She laughs as she steps back outside, going to the centre. "This is going to be amazing once it's lit."

The fire pit is another feature I'm proud of. The beige stone looks perfect against the black that was used on the inside. The seat logs were the hardest for us to get a hold of, but luckily, we managed to get some. After hours of sawing and carving, we managed to build six sturdy seats.

"Personally, I'm hoping she lets us come here once it's open. Once we finish a job like this, we're done with it. We never go back unless there's an issue. So we never get to see it in its final stage. It's nice to know once Paisley has put her touch on it, we will get to come back and see it."

"I bet that will be nice for you. And who wouldn't want to come back here. I know it's not finished but it's surreal," she tells me, her eyes sparkling. When she gazes over the bed and breakfast, she points to the stairs. "What's that?"

"It's the stairs leading up to Paisley's and Landon's room. They're hoping to take the room to the left and add additional rooms onto theirs."

"I guess if they want kids, they'll need to," she tells me. "But that's not what I was talking about."

"What do you mean?"

She heads over to the stairs, and I can feel a blush rising in my cheeks. This is the part I've been doing in my spare time. It's not something Paisley asked for, but I couldn't help it. I see something that has potential and I have to do it. In this case, it's a large stone feature. When it rains, it will turn into a waterfall that pours into the pond at the base.

The feature is in three steps. The bottom has the pond that is surrounded by wild flowers and a few things I made, one being a wooden ladybug. The second is the waterfall, and this one has a miniature barrel, a tiny cottage that sits next to a miniature tree of life, and a wishing well. The top level has a large windmill that I made out of bamboo.

Surrounding all of that are solar panelled lanterns hanging on metal hooks. There are a few solar panelled lights in the rocks, and some even in the water. But since it's light out, she won't be able to see those.

"Where did you buy all of this? I've never seen anything like it."

I clear my throat when she bends down to take a closer look at some of the things I made. "Um, I made them."

She pauses from reaching for a figurine, slowly turning to face me, her lips parted. "You made these?"

"I did."

She stands, taking my hands in hers. "Maddox, these are incredible. Do you sell these for people to buy?"

I snort. "No. They're just things I like to do in my spare time."

She shakes her head, letting go of my hands. "Maddox, you have a real talent here. You could set up your own online store for these."

"I'm pretty sure people would return them."

"I don't think I've ever seen you look so vulnerable," she comments.

"I'm not."

She grins. "Yes, you are. Maddox, you've got nothing to be shy about. You've got talented hands."

It's my turn to grin now. I wink, causing her to blush. "I get told that a lot."

She lightly slaps my shoulder, careful not to startle Asher. "Now there's the Maddox I know."

"And love?" I finish.

She rolls her eyes. "You never stop."

"It's in my blood," I tease.

Her smile slips, and she stares up into my eyes. My heart stops for a second, and I brace myself. "I'm being serious about the features. They're beautiful."

I swallow past the nerves—nerves I never normally get. "It's just pieces of wood."

She steps closer, her eyes glazing over as we continue to stare into one another's eyes. "No. It's art. What I don't get is why you never show this side of yourself to people. You give off this fun, loving, carefree personality, but you, Maddox Carter, are so much more."

I try not to let her words, or the way she's watching me, get to me. It's hard with her gaze boring into me, pleading with me to see what she sees.

"Are you saying I should do other stuff with my hands, other than give women pleasure? Because I'm sure that will upset a lot of women."

Her expression drops before she shakes her head a little, then takes a step back. "Wouldn't want to disappoint the masses."

I open my mouth to apologise, but Max pokes his head out of the kitchen door. "I thought we were going shopping? You just left me."

"*We* are going shopping."

His brows pull together. "I just said that, dipshit. Come on. I need to go today. I've got work tomorrow and Lake's definition of shopping for the week is more like for the night. She never gets enough."

He shuts the door behind him, and I turn back to Amelia. She forces a smile. "We wouldn't want to keep him waiting."

"Amelia," I call out, but she ignores me, heading inside.

I run a hand through my hair, wondering why I feel like this. I speak to every girl who isn't related like that. It lets them know I'm not interested in more than a fuck. But for some reason, having Amelia thinking that of me is bothering me.

I glance down at Asher, letting out a sigh. "I don't do relationships." He yanks his fist out of his mouth, making a gurgling noise. "I know she's hot and can cook, kid. But I'm not a relationship kind of person."

He babbles again, and I steel myself against the guilt eating me up. "Nope. I'm a single pringle."

And nothing is going to change that.

Not her round arse in those jeans.

Not her laugh.

Not her seductive voice in the morning.

Or how great her tits are.

I'm staying single. And she isn't going to bewitch me into anything else.

TWENTY

AMELIA

As we wait inside the doors of Morrisons for Maddox's uncle and aunt, I can't help but run over what happened before we left. I stupidly thought we were sharing a moment, but I was wrong. I let myself picture being with him; something impossible, since it's been made abundantly clear that he doesn't do relationships.

I have two choices: put an end to the friendship or try to move on, and since I don't want to explain why I don't want to be friends anymore, I only have one option. Even though I could keep torturing myself by being around him.

My mum was right, I don't want to be alone for the rest of my life. Maddox being in my life, evoking these feelings, is proof of that. It might be too soon after a baby, after Cameron, but I don't care. I don't have to commit to anything. I could go out on a few dates and see how I feel. It could be that these feelings were evoked because of Maddox. However, I won't know until I put it to the test.

"You've been quiet," Maddox murmurs. "I'm sorry if I said something to offend you."

"You didn't," I tell him, and it's the truth. Nothing he said offended me, it just made me realise that what I've been feeling is useless. It will never amount to anything.

"Is it because Jasmine wanted to stay with Paisley?"

I smile, remembering her face when I said yes. She was so excited. I haven't trusted anyone with her other than my parents and child minder since Cameron. But keeping her secluded will probably do more harm than good. And Paisley is a good person. She has Charlotte there, and I know Landon is going back. I know they'll look after her. I just hope she doesn't cause too much of a mess in the kitchen, although Ella seemed to enjoy the company.

"No. She was loving it there. Once Paisley mentioned showing her the pigs, there was no way I would have gotten her to leave."

"Maddox," a woman calls out, waving.

The extremely good-looking guy next to her, grits his teeth, groaning. "Fuck!"

Maddox chuckles under his breath. "Hey, Liza."

"Oh, who is this?" she asks, turning her attention to me.

"This is my friend, Amelia, and her little boy, Asher. Her daughter, Jasmine, is with Paisley," he introduces. "Amelia, this is Paisley and Jaxon's mum."

Hearing the word 'friend' stings. "It's nice to meet you."

"You too," she tells me, her voice soft.

"Are you feeling okay?" the guy rumbles, looking sexier when he arches his eyebrow at Maddox.

"Worried about me?" Maddox asks, grinning wide. "How thoughtful of you."

He gestures to me. "I mean, you've not set on fire or anything and you're with a chick who has kids."

"We aren't together," Maddox grits out. "And she's cool."

"So, you won't mind if I ask her out?" he asks, turning to me and winking. I have to admit, my lady bits twitch. "You free sometime? Maybe Maddox can babysit."

"She doesn't date arseholes," Maddox snaps, grabbing the trolley.

"Reid, let's go before you put your foot in it again," Liza warns, giving the guy a disapproving glance. "It was nice to see you both, and I hope to see you again soon."

"Always up for your breakfasts," Maddox calls out, winking at her.

The Reid guy goes to take a step towards Maddox, his fists clenched, but Liza grabs his wrist, pulling him along. "Really, Reid. We are out in public."

"But, Mum," he growls.

They leave, and I turn to Maddox, arching an eyebrow. "Who was that?"

"That's one of Jaxon's younger brothers. He's the one who damaged Landon's car."

"Was that Reid?" Max growls, up on his tip toes to look through the crowd.

"Don't you dare," Lake warns.

"I dare. It's going to cost him a few hundred quid to replace that part."

Maddox rubs his hands together, grinning. "Let's go."

When they head off, Lake and I rush to keep up. Once they're a little behind Liza and Reid, they slow down, giving us a chance to browse the aisles.

"I swear, they never grow up," Lake comments.

I chuckle under my breath. "I'm good with that," I tell her, smiling down at Asher sleeping in the baby seat.

"He's beautiful. Max told me how Maddox delivered him and how good you handled it all."

I glance at her, eyes widening. "Really? Because Max kept screaming at me to close my legs."

She laughs. "Sounds like him. He didn't handle the birth of the triplets well," she states, but then pauses, shaking her head. "He didn't handle any of it well, but that's another story. He has a tendency to dramatize everything, but it's one of the things I love about him."

"I can see that," I agree, stopping short when I notice Maddox dodging another trolley to get to Liza's. He drops a fresh fish into the trolley before racing away, hiding behind another post. "What are they doing?"

Lake lets out a sigh. "I've come to learn to never ask. I was so scared my kids would take on Max's nutty behaviour, but out of all the family, it's Maddox who is the closest to his personality. But they also clash, so if something happens, walk away."

"Walk away?" I ask, unsure if being here is all right now.

"Trust me," she gently orders.

"Oh my God," I whisper when I see Max slide out from under one of the stacks of shelves, throwing a pack of biscuits into the trolley. I glance around for Maddox, but he's nowhere in sight.

"Reid, I said I wasn't buying all this crap," Liza snaps, taking the biscuits back out and slamming them down on the shelf.

"W-what? I didn't put them there," he argues.

"Don't," Liza warns, before heading forward.

"So, you and Maddox," Lake begins. "He said you're just friends, but I saw the way you were watching him at breakfast."

Flustered and feeling my cheeks heat, I shake my head in denial. "We are just friends."

She chuckles, giving me a knowing look. "If you say so."

"I do," I rush out. "I mean, you know him. He's your nephew. He doesn't do relationships."

"But you want to," she adds on, then snorts, watching as Maddox does some sort of spin dance, drops a pack of donuts in the trolley, then races off.

Keeping one eye on the things I need, I answer Lake. "We're just friends."

"Word to the wise: don't fight it. He might not realise he's into you yet, but he will. Then you need to be ready."

"I-I don't know what to say to that."

She reaches over, placing her hand over mine. "Nothing to say. They're hard not to love. Trust me."

I take her word for it and watch as Max reaches for the crisps, dumping two bags of twenty-four in the trolley before racing off.

We come to a stop at the end of the aisle, watching as Liza spins around to Reid and leans up to clip him around the ear. "Reid Hayes, if you put one more thing in this trolley, I am going to wring your neck."

"Mum! But it wasn't me."

"Don't 'it wasn't me', Reid. It's only us here," she snaps, before walking off.

Reid pauses at her words and spins around, facing us. Realisation hits him, and he storms towards us. Reflexes have me taking a step back when he reaches me, pulling the trolley and Asher with me.

"Where are they?"

"Somewhere," Lake tells him.

When he turns to me, a squeak passes my lips and I shrug. He growls, storming past us. "Wow."

"Hopefully nothing else happens."

Ten minutes later, Lake is eating her words. We're nearing the end of the shop when we hear a commotion in the aisle over. Racing around the corner, we come to a stop at the scene in front of us.

"Stop smashing the jars," Max yells. "That's good food going to waste."

Glancing down at the floor, my eyes widen. There's a smashed jar of bolognaise sauce at Reid's feet. When Max drops another jar, I startle, gaping at the scene.

"Stop trying to attack me," Max yells. "Look, he's attacking me."

A shop assistant rushes over. "What is the problem?"

Max, shockingly, starts to cry. "He keeps smashing these jars at my feet."

"Oh, sir, are you okay?" she asks, before glaring at Reid.

"No," he blubbers.

"Fucker did it," Maddox rumbles close to my ear, and a shiver races up my spine.

Lake glances from Maddox to me, before giving me a knowing look, which I ignore. "Did what?" I whisper.

"Watch."

Reid grits his teeth. "No need. Pass me two jars and I'll go pay for them and leave them at the counter."

"Thank you. Off you go."

Reid storms off in our direction, pausing when he sees Maddox. "You are going to pay for setting that lunatic on me."

Maddox chuckles. "Try it. You've still got Landon to deal with."

Reid snorts. "Like hell. He's gone soft."

"We'll see," Maddox sings, clearly enjoying himself.

Once he's left, I turn on Maddox, shaking my head. "You two are terrible."

He chuckles. "This is tame compared to what it used to be. This would have ended up in a brawl any other time."

"His face was priceless," Max declares, laughing uproariously when Lake slaps his shoulder.

Maddox nudges my shoulder as he watches Asher sucking on his fist. "Have you finished?"

I nod. "I have. Although, I'm a little traumatised after that. Does your uncle take acting lessons?"

Maddox shrugs. "He's just that crazy."

We head over to the tills, Maddox walking ahead of me with his uncle. Lake uses the till next to me to unload her shopping onto. Maddox stops, helping me put it all onto the belt.

"Excuse me, sir," a deep voice demands, and I glance up from the trolley, seeing two security guards standing at the end, hands on hips.

"Me?" Maddox asks, straightening.

"And you," the younger of the two says, jerking his head at Max.

Oh God.

I glance at Lake for answers, but she doesn't seem fazed, unloading her trolley onto the belt without a care.

What on earth is happening?

The older guy steps forward. "Could you two please step this way?"

"Why? We've not done anything wrong," Max argues.

Maddox lets out a sigh. "What did that little dweeb do?"

"Please, sir, don't make this difficult," he warns, keeping his tone even.

"I'm a respectful P.E. teacher. I won't be manhandled," Max argues as one reaches for his arm.

"Max," Maddox hisses.

"No, I've done nothing wrong," Max snaps, dodging the guy.

My lips part as they restrain Max, pinning him against the wall. "What are you doing?" he screeches. "Why are you touching me?"

"We were informed you have been shoplifting, sir."

"Shoplifting?" he asks, snorting. "I don't need to— Hey!"

"Sir, please keep still," the youngest grits out.

"Help!" Max yells. "Help! He's touching my junk."

"Oh my God," I breathe out.

"Just do your shopping," Lake whispers, acting like she doesn't know them.

Slowly, I do as she says whilst keeping an eye on what's happening.

"Lake! Lake! Aren't you going to defend your husband?" he barks out, squealing as the guard pats down his legs. "Stop trying to cop a feel."

"Clear," the oldest guy announces, turning to Maddox now.

Maddox steps forward, groaning. He lifts his hands into the air, letting the guard pat him down. When he gets to his chest, Maddox's eyes widen. "Hey, watch what you're touching."

"We are doing our job," the youngest grits out.

"Oh my God, you just touched my knob," he yells, trying to get away. "What are you doing?"

"This is harassment," Max hisses. "You can't do this."

"You are acting dramatic. We are doing everything by the book," he replies, but he can't hide the nervous look he casts at everyone watching.

"I bet you don't feel everyone up like that," Maddox bites out. "Or is it just me?"

"All clear," the youngest announces, stepping back. "It seems there was a mistake."

"I told you that," Max hisses.

"Do we need to call the police or are you going to calm down?" the oldest reacts.

Maddox flinches when the closest guard to him hands him back his phone. "Yes, so we can tell them how you like touching defenceless men."

"Hi, I'm the manager. Can I help you?" a woman asks, stepping into the huddle.

Max jabs his finger at the guard. "He was touching me inappropriately."

Maddox flinches away from the guard. "Me too. Me too."

The guards sputter. "We were doing our job."

"You work in a supermarket, and we aren't a slab of meat," Max yells, before bursting into tears. "I'll never come here again. He touched me."

"That's sixty-four pounds and twenty-eight pence," the cashier announces, and I startle, turning to find she's packed my bags for me. She grimaces, looking at the scene. "I thought you might need some help."

"I-I—"

She waves me off as I begin to pay. "It's okay. They've been in here before. The security guys are new, so they aren't aware of them. So is the manager. It will be entertaining to see what she does."

I unload the bags back into my trolley. "Thank you."

"Have a nice day," she tells me, before beginning to put through the customer's food behind me.

Lake steps up beside me. "Let's go before they call the police. With any luck, Max will realise his food is running away and begin to chase it."

"He didn't do any shopping," I remind her. Come to think of it, I only saw her put a couple of things in.

She laughs, shaking her head at me. "Darlin', most of the stuff put into the trolley was from him. He's sneaky when it comes to food."

We reach the exit when we hear him. "Where's my damn food?" Max yells. "Where's that wife gone?"

I begin to laugh, staring at her in amazement. "You are a queen for putting up with his antics."

She laughs along with me. "He makes life interesting, that's for sure."

"There she is," is snapped, and I inwardly groan, recognising the voice.

"Are you following me?" I ask, staring into the hard eyes of Cameron's mum.

Glancing to her left, I spot someone I've not seen in years, long before

Cameron and I broke up. Nessa, shortened from Vanessa, is fifteen and one of his youngest siblings, and unlike Cameron and Devon, who tried to stay on the straight and narrow, Nessa isn't one of them. At the age of ten, she was getting into fights, got caught stealing more than once, and was always skipping school.

And by the looks of things, her behaviour hasn't improved. Her rounded stomach is on show, her top having risen above her pregnant belly. Her ginger roots are showing, and her skin looks aged yet young.

"Why the fuck are you keeping Cam's kid away from my mum, bitch?"

My cheeks heat, knowing Lake is listening to this. She takes a step closer, coming to my side.

"I'm not sure how many times I have to tell you this, but Cameron doesn't have rights to the kids," I tell them, keeping my voice calm.

"From what Devon found out, that's only in effect with Jasmine. You hadn't had this one yet. So, we can take him with us. He doesn't need a stuck-up mum like you," Nessa snaps.

"No, he has one that loves him and takes care of him. He doesn't need people who can't mind their language, don't have any common sense, and look like they're out of an episode of *The Walking Dead*," Maddox snaps.

Nessa gapes at Maddox, her cheeks flushing. She tries to pull her top down, showcasing her little bit of cleavage. A smile lights up her face, showing a row of yellow-stained teeth. "This is between us."

"No," he tells her, placing a hand on my shoulder. "Stop harassing her."

Carol steps forward, glaring. "We want to see our grandchild," she demands.

He leans forward, getting in her face. "That sounds like a *you* problem."

"It's going to be her problem."

"No, it's not," Max pipes in.

"You again," Carol hisses.

Max grimaces. "Let's not announce we've met each other before. I've got a reputation."

"You're married," Lake mutters dryly.

He grins. "And you, my darlin' wife, are all I need." He turns back to the unwanted guests, narrowing his gaze. "You go near Amelia or any of her kids again, and you'll have the Carter's to deal with."

"The Carter's?" Nessa breathes out, her eyes wide before they go hard, turning to me. "They got my brother sent to prison, didn't they? They set it up."

"Little girl, go back home and finish playing with Barbies. We have nothing to do with your sick brother. Now run along."

"You can't speak to me like—"

Her mum grabs her arm, pulling her back. "Let's go," she demands, before glancing at me. "We will be speaking to our lawyer."

"Like you can afford it," Maddox mutters. When they are gone, Maddox turns to me, taking me in. "You okay?"

I shakily lift my hand to my mouth. "She's right. Asher wasn't born then. It only ever mentioned Jasmine."

"It won't matter," Max assures me. "Talk to my brother, Myles. He's a social worker."

"What if they—"

"No social worker in their right mind would give them any kind of access. Hell, she shouldn't have custody of her own kids. How young was that girl?"

"Fifteen," I tell him. "I hope what they said isn't true."

"Come on. Let's go get Jaz from Paisley's, then you can work out your anger by baking and cooking for me."

A smirk teases my lips. "Shouldn't you be cooking for me to cheer me up?"

He wraps his arm around my shoulder, pulling me against his chest. "No, because my cooking would only make you miserable. My company, however, will cheer you right up."

I laugh despite what just happened. "Okay then."

"We'll catch you in the week," Lake tells him, and when her gaze lands on me, I find myself blushing and turning away. It's that knowing look again.

She's wrong though. There is no way Maddox will push everything he believes in aside to settle down with a single mum of two.

No chance.

TWENTY-ONE

MADDOX

Sweat pours down my back as I heave the last bag of plaster into the spa. Landon drops his bag down on top, not breaking a sweat. I guess all those extra hours at the gym are paying off, that and the fact he wasn't here at six this morning like I was.

I glance up when I hear Landon's name called by our cousin Jacob. "Please don't tell me he and Trent have gotten into trouble again," I grumble under my breath.

"In here," Landon calls out.

He strolls in, his eyes tight and worried. "I've met him," he rushes out, panting for breath.

"Who?" Landon and I ask, sharing a glance with each other. The only time I've seen Jacob like this was when he thought his mum and dad caught him sneaking out to a house party.

"That Scott guy."

Landon's posture tenses. "You did?"

"He's a fucking suit," he rushes out. "But something is definitely off. He was all nice, too nice, acting slimy. I knew something was up. No one is ever that nice."

"Calm down and tell me right fucking now what's happened," Landon grits out.

"I went to Charlotte's house to get an A-level textbook for my Geography class, and *he* was there. She didn't once ask me if I wanted something to eat or drink—"

"We already know she's not herself," I tell him.

"You don't understand," he yells, pulling at the ends of his hair. "She always mothers me. Always. Even as a kid Mum said she would pretend I was her baby, always keeping me occupied. She's not just acting differently, something *is* different."

"Jacob, mate, calm down," Landon demands. "We'll get to the bottom of this."

He breathes out heavily, leaning against the plasterboard. "She went to get changed because the book was at the library and she was going to get it for me. She wore normal day clothes."

"And? It's a library, not a bank. She can wear what the fuck she wants."

"It was her favourite 'World's Best Cat Mum' jumper. She walked out, and he pulled her into the kitchen. I followed, and that fucker asked her if she was really going to wear it out of the house."

"He did fucking what?" Landon grits out.

"Is he still there?" I bark out.

"No, he left, but she got changed. You should have seen her face. And when I told him where to go, she said it was fine, that it was a childish jumper."

"I'm going," Landon declares, taking his work belt off.

I follow, nodding. "Jacob, can you go tell Mark he's in charge. Don't tell him why because he'll want to come, and she doesn't need everyone there. I'll drop you back home after."

"Is he hurting her?" Jacob whispers. "Did I not protect her?"

I grip him around the neck, bringing his forehead to mine. "You did the right thing coming to us. We know nothing about him or what he's capable of. Let us go see what's going on. Okay?"

He nods. "Yeah, and, um, don't tell her I got all emotional and that."

Landon chuckles, punching him lightly on the shoulder. "She knows you care."

We leave Jacob to look for Mark as we head for my truck. "We need to pick someone up first," I tell him.

Someone I haven't seen for a few days. I'm being paranoid, I know it, but it feels like she's avoiding me.

"Who?"

"Amelia."

I dial her number on my Bluetooth, and listen to it ring… and ring. I flick a glance to Landon, forcing a smile. "She's always playing these kinds of games with me."

"She's funny," he mutters sarcastically.

I hit redial, before tapping my fingers on the steering wheel. *Please, answer.*

"Hello?"

"Hey, it's me, Maddox."

"I know," she tells me, chuckling. "Everything okay?"

"No. I need to ask a huge favour."

"What is it?"

"Charlotte's brother just came to the site I'm working on, upset. He met Charlotte's boyfriend, and what he said has raised a red flag. We want to talk to her, but it will be too obvious if we go in guns blazing. We thought she might open up to you with the kids there."

"Jasmine is at school."

"That's okay. Asher's cute too," I tell her.

"Thanks," she replies sarcastically. "I'll let him know."

"He knows," I assure her.

She lets out a sigh. "She's not going to appreciate a stranger getting in her business."

"We'll be there," I tell her.

"Please," Landon pleads. "I've tried but she just pushes me away."

"All right. I'll get Asher ready. Where do you want me to meet you?"

"We'll be at yours in fifteen minutes," I tell her, before ending the call.

"Rude much," Landon comments.

I take my attention off the road for a second, seeing him smirking at me. "What?"

"You didn't even say goodbye."

My brows pinch together. "Why? I'll be seeing her soon."

"Jesus, there is no talking to you," he mutters, kicking back in the chair.

Whatever.

"I HOPE THIS doesn't upset her," Amelia murmurs as she pulls up outside the library.

"She'll be fine. We just need to get her to see reason," Landon explains from the back.

Amelia turns to me. "Are you seriously in a mood because I wouldn't let you drive?"

I huff out a breath. "I don't get in moods. I just think I should have driven."

"Why? Because you're a man?"

I open my mouth to answer but my brain suddenly connects to what she said. Landon slaps his hand down hard on my shoulder. "Wise man. Wise man."

I roll my eyes and shove open the door. "Whatever."

I grab the pushchair out of the back, making quick work of putting it together. Amelia pauses near the back of the car, watching me with her lips parted. "When did you learn that?"

I rub the back of my neck. "I, um, kind of practiced."

"Practiced? When?" she asks dubiously.

"This should be good," Landon comments.

I send him a glare before turning back to Amelia. "I, um, kind of borrowed your car keys to get the pushchair and took it to mine. I spent the night figuring it out then timing myself," I explain, puffing my chest out. "I got down to five seconds."

She glances from me, to the pushchair, then back to me. "I don't know whether to be pissed you stole my keys and pushchair or impressed."

I swing my arm around her shoulders, causing her to clutch the car seat tighter. "Always impressed."

She pushes out of my arms, clipping the car seat to the pushchair before stopping to watch me. "Why? Why would you even go to that trouble to learn? You don't have a baby."

I have Asher.

I don't voice that. I don't even know *where* that came from. He isn't mine. He isn't anything to me. He's just a kid I delivered who belongs to my hot neighbour. "I guess I just wanted to know," I tell her absently, wondering where my earlier train of thoughts came from.

"Let's go in."

"This place is huge," Amelia comments as she pushes the pushchair onto the pavement.

There are two entrances to the library. One through the small café set on Main Street and then this one.

This place would have been knocked down like the rest of the old factories, but it held sentimental value to some guy thirty years ago. He decided to sell to Charlotte when he saw the passion she had for the building.

I push open the heavy door, holding it open for Amelia to get through with the pushchair. "She runs this by herself?"

"She has a few sponsors, but other than that, yes," I tell her.

"She gets custom through doing parties, letting people hold meetings, and has a selection of books from indie authors," Landon adds, unable to keep how proud he is from his voice.

"I have got to browse these shelves," Amelia whispers.

"You don't have time for that," I tell her, and she turns to glare at me.

"Shush. Did no one ever tell you it's disrespectful to speak loudly in a library?"

I rear back. "Huh? I thought it was a rule at school 'cause of people studying."

Her gaze hardens a tad. "It's principle. Just shush."

I hold my hands up, stepping away from her. "Okay then."

We walk up to the reception area, finding a girl with purple-streaked hair blowing chewing gum from her mouth. She stops flicking through her magazine to look up, looking put out by us being here.

"Is Charlotte around?"

"Charlotte?" she asks, sounding bored.

Landon gives me a 'what the fuck' look before turning to her. "Your boss. The chick who runs the place."

"Wow, I've been calling her Farley," she tells me, before tilting her head further up. "Charlotte! Charlotte! You have guests here."

We turn to the main room, rows and rows of books lining the bottom level. Charlotte comes running out of the stacks on the upper level, breathing hard. "I told you not to yell in the library. It's disrespectful."

"To who?" the chick yells back. "There's no one here."

"To the books," Charlotte and Amelia argue.

"Landon, Maddox, Amelia, what a pleasant surprise," she greets, beaming at us. She's wearing a white blouse with cream slacks, something I'm sure she's only ever worn once.

When she reaches us, Amelia wastes no time in stepping forward. "Why didn't you tell me about this place? It's incredible. And you do kids parties?"

"Did I not mention it? It is an awesome place. You should check out the audio selection. With the baby, you can listen to it whilst doing what you've got to do."

"That would be amazing," Amelia breathes.

"We aren't here to talk about books," Landon growls.

Amelia rolls her eyes and pushes the pushchair towards me. "Watch Asher for a moment. We're going to check out the audio selection," she tells me, before grimacing, turning to Charlotte. "If that's okay with you?"

Charlotte bounces on the balls of her feet. "Of course it is. Oh my God, you have to see the new selection we have in."

"I'm looking forward to it," Amelia gushes, and Landon and I slowly follow them to the back.

"So, Landon said you do parties and such. I guess that includes school outings?"

Charlotte looks impressed. "It does. Most of the kids will borrow a book. The more we get, the more chance we have of sponsors sticking around."

"So, would you consider letting some OAPs visit from the care home I work at? Some won't be able to, but I think an idea one of the workers had would really work. We could play Audiobooks for those who are limited with movement."

Charlotte stops, her eyes tearing up. "I have some old historical romance audio I can lend to you. They're normally between three-ninety-nine or nine-ninety-nine. But there are some that are old that we took off the shelf to put into the sale bin. But I'll get them out for you."

"We can work up a payment plan after," Amelia assures her. "Now, where are these audio books."

"You should read this book by Amy something. It's not a new one but it's so good. It's about this guy who was an assassin, and he—"

"Oh my God, the one with the corrupt step-sister? She turns on him?"

Charlotte's face lights up. "Yes! Isn't he hot?"

"Oh my God, when he—"

Landon steps forward. "We didn't come to talk about books."

I grin, slapping him on the chest. "No, no. Don't stop. What were you going to say, Amelia?"

Her face goes beet-red and she glances away. "It doesn't matter."

Charlotte's smile drops. "It does matter. Why don't you two go get something to eat in the café?"

"Yeah, we can talk about *books*," Amelia adds, glancing at me funny.

"Are you okay?" I ask.

She rolls her eyes, letting out a deep sigh. "Yes, Maddox, now go get some food and a drink. Leave us alone."

"You want me to go?" Landon asks, shocked.

Charlotte bites her lip. "I didn't ask you to go, go. I just never get to speak to someone who is into books as much as me."

Landon can't argue. It's written all over his face. He wants her to have everything she's ever wanted. His friendship with her is like mine and Lily's. She balances him, like Lily balances me. Or at least she used to. Now I'm not so sure anymore. I glance at Amelia, narrowing my gaze on her. *Is it her who had made the change?* Since I met her, I don't crave attention in other aspects of my life; I don't smother Lily and demand she spend time with me. I'm content with just her.

"What?" she mouths.

I jolt, not releasing I was staring. "Nothing," I mouth back.

"We'll be in the café then, when you're finished," he tells her, his shoulders slumping.

We begin our way to the café, and once the girls are out of sight, Landon pushes me, nearly causing me to fall into the bookshelf.

"What was that for, dickhead?"

"You brought a chick who talks books. How can we speak to her now? It will kill her mood."

"I didn't know that would happen. Let's just see what Amelia says after."

"You'd better be right, otherwise I'll find this fucker and go back on my word and end him."

I grimace. "It doesn't end well. Look at me and Lily. Do you want that with you and Charlotte?"

He runs a hand through his hair. "No. But I also don't want her hurt either. She's too kind, and I'm worried he'll change her." He pauses, stopping at the door that leads into the café. "It will be my fault. Since Paisley, the gym and the extra work, I've not had as much time to spend with her as I used to. I feel like shit, man."

"We won't let that happen, Landon," I assure him. "And this isn't your fault. She must have known that at some point in your life you'd find a girl who took up your time."

"But I promised I'd always be there for her."

I clap him on the back. "I know, man. I know." I push open the door, and stop, breathing in the sweet aroma. I turn back to Landon. "You are so fucking paying."

"Fuck!" he grouches, sulking behind me.

TWENTY-TWO

AMELIA

THE LEAVES RUSTLE, THE SUN WARM with a chilly breeze as I head across the road to Maddox's. Yesterday, I had to go pick up Jasmine and go to my aunt's for dinner with the kids, so I never got a chance to talk to him about my conversation with Charlotte.

"Can I eat the cookies?" Jasmine asks as I push the pushchair up the kerb.

"No, baby. Not until you've had lunch at Nanny's, and those are Maddox's."

"Not fair," she grumbles, making me smile.

"Yo, bitch," Cassie calls out, her hair knotted and sticking out.

Her red-rimmed eyes narrow on me, her jaw clenched. I let out a sigh, not bothering to reprimand her for her language. "What do you want, Cassie?"

"Just to let you know we aren't going anywhere. I don't care what the council say."

"I'm sorry to hear it," I lie. "But it has nothing to do with me."

"Like I believe you. Pregnant and spreading your legs to that fucking prick. You'd do anything."

"Cassie," I hiss out, covering Jasmine's ears. "Leave us out of this."

I ignore her reply and rush up Maddox's path. I bang on the door, not wanting to give her a chance to say anything else.

He opens the door, wearing his work clothes. The cut on his arm has me wincing, and the nurse in me coming out. "Oh my God, what did you do?"

He moves his arm out of the way, but I snatch it back. "It's nothing."

"That's not nothing."

He chuckles. "Look at you, all bossy."

"She bosses to me too," Jasmine adds, and I send her a disapproving look.

"Let me take a look at it," I demand, pushing Asher up the step. When he doesn't budge for a moment, I begin to think he's not going to let us in, but then he steps aside, letting us through. I head straight for the kitchen I can see down the hallway, leaving a sleeping Asher just outside the door. "Jasmine, go watch *Peppa Pig* on your tablet."

"It's fine," he assures me, taking a seat at the table where supplies are scattered all over the place. "It's just a scratch."

"It needs stiches," I warn him, bringing his arm closer. "And a deep clean. How did you do it?"

He groans, sitting back. "The guy I fired? He came back to dispute his last paycheque and ended up taking a swing at me with a steel bead."

I begin to sort through the supplies. "I hope you called the police. This is bad."

He tries to pull back again, but with one hand, I grab his wrist, keeping a tight grip on it. I grab the sterile water, and quickly soak the wound.

He hisses out a breath. "Shit. That hurts more than the time they took those cheesy things off the McDonalds menu."

I chuckle, dabbing it dry. "Are you okay with me stitching this together?"

"I'd rather sit round next door for the day, but I guess."

I chuckle under my breath and get the needle ready, pulling it out of the packaging. "I'm not even going to ask how you have all the equipment to do this here. Or how some of this is hospital issue."

"Fuck," he hisses, and I grimace.

"I'm sorry. You don't have any numbing cream here."

"It's fine," he tells me, making eye contact with me. My thumb rubs in a small circle along the top of his hand. Clearing his throat, he breaks the spell between us. "And to answer your *non*-question; Landon got into a lot of scrapes before Paisley. We kept these in stock just in case."

"Why do I feel like there's a but?" I tease.

He chuckles. "Because there is," he admits. "Remember I told you about the feud with the Hayes family?" I nod, and he continues. "Well, that was another reason we had them on hand. Couldn't let the hospital document injuries."

I finish up with the last stitch just as my phone begins to ring. "Don't move. I just need to get that," I tell him. I rush over to the pushchair, grabbing it out of the bag I've hung over the handle.

Seeing Mum's name, I quickly answer. Jasmine and Asher are due over there soon, but she may want to get them sooner. "Hey, Mum, is everything okay?"

She coughs into the phone. "I'm sorry, darlin'. Your dad is in bed with the flu. Is there any way you could drop the kids over to us? He's not going to be able to drive and my car is in the shop being fixed. You know I can't drive manual."

"Mum, you don't sound too good yourself," I tell her, clicking my fingers and pointing to the chair when Maddox goes to get up.

"I'm hungry," he grumbles.

I inwardly sigh, stepping back and grabbing the pasta and the tub of cookies I made for him earlier. I hand them to him before pulling open the first drawer I find and hitting the jackpot for a knife and fork.

Mum finishes her coughing fit, followed by a sniffle. "I'm fine. Honestly."

"Mum, I love you, but you need to rest. I'll make you a pot of soup and bring it over once it's done."

"What about the kids? You have work soon and you can't take them with you."

I pace the small space of the kitchen. "I'll call in sick. I'm sure Auntie Tracey won't mind."

"Are you sure, sweetie? You've only been back a few days and you're still struggling to get sleep."

"I'll handle it, Mum."

"All right. I love you," she tells me.

"Love you too, Mum," I reply, before ending the call.

I drop back down in the seat, feeling a heavy weight on my chest. I need these hours, especially since I can't work the long ones I normally would.

"Everything okay?" Maddox asks around a mouthful of food.

"No. Yes. It will be fine," I tell him.

He arches an eyebrow. "What's going on? You said you'd call in sick, but you aren't sick."

"Mum and Dad are, and they were having the kids for me."

"Don't they have a child minder?" he asks.

"Normally Jasmine does, but she's having a few issues there, so I decided to pull her out. And Asher is too young to go there."

"I'll have them," he blurts out.

"W-what?" I stutter, wondering if I heard him right.

"I'm not allowed back into work. It's company policy," he explains, shrugging. "And it's not like I've not had them before."

"Yeah, but I'm always in the house," I state.

"Not when you went to the hospital after you gave birth. I did good then."

I snort, rolling my eyes. "You also had a house full of people to help."

He glares at me, sitting forward. "I'll have you know, I did everything myself. No one helped me with Jasmine at all."

"I don't know. It's a big responsibility," I murmur, unsure.

"I have over forty-seven employees and a business to run; I'm pretty sure I can do this." He pauses, looking at me closely. "Unless you don't trust me."

"Of course I do," I tell him truthfully.

"Then it's settled," he declares, getting up.

"Fine," I give in. "But sit down and let me wrap that up."

"Thank you."

I glance up at his soft tone. "Shouldn't I be the one saying thank you to you?"

He chuckles, his eyes sparkling. "No. Doing this, I… thank you."

"You're welcome," I reply. "Now, let me wrap this up and then I can share of some of the things Charlotte and I spoke about."

"She spoke to you?"

"In confidence," I add. "So, I won't be repeating all of it."

"We want to help her," he demands, his tone light though.

"I know you do. But you can't overwhelm her. I don't know her all that well, but in most cases, it could lead to you pushing her closer to him."

"I'll kill him if he's touched her."

"I don't think he's physically hurt her, but that doesn't mean abuse isn't there."

"So *he is* abusing her," he concedes, going to stand up.

I grab his arm, sitting him back down. "Stop. I'm not going to tell you anything if this is how you're going to react."

"What can you tell me?" he asks, sliding forward in his chair. "Because we're getting worried."

"I know. And I'm sorry I couldn't tell you yesterday, but I didn't feel comfortable talking about it in front of Landon."

"Why? He's her best friend."

"Because I didn't push Charlotte to talk to me. I talked about myself in the hope to gauge her reaction."

"I, I didn't know," he murmurs.

I begin to clean up the mess, busying myself as I talk. I can't look him in the eye whilst talking about this. "We began talking about a love interest in a book we had both read. She had this dreamy gaze in her eyes as we were talking about him. I knew that look."

"What do you mean?" he asks, keeping his voice low.

I force a smile as I get up and put the stuff in the bin. I stare outside the window into his spacious, tidy garden. "Reading romance sucks you in and keeps you there. It gives you the misguided notion of what love is and what it should be. It's not all happy endings. The endings are only the beginning in the romance world. The things that come after stay a mystery for a reason. It's to give you hope. Because not all love is boy meets girl, girl meets boy. It has obstacles, hardships, and mountains to climb. For there to be highs, there is always a low.

"I took one look at Charlotte and I knew she wanted a love like that, so much so that she'd do anything—even put up with a dickhead—to have it. So I told her how reading helped me escape while I was recovering. I shared my past about Cameron and how stupid I was for believing it could be how it's like in the books." I turn around, wiping the tear rolling down my cheek. "I explained how I let my dreams of a picture-perfect family brainwash me, and that it nearly cost me everything."

"I-I... Amelia," he breathes out, pushing back in his chair.

When he begins to walk over, I back up against the sink. "This isn't about me," I tell him.

"I didn't mean for this though. I wanted to help Charlotte but not at the expense of bringing up painful memories."

I force out a dry chuckle. "The trouble with that is Charlotte only sees love in your family. She sees it in her parents, her aunts and uncles, and now her cousins. And she craves it. She's not going to listen to people who have it when she wants it. I wanted her to know my story. If you want her to listen, to really listen, she needs to know not all love is like your family's. It can be cruel, hard, and manipulative."

He steps closer, getting in my personal space. When he places his hands on my biceps, a shiver runs up my spine. "What did she say to that?"

I blink up at him, and time freezes as I stare into his eyes. He's watching me like it's his first time. I swallow down salvia to cure my dry throat. "She didn't say anything. She didn't need to. Her body language and eyes said it all."

"What does that mean?" he asks, his chest rising and falling as he steps closer.

I don't think he's even aware of what he's doing, especially when he begins to run those hands up and down my arms, offering me comfort.

"It means you need to give her time to see it's not love but a consolation prize. I told her I was wrong not to listen to my gut. I had my doubts about Cameron. It was a tiny voice in the back of my head that told me he wasn't the one."

He tilts my chin up with his knuckles, then bends until we're eye level. "He was a fool to do what he did to you," he croaks out.

"Maddox," I whisper, stepping closer, placing my hand on his hips.

"Mum, are we going? I want my cookies."

A look up and horror washes over his expression. He jumps back, clearing his throat. I straighten my top, forcing a smile for my daughter. "Change of plans, Jasmine. Maddox is going to watch you today," I inform her, before turning to Maddox. My stomach clenches when I see the look of disgust on his expression. "If that's still okay?"

He looks up, and quickly rushes to confirm. "Wouldn't want to do anything else."

Jasmine pumps her hands into the air. "Best day ever."

Maddox meets my gaze, locking me in place to the point I'm not sure I can catch my next breath. "Yeah, best day ever."

"*We have* to watch one of my movies today," Jasmine announces. "That gun movie was okay, but not as good as mine."

I arch my eyebrow at Maddox, who has the nerve to go red. "It was a Christmas movie," he defends himself.

"Christmas movie?"

He lets out a sigh, narrowing his gaze teasingly at my daughter. "It was *Die Hard*."

"I'm not even going to comment," I tell him.

"She loved it at the end when the good stuff happened," he explains, stepping closer to me.

I awkwardly stand there, trying to force my emotions down. "I bet."

"Amelia," he murmurs, and I know in my gut he's about to talk about the moment we just shared. And I can't have him tell me I'm just a friend once more.

I quickly grab my phone off the table, forcing a smile. "I need to get some things done before I have to get to work. I'll make lunch for the both of you. Forty minutes?"

He nods, looking away. "I'll be there."

I grip the handle of the pushchair, pushing Asher back down the hall. Maddox jumps in front of us, pulling open the front door.

When I get outside, I turn back to him. "Don't get that arm wet. I'll check on it later after work."

"Wait," he calls out when I begin my descent down the path.

I pause, my legs feeling like they are about to give out beneath me. "Thank you for having the kids for me."

"That's fine. I want to, but—"

"Say bye to Maddox, Jasmine."

She looks up from her tablet. "See you later, alligator."

He grins. "In a while crocodile."

"Why are you walking so fast?" Jasmine asks as we cross the road.

"Because I know how much you want those cookies," I tell her.

She slaps the palm of her hand over her forehead. "I left them on Maddox's sofa."

I chuckle, pulling my keys out of my bag. "Bit of a good job we have more."

"We could go back and get them."

I pause with the key halfway into the lock and look down at my naïve, beautiful daughter. "They will be gone."

She lets out a sigh, glancing wistfully at Maddox's. "Yeah. He eats everything."

TWENTY-THREE

AMELIA

I STIFLE A YAWN AS I TEAR OPEN another box. My aunt has a trainee working so I thought I'd let her get experience by following Hope around. I volunteered to stock our medical storeroom.

There's a light knock on the door and I startle, glancing to the door. "Yeah?" I call out.

My aunt pushes open the door, peeking her head round. She smiles when she spots me at the far back. "There you are. Hope said you were here but when I came by earlier, you weren't."

"I had to go sign for an order," I explain, pointing to the boxes.

"Talk to me," she demands softly.

I'm taken aback by her words. "Um, we are."

She snorts, and steps further into the room, closing the door behind her. "You have been a zombie all day. It's like you're in a world of your own. Did Asher keep you up all night?"

Surprisingly, no. The neighbour's music was drowned out a little by the ear buds I bought. Maddox is the reason for my mood. I was stupid to think he was going to kiss me, stupid for letting myself feel like this towards him.

"No, Tracey. I'm just not with it. I must be having an off day."

She gives me a knowing look as she takes a seat on the stool. "Is this about a boy?"

I rear back, shaking my head vehemently. "No. Of course not. What made you think that?"

She chuckles, shaking her head disbelievingly. "You might have pulled the wool over your mum's eyes over the years, but you've never been able to do it to me. I know about the hot neighbour. One your mum said has been doing a lot for you," she states, arching an eyebrow when I go to deny it. "She even said he has stayed over."

"It's not what you think," I defend, unable to look at her. She's right. There were times I could fool my mum, but I've never been able to do it with my aunt. She could always see past the façade.

"Tell me what's going on."

I drop the bandages onto the side and turn to her, knowing she'll never drop it until I answer. "He's so frustrating. He showed up one day and offered to help me. I let him. A complete stranger," I rant. "Then, he happens to turn up the day I go into labour and delivers the baby."

"I'm not hearing anything bad," Tracey comments, smirking.

I let out a growl. "I'm not finished. He keeps coming over. He's good with my kids. Asher can't bloody sleep without him. He gets in my personal space and he eats all our food. He never listens, always demanding to pay for everything, and never hears me when I tell him no. He just does it anyway."

Tracey gets up, pulling me to a stop. I hadn't even realised I was pacing until she brings me to a stop. She bursts out laughing, and I look on, stunned and maybe a little hurt she'd laugh at my dilemma.

"You, my sweet girl, like him."

I scoff. "I do not."

She grips my chin gently, turning my head until I'm facing her. Her gaze softens and she gives me a small smile. "Yes, you do. Your uncle drove me nuts too. It's kind of what made me fall in love with him."

"I'm not in love with Maddox." She gives me a pointed look, and I let out a sigh. "It doesn't matter how I feel towards him. He doesn't do relationships or any kind of commitment. I'm pretty sure even being friends with me is new for him."

"You don't know that," she softly scolds.

I step back out of her embrace. "Yes, I do. Because he tells me any chance he gets. You don't know him, Aunt Tracey. He's a free spirit with zero regrets. He lives his life to the fullest and makes sure he gets the fullest back. He doesn't want to lose that by settling down, and he certainly won't do it by being with a single parent. He'll want kids of his own."

"You could have more kids," she tells me. "It doesn't mean anything in this day and age."

I scrape my hair up into a bun on the top of my head. Now that I'm finishing soon, it doesn't matter what it looks like. "It doesn't matter. He doesn't see me like that. No one will."

"Nonsense. Debbie's son is coming to town—"

"No. No, no, no, no. I told you—"

"Just hear me out. His sister has just opened a restaurant up in town and he wants a date to go with him when he visits. He came in to see his mum and offered to take her, but she has an out-of-town conference to get more sponsors. I told him you'd love to go."

"You did what?" I screech.

She grimaces, holding her hands up. "Just think about it. You know it's only a friendly date. It's nothing too serious. And maybe it will give this neighbour some incentive to ask you out."

"Oh God," I groan, glancing away. "I can't believe you've done this."

"Well…" when a flash of guilt flashes across her expression, I narrow my gaze on her.

"What?" I whine. "What else did you do? Promise my firstborn to him? Because I've got to tell you, she might be mini, but she will fight him."

She waves me off. "Your mum also agreed."

"Mum knows about this?"

"Yes. She was here when he arrived. I'm sorry. I just think it will be good for you."

"Ring him and tell him no," I demand. "I don't even know him."

"You've met him once," she tells me, snorting.

I had, and although handsome, he didn't spark my fancy. He was just Nolan, Debbie's son, to me.

"I don't care. I'm not going on a date with him," I tell her.

"Um, well, it's next weekend so you can't cancel now."

"What? That's seven days away."

She sheepishly shrugs. "You can't let him down now. He was so excited."

"I can't believe you've done this."

"Just think of it as a test run. You'll get to break the fear of going on a first date and do it with someone you know is a respected gentleman. You don't have to be worried about calling him back because it's only a favour—unless you want to go on a second date. And you'll get a free meal," she tells me, trying to persuade me into this. "And let's not forget that you'll know once and for all if your neighbour has feelings or not. If he lets you go on a date with some other guy, then it's only friendship he wants. If he stops you, well, you'll know he wants more."

She's right. She is horribly, connivingly right. Still, I can't do this. "You'll have to cancel, Tracey. I won't go. I'm not playing games with someone like that."

"But—"

"Please, Tracey."

"Okay," she breathes. "I'll go speak to Debbie now."

I nod, waiting for her to leave before leaning against the shelves. I can't believe my mum and aunt did that. And Debbie. I expected more from her. She is the other owner at Nightingale Care Home and has been best friends with my aunt since nursery.

"At least I got out of it," I mutter, before getting back to work.

Slamming the car door shut, I begin to drag my feet up to the door. I'm exhausted, and now I have to go and do some cleaning, make sure Asher is okay, and get dinner on.

I push through the door, expecting there to be chaos, but all I'm greeted by is the sound of the T.V. playing.

I slowly shut the door, the click of the lock echoing in the small hallway. Stepping into the front room, I come to a stop at the sight of Maddox sitting on the floor, Asher lying between his legs, content with just looking at Maddox's face. My daughter sits behind him on the sofa, combing his hair. I bite my bottom lip to smother the giggle threatening. I hadn't seen it as she was combing, but there are also plastic butterfly clips scattered in his hair.

I glance back at Maddox, trying to see if he's uncomfortable, but he's glued to the T.V., his eyes sparking with amusement.

Turning in the direction of the television, I chuckle. Jasmine had finally won him over and gotten him to watch Frozen. Number two as well.

"I'm back," I call out when it becomes evident they haven't heard me.

"Shush," Maddox hisses, not looking away from the television.

"Hey, Mummy," Jasmine greets, before going back to her task. She sticks her tongue out, biting down on it as she concentrates.

"Let me watch this," he calls out. "It's not long started so you can join us if you're quiet."

"Well thanks," I mutter dryly.

Maddox begins to laugh uproariously, and Jasmine giggles, falling onto her side on the sofa. "This guy is a hoot," Maddox declares, before snorting. "Samantha."

The ground beneath Olaf opens up and he glances down into the hole. When he calls out 'Samantha', Maddox tilts his head back, bursting into laughter. "I need an Olaf in my life."

I leave the room to get out of my work clothes, and as I reach the stairs, I hear Jasmine reply, "Me too. Me too. I'll ask Santa again."

"Ask for me too," he demands.

I stop on the stairs, a smile pulling at my lips when she replies, "Why can't you ask him? He might not bring me mine if you want one too."

Maddox snorts. "I got put on the naughty list."

"The naughty list?" she whispers, her voice trembling. "It's really real?"

Maddox chuckles. "Yeah, Jaz. It is."

"I'm going to be the best girl ever."

I hear a shuffle before Maddox replies, "Jasmine, you already are."

"Really?"

"Hell yeah. Your mum couldn't be luckier to have a daughter as good and as cool as you."

"Maddox, you're the best," she gushes out.

"Tell your mum that," he grumbles.

"She knows. She talks to Nanny about you all the time."

I inwardly groan. My daughter and those big ears. And Maddox… not two minutes ago he was telling me to shush. Now he's chatty Cathy.

"What does she say?" he asks.

"Last night, she told Nanny she'd kill for you to be here."

"She did, did she."

"Uh huh. Asher wouldn't go to sleep," she declares, and I hear the dejected sigh come from him. I smile a little, picturing his crestfallen expression.

"Did she say anything else?"

"She said her lady bits stopped hurting," Jasmine reveals, and I slap my forehead. I need to get changed and get back in there before she tells him about the time I cried on the phone to my mum because it felt like one of my stiches had torn. It hadn't. But the pain was real.

I race to my room, throwing my clothes onto the floor in my dash to get dressed. I throw on some pyjamas before racing downstairs.

Maddox is still in the same position but now Jasmine is sitting next to him, glued to the television. When he glances up at my entrance, his cheeks flush.

Oh God, she told him about the rest of the conversation.

"I'm, um, putting dinner on. Did you want something?"

"Dinner can wait," he tells me. "Just come sit and relax. You just walked in from work. And this is good. This Olaf dude is hilarious."

"I'll tell everyone you said that," I warn teasingly. "And Jasmine needs feeding, so I've got to get something on now."

He shrugs. "Tell anyone. I'm masculine enough to not give a sh—sugar. And Jasmine had a big lunch."

"I made her lunch," I point out. "She didn't eat it."

He bites his lip, glancing away. "We, um, kind of went to see my mum, and she fed us."

My body tenses. "You didn't tell me you were leaving the house."

"I didn't think it would be a problem. I'm sorry," he tells me, looking unsure.

I slump, feeling bad. "It's fine. It's no trouble."

"Are you going to watch the rest of the movie?" Jasmine asks.

"I, um—" I squeal as Maddox dives for me, knocking my legs out from beneath me. Instead of hitting the floor like I assumed I would, I land on Maddox. "Maddox. What on earth?"

"Are you going to watch the movie with us?" he demands, grinning up at me.

"I have things to do."

He tilts his head up to look at Jasmine, rolling his eyes at her. "She has things to do."

She folds her arms over her chest, her expression filled with determination. "Mummy," she calls in a sing-song voice.

"Jasmine," I warn when she steps closer to me.

Maddox pokes me in the ribs, and I curl up, my stomach tensing. "Don't you dare," I warn, struggling to get free.

The grin that lights up his face stops my heart. He is breath-taking. Before a moment can be shared, he digs his fingers into my ribs lightly, and begins to tickle me. "Are you going to watch the movie?"

"Never," I choke out, squirming as laughter pours out of me.

He rolls us until he's above me, situating himself between my legs. "Then I guess we'll have to keep this up until you say yes."

My eyes widen. "You wouldn't?"

He glances up at Jasmine, the wicked grin on his lips causing my thighs to clench. "We will, won't we?"

"Yes," she roars, before diving on Maddox. He lets out a gruff breath, but then begins to laugh as he dives for my waist.

"No," I cry out, the pressure of my bladder increasing each time he tickles me.

"Say yes," Jasmine cries out.

Oh God, I'm going to piss myself.

"Yes. Fine. Yes. But Maddox is doing dinner."

Maddox stops his onslaught, but Jasmine stays wrapped around his neck. He glances down at me, his eyes sparkling with happiness. "I'll order take-out."

I roll my eyes. "That's nothing new. Now, would you get off me?"

He smirks, putting more pressure on top of me. "I don't know. I'm kind of comfy," he states. "How about you, Jaz? Are you comfy?"

"Yes!"

I place my hand on his chest, my breathing escalating at the warmth seeping through his T-shirt. "Maddox," I whisper, and his pupils dilate, filling with desire.

My brain fizzles, and I forget my left from my right. It's him. All him. His large frame covering mine, his touch so gentle as he tries not to squash me, and his scent.

God, he smells so good.

He lifts his hand to my cheek, his thumb slowly sliding over my jawline. I flick my tongue over my bottom lip and his eyes watch the movement as his chest vibrates with a groan.

He leans forward, and my heart races as his gaze burns into mine, lost in the sea of emotions.

He stops abruptly, his body jerking, and my brows pull together—until Jasmine swings further over his shoulder, her face popping up next to his, lit up with a smile. "Mummy. Come on. It's the best song."

I clear my throat and slowly Maddox rises, unable to look at me. I wouldn't be able to either. I pull down my shirt, covering my stomach that had been bared to him during our little scuffle.

"You know what? I'm starving," Maddox states, getting up off the floor. "I'll order us food. Yeah?"

As he leaves the room, my heart stutters. I close my eyes, my aunt's words from earlier playing through my mind.

She was wrong. There is no way he is attracted to me. He wouldn't act revolted each time we get close if he were.

"You okay, Mummy? You look sad," Jasmine asks, coming to sit on my lap.

I press a kiss to her cheek. "I'm not sad. I'm always happy around my babies."

She giggles, snuggling into me. "I'm not a baby anymore."

I let out a sigh. "Jaz, you'll always be my baby."

"And Asher?"

"And Asher," I agree, leaning over to pick him up. He coos, his little legs and arms kicking about in excitement. I laugh, pressing him closer to my chest and kissing his forehead.

I don't need a man to complete me. My life is complete with these two. I'll go on this date, but I'm doing it without expectations. Because one thing is for sure: I'm not going to settle. I'm not going to be with someone until I'm absolutely sure they are the one. People might say I have my head in the clouds, but this is life. And it's a life I want to spend surrounded by love and happiness.

And right now, I couldn't be happier.

If Maddox doesn't want me, it's his loss. I'm content with being friends. Because as much as I am attracted to him, I value his friendship more.

Knowing I need to move, I place Asher back on his blanket and Jasmine on the floor next to me. I get up, heading to the front door, to where I dropped my bag. I pull out my phone, bringing up my chat with my aunt.

Amelia: Can you tell Nolan I've changed my mind. I'll do it. I'll go with him. But just as friends.

Aunt Tracey: I knew you'd come to your senses. I'll pass along your number.

Amelia: You didn't cancel?

Aunt Tracey: I'm your aunt and I love you. You'll have fun. See you tomorrow.

I glance down at my phone, biting my lower lip. I've done it now. I can't keep changing my mind.

There is no going back now.

TWENTY-FOUR

MADDOX

My spoon clinks against the bowl filled with ice cream as I dive in for another scoop. It's my second bowl—okay, maybe fifth. But I have my reasons goddammit.

Amelia.

She's fucking with my head, and I'm letting her.

Why does she have to be sexy without meaning to be? Why does she have to make me laugh and enjoy my time with her? She doesn't bore me. Her kids—believe it or not—also don't bore me or scare me. Life with her is just that... life.

I had the house, the car, a business, and family who loved and adored me, but until her, I never felt like I was living life. A car, a job, a house... it was all society's steps. It was a routine mapped out hundreds of years ago, and people continued to do it. It was all about the next step in life. It was about when you were going to settle down and have kids. All of that sounded boring and exhausting.

Why can't we just live for the now?

I work because I like what I do. I love building things and seeing something come together. I love my car because as fit as I am, no fucking way will I walk everywhere. It killed me as a kid when one of the parents couldn't pick me up. And I got a house because I wanted my own space. I wanted peace, even though I had been wrong about that.

Maybe you are wrong about this.

A low, guttural growl rises up my throat. I'm not wrong. *Am I?* I have never felt so exhilarated, so at peace, or needed, as I do when I'm with Amelia and the kids. Is that what people strive to have; to be? Because although it kills me to admit, it doesn't feel like I'd be chaining myself down. It doesn't feel like I'd be giving anything up, only gaining so much more.

I slam my spoon down in the bowl. This is my dad's fault. Not Amelia's. He told me I'd never get a girlfriend, and it's clearly playing on my mind. It has to be the reason I'm so attracted to her, why my stomach sinks every time I leave them in that house. Why I'm imagining a life where it's just us. Only us.

It's like the time Dad told me I couldn't touch his spring onions. He knew I hated them, but he put the dare in my head and pushed me to eat the jar. He's doing it again with Amelia.

That has to be it.

I don't want to give up single life. I love fucking different women. I like the variety, the no commitment. With Amelia, it's all a massive commitment. I can't just have a fling, get her out of my system, and move on. There are kids involved, and I couldn't do that to them.

Or to her.

I'd also have to give up our friendship, and that's something I'm not prepared to do. She means too much to me.

All my thoughts about commitment and accepting it as something I want is my dad's voice in the back of my head. It's like being told you can't have something. You only want it more.

I can't let him get into my head.

I groan over the noise going on next door. It has been going on for over an hour now. I can't even get a moment to drown in my own misery.

When the picture in the hall falls and smashes to the ground in the hallway, I don't even blink. I should have learned and stopped replacing it every single time it got broke.

My phone beeps with a message, and I slide back in my chair. As I race to get my phone, I trip over my feet, falling flat onto my stomach as I slide across the kitchen floor. "Fuck!" I grouch, getting myself and my pride up off the floor. I reach for my phone, my shoulders deflating when I see it's a message from Mum and not Amelia. I had hoped she would cave and admit she was missing me.

Mum: Just to let you know, your dad left about ten minutes ago, and he was acting weird. I thought nothing of it until I saw Trent's hockey stick gone from by the front door. Both of them. I'm pretty sure they were there when he left though. He might have come back, I'm not sure. I've been upstairs.

"Shit," I murmur. He did say he was dealing with next door tonight, and I forgot about it.

Maddox: I'll make sure he doesn't get arrested, Mum.

Mum: That doesn't reassure me. I'm just glad he went alone and didn't take your uncle Max with him.

She isn't wrong there.

A screech of tyres spinning on the tarmac has my blood running cold. I shove my phone into my back pocket instead of calling Dad. I race through the hallway, to the front door, swinging it open. Lights blind me for a second before the car shuts down.

I gape as my dad steps out with Mason sliding out of the passenger side, both with a hockey stick in their hands.

"Fuck!" I grimace, shutting the door to.

He promised he wouldn't go over the top. I don't want to get arrested.

Whispers begin next door, and I watch as Kayne and his mates get up from their deck chairs, going on alert.

"Turn the fucking music off and keep it fucking off," Dad orders, slamming his car door shut.

"Who the fuck are you?" Kayne barks, just as his mum comes barging out of the front door, a can of cider in one hand, a fag in the other.

Dad stops at the edge of the path, Mason next to him, both looking menacing. "Your worst fucking nightmare if that isn't turned off."

Cassie laughs, dropping her fag to the floor and stomping on it. "You can't stop us from having a party."

Mason turns to Cassie, his lip curling with disgust. "It's after ten, so we fucking can."

"You don't even live here," Kayne snaps.

"No, but you've got plenty of other neighbours who are fucked off hearing it," Dad replies, taking a step onto their path.

"Are you going to turn it off?" Mason demands.

"You wanna fight, old man?" a gangly kid with yellow teeth asks.

Dad doesn't even spare him a glance. "Pipe down, little boy. You're embarrassing yourself."

The kid throws his can to the ground, puffing his chest out. "Who the fuck do you think you're talking to? I'll knock your head off your shoulders."

When he rushes at Dad, I step out of the door, readying to jump in. Dad grips him around the neck, squeezing until the kid's eyes begin to bulge.

Just before anyone else can make a move, tyres skid along the road. The car comes to a stop over the pavement and half of the garden. I gawk as Max comes out, a bat swinging over his shoulder.

But that isn't even the worst of it.

"What the fuck?" Mason breathes out, his eyes widening.

"You tryin' to fuck with my nephew?"

"Fucking hell. We just want to chill out," Cassie screeches as she turns to me. "You can't man up, so you have to send the calvary?" Her eyes go to Max, her lip curling. "And a member of the Village People."

My lips twist in disgust. "Like I need them to sort you lot fucking out. I'm just done with your shit. It's time you had a bit of your own medicine."

"Are you going to turn it off?" Dad repeats, dropping the hockey stick to his side.

"Am I fuck," Cassie screeches. "It's my home. I can do what the fuck I like."

"And as a public citizen who is fed up of your shit, so can I," he tells her, throwing the lad to the side.

The girls screech, racing off the garden as Dad charges at the sound system, swinging the hockey stick and shattering it to pieces.

"Stop!" Cassie cries, stepping away from the broken plastic flying everywhere.

Kayne and his mates go to intervene, but Mason and Max step in, stopping them from getting to Dad.

"You want to party?" Max screams, smashing the bat against a chair, causing it to fly across the garden.

Dad grabs the extension lead wire that is hanging out the window, yanking it hard. Something smashes inside and screams echo into the silence of the night. A few girls and a couple of guys come racing out.

I'm frozen on the spot, still shocked at the sight of my uncle Max. He swings at another chair, cracking the cheap plastic and breaking it before getting into a lad's face. "You want to listen to music, go to a fucking club like normal people."

"You can't do this," Cassie screeches, going for my dad when he swings the hockey stick up before bringing it down on the speaker. "You are going to pay for that."

He gently pushes her away, and the look in his eyes stops her short. "I can do this. You've had chance after chance to turn this crap off. You didn't. Now, if I find out this has been replaced, I'll be back, and it won't be as civilised."

"You can't stop me," she snaps.

"He's crazy," I hear whispered, and I turn to see a couple of girls gaping at my uncle, who is now jumping on the roof of Kayne's car, banging on his chest with one fist and holding the bat up with the other.

"Are you not entertained!" he yells, before slapping his hand over mouth repeatedly as he howls.

"I'm calling the police."

Dad leans down, getting in her face. "Call them. I dare you. In fact, my niece's fiancé is a cop. I'll call him."

"This is ridiculous."

"You partying like you're still a teenager is what's ridiculous," Dad snaps.

Max roars, jumping down from the car in front of one of Kayne's mates. The guy staggers backwards, tripping over some rubbish left on the weeds. He falls on his arse, crawling backwards with fear etched onto his face.

"Yeah, you know it," Max barks, before bursting into crazy laughter.

"Don't make me come back," Dad warns.

Kayne sways on his feet for a moment before marching over to his mum, blood pouring out of his nose. She takes one look at him and her eyes harden. "Get the fuck off our garden before I set them all on you."

Dad shrugs, and walks over the grass to get to mine. I watch as the others either leave or follow Cassie and Kayne inside.

My lips are still parted as Max walks up to us, his outfit squeaking. He reaches back, pushing his hand down the back of his trousers.

Leather trousers.

"Wedgy," he mutters. Dad comes to stand by my side, Mason on the other as we stand gawking at him. He blinks up at us. "What?"

"What the fuck are you wearing?" I burst out.

"How do you even own that?" Dad asks, then pauses, closing his eyes. "Don't answer that."

"I'm speechless."

Max growls low in his throat, narrowing his eyes into slits. He pulls the leather vest closed over his naked chest. The squeak from the leather rubbing together echoes through the air. He has a chain going from the little pocket on the front of his vest to the hoop on the trousers.

"Lake likes it when I dress up," he mutters defensively.

"So she can have a laugh?" Mason retorts.

"No, she gets—"

"Eww," I cry out, turning away from him. "I don't need to hear this shit."

"You asked," Max snaps.

"What made you wear it fucking here?" Dad asks. "In fact, how the fuck did you know I was here?"

"Harlow messaged to threaten me. She thought I was with you and said if I got you arrested, she was cutting off my food supply at her house. Like she would ever go through with it."

"Shit!"

"Well, if seeing Max in leather doesn't scare them, nothing will," I let out, grinning.

"I think I look pretty hot," he replies, jutting his hips side to side.

I can't help it, laughter bursts out of me, and Dad and Mason do the same, doubling over.

"You look like a dickhead," Dad comments.

"A crazy, demented dickhead," Mason adds.

"I can't," I gasp out through laughter.

"Fuck you all," Max growls. "If they don't stop, I'll be back."

"As Tinker Bell?" I ask, laughing harder when his expression turns to stone.

He storms off with our laughter filling the air. He stops at his car door, turning to give us one disgruntled look before getting in. The squeaking of his outfit sets us all off again, tears of laughter running down our cheeks.

"I swear, he was dropped way too much as a baby," Dad declares, wiping under his eyes before turning to me. "If it starts up again, call me."

"Shit!" Mason growls, closing his eyes.

I give him a sideways look. "What?"

"I didn't get a fucking picture of Max."

"Fuck! Me neither."

Dad snorts. "My dash cam was recording."

I laugh, clapping him on the shoulder. "Send it to me."

"See you tomorrow," he tells me, before he and Mason head down the path.

I lift my hand, giving them a wave as they pull out and drive away. My gaze goes to Amelia's, and I jerk on the spot when I see her standing on the doorstep, Asher getting rocked in her arms.

I hold my hand up to tell her to give me a minute. I race to the door, leaning in to grab my keys before jogging across the road to hers.

"Hey," I greet, leaning down to kiss Asher on the head.

"Um, I'm tired, so excuse me if I sound crazy, but was your, um, uncle acting like a lunatic across the road?"

I sigh. I had hoped she missed the whole thing. "Yeah. I'm sorry if he's disturbed you."

"And wearing leather?" she asks, still bug-eyed.

I rub the back of my neck. "He got in an accident and it was the only clothing they had left. He's a good sport."

"Leather? Accident?"

I nod. "It's okay. What's one more bump on the head for him," I comment, before reaching out to pick up my favourite little man. "You miss me?" I laugh, shaking my head. "Of course you missed me."

"I don't even know what to say," she whispers.

"Want to watch a movie in bed?"

"W-what?" Amelia stutters. "But there's no music, and Asher is fine tonight."

I push my way through the door, keeping Asher close to my chest. "I'm bored. C'mon."

She slowly shuts the door, a pained expression on her face as she groans, "Oh, all right then."

TWENTY-FIVE

AMELIA

The keys clink on the table as I drop them there. My feet are sore from being on them all day, and my back aches. All I want to do is go to bed, but I can't. On my way out this morning, I ran into the postman, who handed me our mail. I forgot all about it until my lunch break. What I read had my blood boiling.

I pad into the living room, inwardly groaning at the sight of him lounged back in the chair, his headset over his head and the controller stuck to his hand. It's the same position I left him in this morning.

I stand in front of him, slapping the invoice down on the coffee table, startling him. He grits his teeth, pressing pause on his game. "What the fuck, Amelia."

"What is this?"

I scan the room, my face heating when I see not one thing has been done, which means bedtime is looking later and later.

"It's an invoice for my subscription," he mutters dryly.

"I told you I couldn't afford it this month, Cameron."

He throws his controller onto the coffee table, glaring up at me. "Sorry, mum."

"Don't," I warn him, keeping my voice low, even.

He gets up, moving into the kitchen. "I swear to fucking Christ, Amelia. I'm trying. I'm really trying. Do you think I like having you support me? Because I don't. Yet you constantly bring me down. You rub it in my face every fucking chance you get."

I take a step back. "That wasn't what I was doing."

He jabs his finger towards me. "Yes, you were. You always do it. Do you get a kick out of making me feel low? Do you? Because I'm fucking sick of it."

"We have electric to pay for, Cameron. You can't just purchase a gaming subscription. We have a two-year-old to think about."

He pushes off the counter, storming up to me. "Don't bring Jasmine into this."

"Cameron," I whisper, my voice shaking.

He throws his hands up, shoving his face into my space. "You aren't the one here all day. You aren't the one who has to deal with her crying, messing with shit. I am. You go to work, but I'm doing the hard part."

"Cameron," I repeat.

"And then you come in here all high and fucking mighty, spitting shit at me. I don't need this crap."

I flinch when he moves forward, gripping me by the chin with enough force to bruise. "Cameron," I repeat, seeing that far away, dead look in his eye.

"I've fucking had it. Is it too much to ask for you to treat me like a man?"

"I-I'm sorry," I croak out.

He forces out a laugh before his expression turns to stone. "No, you aren't."

I try to nod but his hand keeps my head in place. I try to grip his wrists to push him away, but he slaps them away with his free hand. "Please, Cameron. We can talk about this. Maybe we have time to cancel the subscription."

His nostrils flare, and he backhands me across the face, causing me to drop to the floor with a thud. I cup my cheek, tears streaming down my face.

"Fuck's sake," he growls, turning his back to me. "Stop fucking crying."

I sniffle louder, unable to look in his direction.

"I said, stop fucking crying!"

"Amelia!"

I catapult awake, landing on the floor with a thud. I blink my eyes open, glancing around the small office.

"Amelia," Tracey cries, bending down on the floor next to me.

I flinch, and it takes me a minute to remember this is my aunt. It isn't Cameron. *It was just a nightmare.*

I inwardly groan, wiping the sleep out of my eyes. "I'm so sorry, Tracey. I came in for my break and I must have fallen asleep."

She helps me back into the chair as tears gather in my eyes. This is my third week back, and I am both physically and emotionally exhausted.

"Sweet girl, you have so much to juggle. Maybe coming back now was too soon."

I sniffle and reach for the box of tissues beside me on the desk, pulling one out to blow my nose. "I need the money, Tracey. I can't miss any payments. I don't have much left to pay off. I should have them cleared by the end of the year, thanks to Mum and Dad not taking rent off me."

She swipes my hair out of my face, tucking it behind my ear. "I have money I can give you. You shouldn't be working yourself into the ground."

"I need to do this," I tell her.

"What about letting us pay it off, save you paying the interest, then you pay us monthly? Would that help?"

I shake my head, almost tempted. "No. I can't let anyone do that."

"Let me," she pleads. "You're so young, Amelia. You have two beautiful children and it's going to fly by. Don't spend it worrying over debt that wasn't yours to begin with. Let me help you. Please."

My head hangs low and my shoulders shake as sobs tear from my throat. "I've tried so hard. So, so hard. When I became pregnant, I was determined never to receive government help. Not because I think there is something wrong with it but because I wanted to prove it wasn't me. Everyone I know turned on me. There were whispers. I heard them, Tracey," I explain, sniffling.

"'*That's her sat on her arse at home, living off tax-payers*'. '*I always knew she would end up a dosser*'. '*Wouldn't surprise me if she got pregnant on purpose to get the benefits*'. '*Oh, why am I not surprised another teenager is pregnant. Another person a tax-payer has to provide for'*. It hurt. I didn't believe anything they said. I still don't. What choices people make, it's up to them. But I wanted to do it on my own."

She grabs my hands, squeezing them. "You're killing yourself doing it, sweetie."

"I'm failing," I cry out.

"Oh honey," she whispers, pulling me against her chest. "You aren't failing. And asking for help isn't failing. It's living. Women have been doing this for years and it comes with highs and lows. It comes with laughter and tears. And it tears your heart open in the worst and best possible way. Parenting is kind of like Bipolar; it has its ups and its downs. This is just a down moment. And it will pass, my sweet child."

"It doesn't feel like it."

"Let me help you."

"I can't let you," I whisper, unable to meet her gaze.

She pulls back, kissing my forehead. "Please, Amelia. It's breaking my heart watching you exhaust yourself into the ground. Your mum is beside herself with worry. Your dad is getting twitchy. They've left you be because they respect your wishes, but, sweet girl, they are worried sick."

I wipe at my nose, meeting her gaze. "What? I-I... why didn't they say anything?"

Her eyes drop a little, her lips tipping down. "Because they love you."

I can't bear them going through anything else because of me. I can't. "I didn't mean to. I just want them to be proud of me. I messed up with Cameron. Big time."

"You didn't mess up; he did. You've overcome so much, but that... It's not people judging you, it's you," she tells me softly. "And your parents couldn't be prouder. You are a wonder and such a beautiful, kind, caring woman."

"Tracey," I whisper.

"It's time to lean on people, Amelia. The ones who love you have their arms wide open waiting for you to catch on. We are here for you."

I wipe under my eyes, feeling a weight begin to leave my shoulders as I sag against the chair. "And you'll let me pay you back?"

To my shock, Tracey's eyes begin to water. She grips my hands so tightly I almost flinch. "You're saying yes?"

I nod. "Yes. As much as this is killing me, it's something I know I need to do for my children's sake. The interest fees keep climbing, and I can't up my monthly payment," I admit, glancing away. "I-I'm so grateful."

She tucks my hair behind my ear. "Go home. Get some rest, and I'll get Mary to cover your shift. She's been wanting extra hours."

"I can't do that," I tell her.

"You can. It's an order. I'll get the information off your mum on what bills need paying, and together we will get them sorted and work out a payment plan for you. Does that sound good?"

I reach for her, pulling her into my arms before squeezing her tightly. "Thank you."

She stands, wiping off her trousers. "You are more than welcome. Now get home. I'll call your mother and tell her you're leaving early."

"Yes, boss," I tease.

She smiles before turning on her heel and leaving. Once she leaves, more tears begin to fall. It does feel like giving up in my head, but in my heart, I feel like the vice that had been wrapped around it is finally loose, giving me room to breathe.

Groggily, I make my way down the stairs. I came home, got changed, and immediately fell asleep on top of my bed covers. Until I heard my mum walking in with the kids.

I rub sleep out of my eyes as I step into the front room, coming wide awake when I see the bags scattered all over the floor.

Mum looks up from a bag, beaming wide. "Darlin', Tracey told me what you agreed to, so I thought I'd go out and get you some things."

"What?" I ask, stifling a yawn.

Jasmine walks up to me, hugging my waist. "Hey, Mummy."

"Hey, baby," I greet, and watch her jump on the sofa, flicking on the television, before turning back to Mum. "What are you going on about?"

She walks up to me, cupping my cheeks before leaning in to kiss my forehead. When she pulls back, tears are in her eyes. "You're finally accepting help."

"Mum, you help me all the time," I defend, realising where this is going.

She sniffles dramatically as she pulls back. "I've worried about you for so long. You are one of the strongest, most determined women I know, but you worry me. You not letting me and your father help… we lost sleep because of it. Now you are letting us and Tracey."

When she begins to cry, I pull her down on the sofa, keeping her close. "Mum, you cared for me when I got out of the hospital. You did it whilst helping raise my daughter. You helped me get back into work. You looked after my daughter and now my son, so I could continue to work. You saved me from myself. You were helping. More than you'll ever know."

When she turns into a blubbering mess, I pull her into my arms, holding her close. "I love you."

Laughter spills out of me at her reaction. "I love you too, Mum. Always."

She pulls back, dabbing her eyes dry with a tissue she pulls out of her pocket. "Look at me, getting emotional."

"It's fine," I assure her, leaning against her. I take in the bags again and pull back. "But, Mum, what on earth is in those bags?"

"I got you a date outfit. It's beautiful. Whilst I was there, I got you new shoes, a bag, and a few other bits and bobs. When Tracey told me the news, I knew I could do what I've been wanting to do for a long time."

"And what is that?" I ask, turning from the bags to her.

"Spoil you."

I laugh. "Mum, you do spoil me."

"Not in the way we'd like to. You give restrictions," she explains, before dragging the closest bag over. She opens it and pulls out a bedsheet. "Now you can stop using the one you took from my house. This one is more your style."

It is. "Mum," I whisper.

She pulls another over. "I got you that salt lamp you eyed up when we went shopping too. It will look amazing in your bedroom."

My eyes widen as I take a look around the front room. "Mum?"

"Don't you dare moan at me. I get to do this—"

"Mum," I yell, getting up.

She stands, yelling back. "You don't need to yell. I'm right here."

"Where is Asher?" I breathe out when panic begins to rise in my chest.

"Your Maddox bumped into me when I came to get your size out the wardrobe."

I gape at her. "You came here whilst I was asleep?" *And I didn't wake up?*

"Yes."

"And Maddox?"

"Was on his way to work and offered to take Asher."

I press my hands to my cheeks, feeling them heat, before I rush to my phone. "Mum, Maddox works in construction. All that dust and whatever won't be good for the baby."

"I don't think he's actually going to put him to work," Mum mutters.

The phone rings in my ear, and I tap my foot restlessly on the floor. "Evening, sunshine."

"Maddox, please tell me you didn't let Asher around your workplace," I rush out.

"Does being in the bed and breakfast count?"

"So, he wasn't inside the new build?"

"No," he answers. "Everything okay?"

I run my hand through my hair, narrowing my gaze on my mum. "Yeah. I was just worried."

"He's safe with me. And we didn't stay long, just long enough to let Mark know he was in charge. Then we went to Lily's."

"You're at Lily's?"

"No, I'm at my mum's now."

My brows pull together. "Wait, I didn't pack enough stuff for him to be gone this long. Have you changed his nappy?"

"No," he admits.

I slump down in the chair. "Maddox, you need to bring him back now. Being in a nappy that long can cause problems."

"Your mum said he had been changed before she left the house, then Lily changed him when we got to hers, and my mum just changed him. I didn't need to do it."

"How did you have enough stuff?"

"Why are you acting weird? I got what he needed from the box of stuff beside your sofa."

My brows pull together. "What? How? I thought you were out."

"I was, but after we used the last nappy at Lily's, I drove to yours and grabbed more."

"I was asleep," I push out, wondering if I'm still asleep because this conversation is confusing as hell.

"I know. I didn't want to wake you, so I let myself in."

"Let yourself in?" I repeat, gaping.

"Yeah, with your spare key. I nabbed it the other day. Anyway, we're coming back soon. I've got a surprise for Jasmine."

"What?"

"One of the neighbours' kids has outgrown her bike, so she put it out the front for free. I've grabbed it. It's that ice princess too, so she'll love it. I'll check it over to make sure everything is okay before I give it to her."

"I—what?"

I hear his heavy sigh into the phone. "Look, if you need another hour to get more sleep, let me know. You're acting weird."

"This conversation is weird."

His soft chuckle sends a shiver up my spine. "Be back soon."

Mum looks at me knowingly when I hold the phone in my lap. *He put the phone down.* "I'm going to head back, but I'll be back in the morning to help out."

"You don't need to do that. You're already babysitting tomorrow night."

She waves me off as she grabs her handbag off the floor. "I'm happy to."

After saying our goodbyes, I head back into the room, flopping down on the sofa. Jasmine tucks her legs up over mine, and arches her eyebrow. "Mum? What's a bikini wax?"

"What? Where did you hear that?"

She shrugs. "Nanny said she's going to book you in for one."

I groan, covering my eyes with my arm. I'm going to kill my mother.

TWENTY-SIX

MADDOX

Freshly showered and changed, and finished for the day, I leave to head over to Amelia's. I'm hoping she's in a better mood this evening. This morning, she had been tense, on edge and acting weird. If I snored through the night, all she had to do was say. I could give her ear buds.

Locking up, I take one step onto the drive, and stop at the sight of Kayne running out of the house. "What is this?" he cries out, wiping white gunky stuff off his face and chest.

"The smell," Cassie cries, opening the upstairs window. She gags with her head out of the window.

One of Kayne's friends stops at the end of the path, eyes wide and unblinking. "Why the fuck does it look like you've got a bucket of spunk tipped all over you?"

"He likes the boys," is whispered, and I inwardly groan.

The lad looks around as he takes a step back. "I'll, um, I'll speak to you later."

My attention goes back to the house as other windows upstairs are opened, the same with the two downstairs facing the street. Three girls and two more lads hang out, their eyes red and their skin a sickly green colour.

"Colour me amused," I hear hissed from close by, and I spin around to the sound, just as a cloud of neon green glitter explodes all over Kayne.

"What the fuck?" Kayne roars, trying to wipe it away. It only makes it worse. "You!"

I point to my chest, unable to hide my amusement. "Me?"

"You did this," he hisses.

"Sorry, princess, but I've got no hand in this," I admit.

"I'm not a fucking princess."

I lean over the fence a little, whispering. "I'm not sure if you're aware, but you look like a female unicorn that just got gang-banged."

"You fucking prick," he roars, going to take a step towards me, but another cloud of glitter explodes, leaving him blind and tripping over his own feet.

Laughter spills out of me when I hear screams coming from inside the house. Another glitter bomb is catapulted through the window, then another, and another.

"My bed," Cassie cries.

I squint into the branches, chuckling when I see my uncle lying on his stomach, the gun he and my uncle Myles built in his hand. It was meant to be for water bombs, but clearly, he changed it to hold glitter bombs.

"What is that smell?" someone yells.

"Get it off me!" Kayne screeches. "My balls are burning." He begins to choke, pink glitter shooting out of his mouth.

I watch him stagger back to the house, tail between his legs, before heading over to the tree. I look up, arching an eyebrow.

"How long have you had that camouflage hazmat suit?" I ask.

Max grins, jumping down from the tree. Looking back, he did it with finesse, with the grace of a cat, but when he lands like a baby deer walking for the first time, it's anything but smooth.

I hold my hand out to him and he takes it, before wiping his hands down his suit. He lifts the goggles up, grinning like a cat who got the cream. "Glitter is a fucking bitch to get out. And did you see the new concoction me and Hayden came up with? It really does look like thick semen."

"How do you even have time for this?"

"How do you not?" he argues. "You're just jealous that I came up with something good."

I snort. "I have an idea myself you know. I just don't have time to pull it off."

"Yeah right."

"I do!"

He crosses his arms over his chest after sliding the gun over his back. "And do tell us what this plan is."

"No, because I can't do it anyway, and I'm not having you talk me into it. I'm getting sick of being taken to the station because of you."

He smirks at me with that cocky look of his. "You didn't have anything good, did you?"

I narrow my gaze on him. "Yes, I did. Our lofts are connected. I was going to sneak in each night and make them think they are being haunted."

"Don't they party all night?" he asks.

I sigh, leaning against his car at the end of the drive. "Yeah, and I'm working all day, hence the reason why I can't do it."

He glances up at the house, looking deep in thought. "So, they're connected, huh?"

"Max," I warn. "Dad's dealt with it."

"Doesn't seem like it. They're still living there."

"Whatever," I mutter. "I need to go."

His grin spreads. "Over to Amelia's?"

"Yes. I have dinner there."

He straightens with that look I know all too well. He's hungry. He licks his lips. "I heard her food was good."

I snort. "Hate to tell you this, but they were lying. It's her mum who's the cook. Amelia's food is crap. Its why her mum normally leaves edible food around."

He scratches his head. "I must have heard wrong."

"Right. And don't you want to do the back windows before you leave?" I offer.

He swings the gun to the front, putting his game face on. "Those fuckers are going to shit glitter by the time I'm done with them."

"Have fun," I call out, taking a step into the road, ready for my dinner.

"Always do, kid. Always do."

I shake my head as I pick up speed, running up Amelia's path. I knock on the door, and seconds later, I hear Jasmine. "It's Maddox!"

I grin, jumping forward when she opens the door. "Roar!"

She squeals, jumping back. "I'll get you back for that."

Breathing hard, Amelia races to the door. "Jasmine, what have I told you about opening the door."

Cocking her hip, Jasmine rolls her eyes at her mum. "But he always comes for dinner."

I push my way inside. "I really do."

Amelia's cheeks turn pink as she steps back. She's still acting weird, not looking me in the eye. "I'm doing jacket potatoes and chicken."

I rub my stomach and kick the door shut behind me. "Sounds amazing."

Just before the door clicks shut, Amelia's eyes widen. "Is that your uncle in a camouflage hazmat suit?"

I wave her off. "No. Next door have a flea infestation."

Horror washes over her expression. "Really?"

I nod. "Horrible."

"Yeah," she murmurs, before a shiver rakes through her body.

"Want any help?"

"If you don't mind. Asher's down for a nap so I'll have time to prepare everything."

Jasmine races ahead, diving onto the sofa to watch the cartoon channel. Before I let it pull me in, I follow Amelia into the kitchen. Everything is set out on the counter. There's cucumber, lettuce, tomatoes, red onion, carrots and a mix of veggies to make coleslaw.

The door knocks again, and Amelia looks up, her face paling. "I'll get that. It will be my mum."

"You okay?"

She forces a smile, wiping her hands on the dish towel. "Yeah."

I grab the chopping board as she leaves to answer the door. I relax when I hear her mum. "Sweetie, what did I tell you? You need to pamper yourself."

"I have two kids and things to do, dinner to make," she tells her. "And can we not talk about this."

I beam at her mum as she comes to a stop in the kitchen doorway. She shares a look with her daughter, making me question whether there is more to Amelia's behaviour. "Maddox, what a pleasant surprise."

"You staying for dinner?" I ask, as I hand Amelia the knife.

She begins to work on chopping up the salad, handing me the bowl to put the coleslaw ingredients in.

She holds out a piece of cucumber, and I close my lips around it, not taking my gaze away from the task. I place the ingredients into the bowl, and she passes me the mayo before pulling out another bowl and emptying some tuna into it. I finish mixing the coleslaw before grabbing another plate, then reach for the cheese grater Amelia hands me.

We make quick work of putting dinner together when suddenly, her mum begins to laugh. We stop what we're doing, glancing up at her. She's watching us in amusement, her eyes alight with happiness.

"What?" Amelia asks.

"How long have you two been married?"

I choke on the piece of onion I stole from Amelia's board. I bang my chest as it heaves, and my nose begins to burn. "Shit!" I croak out.

"Me and your father have been married for many decades, and we still don't have that kind of rhythm together. If your father tried to help me in the kitchen, it would be a disaster."

"Mum," Amelia groans.

"To be honest, I'm normally a disaster in the kitchen. Don't get me wrong, I can pick up a plate with food on, even watch someone cook, but the minute I put my hands on any cutlery, it's over. Amelia makes it kind of easy."

"I bet," Nita murmurs, smirking at her daughter.

I clear my throat. "Are you staying for dinner? Amelia makes loads."

Her brows pull together. "Of course. I'm here to babysit the kids."

My attention snaps to Amelia. "What? Where are you going?"

"Um, nowhe—"

"She has a date," Nita interrupts, staring at me weirdly.

I rear back, glancing at Amelia. She's going on a date? With who? Why didn't I know about this?

"*You're* going on a date?"

"Yes, my—"

"He's so handsome. He has a respectful job, is polite, and did I mention handsome?" Nita comments as she grabs the jacket potatoes out of the oven.

I can't believe she would do this to me. To us.

"You can't go on a date," I demand, my tone high, screechy.

"Why not?" she asks, slowly placing her knife down on the chopping board.

I gulp, stepping back. "Because you have kids?"

"I'm going," she tells me, straightening her shoulders, the uncertainty from the past two days leaving her body. Now, in front of me stands a determined, confident woman.

What is going on?

"I'll babysit the kids," I blurt out.

Maybe then I can see who this dick is.

"You will?" Amelia asks, her eyes wide. "But you just said—"

I shrug, trying to play it off. "Yeah, why not. I live across the street. The kids love me."

"Perfect," Nita calls out, clasping her hands together. "Me and your father can go and watch a movie together. We've not done that in a while."

"Um, I'll be back. What time are you going?" I ask her.

She watches me closely, her brows pulling together. "At seven."

"I'll be back at six."

"Hey, what about the food?" she calls out when I go to leave.

Trying to clear my head, I force a smile. "Just pop some in the oven. I'll eat it later."

I leave before I say anything else I'll regret. I need to know what's going on in my head.

"You," I roar, lifting my dad off his chair. "What did you do to me?"

He shoots me a furious glare, pushing me back. I stagger back, bumping into the fireplace.

"What the hell are you doing, son?" he bites out.

Mum stands, coming between us. "What on earth?"

I point at Dad whilst addressing her when I answer. "He put it in my head about being in a relationship. That I could never do it. Then he crawled into my head and messed with it. He made me look at Amelia differently. And now she's going on a date and I feel… I feel… I don't know what I feel."

"You're jealous," Dad muses.

I take a step towards him, clenching my fists. "You did this."

"Sit down," Mum barks, using her mum voice.

I take a seat in the chair, running my fingers through my hair. "Why do I feel like this?"

Mum kneels in front of me, placing her soft hands over mine. "Because you love her."

I lift my head, snorting. "No, I do not. Why are you being ridiculous?" I ask, glancing at Dad. "Did you let her drink again?"

"She's right. You love her."

"No, I don't."

"Do you want her with anyone else?" Mum asks, standing to step next to my father.

"What? I, I… it's not up to me," I admit, unable to look at her.

"Maddox, answer the question," Mum orders softly.

I stand, throwing my hands up. "No, okay. No, I don't. But I'm not saying she should be with me either. The only reason I'm feeling this way is because of him."

"I didn't do anything," Dad states.

"Yes, you did," I yell. "It's just like that time you told me not to climb the tree outside, saying that I'd never make it."

"Because you wouldn't have, and you didn't," he barks. "You broke your leg in three places. I don't say these things to egg you on. I'm not Max. Life isn't a competition."

"But she's the prize," I yell, my shoulders slumping. "She's the prize."

"Oh, honey."

I wave Mum off when she goes to take a step towards me. "Don't. It doesn't matter anymore. She's going on a date. She'll probably go on more and have hot, sweaty sex. He'll be a father figure to the kids, and they'll like him more than me. She'll cook him meals, and make him laugh. I'll just be the neighbour."

"Stop her. It's only one date."

"I'm not doing that to her. He must mean something to her if she agreed to it. She's been through a lot."

"Honey," she murmurs.

"It's fine."

Dad claps his hands, forcing out a laugh. "Well, you are just like your uncle Max."

I narrow my gaze on him. "Take that back," I hiss.

"No. He gave up Lake, you know. She went back home. You're doing the same," he tells me, stepping out of Mum's arms. "I'll tell you the same thing I told him. We are Carter's. We don't give up, and we fight for what we want."

"I'm not giving up," I grit out.

"Sounds that way to me," he retorts.

My entire body tenses. "I'm not."

"Then go and babysit those kids while she goes out on a date. Keep telling yourself it's me who pushed these feelings onto you. Hide what you really want. You've been doing it for a while."

"What is that supposed to mean?" I screech.

"You moved out because you wanted 'peace', yet we all know you've regretted it ever since. You missed us, missed your family, missed the noise that comes with being surrounded by love. Yet your stubborn arse stayed there or used Lily's pad as an excuse for company."

"I did not," I deny.

Mum sighs. "Honey, you really did. You want this. You want Amelia."

"I'm happy being single."

Dad snorts with disgust. "No, you aren't. You have been older than your years since the minute you could walk. You bought a house, and started up a business—hell, you started your driving lessons way before any of your cousins. And yet, none of it was enough. You want more."

"No," I deny, breathing heavily. I hadn't come for this.

"Yes, Maddox." I go to leave, and he growls low under his breath. "You let her get away, and you are a fool."

I stop in the doorway, my nostrils flaring as I glance over my shoulder at Dad. "I'm not going to let her get away. I'm a Carter. I'm going after what I want."

"That'a boy," Dad booms as I head out the door.

TWENTY-SEVEN

AMELIA

A GENTLE BREEZE BLOWS THROUGH my open window as I get ready. My anxiety and nerves have made showering pointless. I've already rolled on deodorant three times.

I'll babysit.

Those words are carved into my brain. I was stupid to believe he'd fight for me, for us. It cemented the realisation that he doesn't see me as more than a friend. I can't fault him for that. I was stupid to hold on to the hope that he did.

I'll babysit.

I close my eyes as I drop down on the end of my bed, glancing down at my black cotton trousers.

I'm going on a date. Yes, granted it isn't with someone I have a connection with, but it still feels real. The nerves are real.

It's for the best. Maddox made it perfectly clear that we are just friends. And I cherish that friendship. He has done more for me than anyone else, other than my family, has ever done. He has been there and truly listened. I can't lose that. But I also have to come to terms with the fact that we will only ever be friends. And going on this date is the start I need.

There's a light knock on the door, bringing me out of my downcast thoughts. "Come in," I call out, sliding my feet into my ankle boots.

Mum pops her head around the door, smiling wide. "You ready? It's nearly six and you have to get there."

I stand, grabbing my bag off the bed. She's right. When Nolan text me in the week, it was to confirm meeting arrangements. Since I didn't feel comfortable with him coming to the house, I told him I'd meet him there. The restaurant is a ten-minute drive, plus the time it will take for me to find a parking space. "Is Maddox here?"

Mum steps further into the room, checking behind her quickly to see if anyone's there. "I like Maddox, I do, but are you sure about leaving him with the kids?"

I stare at her, bewildered. "Earlier you couldn't have been more excited."

"That was before he came back and looked like he was ready to pass out. Jasmine's movie just finished. When the prince and princess got married, he bolted off the sofa like he had a stick up his arse."

"Mum," I scold lightly, unable to keep the amusement off my face.

"He's sat down there eating all the junk food."

"He's good with them, Mum. Hell, for someone who was petrified of kids and didn't like them, he does better than me."

"Okay, okay," she concedes, then pauses, scanning me from head to toe. "Oh, sweetie, you look beautiful."

I glance down at my plain trousers, scrunching my nose up. They're all I have and are the only bottoms that go with my purple silk halter neck. Mum bought me a beautiful red dress, but it seemed too formal to wear for a dinner date, so I decided to wear the top she bought with a pair of trousers I already had stored in my wardrobe.

"I don't know. It feels weird," I admit, twisting the infinity necklace around my neck.

She cups my cheek after brushing my curled hair over my shoulder. "It suits you, darlin'. Now come on. Let's get you moving. I have to get back to your father. He booked us tickets."

I grip her wrist when she turns to leave, taking a deep breath. "Thank you," I declare, my throat tight with emotion.

She scans my face, her brows pulling together. "Whatever for?"

"For being my mum. For loving me. For pushing me when I was close to giving up. For being you."

Her eyes begin to tear up as she takes a step forward. "Always for my girl." She leans in, kissing me on the cheek. "Now, have fun, and call me to let me know how it goes."

I nod when she steps back. "I will."

I follow her down the stairs and into the front room, my heart racing when I hear Maddox's voice.

I'll babysit.

I inhale before exhaling slowly. Just because he didn't hesitate to say it, didn't care that I was going on a date, doesn't mean I should let it ruin my night.

Maddox shoots up from the sofa, gawking at me. "Amelia."

"Mummy, you look pretty," Jasmine sings, dazedly looking up at me.

"Thank you, baby."

"I need to talk to you," Maddox blurts out, before his gaze goes to the door, just as there's a knock.

"I'll get it," Mum calls out.

"What did you want to talk about?" I ask, placing my bag on the arm of the sofa.

"Honey, it's Nolan," Mum calls out.

"Nolan?" I repeat, staring in shock. I glance at the clock above the fireplace, seeing I'm not late.

"Amelia," Maddox calls.

"I need to go see what's going on," I tell him, just as Asher begins to stir.

Maddox looks conflicted, but in the end, my son wins out. While he heads over to pick him up, I head to the door.

I sidle up next to Mum, smiling at Nolan, who looks sharp in his two-piece suit. I'm glad he opted for no tie, because then I would have definitely been underdressed. He's good looking in a nerdy kind of way. His has a sharp jaw, brown slick hair that's gelled into style, and the most piercing blue eyes I have ever seen. They're just like his mum's.

"Nolan, I thought we agreed to meet at the restaurant? Did I miss a call or text?" I ask, glancing behind me when I hear Maddox approaching.

"I know. I know. But it didn't feel right meeting you there, so I thought I'd surprise you. I got your address off my mum."

"That is so sweet of you, Nolan," Mum announces, before pressing a kiss to my cheek. "Speak to you later, honey."

"Bye, Mum."

"I'm sorry, have I messed up plans?" he asks, glancing from Mum to me.

I wave him off, pushing my annoyance about him being here aside. "No, no. Of course not. Let me get my bag and we can go."

"Hello," Maddox rumbles, rocking Asher in his arms.

The look on his face has my feet freezing in place. I have never seen him look so… so angry. Or at least, that's how it's coming across. I bend down to Jasmine, whispering, "Can you get my bag off the sofa, please?"

She nods, racing back inside.

"Nolan, this is Maddox. Maddox, Nolan."

"Is this your little one?" Nolan asks, pushing up on his toes to see him.

I force a smile and take the bag Jasmine hands me. "It is."

"He is adorable. I just want to eat him up."

Maddox steps back, holding Asher closer. "You want to eat him?" he asks, horrified.

"I didn't mean literally. I like babies."

Maddox hisses under his breath. "You *like* babies?"

"Not like that," he rushes out, glancing at me briefly with a pale face. "Stop twisting my words."

Maddox holds his hands up, giving Nolan a pitying stare. "I'm not twisting anything."

"Who are you again?" Nolan asks, his cheeks getting colour now.

"He's a friend," I interrupt, pushing Maddox out of the way so I can step out onto the front step.

"He sleeps over," Jasmine declares.

Nolan glances from Maddox to me, his brow puckered into a frown. "I thought you were single. Mum said—"

My eyes widen. "I am. I am. He sleeps on the sofa."

"And in her bed," Jasmine sniggers, and Maddox chuckles.

I turn my back to Nolan, glaring at him. "Why don't you take the kids inside, Maddox, and I'll see you later. All the information you need is on the fridge. If you have any questions, call me or call my mum."

He nods, still staring over my shoulder. "Where are you taking her?"

"Maddox," I quietly call under my breath.

Nolan clears his throat. "I'll go wait in the car."

Once he's out of earshot, I turn and narrow my gaze on Maddox. "What are you doing?" I hiss out.

"He's not your type," he states.

"You don't even know what my type is."

"I know it's not him," he retorts. "I mean, 'I like babies'. Does he want to be on a register someday?"

"Maddox," I cry out quietly. "Please, stop. He's a family friend's son. I can assure you, he's harmless. Please, this is hard enough."

Something flashes in his eyes before he closes them briefly, letting out a sigh. When he opens them, his pupils darken. "I'm sorry."

"Thank you," I reply, before bending down and kissing Jasmine on the forehead. "Be good for Maddox."

She places a hand over her chest. "I promise."

I let out a breath and lean over, kissing Asher on the head. "See you soon, little man."

I take a step back when Maddox's voice stops me. "Don't I get one?"

I stagger, shakily turning to face him. "W-what?"

He holds his free hand up, grinning. "I'm joking. Have fun."

"Y-yeah, thanks," I murmur, shaking away the turmoil going on inside of me.

I head down the path towards where Nolan is standing, waiting for me. "Amelia?" Maddox calls out.

I stop, my heart in my chest as I turn around. Something inside of me is hoping he'll ask me to stay, tell me not to go.

"You look really beautiful tonight."

I give him a nod, tucking a strand of hair behind my ear. "Thank you."

My legs feel like jelly as I head back down the path, forcing a smile to Nolan. I try to steel my nerves, but on the inside, all I want to do is run back to the house and ask, *Why can't I be enough?*

Why can't he want me?

Half hour in his presence, I began to relax. An hour in, and I was laughing and joking around. It's now hour two, and we've eaten our starter and main and gotten to know each other. I've met his sister, who owns the restaurant, and she was a blast.

All in all, I'm enjoying myself. All that tension from earlier seems ridiculous now I'm in his company. He's smart and kind. A little nerdy, but I like it. He's fun to be around.

It's also a nice change. Cameron and I didn't do anything like this, so technically, this is my first date. It's nice to be treated.

Nolan places his drink down on the beer mat, a soft smile playing on his lips. "I just want to say sorry again if I made you uncomfortable earlier. I thought you were just being polite about meeting me here."

I wave him off, placing my Coke down on the mat. "Don't be. I was just being paranoid. I've never been set up on a date like this, or any date."

He lets out a dry laugh. "I swear, my mum would have me married with kids by now if she could."

"You don't want those things?"

"I do. But I also want it to be on my terms," he explains. "What about you? Mum said you broke up with your ex nearly a year ago. You've got a new baby. It must be hard on your own."

My lips tip down. "It is and it isn't. It's the best kind of hard because you are constantly rewarded. I have two amazing children. It makes up for the hard work and stress you go through."

"I get that," he replies.

"What about you? You said your job is taxing, so what do you do to wind down?"

He grins, flashing his pearly whites. "I'm boring. Honestly."

I chuckle, leaning forward. "No, c'mon, you have to tell me now."

He groans through a chuckle. "Promise you won't laugh?"

I place my hand over my heart. "Promise."

"Just remember, I said I was boring," he warns me. "I like to read SYFY. By the time I get back from the office, I'm mostly too wired to do much else. If I do have time off, I spend it with family and friends."

It's funny how kind of perfect he is for me. So far, we have a few things in common with each other. Sadly, the one thing we don't is attraction, but this is only the first date. I don't get the vibe that he likes me in that way either, so it's mutual.

"That's not boring. That seems practical."

He tugs at his shirt collar as he clears his throat. "Um, what about the guy at your place? What's going on there?"

My breath hitches. "Nothing is going on there."

"Are you sure? Because he didn't seem happy about you going on a date," he tells me, arching an eyebrow.

I shrug, swirling the paper straw around my drink. "He's just a friend."

"He seems more than a friend," he tells me, and I hear a hint of something else in his voice.

I tilt my head up. "What makes you say that?"

His gaze flicks over my shoulder. "Because he's just barged past the hostess with your kids in tow."

"W-what?" I rush out, spinning around in my chair. My eyeballs bug out at the sight of him holding Asher to his chest and Jasmine holding his hand. "Oh my God."

"Mummy," Jasmine calls out, grinning. Her T-shirt is inside out, and she has on pyjama bottoms instead of jeans or a skirt.

I push back in my chair and get up, feeling the blood rush from my face. "Is everything okay?"

Maddox's brows pinch together. "No, it's bloody not."

I rear back at his harsh voice. The kids look fine, but still… "What's happened?"

"Why didn't you tell me you had an Xbox?"

I gape at him for a moment, before answering, "Please tell me you didn't come all the way down here and interrupt my date to ask me why I have an Xbox."

He pats Asher's back, ducking his head a little. "Yes and no. You've been gone a while and we were getting worried."

I pinch the bridge of my nose. "Worried about what?"

He glares over at Nolan. "I'm allowed to be worried."

"Maddox," I warn.

"No," he bursts out, causing Asher to jump. "I'm home all night with the kids while you come out to this fancy-arse restaurant and you can't even answer your phone."

I grab my bag to get my phone. When I pull it out, I see I have ten missed calls from Maddox. I inwardly groan. I forgot to put it back on loud after Asher woke up from his nap. "Maddox, I'm fine."

I glance around the restaurant, noticing a few people watching on. Maddox sniffles. "We've been worried sick all night. I was going out of my mind. The kids were going out of their minds."

"Oh my," a woman whispers from close by.

My cheeks and neck heat as I fiddle with the hem of my shirt. People are staring with judging eyes. "Maddox, we don't need to do this here. Why don't you take the kids home and I'll meet you back there?"

"Why?" he asks distractedly, reaching for the bread roll on the table. His eyes widen. "This is good bread."

"Excuse me, but kids aren't allowed in here at this time," Nolan's sister, Hetty, announces, walking up to the table.

"I'm sorry," I rush out, but I notice Nolan leaning down and saying something to her. "I can't believe you've done this, Madz," I hiss out.

"Done what?"

"You've ruined my date," I snap at him.

He snorts. "Like it was serious. You aren't even in his league. You're too hot for someone like him. And I bet you're bored as hell. You're welcome."

"For what?" I cry out, failing to keep my voice low.

"For saving you from boredom."

"Hey," Nolan retorts.

I'm too angry to even answer Maddox. Frustrated and feeling tears well up in my eyes, I turn to Nolan. "I'm so sorry, Nolan. Is it okay if I bail early?"

His smile warms my heart. "Go ahead. Maybe we can do this again another time?"

"No, she won't," Maddox answers, lifting my bag.

"Maddox," I hiss out.

"Uh oh," Jasmine whispers. "You are in trouble."

I turn to Nolan, forcing a smile. "I'd love to," I answer. "Let me pay for my food."

He waves me off. "It's fine. It was on the house anyway."

Maddox snorts. "Can't even pay for food."

"It was my gift," Hetty retorts, her gaze hard on Maddox.

I grab his free arm, taking Jasmine's in my other hand. "I'm really sorry about this. I'm going to take all three kids home."

"And put me to bed?" Maddox teases, winking down at me. I'm too mad to find his comment amusing.

"I'm going to strangle you."

"She likes it rough," he calls out, and I groan, pulling him towards the door. I'll apologise later to Nolan and hopefully fix the mess Maddox has made.

Because as reluctant as I was to go on this date, I'm glad I did. He's a good person, a good guy, and he doesn't deserve to be treated like that.

TWENTY-EIGHT

MADDOX

YOU KNOW THE EXACT MOMENT you fuck up. It's like your insides twist and your stomach turns like you've driven over a hill too fast. It's a sixth sense. Yet, you do nothing to correct it. Or at least, I'm not. But that's more out of self-preservation and years of watching my dad and uncles get out the shitter with the wives.

Which is why I know I'm six feet deep in shit. Luckily, I know when to keep my mouth shut.

The silence was deafening on the ride home and worse when we got inside. She hasn't spoken one word to me since we left the restaurant, and it's beginning to make me want to crawl the walls.

I've seen my mum in moods, my sister, hell, even my cousins, but none of them, and I mean none, have ever made me feel like this. It's torture in itself, and all I can do is sit here and wait for her to explode.

Because it is coming.

I can feel it like a storm brewing. And I'm man enough to admit I'm scared shitless.

There is nothing worse than a woman's silence.

She's currently stomping around upstairs, putting the kids to bed. I'm not even sure she realises moving around like that is not going to soothe the little monsters to sleep. But telling her that seems like a death wish.

I don't regret anything I did tonight. Maybe. Kind of. I guess I could have done it a little differently, but in my defence, I was going out of my mind. What was just over two hours felt like ten to me. My eyes barely drifted away from the clock, watching the minutes tick by. I kept wondering what she was doing; if he would try it on with her; or if she needed me.

I never get like this.

She doesn't want a guy like that; she wants me. And now she can have me. We're perfect together.

I'm giving her all of me, something I have never given another chick before. More importantly, I want her. I don't want anyone else to get my dinners, to get my laughs, to get my cuddles. I don't want anyone else to have the bond I share with the kids, that I share with Amelia. I don't want them to have Amelia. I want her. I need her. She is mine. And if I have to play dirty to get her, I will.

I just have to get out of my earlier spectacle.

I knew going to the restaurant was a bad idea. I talked myself out of it three times before finally giving in and going. I had hoped she would take one look at me, then fall to her knees and beg me to take her home. I guess bringing the kids, having Jasmine wearing her clothes inside out, and yelling crap, put her off. But I can make all that okay once I tell her how I'm feeling.

She stomps into the living room, picking up toys as she goes, before forcefully throwing them into the basket tucked under her arm.

"Amelia," I call out softly, standing from the sofa.

She ignores me, cleaning up the mess I made from changing Asher earlier, her movements harsh and filled with anger.

"Amelia?"

She throws the dirty clothes onto the sofa, her breath ragged as she turns to face me. I flinch, holding my hands up.

"No, Maddox. Just no. You've done a lot of crap, most I find endearing, but tonight you embarrassed me. You ruined a perfectly good date, and for what? What did you hope to achieve? If you didn't want to babysit you could have called my mum to come and get them."

"I didn't mean to embarrass you, and I love looking after the kids," I murmur. "I was just—"

"Being you, I know," she snaps. "You need to leave."

Straightening, I take a step forward. "No, you don't understand—"

"No, I don't understand. I don't understand how after weeks of friendship, of letting you in and telling you my insecurities, you'd do this to me tonight. You must have known what a big step this was for me to take. I don't get why you would do it. I truly don't."

"Because it should have been me," I blurt out, lowering my voice when it rises. "It should have been me you went out with."

"W-what?" she stammers, gawking at me.

I walk over to her, placing my hands on her cheeks. "I want you."

"Maddox," she whispers, gripping my biceps.

A low, pleasant hum warms my blood. This isn't like the times before when I had her in my grasp. It's like a barrier has been removed and opened me up to her. It's like seeing her for the first time.

"I couldn't let you be with him a moment longer," I murmur, closing my eyes as I tilt my head down.

She palms my face, pushing me away. When I glance at her, I don't expect her to be staring at me in disbelief.

"W-what?"

"I want you," I tell her, taking a step closer again. I need her in my arms.

"No," she whispers, taking one back.

"I don't want anyone else taking you out. I don't want anyone else to be with you. *I* want to be with you."

Something flashes behind her eyes before her entire body tenses, and she grits out, "Get out!"

"W-what?" I reply, finding it hard to believe she wants me to go.

Maybe she didn't hear the part where I said I wanted to be with her?

And she did try to kiss me.

"I said: get out," she hisses. "Get out!"

"I just told you I'm into you and you're telling me to get out?" I ask, shocked by her reaction. "I know you want me too. You were going to kiss me. I could feel you melting into my arms."

She shakes her head, tears gathering in her eyes. "I can't believe you'd do this to me," she whispers brokenly.

"Do what? Want you? We are perfect together."

"You don't like me, Maddox. You are just scared of losing me. You've made it perfectly clear time and time again that you only see me as a friend."

I run my fingers through my hair, letting out a frustrated breath. I knew that would backfire eventually. "No, that is not it at all, Amelia. I swear to you. I want you. I want you so goddamn bad it hurts inside. I've never wanted anyone like I want you. I lo—"

Her expression is livid. "No! You only want me because you were scared someone else would. You just admitted it yourself," she breathes out.

"That's not true, Amelia, and you know it."

"Oh? So this isn't you being scared of losing another friend like you lost Lily?"

"This has nothing to do with Lily," I tell her adamantly.

"It has everything to do with Lily. I was just a replacement, remember," she argues, pointing at me. She forces out a laugh. "I'm so fucking stupid."

"Amelia," I breathe out, struggling to find words.

My heart stutters when she glances at me, her expression drawn in agony. "You are cruel to do this to me, to us. It's clear I like you—who wouldn't. But to play on that just to keep me in your life… no, Maddox."

"No," I reply hoarsely. "You're twisting it. That isn't what this is at all. I know what I've said in the past, but I'm serious."

"Then what is it, Maddox? Because from my point of view, it seems like you've done it because you're worried someone else will snatch me up. Convenient how after weeks of spending time together, you wait until tonight to say all of this."

"Of course I'm worried someone will snatch you up. I'm petrified. But that isn't my reason for this revelation. It's you. It's always been you," I plead, my father's words coming back to bite me in the arse.

'Some girl will knock him on his arse, and she'll reject him. He'll regret ever being a player, and will come crying to his mum for help.'

He was right. He was so right. The realisation of that is so strong I struggle to find my step, nearly colliding with the coffee table.

"You said you didn't do relationships," she tells me, her eyes glassy with tears.

"I don't. You're different," I tell her, my voice low, almost pleading.

She turns her back to me, forcing out a laugh. "I should have seen this coming. Why me? Why?"

"What are you talking about?"

She turns to face me, and I'm taken aback by the tears running down her cheeks. "You have had so many chances, Maddox. Hell, we've had moments where I could have sworn you were going to kiss me. But you did nothing. You said nothing."

"Because I didn't know how I was feeling then. I was confused," I argue.

"I think you still are. You can't play with women's feelings like this. I'm not a toy, Maddox."

"I don't think you are a toy," I grit out. "God, this isn't going as planned."

She laughs dryly. "How did you picture it going? You waited until I was on a date and embarrassed me."

"Amelia," I whisper, wondering where I went wrong. How did it get to this point?

"Please, leave," she orders, not meeting my gaze.

I know I'm not going to win this fight, not now, not this second. I also don't want her to feel trapped or pushed, not after everything she's been through.

I stop when I reach the door, resting my head against the doorframe. "I never meant for this, you know."

"I know, but you still hurt me tonight," she whispers.

"I don't mean that," I tell her, looking over my shoulder at her. "I meant falling in love with you. You're right. I never wanted a girlfriend. I didn't want to commit. But you came into my life and you wormed your way inside."

"That's friendship, Maddox. That's not romantic love," she tells me softly.

I shake my head. "If you could feel what I feel right now, you'd know that isn't true," I admit, letting it pour out. "Please, just give me a chance."

"I can't," she tells me, and it comes out like a broken plea.

"Why? Why can't you? I know you feel the same way."

"That may be true, but I'll never be able to trust that *you* do. You want the idea of me. You want what you had with Lily, and you don't want the same mistake to happen. Because that's what I was. I was just a replacement of the friend you lost. That was the deal, remember."

"Please—"

"I've had my heart broken and hurt too much, Maddox. I'm not going through that again," she tells me, running her fingers over Asher's blanket. "Can you please leave."

"I will," I whisper, gripping the handle on the door. "And, Amelia?" She looks up, tears streaming down her face. "You were never a replacement. You were more than just some deal. You were you. And looking back, you've always been more than a friend."

I leave at the sound of her broken sobs, clenching my fists at my sides to stop myself from going back in there.

For years I played the field, fucked who I fancied and fancied who I fucked. It was nothing more, nothing less. It wasn't meaningful, it wasn't cheap. It just was.

Dad wasn't the only one who swore a girl would knock me off my feet, but it was only him who said it like a prayer. It was like he knew it would come true. And it has. Only I wasn't just knocked off my feet. My world has slipped off its axis.

I jerk to a stop at the end of my path, noticing my dad sitting on my doorstep. "You fucked it up, didn't you?" he states, pity filling his eyes.

"I guess I'm predictable," I spit out.

"No, you're a Carter, and we always fuck up in some way. But we make it right."

"She didn't even take me seriously," I admit.

"Because you've never taken anything but work seriously. I'm not saying it's a bad thing. I love who you are, who you've become. I wouldn't change that."

I twirl the keys around my finger, forcing out a laugh. "That's basically what she said. I've done nothing but tell her we're friends, that I never want a relationship."

"And you told her that you do now?" he asks, brushing dirt off his hands and onto his jeans as he gets up.

"Yes. No. Yes. It was intense over there. She hates me, and I don't blame her."

Just as I finish, the music comes blaring from next door, playing some rock band I've never heard of. Dad's jaw clenches as he glances in that direction. "What do you want to do? Do you want to go get shit faced, go inside and be alone—what? I'm here for whatever you need."

"Mum ordered you to, didn't she?" I tease.

He scoffs, before his shoulders drop, and he lets out a sigh. "Yeah, but let's not go there."

I lean against the car. "I don't know what to do. I've not only fucked up my chances with her, but I've just lost her as a friend too. She couldn't even look at me."

He claps a hand down on my shoulder. "Then fight for her. Show her you aren't some small-minded man-whore who only thinks with his stomach and dick. Let her see how serious you are."

I narrow my gaze on him. "She didn't say I was small-minded."

Dad smirks, shrugging. "Just show her."

"Fuck that," Max barks out, and I startle, turning around to find him and Landon leaning against my truck.

"How long have you been there?" I ask, gritting my teeth.

"Long enough to know dipshit gave you shit advice," he retorts.

"Fuck you, Max," Dad barks.

Max rolls his eyes at Dad before turning his attention to me. "You need the big gesture. The one that will have her telling people for years to come."

"I think he did that when he delivered Asher," Landon murmurs.

"He's right."

Max snorts. "That was child's play. I'm talking about something romantic, something that screams commitment."

"He watches a few Hallmark movies, and he thinks he's Cupid," Dad mutters beside me.

My eyes widen as I stare at my uncle. "Are you trying to get me to propose to her, because, dude, it will end up with me stabbed in the chest," I tell him. "Plus, I'm not ready for marriage."

"Fucking hell," he breathes out. "I'm surrounded by idiots."

"Max, just spit it out, for God's sake, so we can go to the pub," Dad barks.

"Jesus. Chill, Mally," he replies, before saying, "Open up to her. You need to find the right words, the right gesture, *the romantic* gesture."

"You've said that, but what are those things?"

His face scrunches up. "Do I look like the love doctor? Figure that shit out yourself."

I glance to Landon with nothing else left to lose. "What would you do?"

"I wouldn't have fucked it up."

I arch an eyebrow. "Do you need me to run through yours and Paisley's love affair."

He sighs, pushing off my truck. "Figure out what you truly want, what she means to you, what you picture for your future. Don't let her go. Once you've figure that out, you'll know exactly what to do." He shoves his hands in his leather jacket. "Now, are we finished with the heart to heart, because it's making me uncomfortable."

"When did you get so romantic?" Dad questions, smirking at Landon.

Max claps Landon on the shoulder. "Gets it from his dad."

The music next door gets louder, and I swear I hear Dad's knuckles crack when he clenches his fists. "Can we please do something about those neighbours."

Max rubs his hands together. "I have the perfect thing in my car."

"It better not be glitter," I murmur, pushing away my thoughts of Amelia. Maybe this will help clear my head.

"I need you guys to distract them. I'm going to plant some things inside their home. They'll be gone by the end of the week."

"How—" Dad begins.

"You don't want to know," I tell him, following Max down the path to his car that's parked up a bit from mine.

He pushes the boot up, grinning like a mad man. I gape into the back of the boot. "Why do you have all this in here?" I question.

Inside is a bucket of waterbombs, four guns, and a bag filled with things I don't want to know about.

"Why do you have handcuffs, Dad?" Landon asks as he lifts a pair out of the bag. He drops them quickly, frowning. "Never mind."

"They aren't my main set, don't worry," Max murmurs, bending further into the car and grabbing another bag. He pulls it to the edge of the car before reaching in for something else. He comes back with a black jacket. While he shoves it on, I pick up a gun, holding the handmade device in wonder. They have never let us play with these before; said they were too strong.

"I'm not going to ask why you have all this just lying around in your boot," Dad murmurs, reaching for a gun.

Max hands us each a bag. "Be careful with those. They have my new concoction in. They have glue inside, which will be a bitch for them to get off."

"How is that going to burst?" Landon asks.

Max just looks at his son like he's stupid. "Because I'm a genius. It's all about the right pressure when blowing them up."

"If you say so," I retort, carefully putting the bag over my shoulder.

Max stares at the bag a moment longer. "Maybe don't burst one on yourselves. Although the glue eventually comes off, it can take days for the smell to wash away."

"Max," Dad warns.

Max nods like he's silently agreeing with himself. "Malik, you take the back. Landon, go hide in those bushes over there. You, Madz, climb up that tree. It's the best vantage point."

Before any of us can argue, he's gone. I turn to my dad, clutching the gun higher in my arms. "Shall we just go?"

"Move it," Max hisses from somewhere.

Dad groans. "Let's just get this over with. You know how he gets if he doesn't get what he wants."

My mind flashes back to the time we went abroad. There was a storm, and Max, not being able to go swimming, lost it. He went down into the cafeteria, and I'm not sure what happened, but the next minute we were having to relocate to another hotel.

I give Dad a nod before jogging off to my designated spot. Landon stops midway to his spot to give me a leg-up. Just as I'm swinging my leg over the thickest branch, Landon is diving behind some bushes, his dark hair popping up from the branches.

"This is so fucking stupid," I whisper to myself.

Another five minutes pass, and I begin to think nothing is going to happen. Just as I'm about to pull my phone out to call Dad, screams erupt from inside the house, the music turning down a notch.

"Who was that?" someone yells.

A girl begins to squeal. "Oh my God, something touched me."

"Fuck! The television just switched on."

The music suddenly stops, and I swear, you can hear a pin drop it's gone that silent. "Where did the new music player go?"

"Alexa?" Kayne calls out, and I chuckle to myself, wondering if he's waiting for a reply.

My fingers tense around the trigger, and I lift the gun a little, aiming it towards the door. As soon as the door flies open, I begin to shoot, pelting the glue bombs at anyone who leaves the house. When the filter is empty, I load more inside, grinning when Landon takes up my leave, shooting at them.

"Back inside, back inside," Cassie screams. "Go out the back."

"They are so fucked," I whisper.

"Oh my God, who is doing this," a woman yells, and I hear tears in her voice. "They've ruined my spliff."

"Can you smell that?" Kayne calls out, sounding close to the front of the house.

"I have had it with that fucking neighbour," Cassie screams.

"There's a ghost in here," a lad declares.

"There are no fucking ghosts in here. It's that fucking neighbour," Cassie cries out. "Oh my God, what is that?"

A throat clears below the tree, and I startle, slipping from my perch. I quickly grab the branch, hanging off it, my eyes widening when I see the two cops below. One female, one male.

"Evening," I greet, smirking.

"Maddox," PC Marker greets.

I squint through the darkness, and groan when I see it's really him. "Oh shit!"

"Get down, Maddox."

"I swear, this wasn't my idea," I defend, landing on the balls of my feet.

"We came about a noise complaint," he tells me once I've straightened my jacket. "Instead, we find you up the tree and your cousin in the bush shooting at the house we were called out to."

"And you decide today, of all days, to come and actually follow through with the noise complaint?" I mutter sarcastically.

"Arrest him!" Cassie screeches, charging out of the house.

"He should be arresting you," I bite out.

"You've destroyed my home," she declares, and I inwardly groan. It was hardly a palace to begin with.

"What is that smell?" the female officer asks, covering up her nose.

"It was him," Cassie accuses.

I smirk at the female officer. "You can sniff me if you want, baby. I promise I smell nothing like that."

"You—"

"Step back," PC Marker warns before turning back to me. "We are going to need to take statements."

"That's fine," I tell him, tugging the bag behind me out of sight.

PC Marker notices and narrows his gaze. "Show me what's in the bag."

"You really don't want to know," I warn him, wincing when Cassie's screeching gets higher. Luckily, her son has a brain cell because he holds her back from attacking me.

PC Marker reaches for the bag, gripping the handle. I pull it towards me, and in a game of tug of war, PC Marker wins. The bag smacks against his chest, and two of the balloons explode all over him.

"Fuck," I hiss.

His jaw tight, eyes narrowed into slits, he takes a step towards me. "Turn around!"

"Fucking Max," I grouch.

TWENTY-NINE

AMELIA

I HOP INTO THE LIVING ROOM, struggling to get my shoe on at the same time. I hiss out a breath when I trip over the changing bag, thankfully landing on the sofa and not on the floor.

This was not the way I hoped this morning would go.

"Jasmine, get your shoes on," I yell.

"I am," she yells back, before she comes storming into the living room.

I scan her attire and inwardly groan. "Jasmine, I said to put something warm on. Nanny wants to take you out."

"I want to wear this," she tells me, twirling in her Elsa dress.

I close my eyes, fighting back tears. I'm running late, and I'm exhausted, not only from the commotion going on outside last night, but because I kept replaying Maddox's words over in my head. I couldn't get a wink of sleep and spent the entire night tossing and turning. At around six this morning, I dozed off after feeding Asher and slept through my alarm.

I don't have time to get her changed.

"Get your coat," I order.

Her bottom lip trembles. "Are you mad, Mummy?"

I let out a breath before turning to her, forcing a smile. "No, baby. Mummy is just really late," I tell her.

I quickly grab the changing bag, my keys, and handbag before bending down for the car seat Asher is strapped into.

"I'm ready," Jasmine declares, shoving her arms through the sleeves of her coat.

"Let's go."

The sky is clear, and the birds are chirping into the morning breeze as we race out the door. The keys slip out of my hand as I reach back to shut the door. "Fuck!" I hiss out quietly.

"Don't speak to me!" Maddox yells, and I straighten up, swinging around to face the street.

He's just getting out of his mum's car, but it isn't me or her his comment is directed at. It's his uncle, who is sitting on the back of his truck.

I'm frozen, my feet glued in place at seeing him. My heart constricts at the sight of his rugged yet handsome appearance.

It has only been one night, and I miss him.

But I'm angry with him more.

Max jumps down from the truck, grimacing. "It's not my fault you got caught."

"You didn't exactly take responsibility either," Maddox snaps. "They were rough."

"Don't be such a baby," Max retorts.

Maddox throws his hands up. "I'm going to get you back for this."

"Look, I'm—"

"No, Uncle Max. No."

"Max, if you get my son arrested again, I will personally make your life a living hell; starting with cutting off your home baked goods," Harlow snaps from inside the car.

"You wouldn't?" Max gasps out.

"I would," she replies, before turning to her son. "I'll see you later for dinner."

He gives her a chin lift as she drives off, leaving dust in the wind. I jerk into action when our gazes meet. He tenses, taking a step towards me.

I quickly heft Asher up my arm, making my way to the car.

"Maddox," Jasmine calls, racing towards him.

"Jasmine," I call out.

She ignores me, waiting for Maddox to meet her on this side of the road. I finish strapping Asher in, double checking he's secure before closing the door.

"Jasmine," I call out.

Jasmine puffs out a breath before tilting her head up to Maddox. "Do you like my dress?" she asks him.

"You look like a princess, Jaz," he replies, his voice low, and the pain I can hear, hurts.

I close my eyes, breathing through my nose when it begins to sting with tears. "Jasmine," I croak out. "We're late."

"Amelia," Maddox calls.

"Jasmine," I demand, pulling open my car door. I can't look at him right now, let alone talk to him. It's killing me inside.

My feelings for him were crushed the minute he was selfish enough to use them against me. He doesn't want me romantically. He just wants the idea of me.

And that hurts the most. That I'm not enough. That I'm just a consolation prize.

"C'mon, Jaz, we're late," I tell her, helping her into the back of the car.

"Mummy? Are you mad at Maddox?"

"Jasmine," I groan, clipping in her belt.

"But, Mum—" she whines.

"Please, Jasmine," I plead.

She takes one look at my face and relaxes back into her seat, her tiny little face scrunched up in a frown.

"Amelia," Maddox calls again.

"I'm late," I tell him, sliding into the driver's side. I slam the door shut and clip in my belt.

My entire body shakes as I begin to pull out of the driveway. The whole world seems to move in slow motion as I slowly pull out of the driveway, briefly making eye contact with Maddox. He stands at the end of the drive, his shoulders hunched forward, his lip tipped down. Just seeing him like that has my heart yearning for him. It's like my world is spinning out of control and there is nothing I can do to stop it.

He's just one man.

One man who managed to break down my defences and open up my heart. He doesn't demand power over me, he gave me power. He doesn't see me as broken, but as someone who is whole. He doesn't see past the single mum, he embraces it, and yet it isn't *me* he wants.

He can't.

It's not even the family I can give him that he wants. He has enough family.

Which leads to more questions in my head. Does he really want more or is this his attempt to not lose another friend?

I glance away as I pull out into the road, tears burning the back of my nose. No, that look on his face meant nothing.

"Mummy, did Maddox do something bad?" Jasmine whispers, and when I glance through the rear-view mirror, her bottom lip trembles.

"No, baby, he didn't do anything wrong. I promise."

"Good, because he's my friend and I love him," she tells me.

"I know, sweetie."

"And I wish he was my daddy."

My breath hitches at those words. I can't answer her, too choked up. She is too young for this, too young to be hurt. Because even if I trust that Maddox wants more, there would be a time when it could end between us, and where would that leave her? Where would it leave Asher?

By the time I reach the care home, I'm a hormonal mess. Mum is waiting outside with Aunt Tracey, both looking concerned. I shut the car off and get out, slamming the door behind me. Seeing my mum, the one person in this world I can count on, who I know has my back through everything, I break. I burst into tears, clutching my stomach.

"Amelia," Mum cries, racing across the car park with Tracey in tow. "What on earth!"

"Nita, you get Amelia into the office and I'll take the kids to the T.V. room," Tracey whispers.

Mum supports my weight, and together we make it inside and through to the office. Once I'm sat down in the chair, Mum wastes no time in demanding I tell her what's wrong.

"Please, Amelia, I'm worried. Is it Cameron's mum and aunt again? Did they do something?"

I wipe at my tears, digging my fingers into my thighs. "No. No. I'm just tired," I admit.

"No, honey, this isn't just exhaustion."

I blink through my tears and tell her the truth. "It's Maddox. I think I've lost him."

"What? Why on earth would you think that? That boy loves you and those two children."

Her words only make me cry harder. "He ruined the date last night. He said he wanted to be with me."

"I don't understand why you're crying, sweetie."

"Because it's not real. He saw another man stepping in and panicked. He lost Lily—his cousin—to her husband, and I bet he saw the same thing happening with Nolan. So, to keep me, he made this rash decision. He had all evening to tell me not to go on that date, but he waited for me to go. He came to the restaurant and embarrassed me."

"I'm sure that's not the case," Mum replies, running her finger down my cheek.

I close my eyes at her touch. "We argued when we got back, and I kicked him out. Now I can't even look at him. He has done nothing but friend-zone me during our entire friendship, but now he wants more. How can I trust that?"

"This isn't about what he's said or him declaring he wants you."

My brows bunch together as I open my eyes and gape at her. "I'm sorry, what?"

"This is about trust. You are too scared to trust."

"Can you blame me?" I cry. "He said he didn't do relationships, that he liked variety and the single life. He has called me friend so many times that if I had a pound for each one, I'd be a millionaire. Now he wants me? Yeah, I don't believe that. Now our friendship is ruined, and I…"

"You love him," Mum finishes.

"No," I deny, looking away.

"He might have done those things, sweetie, but he's been more than that. He has stayed to get your son to sleep, he has bought you items you refused to splurge on, and he has been there for you and the kids. He has fixed what is broken inside the house. He got your daughter a bike. He built you the pan unit for your kitchen. He's been everything Cameron wasn't but everything you wished him to be. You love him."

"I think I've lost him," I cry out, wiping away my tears. "How can I trust this is what he wants now? I'll always wonder why. I don't think I can do that."

"Because Maddox doesn't do anything he doesn't want to do," Hope answers from the doorway.

I meet her gaze, hating the pity staring back at me.

"Hey, Hope," Mum greets.

"I saw the kids in the T.V. room and thought I'd come and check that everything is okay," Hope explains. "I don't know the full story, but I can promise that with all his immaturity and questionable behaviour, he is not someone who would string you along. He's too brutally honest. You and the kids mean the world to him."

I wipe at my eyes, shifting in my seat. "I'm not sure what to believe. All the times he mentioned staying single, he was adamant."

Hope rolls her eyes. "He's also adamant Tupac is alive. We let him roll with it," she replies softly. "Just hear him out, or at least think about it."

"And you can think about it while you are at home in bed," Tracey interrupts.

"W-what? I have work," I argue.

She shakes her head, her gaze soft and filled with kindness. "No. As of today you are going on paid leave for two weeks. I don't care what you say," she tells me when I open my mouth to interrupt. "You haven't recovered from giving birth. And I don't mean the actual birth, but the hormonal side that comes with it. You're all over the place. You're tired, stressed and beyond exhausted. It hurts, my girl."

"She's right," Mum continues. "You have taken on so much by yourself. Now you've let people in to help, I want you to take it easy, enjoy being a parent without any stress for a little while. Jasmine wants to go to the fair at the weekend. Take her."

"But I…I—"

"Honey, you look like you haven't slept in a week," Mum declares.

"And I bet that's another reason why this thing with Maddox has hit you so hard," Tracey explains.

"That, and he has been a rock for you," Hope interjects softly. "Thinking you've lost him has probably pushed you over the edge."

I wipe at my eyes. "I'm so tired. I'm tired of it all. I had all these expectations, all these notions of what I'd be like as a parent. But I'm failing. I'm failing at it all. And now the one person who I had that was mine is gone."

"He's not gone," Hope tells me.

"Then why does it feel like I've lost him?" I ask, meeting her gaze.

"Because you haven't processed what it means yet," she explains.

"You went through so much with Cameron, and although it doesn't seem like it right now, I can bet my house that this is about him. It's what he did to you. You are so sure no one will want you for you. And they do."

I scrub my hand down my face. "I can't even think about any of this right now."

"Go home. Get some sleep, and I'll be round later with the kids to cook you dinner."

I lean forward, hugging my mum. "I love you."

"I love you too."

I groan as my back protests when I stand. Tracey hands me my car keys. "Take care of yourself for us."

"I will, and I'm sorry for leaving you a staff member short."

Hope snorts. "Are you kidding? We've got this. We just want what's best for you."

After giving Tracey a short hug, I then move to Hope, pulling her into my arms. "I know I shouldn't ask this of you, but could you please not tell Maddox what happened."

"Of course I won't," she replies, hugging me a little tighter. "Why don't I walk you to your car?"

I give her a nod before saying goodbye to Mum and my aunt. As we head down the corridor, Hope turns to me. "He really does care for you."

I glance down at my shoes. "I know he does. But he can be impulsive. I'm not sure if what he wants is real or not."

"If it was for selfish reasons, he wouldn't be staying with you instead of going out with friends. He's cancelled on family meals, which he never does, and when he's with us, he does nothing but talk about you and the kids."

The wind blows my hair off my face when we step outside. "I-I can't talk about this."

She reaches for my bicep, giving it a gentle squeeze. "I understand. And if you do ever want to talk, I'm always here for you. I promise."

"Thank you, Hope."

"You're welcome. Now head home and get some rest."

"I will."

I make sure Tracey has all the kids' things and sigh with relief to see she has. Getting in the car, I let out a tired breath. She was right, I am exhausted. I'm exhausted from it, from weaving my way through this world to keep on living. It's hard. Life is hard.

And yet, I know once I've slept off this exhaustion, I'll have to start all over again. Another day, another fight.

It was easier with Maddox. I felt like I could take on anything.

Now… now I'm not sure I can handle one more thing.

THIRTY

MADDOX

I TWIST MY HEAD FROM LEFT TO right, cricking my neck. To keep busy, to keep my mind from going to Amelia or succumbing to the loneliness I feel without her, I've exhausted myself with work.

My men had long left to go have a beer or go home to their families. I just don't have anything to go back to, not anymore. It's strange how someone, in such a short amount of time, can change your perspective on life. I was happy before, I know it. And yet here I am, sweat trickling down my back, missing the times I had with Amelia; my nights with her and the kids. For me, with them I had never been happier.

She isn't answering her phone or replying to my messages. I'm too scared to go over there. I don't want to unsettle the kids or scare them if Amelia gets upset. The distance is killing me. If I can't get her to listen to me, what chance do I have of making this right?

Breathing hard, I lean against the reception counter. I miss her. I truly fucking miss her. And the kids.

I turn my back to the counter, sliding down the sleek wood, my arse hitting the cold concrete floor. I shove my knees to my chest, resting my elbows on my knees as I grip my hair.

I fucked up so bad and I don't know how to fix it. I don't know what the grand gesture is or what it means. Hell, I'm not even sure anything will work right now.

Going home to that empty house isn't an option. I stayed at Mum and Dad's last night after my neighbours' horror-filled screams rattled the paper-thin walls. I'm not sure what was going on over there, but whatever it was, it made me miss the loud music.

My phone alerts me of a message, and I tilt to the side, pulling my phone out of my back pocket. It's our family group chat.

Lake: Have any of you seen Max? He left last night with a bag and hasn't returned. I'm getting really worried. He's not answering his phone.

Landon: Mum, I've told you to stop worrying.

Hayden: Mum, he's right. He'll be back later and yapping on about how the aliens wanted his love juice or some shit. Did you get in touch with Liam to see if he's seen him?

Lake: I'm really worried.

Maverick: Did you check the police station?

Lake: Yes. He's not there, and when I asked them to double check, they said they weren't mistaken. They've had his picture on the door of every cell ever since he conned those officers to let him out and he ended up hacking into everyone's records.

Malik: Hospital?

Lake: Checked the closest three.

Mason: Mental institution? It wouldn't surprise me.

Lake: As soon as I said the name, she said he is not welcome there and put the phone down.

Hayden: It's Dad. He'll turn up. He needs feeding.

Liam: Um, I kind of threw out a note he left this morning. I thought he was just being a twat.

Lake: What did it say?????

Liam: For you not to worry that he's left you. He hasn't, and he ate all his food. And that it shouldn't take more than another night. He mentioned something about setting up the sound system.

I close my eyes. Fucking Max. He was responsible for the noises I heard coming from next door. I don't need anyone to confirm it. I can feel it in my gut.

Maddox: He's in my fucking loft.

Lake: What????

Hayden: Dude!!! Creepy.

Maddox: I thought I was hearing things, but now that you've mentioned the sound system, I think it was him. There have been some spooky sounds coming from next door.

Harlow: It would explain why your neighbours have been going out of their minds with fear. Didn't you say they were screaming last night?

Maddox: What should we do?

Lake: Nail your fucking loft shut because he'll be safer up there.

When I see her go offline, I chuckle to myself.

Landon: Anyone else feel awkward?

Maddox: Do you not care that your dad is missing?

Landon: It couldn't have happened to a better person.

Hayden: I'll remember to mention that to him.

Landon: Fuck! I was joking.

Malik: So, he's not missing?

Mason: I just cancelled the balloons.

Maverick: I cancelled the beer.

Myles: I knew I shouldn't have opened that whiskey.

Max: Guys, guys, guys! You don't have to pretend; I know you're secretly sobbing into your pillows.

Malik: With so much joy!

Max: I fucking hate you all.

Lake: ...

Max: Fuck!

Lake: ...

Maverick: You know it's bad if she's still typing.

Max: Double fuck!

Maddox: Someone bring the popcorn.

Max: I'm doing you a fucking favour, you traitorous bastard. Do you know how much money I've spent on cling film and glue? And let's not include the energy I've put in turning items upside down while they aren't looking or are asleep. Gluing the tele to the T.V. stand wasn't easy, you know. And I might lose that sound system. You kids are so ungrateful.

Landon: You got that cling film through bulk order thanks to me.

Malik: He's not a bastard.

Max: Not the point. And are you not going to comment on my brilliance?

Maddox: No, because that spooky ghost music was freaking me out.

Max: Ordered it off the internet. So authentic.

Lake: I am going to wring your fucking neck if you come home. I've been going out of my mind, worried you'd ended up in prison, or worse, the mental institution. You know what happened the last time you were there.

Lake: Did you know the police nearly arrested me for harassing a police officer? If it wasn't for Beau, I would be in a cell right now. I am cutting you off home baked meals for a month. I'm giving the kids all your snacks.

Lake: Including the hidden ones.

Max: ...

Lake: And no sex at all.
Hayden: Mum!
Landon: Kill me!
Liam: removed himself from the group chat.
Max: Fuck!!!!!!

I put my phone into my hoody when I hear someone heading inside. The floodlights light up the entire room, but the rest is blanketed in darkness. I rise to my feet, holding my hand up to cover my eyes.

"Lily," I murmur when she steps into view, her red coat wrapped around her. "What are you doing here? Does Jaxon know?"

"He's at his mum's," she tells me. "Mum told me what happened with Amelia. I wanted to come and see if you were okay. I was worried."

I rub the back of my neck. "What can I say, I fucked up."

Her gaze softens. "Nothing is ever fucked up."

I force out a laugh. "How can you, of all people, say that? I know you haven't forgiven me for what I did. I'm always fucking up."

She lets out a sigh before taking a look around the room. When she spots an old plastic crate, she heads over to it. Seeing what she's about to do, I pick it up, taking it back over to the counter.

She takes a seat, and I take my place back on the floor. "I don't hate you, Maddox. What you did hurt me, but I know you did it out of love. Was it right? No. Was it wrong? Absolutely. But it doesn't make you a bad person. And it all worked out in the end," she tells me, before her expression turns to hurt. "Is that why you didn't tell me what was going on with Amelia?"

I scrub a hand down my face. "No. I just haven't wanted to speak to anyone. I didn't want anyone to tell me, 'I told you so'."

"You make it sound like it's over."

I snort. "It never really began. She doesn't trust me, and why should she?"

She reaches forward, grabbing my hand. "Because you are the best person I know. You were my rock. You filled my life with laughter when all I did was weep inside. You made me strong when I felt weak. She will see that, Madz. There's no way she can't see what a great person you are. You may, um, sleep around, but you've never purposely hurt anyone. She'd be a fool to let you go."

"You really think so?"

"I know so," she states, smiling softly.

"Max said I'm supposed to make a grand gesture," I tell her.

Her eyes twinkle. "It amazes me how knowledgeable he is."

"Don't let him hear that," I warn her, chuckling under my breath.

She places her hand over her chest. "I won't. Promise."

I groan, closing my eyes. "How am I going to make this right?"

"Tell me what happened," she demands lightly. "Maybe we can work something out."

I take in a lungful of air before diving into everything, guilt eating away at my chest when I start with Amelia's ex. I then run through our time together, how easy she was to be around, how nice it was to be needed and not just wanted.

Halfway through the story, I feel like a massive idiot. I hadn't realised my feelings for Amelia during my conversation with Dad, but I'd had them all along, from the minute we shared one of the most traumatic yet beautiful experiences a person can go through.

Childbirth.

I end the story with mine and Amelia's argument, before forcing out a laugh. "It was there the entire time and I didn't even see it."

"But now you do," she states. "She sounds like she's scared, Maddox. You can't give up."

"I don't want to push her. She told me how her ex would emotionally manipulate her into getting back with him," I explain. "I'm going to respect her wishes. She doesn't want to be with me."

"Maddox, do you think I wasn't scared of being in a relationship? I did it because I had my family and Jaxon. He made me feel safe enough to take that step," she begins. "You need to make her feel safe enough to love you."

"How am I going to do that?"

She shrugs. "Be honest with her. Tell her everything you told me."

I rest my head against the counter, closing my eyes. "You make it sound so simple."

She laughs, and its music to my ears. "It's not. Can you remember what happened with Jaxon?"

"I really am sorry about that. I just wanted to protect you. I guess I couldn't see that you didn't need protecting from him."

"It all worked out okay."

When I meet her gaze, I give her a pitying stare. "How will I get her to listen to me? She isn't answering the phone or replying to my messages."

A sly smile reaches her lips, and she leans forward. "I have it on good authority that she'll be taking the kids to the fair tomorrow."

"What? How do you know this? Have you spoken to her?"

"No, no. I haven't. But Hope has. I guess she knew I'd come straight to you and tell you."

"I need to go. I need to get her to listen."

"Did you hear me when I said it was tomorrow?" she asks, letting out a giggle.

"I need a plan then. Something to get her to listen."

She shrugs. "Do what you always do."

"And what's that?" I ask.

"Wing it."

"I really do love you," I tell her, chuckling. "I hope this works."

"Me too."

I let the silence fill the air for a moment before glancing over at Lily. "How come you've not told anyone else about the pregnancy yet?"

She fiddles with the hem of her coat. "I'm not sure. I guess I'm waiting for the right time."

I curse under my breath. "Lily, what we did to Jaxon was wrong. We know that. It hurt us more than it hurt him too. Trust me," I tell her. "You don't have to be scared we'll overreact again."

Her chin trembles a little. "It's not just that. I am scared to tell the rest of the uncles. I mean, did you hear Max at breakfast a few weeks ago?"

"Max overreacts about everything," I remind her. "And he's currently haunting my neighbours, so you shouldn't really worry about what he thinks."

She chuckles. "I read the messages outside. Aunt Lake is so mad."

"Yeah, she is," I confirm.

"It's not just that. I want to make sure everything is okay. We had the scan, and everything is going well. I'm due in December. But I don't know…" she trails off, looking interested in the counter.

"It's because we failed you," I tell her. "I'm sorry."

Tears gather in her eyes. "Don't. It's me. I'm being silly. Even Jaxon said we should be shouting it from the rooftops."

"Lily," Jaxon calls, as I hear the front door open.

Lily stands, brushing off the back of her coat. I stand too.

"We're in here," she calls out softly.

I head over, pulling her into my arms. "Tell everyone when you're ready. Just don't leave it too long," I warn her, keeping my voice low. "They are all going to be happy for you, just like I am."

"Thank you," she whispers, her voice filled with emotion. When Jaxon steps past the floodlights and into sight, she turns to him. "Did you sort Reid's car?"

Jaxon's gaze narrows on me as he pulls her into his arms. "It was clingfilmed to a post outside a gay bar."

I burst out laughing, remembering Landon's comment about his dad ordering cling film through him. I guess it's true what they say: like father, like son.

"How did that happen?"

Jaxon tenses. "I'll be sure to ask Landon tomorrow when I see him. We've only just found the location."

"Did you go help him get it?" Lily asks, her brows pulling together.

"Nah, he and Wyatt have got it covered," he assures her. "Let's get you home."

"Are you going to be there tomorrow?" I call out before they get past the floodlights.

Lily stops, glancing over her shoulder with an angelic smile. "I wouldn't miss it for the world."

I grin back, feeling optimistic about the entire situation now. I'm going to get my girl.

THIRTY-ONE

MADDOX

As always when the fair came to town, it's packed. Children scream and laugh, and parents yell back and forth to be heard over the noise. They have vendors set up, selling all kinds of bits and bobs, but my favourites are always the food vendors. You can smell steaks, burgers, Chinese, Indian and popcorn and candyfloss. It's heaven. Apart from the Christmas market, this is my favourite place to grab food. All that fatty goodness is good for the soul.

I lick my lips, glancing up at one of the menus, finding it hard to choose. There is nowhere free for us to sit and eat, so I have to order only what I can carry. It's a challenge our family has conquered over the years.

"No," Sunday snaps, covering the food in her lap when her dad goes to take some.

Bailey chuckles, handing the little girl her juice. "Here you go, sweetie."

"Did you teach her not to share?" Aiden argues, frowning at his girlfriend.

Bailey, used to his behaviour, snorts. "No. It runs in the family."

"I bet she gives me some," I tease, bending down so I'm eye level with my niece. "Can Uncle Maddox try some of your burger?"

Her cute face scrunches up into a lethal frown. She mimics her dad so well, it's uncanny. "No."

I put on my best puppy dog face. "Please."

"Mine," she cries out, and I flinch, falling back on my arse.

Sheesh, she has a temper when it comes to food.

"Does she know any other words?" I ask.

Bailey sighs. "We've got her to say 'food' and 'pop', but 'mine' and 'no' are her favourites."

Aiden chuckles, wiping the sauce off her mouth. "Lucky we didn't bet anything, right?"

"F-off," I grumble, getting up and wiping the dirt off my arse.

"Aren't you meant to be doing some crazy gesture to win your girl back today?"

I narrow my gaze on Aiden. "How do you know that?"

He grins, shrugging. "I have my sources."

"Have you seen her?"

"Dude, we arrived *with you* thirty minutes ago; don't you think if I had seen her, I would have said something?"

He has a point.

"Do you know what you are going to do?" Bailey asks.

"No. Not a clue. Dad said I need to tell her with words what I'm feeling," I explain.

She nods. "You should. Have you ever watched a romantic movie? They always do something big, something the girl can't ignore."

Interested, I step a little closer. "What did they do?"

She shrugs, finishing off her chip. "Some do things in front of an audience; the bigger the better. It's so they can't run away or say no. And sometimes it can prove the person means what they are saying if they are willing to let everyone know how they are feeling."

My brows pull together. "But isn't that forcing them to be okay. I mean, if someone were to propose in a room full of people, how could the woman say no then?"

Bailey laughs at my reply. "Are you planning on proposing?"

I rear back. "No, I just want her to be my girlfriend."

"*My girlfriend*," Aiden mimics, teasing me.

I shove his shoulder. "You're a dick, do you know that?"

"I tell him at least twice a day," Bailey jokes.

"Oh look, Lily is here with her neighbours' kids," Aiden comments.

Seeing Lily laugh at something Star says brings a calmness to my chest. I hadn't realised how tensed up I was until I laid eyes on her. She always has a way of calming me down when I'm stressed.

So what if I haven't seen Amelia? It doesn't mean she isn't coming. It just means she's somewhere hidden in the sea of people.

Any other explanation isn't acceptable.

As we walk towards their little huddle, thoughts of Amelia are pushed to the side when one guy walks past with a beer can in his hand. His mates, drunk, push him to the side, nearly colliding with Lily and Jaxon. I tense, ready to go to Lily, but pause when she doesn't react the way she normally does. There's no black out, no going into herself, nothing. Instead, she steps closer to Jaxon, trusting him to shield her.

And I get it then.

I get why she kept him a secret. I get why she loves him and why she was so broken up about what we did.

I get it all.

I get what love truly means.

What Amelia truly means to me.

Jaxon watches me closely, confusion written all over his face. The silent question hangs in the air, and I give a subtle shake of my head. I'm not going to draw attention to what happened. Lily needs to come to terms with that by herself. I'm just happy she was able to slay some of her demons or at least trust Jaxon enough for him to do it.

"Maddox," Lily greets, beaming up at me. "Did you try the Balti from the vendor up there? It smelled *amazing*."

"I haven't had a chance yet," I answer, grinning at her enthusiasm. "Hey, kids."

"Hey, man," Miah grumbles.

Jaxon, taking pity on the teenager, hands him a twenty. "Go do your own thing."

His eyes light up as he takes the cash. "Really? Thanks."

"But weren't we going to go on the bumper cars?" Lily asks, pouting.

"Babe, he has mates to meet up with. He doesn't want to be seen hanging out with us," Jaxon explains, chuckling.

"Not that you aren't cool or anything," Miah rushes to add.

"Go on then. We will pick you up at five to take you home."

"Babe," Jaxon teases.

She lets out a sigh. "Okay, but call me if you do need picking up," she tells him, before reaching into her purse. "Here's some extra money, in case you need it."

"You don't need to—"

"I want to," she tells him softly.

Once he's gone, she cuddles into Jaxon's side and stares up at me. "Have you seen her yet?"

"No," I tell her, losing hope that she's coming. "I don't think she's coming."

"We've just seen her," she tells me, and I straighten. "Yeah, there she is."

I follow the direction she's pointing to, and my pulse begins to beat rapidly. She's with her mum and the kids, sitting near the stage where a live band is playing.

She's here.

Although she looks a little tired, I have never seen her look so beautiful. I was a fool not to see this before. It's one thing knowing a woman is hot, but it's another to see past that and see the person they truly are.

And I'm seeing her.

Fuck am I seeing her.

"What do I do?" I rush out, straightening my jacket. "I need a big gesture."

I scan the area, my gaze going back to the stage. My brows pull together when Bailey's words come to mind.

'Some do things in front of an audience; the bigger the better.'

You can't get much bigger than the fair in Coldenshire. It's the biggest event, apart from the family day they do in the summer.

"You could just go over—"

"I've got an idea," I tell them.

"Twenty says he fucks up," Aiden states.

"Fifty says he makes himself look like a dickhead," Jaxon puts in.

"Guys," Lily murmurs. "Maddox?"

I startle, pulling my gaze away from Amelia. "I'm going to sing."

"What?" she asks, her eyes wide. "You can't—"

"Be back," I tell them, before racing around the crowd so she can't spot me. I get near the stage and don't stop, leaping up onto it.

"Hey," the drummer snaps. "You can't be up here."

"I need to sing," I explain breathlessly.

"Every year," the guitarist yells. "Why don't you fuckers come up with a different dare and leave us the fuck alone?"

"This isn't a dare. I need to win my girl back," I tell them, stomping over to the singer and pulling the mic out of his hand.

"Hey," he snaps, trying to reach for the mic.

"Sorry for the interruption, guys, but there's something I need to do," I tell them, still dodging the singer.

He chases after me, still going for the mic. "Mate, you need to give me the fucking mic back. We have a set."

"No," I snap as he reaches me. He grips the mic, pulling it towards him, but I don't let go. "I've got something I need to do."

"Don't make me knock you out."

I snort, "Like that could happen," I tell him. "This is important. Are you really going to deny me my moment of making the big gesture?"

"Give it back," he orders.

"No."

"Now!"

"No!"

He pauses from trying to free the mic when the crowd begins to laugh. We both turn towards it, and my throat tightens when I find them all staring at us.

"Man, just let him make a twat of himself," the drummer calls out.

The singer lets go of the mic with a growl. "You've got five fucking minutes."

I wink. "I only need three."

I meet Amelia's gaze in the crowd. I let go of the mask and open myself up to her. I let her see I mean this, that I'm here, making myself vulnerable for her.

She closes her eyes as pain washes over her expression.

"Whoohooo, take it off," I hear hollered from the crowd.

I narrow my gaze. "I'm not a stripper. Now shush, I've got something important to do," I argue.

In the distance, I see my dad slap his hand over his forehead, shaking his head. I grin, giving him a wave before clearing my throat and turning back to Amelia.

"I wasn't sure what the big gesture meant, but I do now. It's not about doing something for the say so of it. It's not about pushing boundaries to get what you want. It's not just words, but actions. It's about showing the person you're in love with, how you really feel," I tell her, taking a deep breath. "I need you to know I'll help you chase away your fears. I'll be the person you've always known me to be and more. I'm *with you* one-hundred-percent, and I'm here to prove it to you. So, here goes."

I clear my throat before diving into one my nan's favourite songs. "I love you, baby, and if it's quite all right, I need you baby," I sing, my throat rusty. Amelia's lips part and tears gather in her eyes. Jasmine starts jumping up and down, spotting me for the first time. I send her a wink before continuing.

I get to the end of the second verse when the band start playing. I grin at the drummer before jumping off the stage, taking the mic with me. I speed up the beat, getting into the rhythm.

I head towards Amelia, whose cheeks are flaming red. She stands, ready to flee when I reach her, but I jump onto the bench she was sat on, singing louder.

"Go on, Maddox," someone yells from the crowd, and I know it's one of my family members.

The crowd begins to sing along with me as I get up onto the table, bending down until I'm eye level with Amelia. She sniffles, looking too shocked to do much else.

I reach down, taking her hand in mine as I sing the last line of the song: "Let me love you."

The crowd cheers, hollering and cat calling, and I can do nothing but stare down at the woman I'm in love with.

"Maddox," she whispers.

"I'll go take Jasmine on the trampoline," Nita suggests, a smile in her voice. I hear Jasmine protest, but Nita tempts her with two more rides. She leaves, taking both of the kids with her, but not before yelling, "If you see your dad, send him my way."

Amelia's head jerks to her mum for a moment before her attention is pulled back to me. I jump down from the table, coming to stand in front of her.

Her black hair blows around her face, and I push it aside, wanting to see her face.

"I love you. I know I've not done much to prove that, but I do," I tell her, keeping my voice low, calm. "Please, Amelia. Please give me a chance. Give us a chance."

"I'm scared to," she admits, her lip trembling.

I reach for her, taking her hands in mine. "I know you are. But I meant what I said. I'll chase those fears away. You've got nothing to be afraid of when it comes to me. Us Carter's are like wolves; we only have one mate and it's for life. I take that shit seriously if I'm going to pick the right one."

Her brows pull together. "Isn't it only the alphas who mate for life?"

I nod. "I'm all alpha, baby."

Her eyes, glistening with tears, sparkle. "I guess you'd have to be stupid to pick the wrong one."

"No one else has ever been in the running," I admit, watching her pupils dilate.

"Please don't hurt me," she pleads.

I press closer. "The only one who is going to get hurt is me if you don't say you'll be mine. Plus, can you honestly say that being with me doesn't have its benefits?"

She snorts out a laugh. "And what would those be?" she teases.

"I'm seriously hot to look at, especially naked. No food goes to waste. You've seen the amount Jasmine leaves on her plate," I tell her. "I'm good at snuggling. I fix things. I—"

She grins, wrapping her arms around my neck. "Stop," she chuckles out. "You had me at 'hot to look at'."

I grin, pulling her against me. I lean down, ready to do what I've been dying to do since I first met her. She closes her eyes, leaning up…

And a throat clears.

I blink one eye open, spotting the singer holding his hand out. "Mic," he orders.

I groan, slapping the mic into his hand. "Dickhead."

Amelia begins to laugh, resting her head against my chest. "I can't believe you sang to me."

"Just call me Frank," I tease.

"You have the worst singing voice ever," she tells me, her face lighting up.

"I'll let you get away with that, since you're mine now."

"Oh really," she purrs, stepping closer.

"Amelia! Amelia!" Nita cries, racing over to us, pushing the pushchair. Jasmine races beside her, crying.

"Mummy," Jasmine wails, tears streaming down her face.

Just one look at them and I know something awful has happened. I can feel it in my gut. My spine shoots up straight and alarm bells ring in my ears.

Amelia tenses, her body jerking. "Mum?"

Her mum stops near us, panting heavily as tears rush down her pale face. "It's Asher. He's gone."

My heart pummels and I nearly collapse to the floor. The only thing stopping me is my need to find him.

I inwardly cry out.

Asher.

THIRTY-TWO

AMELIA

My chuckle is forced, and my feet feel like they are welded to the ground. "That's not funny, Mum. Where is he?"

Mum hiccups, clutching her chest. "I'm not joking. I was watching Jasmine on the trampoline, and when I went to check on him, he was gone. He was gone. No one saw anything."

"No," I whisper. "No."

"Dad, come over to the stage area where you saw me last. We have a situation," Maddox barks into his phone.

I begin to look around the fair, taking in all the pushchairs, every baby in the arms of a parent, not seeing Asher anywhere. My heart races, and my skin begins to clam up.

"No one just takes a baby," I whisper.

Mum sniffles, her knuckles white as she grips the handlebars of the pushchair.

"I'm so sorry, baby. So sorry," she cries out. "The lady at the trampoline is calling security for us. We should get back there."

This isn't a joke.

My baby boy is gone.

My feet come unglued, and I race away from Mum and Maddox, pushing through the crowd, towards the trampolines. I bump into hard bodies, not seeing the people pass by as I race to find Asher.

I cry out, nearly falling on my face as I push through a small family. "I'm sorry," I cry out, sobs raking through my body.

I begin to search the area in the hope of seeing him, my vision blurred through the tears. Adrenaline surges through my body as I keep going, scanning as I do. "Asher," I scream.

A woman grabs my arm. "Have you lost your son?"

I stop at her words, panting heavily. "My baby was snatched out of his pushchair. He's only a few months old. He has on blue jeans, and a navy-blue coat with a star logo on. He has dark hair. And he has a star and moon blue blanket with him."

"Oh my God," she breathes out. "I'll help you look."

"Thank you," I choke out, moving along to a guy with a little girl. "Excuse me, have you seen anyone with a baby with a star and moons blue blanket around him?"

"I'm sorry, I haven't," he tells me.

"Amelia!" Maddox yells, and I stop, watching him racing towards me.

A sob breaks free as I turn to him, seeing the same haunted look in his eyes as I have in my heart.

"Where is my baby?" I ask him, almost begging him to know.

"My uncle Myles has blocked the car park and he has other members of the family blocking the exits. Hopefully we aren't too late," he explains, and my heart stops.

He could be anywhere.

"We are going to search the car park now," Malik tells me, his gaze soft.

"Why would someone take him?" I ask, feeling my chest tighten even more.

"I don't know," Maddox grits out. "I want you to stay with your mum. She's on the phone to your dad," he orders, coming close. "Jasmine is with my sister."

I clutch at his arms. "I can't breathe. He's just a tiny baby."

"We'll find him, I promise," he declares.

"I'm such a terrible mother," I cry out.

"No, you aren't," he states fiercely. "This has nothing to do with your mothering skills. Your mum even said she only turned her back for a minute. No one could predict that would happen."

"We have to find him," I tell him, my voice breaking. "He's going to be so scared. He cries with strangers."

Maddox jerks, and tension radiates from his body. When I look at him, his jaw is clenched, and his eyes are watering. He looks to his dad, the determination and loss there, clear to see.

It's then that I know he doesn't just love me.

He loves my kids.

"We'll find him, son. I swear it to you," Malik assures him, squeezing his shoulder.

"I'll find him. I will," he rambles, before turning to me, his gaze fierce and ready for war. "I'll find him."

Asher.

"I can't breathe," I tell him, my heart racing. Whereas most kids will have a distinct description, Asher is a baby, still growing into his personality. Although he looks like Asher to me, to others, he is just another baby. He could be anywhere, with anyone, and the only ones who will notice someone has him, are very few.

Maddox jerks his head at his dad. "I'll meet you there," he tells him, before bending down and pressing a kiss to my forehead. "Your mum and dad are walking over. Stay with them. Okay?"

I nod, startling when my phone begins to vibrate in my pocket. When I see 'private number' flashing on the screen, I go to ignore it, but as my finger hovers over the red phone button, something in me screams to answer it.

Sensing something is wrong, Maddox stops, staring at me. "What?"

My hands shake as I answer the call, slowly bringing the phone up to my ear. "Hello?"

"If you want to see your son again, meet me in the car park," Carol orders, before the phone goes dead.

I bring the phone down slowly, staring at the screen as blood rushes to my ears.

"Amelia, who was that?" Maddox demands.

I tilt my head up, wheezing out, "Carol has him. They're in the car park."

"Fuck!"

"They have my goddamn son," I yell, causing him to flinch.

"Let's go," he tells me, pulling me towards the car park.

"How can they do this? Does she have no empathy in that shrivelled up body of hers?" I rant. "If they have hurt Asher, I am going to lose my crap."

"I think you already have," he grumbles.

"I'm a nurse. I know things," I hiss out. "I'm not having another Hudson mess with me or my children ever again. I have lost too much to them. Not anymore."

"We'll get him," he promises, and takes my hand.

Mum and Dad race after us, yelling for us to tell them what is going on. I don't stop or turn back, too busy needing to get to my son.

We reach the car park, and up ahead, in a group, are Carol, her sister, Karen, Nessa, and the guy Carol was dating the last time I saw her. Beside him stands another guy, this one rougher than the first.

I bite my lip to stop the scream bubbling out when I don't find Asher amongst any of them.

"Where is my son?" I yell, and Maddox pulls me back at the last minute.

"He's close," Carol vows.

"Give me back my son, Carol. You have gone too far," I warn her. "The police already know he's missing."

A flicker of panic flashes in her eyes as they dart to the men standing next to her. "All in good time."

"Give me back my grandson now, you good for nothing human being," Mum screeches. "Don't you think you've put my daughter through enough?"

"Nita," Dad murmurs, pulling her back.

"Don't, Gareth. I am not in the mood," she warns him.

The man she used to date—Colin, I think—steps forward. "You've been a thorn in my woman's side," he declares.

Maddox's fingers dig into my hip, and when I tilt my head up, he's looking into the carpark. When I glance that way, I notice Malik jerk his head in our direction before moving off further into the carpark.

"I don't care what you think or what you want. I just want my son."

"And I want mine," she snaps.

The man I don't recognise turns to Carol. "I thought you said this woman would have the answers to your problems."

I shiver at the sound of his voice, stepping back into Maddox. "What is going on?"

"Give me Asher, otherwise you're going to have more problems," Maddox promises as Landon, Reid, Jaxon, Hayden, Mark and Liam come to stand in our huddle.

The guy with his back to us slowly turns around, smirking. When he pulls something out of his pocket, making a flicking motion with his wrist, I gasp in a breath, stepping back at the sight of the knife.

"I brought my own backup," the guy states, not a flicker of fear on his face.

"Carol," I hiss out, as Maddox blocks me from harm. "Why are you doing this?"

"Because you sent my son to prison, and you're the only one who can get him out," she argues, her voice rising.

"He has a special set of skills," the guy wielding the knife announces.

"Skills? Beating women?" Maddox asks.

"Don't talk about my son like that," Carol snaps.

"We need him out," Karen, the tragic aunt, bites out.

"And that sounds like a *you* problem," Maddox snaps.

"Why? Why do you need him so badly when you didn't before?" I ask, close to tears. I just want to hold my son. I want to know he's okay.

When no one says anything, Nessa steps forward, her hand on her rounded stomach. "Mum and Aunt Karen owe this guy money. The only way they can repay him involves Cameron, since Devon won't get involved. Too high and mighty," she bites out. "Cameron can pick any lock."

"W-what?" I whisper, wondering if I'm hearing this right.

"And you're going to help us get him out," Carol finishes. "If you want to see your son again, you'll write a letter to the police stating you lied."

The ringing in my ears gets louder, tuning out Maddox's reply. There's a popping sensation, right before I launch myself towards her. Maddox wraps his arms around me, and Carol takes a step back. "You put my son in danger because you want your son to pick a fucking lock?"

"No, he's my son too, and he belongs at home, you little fucking slut."

"You greedy, worthless piece of shit," I screech. "That's my son. *My son*. He isn't involved in your crap. Nor in your son's. Give him back. Now!"

"You won't see him again if you don't do what we ask," she tells me, her voice hard.

My heart races when I see Myles step into the group. He was meant to be watching the exit. "She will see him again. Did you really think that with all these witnesses you'd get away with kidnapping a baby?"

"He's my grandson. It's not kidnapping."

"It is when you don't have any legal rights to him," he bites out. "Which I happily had confirmed when my nephew informed me about what you were saying."

"No," she grumbles, but from her expression, I can see she isn't sure.

"This is fucking ridiculous," the guy wielding the knife snaps. "I want my money, Carol, otherwise we're going to have some serious problems."

"Again, that sounds like a *you* problem," Maddox snaps.

"I want my son," I bite out, wiping away my tears. "Just give me back my son and leave us alone."

"He's with my wife, Amelia," Malik announces, stepping between Hayden and Reid. "Safe and sound."

His words echo in my ears over and over, and I collapse to the ground. Maddox lifts me up, supporting my weight.

He's okay.

He's safe.

He's with Harlow.

"Where's my boyfriend?" Nessa orders, stepping forward.

Malik grins. "Knocked out and tied up in the back of your van. Don't worry, the police are there."

"You bastard!" she cries out, taking a step towards him.

Hayden steps out in front of him, crossing her arms over her chest. "Touch him, and I will fucking knock you on your arse."

Nessa stops, her eyes widening. "You'd hit a pregnant woman?"

"Your face isn't pregnant," Hayden retorts. "And you're the one acting like a lunatic, kidnapping an innocent baby."

Carol screams at the top of her lungs in a rage. "You silly fucking cunt. You have no idea what you have done," she yells, rushing forward. She snatches the knife out of the guy's hand, coming at me.

I freeze, but Maddox doesn't. He dives in front of me and gets in her way. He knocks her hand sharply, causing the knife to fall out of her grip. When she begins to punch him, I jerk forward, but the chaos erupting around me stops me short.

There are people everywhere, police too.

Colin shoves out of Liam's grip, reaching for something off the ground, at the same time Maddox pushes Carol away, growling, "I don't hit fucking women, so don't make me—"

"Maddox," I scream, my heart in my throat.

"Maddox!" Malik roars, and the sound is one of a terrified parent, one I know first-hand. I've made the same cry three times in my life now. Once the night Cameron attacked me, then when Jasmine was nearly hit by a car, and today, when I realised Asher had been kidnapped.

Malik reaches for Colin, along with Mark and Liam, and pull him away from Maddox, shoving him to the ground.

"He might not hit women, but I do," Hayden snaps, punching Carol in the nose. She cries out, falling to the floor.

I race over to Maddox when he begins to stagger. He turns around, sweat dripping from the side of his face.

Something isn't right. I can feel it.

"Maddox?" I whisper, my heart stopping for another reason.

"Are we going to class this as a first date? Because it sucks," he rasps.

"Maddox?" I call out quietly, taking another step towards him.

I block out the sound of the fight breaking out as I reach for his hand. He wobbles on his feet before collapsing in a heap to the ground.

"Maddox," I cry out, falling to my knees beside him.

He reaches up, and my eyes widen at the blood covering his hand. I glance down at his hoody, my body shaking when I see the small tear.

"Son!" Malik cries out.

Something snaps me into action, and I quickly lift his hoody, hissing out a breath when I see the puncture wound. "Call nine-nine-nine," I demand, and quickly look up, jerking my head at Reid. "I need your top."

"Fuck no. It's my favourite, and blood is a bastard to get out," he tells me.

"I'm fine," Maddox assures me, trying to sit up.

I push him back down and glare at Reid. "Give me your fucking top right now."

"Here," Liam speaks up, throwing me his T-shirt. I press it down on the wound, applying pressure.

"I'm sorry," I sob out, glancing down at him.

"Not your fault," he assures me, wincing when I press down harder.

Reid steps closer to Maddox's head. "Hurts like a bitch, doesn't it?"

"Yours was barely a scratch, you prick," Maddox bites out. "And you were crying like a baby."

"Fuck!" Malik hisses, running a hand through his hair. "Your mum is going to be so pissed."

"I'm so sorry," I repeat.

Maddox grips my hand, his facial features pinched in pain. "It's not your fault."

"This was my mess."

"No, it isn't. This is on them," he assures me, before forcing out a chuckle. "Bit of a good job I'm not a virgin."

"What does that have to do with anything?" Malik asks, his brows pinched together.

"Don't the Sanderson sisters sacrifice the virgin?"

I snort. "Only you."

"I'm not sure there's a spell or even a plastic surgeon that can make them look young," Reid pipes in.

"Are you still here?" Maddox snaps.

Reid pulls away from his phone, nodding. "I'm live on Facebook. People are taking bets on whether it was me who stabbed you or your girlfriend."

"Me?" I screech.

Reid winces. "Maybe tone it down," he tells me, before leaning in closer to whisper, "I want them to believe it was me."

"Honey, you can move away now. The paramedics are here," Mum tells me, her voice soft.

I can't move.

I hiccup, then take a few steady breaths. "I can't let go because of the bleeding."

Malik places his hand over mine. "They've got him, Amelia."

"He saved my life," I whisper.

"And he'd do it all over again," he assures me.

"He really loves me."

Malik smiles softly, something I have never seen him do before, and it takes my breath away. Now I know where Maddox gets his looks. "Like you'd never believe."

I slowly let go and fall back into my mum's supportive arms. I watch as the paramedic cuts up his hoody, whilst the other removes the T-shirt.

He's going to be okay.

Asher is okay.

"Asher," I whisper, right before my eyes roll into the back of my head, and everything turns black.

THIRTY-THREE

AMELIA

It's nearing late evening. Jasmine is asleep, her head lying in my lap, and Asher is in my arms, where he has been since I woke up to the paramedics checking me over. I can't let him go. Every time Mum or someone offered to take him, I couldn't physically do it. I had to feel him against my chest, to know he was really here and okay. I never want to feel that pain ever again. It felt like someone had taken a rusty, jagged blade and scraped it down my heart.

He's here, and he is unharmed, which is all I want, yet it still feels like he is gone. I guess once the shock wears off, I'll come to terms with everything that happened.

Until then, I'm content to have him in my arms.

Everything after I woke up is a blur. I remember the police arresting Carol and her family, and I remember parts of my conversation with the police, but other than that, it's like there is a smoke screen and it's hard to grasp the words or actions of others. A part of that is because of Maddox.

We are at the hospital, and I can't meet the gazes of his concerned family. We have been here for hours with no update from the doctors. His mum is sobbing into Malik's chest, Lily fell asleep after being inconsolable, and the others are tense yet quiet, waiting for word about Maddox.

Yet, I can't form a word or offer them comfort. I can't apologise or leave. I'm frozen until I can hear the words, *he's okay*.

I love him.

I really love him.

I love the way he barged into my life like a hurricane and turned it upside down in the best possible way. I love the way he took to my kids, the way he included them in his life. I love that he put us in his life without a thought. One day we were strangers, the next we were the closest friends.

And life without him these past few days had been dull. It was lonely. So many times I reached for my phone to apologise, to tell him I felt the same way too. I let fear take over my life once again, but instead of inviting more toxic in, I let something good, something so utterly pure, go.

The guilt is eating away at me. It's my fault Maddox is here. If it hadn't been for my issues, none of this would have happened today. He wouldn't be somewhere in this hospital, lying in a bed.

Mum, who hasn't left my side, presses her hand over mine. She's cold, her hands shaking. "Honey, why don't you let us take the kids home. You have one bottle left."

"I'll keep breastfeeding him," I whisper, which is something I need to do once he is due a feed. I need that connection. "I can't leave."

"At least let your mother get you cleaned up," Dad comments, he, too, sounding worried.

I glance down at my hands, my eyes watering at the dried blood caking them. "I'll wait," I choke out.

"Honey, I'm so sorry I let this happen," Mum chokes out.

I tilt my head to the side. "This isn't your fault, Mum, it's mine. They were there because of the choices I made," I tell her, my voice breaking. "Why does he keep doing this? He isn't even here, and he is ruining my life."

"Everyone makes bad choices," Malik announces, and when I look up, all eyes are on us. "It's the way of life. How would you know if you've made a good one otherwise?"

"I got your son badly hurt," I whisper.

"My son is going to be okay," Harlow tells me. "He won't be if he knows you're blaming yourself. Please don't take that guilt on."

I don't know what to say, so I let the tears pour. Even now she's being kind and good-natured.

"Please, sweetie, let us take you home. You're dead on your feet and the kids need their beds," Mum states. "Or at least let me and your father take them home."

"Mum, I really can't leave them," I tell her, letting her hear it in my voice.

Mum begins to sob, throwing herself into my fathers' arms. "I only turned my back for a moment."

"Mum," I rush out, trying to not wake Jasmine when I turn. "It wasn't your fault. That could have easily been me."

"She's right," Lake utters. "My husband and I had triplets. I can't begin to tell you the amount of times he forgot one or lost one during family outings. We went to the beach once. We were *all* there. Still, Hayden got away and we looked for what felt like hours for her."

"Where was she?" Mum asks.

Hayden groans. "Sat in a cooler eating someone's picnic."

Even with the dark cloud hanging over my head, I laugh. I can't help it. It slips free, and Hayden looks further dejected.

Harlow's eyes light up. "Can you remember the time the twins escaped the play pen under Malik's watch?"

Malik chuckles. "I thought you were going to murder me."

Maverick grins. "Wasn't that when they were trying to come to mine?"

Malik nods. "Yeah."

"Family of Maddox Carter?" a doctor calls out. I tense as Harlow and Malik quickly rush to their feet. I gently slide out from under Jasmine and head over to the door. "You can go in and see him."

Both turn to me. "We'll come out as soon as we speak to him," Harlow promises.

"Go. Go. Make sure he's okay," I plead.

She leans over, giving me a kiss on the cheek. "I'm glad he has you."

Malik squeezes my shoulder before following his wife out of the room. I begin to pace the room, fearing the worst.

Lily stands, and Jaxon reaches for her, steadying her. "He's going to be fine," she assures me.

My eyes glaze over with more tears. "How do you know that? It looked pretty deep."

She shares a look with Jaxon, and he lets her go. She walks over to me and rubs her hand up and down my arm. "Because he's one of the strongest men I know. Look around you, Amelia. This family is strong. They've pulled through so much, and this… this will just be added to the list. Because together we get through it. Now is the time for you to be strong for Maddox."

"I don't know how to be," I admit, feeling my lower lip tremble.

She gives me a small smile, her eyes filling with unshed tears. "You're part of the family now. We can be strong for you."

Her words hit me right in the chest, and I nearly buckle at the force of them. She means it. And looking around at the sea of faces, the others stand by her words too.

They don't hate me.

The door bangs open, and I spin around, clutching Asher tighter in my arms. Harlow has tears streaming down her face, and for a moment, a split moment, I picture the worst. But then she smiles, and sniffles through her tears.

"He's going to be okay," she cries out.

Everyone stands, hollering and cheering. "I knew it," Madison cries out, clutching her chest. Hope hugs her, crying along with her.

When Harlow's gaze meets mine, an uneasy feeling settles in the pit of my stomach. "Can I see him?"

"Honey, I let him know you were out here. He's going to be a while still, and he wants you to take the kids home."

My stomach bottoms out, and there's a loud ringing in my ears. "He wants me to go?"

"He wants you to go home and rest," she explains, but all I hear is that he wants me to go.

I jerk my head into a nod. "Okay. Okay."

Mum steps up beside me, wrapping her arm around my shoulders. "You need your rest. It's been a long day."

"She's right. You look worn out and tired," Harlow adds.

"Okay. Okay," I repeat, although my heart yearns for Maddox.

When I turn to leave, Harlow grips my bicep. "I'm glad my son has you and those beautiful children in his life. He'll be okay."

"Thank you," I reply, before clearing my throat, feeling a ball in the back. "Will you… will you tell him I'm thinking of him. And that I'm sorry."

Her expression softens. "He already knows, but I'll pass it along."

"C'mon, darlin'," Mum calls gently, pushing the pushchair next to me.

"I'll carry him," I tell her.

"All right, Amelia."

MUM PULLS THE car onto the drive. The lights are all off, giving the place an eerie feel. We hadn't expected to be gone this long.

"Honey, I truly am sorry for what happened today," she tells me as the lights of my car light up the house.

"It's really not your fault," I tell her tiredly. "I hate them, Mum. I really hate them."

"The police have them now, and hopefully they won't come near you again."

"Yeah," I tell her, just as I hear Dad's booming voice.

"What the fuck are you doing here?"

I startle, glancing at the house. Sitting on the doorstep is the person I least expected to see. My blood runs cold at the sight of my ex best friend, Scarlett.

"I'll get rid of her," Mum bites out.

"It's fine. Will you help Dad get the kids in for me?"

Mum pauses with her hand on the door handle. "Are you sure? You've been through a lot today already."

I push open my door, grumbling, "Might as well get the rest over with."

"I just need to speak to her," Scarlett tells my dad, then spots me. "Amelia, please, just hear me—oh my God, is that blood?"

"Scarlett," Dad snaps.

Her eyes widen, looking from my hands to my dad, then back again. "What's going on?"

"Dad, help Mum," I order gently, before turning to her, noticing nothing has changed. Not her hair, not her Botox, lip fillers or fake lashes. Nothing. She is the same old person. "And what is going on has nothing to do with you. What are you doing here?"

She rears back like she's shocked that I actually spoke to her. "You've changed."

I let out a tired sigh as Mum and Dad pass, getting the kids inside. "What are you doing here?" I repeat.

She crosses her arms over her chest, bouncing on the balls of her feet as her gaze darts around the street. "I wanted to say I'm sorry."

"And it took you the better part of a year to do that?" I ask, not holding back the bitch in me.

"Look, what happened... I'm sorry," she tells me, as tears gather in her eyes.

I snort, stepping past her. "You slept with my boyfriend," I snap.

"It was a one-time thing, Amelia. You need to believe me. I—"

I whirl on her, crossing my arms over my chest. "Don't patronize me. It was more than once. It was on and off for the majority of our relationship. Cameron told me everything after he knocked you out. You were supposed to be my friend, Scarlett. I don't know how you had the nerve to come and sit at my table and eat my food, play with my kid and let me talk about what was going on at home, and actually answer like you were on my side. I trusted you."

She takes a step back. "I'm sorry. I'm so fucking sorry. I had no idea what he was like."

"Yes, you did," I scream. "You knew exactly what he was like, and you didn't say anything. And if that wasn't bad enough, you left us. You left me and my daughter on the floor to die."

She flinches, taking a step back. "I panicked. I had never seen him like that, and I was badly hurt and scared. And I didn't leave."

I snort, glancing at her in disgust. "Only because he stopped you outside."

She shakily lifts the strap of her bag, pulling it higher over her shoulder. "I've come a long way to say sorry, Amelia. I miss you and want a chance to make it up to you. If this is because you're with him again, it's fine. I just want to fix what is wrong between us."

"Back with him?" I ask, unable to keep the fear out of my voice.

She points to my hands. "You have blood. I thought… and you have a new baby."

"You disgust me. I never want to see his face again, and I never want to see yours."

"But I'm sorry. I miss our friendship, our chats. I miss Jasmine."

It then it dawns on me. "You miss having a family. Because that's what we were to you. We replaced the family you no longer have. It isn't because you're sorry at all."

"I don't have anyone, Amelia. No one. Please, let me prove how sorry I am."

I stare at her for a moment, wondering where she gets off demanding this stuff. "No."

"Please, Amelia—"

"No!" I snap. "I have a beautiful life here. I might have crap going on, but it doesn't wash away or undermine the good I have. I have a wonderful man who loves me and the kids. I have two parents who love and adore me. They've been a rock through all of this crap. And my friends," I get out. "You have no idea what a relief it was to know that not all friends are like you. They are so kind, so giving, and they are here for me, as I am for them.

"Today has been the second worst day of my life, and I come back to this. I don't want it in my life anymore, Scarlett. I don't want you in my life. You are toxic. What you did was unforgiveable, and I can't believe you have the nerve to come here. If you were sorry, you would have said it in the hospital."

"He hurt me too," she cries out. "He hurt me, and I had no one. No one to support me."

"I'm sorry he hit you. I wouldn't wish that upon anyone," I admit. "But it doesn't excuse anything. You made your own bed. I told you time and time again what he was doing."

"I thought he did those things to you because he wanted to be with me and he was angry he was stuck with you because of Jasmine," she blurts out. Her eyes widen, and she takes a step back. "I didn't mean to say that."

"Leave," Mum demands.

"I didn't mean to—"

"Leave," I demand. "I'm surrounded by good people. I'd be a fool to let you back into my life, even if I wanted to."

Her bottom lip trembles. "I really am sorry."

"Me too," I tell her, before turning and taking Mum's arm. We head inside, and I lean back against the door, panting heavily.

"Are you okay?" Mum asks.

I open my eyes, staring at her and Dad. "There's something I need to do, and I don't think you're going to like it."

"What?" Dad asks, before sharing a look with Mum.

I run over what I need to do and why I need to do it. Mum bites her lip, and Dad's face is turning a shade of red I have never seen before.

"Amy," he calls out softly, using a nickname for me he only ever uses for moments like this.

"I need to do this," I affirm.

Mum takes his hand, tears gathered in her eyes. "We understand, and we will be with you every step of the way."

I leap into her arms, holding her close. "Thank you. Thank you for always being the best parents to me."

Dad holds us both as he kisses the top of my head. "Always."

Mum breaks the hug and wipes under her eyes. "We're going to let you get some rest. We've put Jasmine in your bed. We knew you wouldn't want to be apart from them. Asher is in his cot."

"Thank you."

We say our goodbyes, and once I've locked up behind them, I drag my feet up the stairs. I reach my room, and the first place I go to is the cot. I pull Asher out, careful not to disturb him, and carry him over to my bed. I lay him down in the middle of the bed before leaning over to flick the light off.

The curtains are still open, letting the moon light up the room. I stare at my two beautiful children, grateful I have them in my life. As the day's events catch up to me, my thoughts on everything that happened, and on Maddox, I burst into tears.

I cry until I fall into an exhausted sleep, my last thoughts on Maddox and hoping he's okay.

THIRTY-FOUR

MADDOX

Limping up the path, I inwardly grimace at the ache in my side. It's still numbed by the local anaesthetic, but that will soon wear off. My dad always drummed it into our heads to never turn our backs on the enemy, and I feel ridiculous for doing it today. I'm never going to live this down.

I tilt my head up at the house, closing my eyes briefly. What she saw today must have been a lot. I lost my cool, and I don't want her to be scared of me because of it. She needs to know I'd never hurt her. Which is why as soon as they released me, I made Dad drop me back here.

It's now one in the morning, and although I need sleep, I need to see her more. I need to touch her. Hold her. When I saw Amelia's bedroom light on, I had to come over.

I also had to check on Asher and Jasmine. The ache in my chest hasn't abated since the minute I realised he was taken. It didn't even leave when Dad told me he was safe. It's an empty feeling inside of my chest, and I can't get rid of it. I don't understand it. All I have is this driving need to see him.

I was glad when the police took my statement and told me they had been charged. Although this will eventually go to court, it's certain they will get a sentence, hopefully a long one. She will never have to worry about them again. On top of assault charges and kidnapping, they were also charged with possession, amongst other things. I guess having a cop in the family comes in handy when you want all the details. When the police wouldn't give us much information, I had Mum bring Beau in, who was all too willing to fill us in on what he could.

I rap my knuckles on the door for a minute before limping away a few steps. The landing light flicks on, and my heart begins to beat wildly against my chest.

The door opens, and there, hair tussled and wearing her pyjamas, is Amelia. Her mascara from yesterday is smudged under her eyes, and her eyes are still swollen from crying. She flinches when she sees it's me, and not in a bad way but like she can't believe it's me.

"I know it's late, and I'm sorry if I woke you," I tell her. "I saw the lights on and—"

She rushes at me, bursting into tears. I grab her before she can hurt me and gently pull her into my arms. "You're really okay."

My arms relax around her, and I press my lips into the crook of her neck. "I'm okay."

She sniffles, pulling back a little. "You didn't wake me. I had just got changed after feeding Asher."

I tense at his name. Mum said he was fine, but I had to know for sure. "Is he okay?"

She melts against me. "He's completely fine," she assures me. "What you did—"

Her eyes close to mask the pain, but I see it. "I'd do it again, Amelia. I'm just sorry I'm the reason you weren't with him. I distracted you, and—"

She presses her finger over my lips. "I'm done with the blame game. It's not our fault. It's theirs. We could have done a million things differently today and it could have been a worse outcome. I'm just grateful you are both okay," she tells me. "*You are* okay, right?"

"I am. It didn't do any serious damage."

"I'm sorry this happened."

"Not your fault," I assure her. "It's so good to see you."

She bites her lip, her gaze darting over my shoulder. "I didn't think you wanted to see me. You asked me to leave."

"I was worried about the kids being around so many germs, and it was getting late. I wanted you to be at home resting, not waiting around for a doctor to come and treat me."

"*Why are* you here and not resting?" she lightly scolds.

"Because I needed to do this," I tell her, before leaning down.

"Go! Go!" Cassie screams across the road.

I groan, narrowing my eyes. "One more person interrupts us and I'm going to take you and the kids to a remote location. Once they are in bed, I'm going to kiss you so hard."

She grins, but the yelling across the road gets louder. "What on earth," she whispers, and we both watch as Cassie trips over the black bag in her hand, causing it to split. Clothes go everywhere, and she begins to scrape them into a pile, picking them up before dashing to Kayne's car. He comes running out next, green dye covering him from head to toe.

"I can't stay here anymore," she cries out.

"What about the rest of our stuff?" Kayne yells, throwing some stuff into the car.

A loud roar comes from inside the house, and they both freeze before racing to the front of the car.

"I don't give a shit. The council can sort it."

"Mum, I'm scared," Kayne cries.

"Kids," Cassie screams.

Her other kids come racing out, and I'm shocked by the sight of them. I've never seen them before, or if I had, I put them off as friends.

"Mum, something touched me," the teenage girl screams. "On my ankle."

"Get in the car!" Cassie screams.

They all squeeze into the small car, the tyres squealing as they spin on the tarmac.

"Fucking hell. He did it," I murmur.

"Who?" Amelia asks.

"My uncle Max. He's been hiding out in my loft, *eating my food*," I grit out. "But he's finally got rid of them."

Amelia forces out a chuckle. "Surely not."

Max decides to come outside, wiping green powder off his hands. He's grinning to himself, and jerks to a stop when he spots us. "And the trash is out," he calls out. "Now, I'd best be getting back to the wife. I've not had sex in days."

"She said you aren't getting any," I remind him.

"She could never resist me," he calls back as he reaches his car. "And I'm glad you weren't too badly gutted."

"Thanks?"

He grins wider. "You're welcome. Haven't had this much fun in years."

"He says that every few weeks," I grumble, and wave as he pulls out.

Amelia gapes at the space where Max's car once was. "Holy crap."

I grimace. "Look, you can't judge me by my family. The rest aren't like him. Well, Hayden is, but she's a little more psycho, although if you see Charlotte mad then you really see the definition of—"

"Maddox, I love your family. I love you."

I slowly turn in her arms, gripping her waist. "Say that again," I whisper.

"I love you."

I close my eyes, letting the words soak in. Although I always knew she'd love me, hearing it is another matter.

"I love you too," I tell her, before leaning down and capturing her lips with mine. They are softer than I imagined, and her taste explodes in my mouth as I massage my tongue against hers.

Tingles shoot up my spine as I deepen the kiss, tilting her head back to get better access.

She pulls back, breaking the kiss, her pupils dilating as she stares up at me. "You should be resting."

I smirk down at her. "I will after."

"After?" she whispers, still breathless.

"After I fuck my girlfriend."

Her eyes darken as I reach down, capturing her lips once more. I lift her up easily, ignoring the slight pinch in my side as I carry her back into the house. I kick the door closed behind me before moving into the front room.

I stop a foot in front of the largest sofa and place her on her feet, and press my lips to hers. Her silk top is soft against my fingers as I grip the edge, lifting it up and over her head.

Her tits bounce free and I inwardly groan. "Fuck!"

"Now you," she replies hoarsely, and slowly—careful of my wound—she slides my jacket off my shoulders, running her hands over my biceps.

I watch as fascination lights up her face, as she watches her fingers trace over the muscle. When she reaches the bottom of my top, her breathing picks up, and she slowly lifts my top up. I bend down a little, giving her help to pull it over my head.

I wince a little when I straighten, but it doesn't stop me from bringing her flush against my chest, revelling in the feel of her bare skin against mine as I bend down to kiss her.

She moans as I slide my tongue against hers, whilst cupping her tits. The sound of her moan has my dick painfully hard.

When her fingers begin to fumble with the elastic on my joggers, I clench my eyes shut. I can feel her nervousness, her vulnerability, and although I'm going to be mindful of it, I can't help but be more turned on. I grit my teeth as the soft cotton slides over my thighs and down my legs, Amelia following as she gently drops to her knees on the floor.

She looks up at me, her round hazel eyes with emerald flecks, and dark lashes, blinking up at me with little hesitation. So much want, yet there is fear there too. It's only slight, but it is there.

"Baby, as much as I want to feel your lips wrapped around my cock, I want to feel *you* more."

She slowly stands, and I waste no time in pushing her tiny shorts down her legs, letting them drop to the floor. There's a sharp intake of breath before she steps out of them, pressing closer to me.

"Now, I'm not in the best shape, so, baby, you're gonna have to be on top," I tell her, sitting down on the sofa, wincing at the pinch in my side.

"I can do that," she breathes out, straddling my lap.

"Are you sure this is what you want?" I ask, running my fingers through her hair and bringing her lips down to mine.

She moans through the kiss, and when she pulls back, she's breathless, her hips rocking gently against me. "I want this more than anything. I want you. But, Maddox, I've only ever been with—"

"I love you," I assure her, kissing her once more. I deepen the kiss, and tingles shoot down my spine at the sensation. She's everything.

Everything I didn't know I wanted or needed.

"I love you too."

"Then trust me to take care of you," I tell her.

Her pupils dilate as she continues to rock over my cock. I can already feel how wet she is, and it's making me want to fuck her hard, but for now, she needs slow, gentle. I need slow and gentle. And not because of my injuries, but because she deserves to be made love to.

"Condom," she whispers.

"Jacket behind you," I reply hoarsely. When she bends backwards, pushing her pussy over my cock, I grit my teeth. "Fuck!"

Yeah, once I'm at full strength, I'm going to fuck the hell out of my girl.

She comes back up, condom in hand, with a sly little smile on her lips. She tears it open and I lean back, watching as she rolls it over my cock.

Her hands shake, and hesitantly, she leans forward. The minute her lips reach mine, that sensation in the pit of my stomach intensifies.

I have missed out on so much. Before, I felt like I had my pick of women, each one unique in their own way because it was different. But kissing her, feeling her flush against me... this is what it means to be kissed.

Now it feels like the others were in search of this.

For this moment.

For this girl.

And to make sure this is real, I keep my eyelids half open, scared this is a figment of my imagination and I'll wake up at home in bed with some faceless chick.

Her warm breath fans across my face when she pulls back, and wordlessly, I reach between us, lining my cock up at her entrance.

Feeling the tip, she torturously slides down, her eyes half closed, and her lips parted. My jaw aches from clenching so tightly. I want to grab her, to thrust myself inside her so hard, but this isn't about that.

It isn't really about sex.

It's about her.

Connecting with her.

Loving her.

I pull her towards me, one hand on her hip to help keep up the rhythm as she thrusts up and down, her movements slow, steady.

Heat rises from my groin to my chest as I stare into her hypnotic eyes, a wave of warmth hitting me.

Her skin feels smooth under my fingertips as I caress her hip. I watch her lips part as I reach between her legs, swirling my thumb around her clit.

"Maddox," she whispers, sweat glistening over her chest. She leans down, claiming my mouth once more, and the fire that erupts between us is explosive.

Her fingers explore my chest, rising up until they are resting on my shoulders, her nails digging into the skin.

I can feel my orgasm building. Just being inside her, finally being with her… it's an exquisite torture.

She pulls back, breathing heavily. Her tits bounce with each thrust, and I lean forward, kissing up her breastbone, licking the sweat off her skin.

She cries out as I press my thumb down on her clit harder, and I pull back to watch her expression.

The intensity shining back at me nearly undoes me. Our noses touch as she jerkily pushes down on me. Her pussy clenches around me, and I know she's close.

A light sound escapes her lips as she drops down, her arse cheeks slapping against my thighs with each bounce. The sound of her throaty moans accompanying the slapping of our skin has me gritting my teeth. I'm not sure how much longer I can hold off.

When her orgasm hits her, I explode, my fingers tightening on her hips as I slam her down on my dick. I groan as she cries out, collapsing against me.

Heavy panting fills the air for a moment, before Amelia leans back, gazing down at me. "That was…" she pauses, shaking her head. "Wow. It really can be like it is in the books."

"Baby, I'm better than the books," I tell her, grinning.

I manoeuvre us so we're lying down on the couch, facing each other. I grimace as I turn to pull the blanket off the back of the sofa, and take a moment to breathe through the pain.

Amelia runs her finger down my chest, content on just being there. "How are you doing?"

She lets out a dry chuckle. "Considering my son got kidnapped, the man I love got stabbed, and my ex best friend turned up on my doorstep, I'm surprisingly doing okay now."

"It was the great sex," I tease. "I told you I can do magic with my cock."

She shrugs, her lips twisting into a sly smile. "It was okay. I wouldn't say it was magical."

I chuckle. "Babe, it was out of this world," I state, before asking, "What about the old best friend? I hope you told her you have a replacement friend now."

She giggles under her breath. "I told her where to go."

"You're okay though? I don't have to set the females in my family after her?"

She leans back, tilting her head to look up at me. "No. Because seeing her made me realise something."

"Realise what?" I ask quietly.

Her lashes fan across her cheeks briefly before she blinks them open, her voice low, soothing, when she replies, "That life goes on. That everything changes, and it can be for the better. I spent years taking Cameron back because

I wanted us to be a family, because I was scared of what I'd become without him. He was all I knew and felt I had. And it hit me today. I'm so much better off without him. I always was. But now I know I don't need him. I don't need to be scared of being alone because I was never really alone. I have two beautiful children who I couldn't possibly love more. Everything outside of them is a bonus. I have great friends, an amazing family, and a man who doesn't take social cues very well."

"You couldn't have gone with ruggedly handsome, has a big dick, and is great in bed?" I ask, feigning hurt.

Her body shakes against mine. "You kind of forced yourself into my life, and it was the best thing to ever happen to me. You opened my world up to better things. To brighter things. There was laughter in my life again. Love. Friendship," she states, before her lashes flutter again. "I'm so sorry for the way I overreacted that night. I was overwhelmed, and I let fear fuel the negativity running through my mind. I still feel stupid whenever I think back on that night. I thought I lost you."

"Never. I'm like glitter. Once you take me out, you'll never get rid of me. No matter what you do, I'll keep turning up."

She chuckles. "Um, thanks?" she mumbles. "I bet you thought I was a right lunatic."

I stroke my hand over her face, clearing it of the loose strands of her hair getting in the way. "No, what I thought was that the girl I had fallen madly in love with was just torn away from her first date with a guy, only to have her best friend blurt out that he liked her. What I was thinking was that this girl didn't deserve to have it done that way after everything she had been through."

Her scrutinising is kind of unnerving. "Your dad told you how you fucked up, didn't he?"

I groan with a nod, but quickly rush to explain. "In my defence, I've only ever had flings. I had been avoiding finding 'the one' for so long that it spooked me. I freaked out, and I knew I had to do everything to win you. My dad always said it would come at me hard and then backfire. And it did."

"I'm not a prize," she whispers.

I glance down at her, my gaze softening. "Amelia, you're the prize worth having. You aren't some cheap teddy at the fun fair. You're *the* prize. The one you'll do anything or pay anything to have."

Her brows scrunch together. "I'm not sure using the terminology to pay for me is romantic. I think."

My chuckle is mixed in with a groan as I drop my forehead against hers. "What I'm trying to say is that you're worth more than anything money could buy. Having you; you being mine…" I take a deep breath. "It's more than I deserve."

"I love you, Maddox," she croaks out, pressing her lips to mine briefly.

"I love you too," I reply, feeling my chest fill with warmth. "Now, as much as I'm enjoying you being in my arms, can we take this to your room?"

She sits up, taking the blanket with her. "Oh my God, your side. I forgot. Are you okay?"

I place my hand over hers when she goes to pull the blanket off my torso. "It's fine. It's uncomfortable, but I just want to lie in a bed with you and sleep for like a week."

She smiles down at me in amusement. "Jasmine is in there. I put Asher back in his cot when I heard the door knock."

I grit my teeth as I sit up, before reaching for her. "You couldn't sleep without them?"

Her lips tip down. "No. I just—"

"I understand," I interrupt. "You sleep in the middle, and tonight I'll have both my girls with me. At least then I'll know you're all safe."

"Thank you," she tells me, resting her forehead against mine.

I lift her chin up with my knuckles, my lips brushing against hers. "You'll never have to worry about that happening ever again. I'm not going anywhere," I tell her, hearing the conviction in my voice. "And they might not be my kids, but they're still mine. I feel it in my heart. I've missed them just as much as I've missed you."

"They've missed you too. They've been such grumps without you."

I smirk, pressing my lips against hers. "Then let's go to bed and not waste another moment."

Her breath hitches, her eyes watering. "I'd love nothing more."

I move as quickly as I can, since the local anaesthetic is wearing off, and get dressed. Once I'm done, I take Amelia's hand in mine, leading her upstairs.

When we reach her room, my heart begins to hammer inside my chest. Jasmine is sprawled out on her bed, safe, and fast asleep. Relief hits me so hard I nearly stagger my way to the cot.

I need to see him.

I grip the bar of the cot as I stare down at Asher sleeping soundlessly. He's okay. He truly is okay. I sag against the cot, staring at him for a moment longer.

I run my finger down his cheek, the knot inside my chest finally loosening. He really is okay.

This is what I want.

All of it.

Amelia, Jasmine and Asher.

And although I'm kicking myself for not giving in to my urges sooner, I know it happened for a reason.

They are my world.

It's a life lesson that love isn't meant to be messed around with. It isn't something that comes easily, not when it's true love. Not when it's 'the one'. If I had made a move on Amelia sooner, we might not be where we are today. I needed to know what it was like to lose her before I had her.

And no matter what life throws at me now, what bad choices I make in the future, I'll always have this.

Because love isn't to be taken for granted.

It's meant to be treasured.

Amelia and the kids have no idea what's to come. They have never been loved by a Carter.

But they are about to be.

THIRTY-FIVE

AMELIA

The chaotic chatter echoes in my ears as I try to tune it out and escape into my own mind. I don't want to think about where I am, what I'm doing. It will become a reality soon, and I'm not sure I'm ready for that.

For two weeks I have been determined and sure, and yet, the time I began to second guess this decision was today.

I'm outside, staring at the ominous building whilst the rain pours down around me. The weather seems fitting considering where I am. Like a bad omen, telling me this is a bad idea.

Or maybe it isn't.

All I know is, I have to do this.

The last couple of weeks have been proof of that. Being with Maddox has turned my life upside down in the best possible way. It's bliss. It's right. And he just fits. There is no adjustment period, no getting-to-know-you stage. It just is.

And I couldn't be happier. In fact, I didn't know this level of happiness existed until now. It's never been like this before. I feel complete, like I'm finally who I was always meant to be. I have everything I have always wanted.

And thanks to my mum and aunt, my debts are cleared, leaving me nothing to stress about. I can pay in my own time and the right amount. It's a relief.

I also feel healthier than I have in a long time. Before I fell pregnant with Asher, I had been under weight. I skipped meals because of work, and grabbed snacks or a piece of fruit on the go. After Asher, I kept my weight on, but with Maddox's sex drive, it's slowly going. Though my figure has stayed. He'll turn up in the day and palm the kids off to either his mum or mine, just so we can spend hours in bed. I can't complain because I love those moments. I love the times we're alone and it's just us. Because I feel like more than a mum in those moments. I feel like me.

And I'm happy.

However, as blissful as life has been, I need to do this today. At first, Maddox wasn't happy, especially when I told him I was going in alone. But in the end, he understood. Or if he didn't, he pretended to. And I love him for it.

I need to see Cameron, to tell him this violent cycle needs to end because it can't go on anymore. We aren't on the merry-go-round. Me and the kids are on a new ride, a new path, and it doesn't include him or his family becoming an obstacle and causing havoc.

It was Scarlett who made me realise it's what I need to do. Since that dreadful night he attacked us, I had wondered why she did it. I never understood how someone who was such a close part of my life could hurt me the way she did. Until she turned up on my doorstep, I didn't realise how badly I needed the closure.

And it wasn't really about the reasons why.

It wasn't about the 'how could she'.

It was about letting go of the toxic in my life and knowing I had the strength and courage to do it.

Because no matter how many questions I had for her, no matter what answers she gave me, the fact remains the same. She won't change. She hasn't changed. And it was a slap in the face when I realised Cameron won't change either. He will do his sentence and come out the same man. Be the same person. If he hides those characteristics after his sentence, he's lying to himself.

But I'd also be lying to myself if I said I didn't want to go in there and face him. I'd be letting my kids down by not doing this for them. I'd let myself down.

He needs to know *I'm* not the same person. And not because I've changed. It's because I've finally opened my eyes and my heart to new things. I'm no longer afraid of letting others in, no longer scared of what they'll think.

"You can go in," the prison guard announces, his deep voice startling me out of my thoughts.

I hesitantly take a step into the room. Rows and rows of tables are lined up in a cafeteria-like room, each inmate wearing grey joggers and a grey jumper, all with 'inmate' printed in bright orange on the back.

I try not to meet the gazes of the other men sitting on the other side of the tables, as I make my way down to row C. I scan the aisle until my eyes land on Cameron, my heart stuttering at the sight of him.

He hasn't shaved or cut his hair. He looks frail, thinner than I remember, and a lot less intimidating.

His eyes narrow into slits when they spot me, and I inhale deeply before exhaling, making my way down.

I pull out the chair opposite him, grateful for the table separating us. He doesn't take his eyes off me, and a shiver races down my spine.

"What are you doing here, Amelia?" he asks, his voice raspy.

"I came to tell you it ends today. All of it. I don't want your family coming after my kids again, knocking on my door or hurting us. I don't want you coming out of here and trying to find us. If you have any feelings towards Jasmine, you'll do this for her," I tell him, unable to keep the plea out of my tone.

He stares at me unnervingly for a moment, before he lets out a tired breath. "Devon told me what they did. I never asked them to do that, for what it's worth."

I shrug. "It doesn't matter. We are finally in a good place."

His jaw clenches. "What? Is the prison not good enough for you?"

"W-what?"

"You come in here and demand shit from me, as always. Never asking me what I want. You put me here, Amelia. You."

"You put yourself here," I retort, before cutting off the rest of what I was going to say. I didn't come here for this.

He leans back in his chair, the metal feet scraping across the marble floor. "No. *You* did. I never wanted to be a dad. I never wanted to be a stay-at-home bitch."

"W-what?" I repeat, unable to process what he's saying or how this got so off track. "But y-you… you fought to stay whenever I broke things off."

He places his hands on the table, and I flinch. "Because I had nowhere else to fucking go. I didn't want to be like my dad. Like my mum. I wanted to try, but I couldn't do it. She did nothing but cry. Then she learned to talk and walk, and it got worse," he grits out. "I'm a man, goddammit, and I was changing fucking nappies and having some snotty-arse kid mess with my shit. I didn't ask for that."

"You aren't a man," I snap, hating the way he's talking about her. I had no idea he felt this way towards her. "You're a boy who is yet to learn what it means to grow up. I *asked* you. I asked you what you wanted to do when I found out I was pregnant. You were over the moon."

"I lied."

I scoff at that. "You lied about a lot of things."

"I loved her, you know."

I grit my teeth. How could he think all of that and still say he loved her? "You've got a funny way of showing it with what you just said."

"Scarlett. Not her," he bites out. "She made it easier, you know. Fucking her, the excitement of doing it while you were asleep in bed, while you were at work, it made it all worth it. It was a rush the drugs couldn't give me."

I can't speak for a moment. It should bother me that he loved her and not his daughter. It should bother me that he's talking to me like this. But looking at the pathetic person in front of me, all I see is a worthless human being. I don't see the Cameron I fell in love with. I don't even see the one who beat me. I see him for who he truly is.

And that's nothing.

Hell, he hasn't even bothered to ask about Asher. As far as I know, he doesn't even know his gender. I'm not sure what his family have been telling him, or if they've told him anything.

"It was like that with you once too," he tells me, shocking me to my core.

I shake my head. "Maybe. Maybe not. I'm not here about that, about us, or about Scarlett. I came to ask you to leave the kids alone. Us alone. I'm not the same person I was. I'll fight back next time. I'll do anything to protect them."

He leans down on the table, and a guard taps him on the shoulder. "Lean back," he orders.

Cameron gives him a nod before turning back to me. "I'll tell them."

I jerk my head and push back in my chair, looking down on him. "His name is Asher, you know."

"Your new boyfriend?"

"No, my son," I grit out.

He shrugs, but I see a flash of emotion before he blanks it. "It doesn't matter because I'll never meet him," he states, sounding callous. "Make sure they never coming looking for me when they're older, because they won't like what they'll find."

I shake my head in pity. "I feel sorry for you."

He smirks. "Right back at you."

I pause after tucking my chair back in. "You were meant to be more than them. More than this. Don't use me and Jasmine as an excuse for your failure."

When he doesn't reply, I go to walk off, but then his voice stops me. "I'm sorry. For all of it."

I turn back, stopping behind the chair. "What?"

He drops the façade, and remorse shines back at me. "For not being the person you needed me to be. For not loving Jasmine the way a parent should. For hurting you. All of it."

"I never asked you to be anything else, Cam. I never had high expectations. I didn't have a list of what you should be doing. I just wanted you to be you before you started hitting me and hurting my daughter."

"It doesn't matter now," he tells me.

I shake my head. "No, it really doesn't."

"Don't come back here," he warns.

I turn to leave, then glance over my shoulder and say, "Bye, Cameron."

He doesn't say it back. He doesn't need to. A smile lights up my face as I head back through security, never once turning back to him.

That chapter of my life is over.

It's done. After today, I'll hopefully never have to lay eyes on him again. I know there will be a day when the kids ask about him. When they'll probably go looking for him. And as painful as that day will be, I'll tell them everything they need to know. I'll make sure they understand my love for them outweighs anything they'll get from him.

"Leaving already?" a guard asks as I step through the second security checkpoint.

I turn to her, a smile lighting up my face. "I guess some things don't take that long to say."

"Well, have a good day," she tells me.

She has no idea how good my day already is.

I feel liberated. Stronger.

I didn't go there to cause an argument, to get confrontational. I went to get my point across, and I did. In fact, I was there longer than expected. I wanted to face him, to tell him face to face to leave me alone. I didn't want it said through his family, through guards or a solicitor. I needed to do it.

I quickly grab my belongings from the locker. It's only a jacket and my phone, but I wasn't allowed to take them in. I pull it on and leave, not looking back.

I push through the doors, expecting to be blasted with rain, but it's stopped. I glance up, a smile still on my face, but come to a sudden stop when I see Maddox sitting back on the bonnet of his truck, one leg cocked up on the bumper, his head bent, glancing down at his shoes.

He couldn't wait in the car like I asked him to.

He is always there for me, no matter what.

I watch him for a moment, soaking him in. In dark jeans and a black hoody, my man looks hot.

He looks up, and his lips tip up in the corners. He pushes off the bonnet as I take the first step down.

The first step to my future.

The first step to freedom.

When I get to the bottom of the stairs, I jump off, racing over to him and meeting him halfway. I jump into his arms, smiling up at him. "I love you."

"Love you too, babe."

And this is my forever.

This is the thing Cameron never understood, that he never got.

Love isn't about what you can do for the other person. It isn't a competition. It isn't about control.

It's this.

Pure and utter devotion and love.

This is only the beginning. I have a feeling there is more to come, more to explore, and that this is only an inkling of what it feels like to love and be loved by a Carter.

And I'm going to love every minute.

EPILOGUE

CHARLOTTE

My phone feels heavy in my hand, the weight of it pulling me under a dark cloud.

He hasn't messaged me.

I knew he wasn't going to come, but I held on to the hope that he would change his mind.

Love is meant to be a secure feeling. It means you've found your companion; your best friend; your life partner; your soul mate. It's about opening up about your feelings, knowing they are safe and that they're mutual. It's about respect. It's a journey, one I have daydreamed about for as long as I can remember.

I never found love like that. Not until I met Scott. I had been leaving the strip club I was doing research in when I bumped into him. He had just finished work and was heading home. He asked me out for a drink, and I said yes.

I said yes because I was always saying no.

I said yes because it was something I'd never do without weighing the pros and cons.

I said yes because I didn't want to be alone anymore.

I said yes because someone finally noticed me.

But that yes is weighing heavily on my heart. It's like there is something missing from our relationship, a void between us that others don't have.

We aren't like Faith and Beau, Landon and Paisley, Aiden and Bailey, Hayden and Clayton, or Lily and Jaxon. But I don't want to give up. I don't want to give up on love or being loved.

Because love is everything. It's a fundamental part of life. I have family I love. A cat I love. Even a job I love. But I want a man to love, a child to love. I want it all.

Maybe I'm doing something wrong?

"Are you okay?" Lily asks, keeping her voice low.

I force a smile, and a thought occurs to me. "Lily, did you love Jaxon before or after you had sex with him?"

Her eyes bug out. "Um—"

"I mean, do you think that's how you know you love someone?"

"Charlotte," she calls out softly, and I shake my head, tilting my head in her direction. "For me, loving Jaxon wasn't about anything sexual."

"But he's so hot to look at," I tell her, bunching my eyebrows together. I mean, he is book cover hot.

I think I've stared at him for way too long, far too many times. I'm worried that's why he stays clear of me.

Lily giggles and nudges my shoulder. "Husband, remember?"

I grimace. "Sorry."

"Love isn't just a feeling. Although I do feel it. I feel it so much that sometimes I'm worried my heart will burst. But it's a connection too. I had that with Jaxon from the minute I met him. Nothing mattered to him but loving me and vice versa," she explains, leaning in closer. "I know he's been with other women. I'm not stupid. But he was happy just loving me. So no, I don't think you need to have sex to know you love someone."

"Is he not very good at sex?"

"Charlotte," she lightly scolds, a pink tinge rising up her neck.

"Sorry," I answer, letting out a sigh.

"Is this about Scott?" she asks softly, and I tense. "Do you love him?"

"I do. I think I do. I want to be with him, but I don't know. We haven't had sex yet. I get too scared. We've done other stuff though."

"You ready? Maddox and Amelia have arrived," Jaxon announces as he reaches us.

My brows pull together. "I thought Maverick and Teagan arranged this family meeting?"

I scan the room, finding the two over at the bar ordering a drink. We were told the other week to book today off and meet here. I assumed it was something to do with Faith's engagement, but she had been tight-lipped about what the meeting was about when I asked.

Lily nervously glances over at me. "We, um, we'll explain in a minute," she tells me, before turning to her husband. "Can you give us a minute?"

He leans down, kissing her, and a wave of envy fills me. I want that. Scott never does that. But he says it's because he doesn't want to scare me, like I get when we go too far in the bedroom. "See you in a second. I'll go stand by your dad."

Her lips press together. "For protection?"

Jaxon shrugs, grinning. "Maybe."

She shakes her head as he leaves, before turning to me. "Charlotte, I love you. We all do. So, I'm saying this out of love. If you have doubts about Scott, then it's for a reason. Listen to your heart. Okay?"

"I will. I promise."

She wraps her arms around me, pressing her lips to my cheek, before heading off in search of her husband.

I move a little further into the room, coming to stand next to Amelia and Maddox. Jasmine runs off as soon as she sees Madison. I, on the other hand, have eyes for Asher. I can't wait for the day I hold my own child. I long for it.

"Can I hold him?"

Amelia beams at me. "Hey, Charlotte. And of course."

She hands him over, and he settles into my arms, smiling up at me. I smile back, my heart filling with warmth. I glance up at Amelia. "He's getting big."

"He is. And he slept like a trooper last night."

"Thanks to me," Maddox puts in.

"Yeah, yeah," Amelia mutters.

"You're so lucky," I tell her.

"Who wouldn't be lucky to have all this in their life," Maddox comments, gesturing to his body.

Amelia rolls her eyes. "He's such a comedian."

"Can I have your attention," Maverick roars, and the noise from the bar quietens. We always use this space for family meals. With so many of us, it's hard to fit into one house, so we use the bar/restaurant space downstairs instead.

"Hurry it up, Mav, I've got shit to do."

Maverick's gaze hardens on his younger brother. "I told you to take the day off, Max."

He snorts. "And I'm using it wisely with my wife, if you know what I mean."

A chorus of, "Dad!" echoes from three different parts of the room, making me laugh.

"Lily and Jaxon have an announcement," he tells the group, before his gaze lands on each of his brothers. "Remember your promises."

Intrigued, I step closer to where they are formed in a huddle. Lily fiddles with the hem of her shirt, her smile wobbly. "Me and Jaxon, we, um, we…" She pauses, gripping Jaxon's hand.

"We're happy to announce, Lily is expecting. She's due Christmas. If anyone has an issue with me getting her pregnant, take it up with someone who cares."

I stagger backwards.

It's happening again.

I'm happy for her. Truly happy.

But whilst they are moving forward in life, I'm rooted to the spot. I want a family. A baby. And while everyone is getting what they want, I'm still the same old Charlotte.

Cheers ring out in the room, but it stops when Dad begins to yell. "Max passed out."

Laughter fills the air over people heading over to Lily to offer their own congratulations. I go next, beaming at her. "I'm so happy for you."

"I'm sorry I didn't tell you before. We wanted to wait," she explains.

"I understand," I reply softly.

And it doesn't hurt.

Not really.

Now Landon is gone, I'm used to it. I'm not needed. Hell, half the time it feels like I'm not wanted.

And it isn't a lack of love that makes me feel this way because I know each of them love me fiercely.

But sometimes I wonder if it's out of duty instead of them wanting to.

I shake away the negative thoughts, wondering where they came from.

Snap out of it, Charlotte.

"For fuck's sake," Max roars, rubbing the back of his head.

"Doing okay?" Dad asks, looming above him.

Max narrows his gaze on his brother. "Laugh all you want, mother fucker, but did you forget the hell we went through when our other halves got pregnant? All the food they hogged? The tears? My God, I still hear her sobs at night."

Dad pales, slowly turning to face Mum. "I forgot about that."

"You're being dramatic," Lake scoffs.

"I am not," Max barks out as he gets to his feet. He goes to open his mouth to say something to Lily and Jaxon, but then stops suddenly, his face paling as he turns to his daughter. "Are you going to tell me you're pregnant too?"

"Do you want me to be?" Hayden asks wryly, leaning back when he gets in her space.

His eyes bulge. "Are you?"

I giggle at how high-pitched his voice goes. He's always entertaining.

"God, Dad, no. Now go say your congratulations to Lily and Jaxon," she snaps.

Closing his eyes for a second, he then turns to the glowing couple. "Lily, from the bottom of my heart, congratulations. You are going to make a fantastic mother, and nothing I say or do from here on out has anything to do with you," he rambles stiffly, before turning to Jaxon. "You're lucky you waited until she was married."

"You aren't even religious," Lake scoffs.

"I am now," he snaps, before storming outside, where he yells into the sky, "If you're listening to me, don't let me suffer the same fate. Don't take my food away from me. It's my joy in life. My joy!"

"I thought I was his joy," Lake mutters, as his ramblings slowly become muffled.

"Did you lock the door?" Maverick asks, glancing at Mason.

Mason nods. "He'll probably be picked up in an hour, after he finishes rambling about pizza."

"He got arrested once," Mum mutters. "And in my defence, I was hungry."

"What are you talking about?" Lily asks.

She lets out a sigh before answering, "When I was pregnant with Charlotte, I had mad cravings. It was how Max found out. He broke down and began to yell outside, just like he is now."

Dad chuckles, continuing the story. "He lost track of time and rambled for so long that one of the neighbours called the police. He acted like a lunatic when they showed up, so they took him in for drunk and disorderly."

"You okay?" Amelia asks, coming to step beside me.

My smile feels heavy as I look at her. "Of course."

"Charlotte, you remember the day in the library, and we were talking about our happily ever after?"

My throat closes up. "Yeah," I croak out. Her words hit a nerve and have stayed with me. I don't want her to be right.

I know if I try harder, it will be perfect between Scott and I.

I have to believe that.

"The wait may be hard, but the result will make it so much sweeter. I found my forever after believing I'd never go near a man again. You will too."

My eyes fill with tears. "So, I just wait."

She jerks her head. "Whoever ends up with you will be lucky, and will feel the wait was so much sweeter too."

She's wrong.

No one wants me. Not like that.

I glance down at Asher, who coos and blows bubbles at me. "This is all I've ever wanted," I whisper.

"And you'll have it."

"I hope so," I reply.

Because I want my happy back. I want my life filled with roses and sweet kisses. I want morning hugs and late-night dinners. I want 'how was your day' conversations. I want the intimacy, the tension. I want passion and more.

I want love.

I want it all.

Yet the burning in the pit of my stomach makes me feel like it isn't on the cards for me. That it isn't my time.

That Scott isn't the one.

Maybe he doesn't need to be the one. Maybe he just needs to be *some*one.

My time has to be coming.

It has to.

I guess I'll just have to wait and see.

ACKNOWLEDGEMENTS

As crazy as 2020 has been, how hard it's been, I hope this book brings you an inkling of joy. I hope you laughed as much as I did writing Maddox's story.

I hope it brought you solace during a time when we all need it.

And I hope you're well.

As always, thank you for following this series, for loving the characters as much as I do. You make all the hard work worthwhile, and I'm grateful for the support.

Please leave Maddox a review once you're finished. I love seeing your thoughts. It also helps authors, so if you have a moment, leave a review on the appropriate platform.

As you may have guessed, Charlotte's book is next. You can expect more nutty and crazy behaviour, but also struggle and love.

For more updates on what is to come, you can find my readers group on Facebook.

Lisa's Luscious Readers. You're welcome to come and join in the fun.

And thank you to Stephanie at Farrant Editing. You're my hero, and I love you. Thank you for all the hard work and hours you've put in to make sure this is completed. You are a superstar. Merry Christmas, beautiful.

And another massive thank you to those who beta read Maddox's book. You guys are awesome.

BOOKS BY LISA HELEN GRAY

A Carter Brother Series
Malik – Book One (New edited version out now)
Mason – Book Two (Newly written and edited version, coming soon)
Myles – Book Three
Evan Book 3.5
Max – Book Four
Maverick – Book Five

A Next Generation Carter Brother Novel
Faith – Book One
Aiden – Book Two
Landon – Book Three
(Read Soul of My Soul next)
Hayden – Book Four
(Read Eye for an Eye here)
Maddox – Out now

Take A Chance
Soul of My Soul
Eye for an Eye

I Wish
If I Could I'd Wish it all Away
Wishing for a Happily Ever After

Forgotten Series
Better Left Forgotten – Book One
Obsession – Book Two
Forgiven – Book Three
(Newly written and edited version coming soon)

Whithall University
Foul Play – Book One
Game Over – Book Two
Almost Free – Book Three

Kingsley Academy
Wrong Crowd – Book One
Crowd of Lies – Book Two

Printed in Great Britain
by Amazon